Praise for Jonathan Rosen's *Joy Comes in the Morning*

Winner of the Edward Lewis Wallant Award
Winner of the Chaim Potok Literary Award

"At a time when best-selling books on the religious life include bombastic visions of the apocalypse or religion as grand conspiracy [*Joy Comes in the Morning*] is a minor miracle. It arrives much like the way birds appear to the characters in the book: with a delicate wonder.... Rosen provides a much-needed glimpse into authentically religious lives. His book is a window into the heart of faith, both its joys and its sorrows.... A deeply moving story."

— *The Boston Globe*

"Rosen's touching novel about Jewish manners thoughtfully addresses the question of whether piety can teach us faith."

— *The New Yorker*

"Beautiful . . . [*Joy Comes in the Morning*] fills the reader with happiness at the most unexpected moments."

— *The New York Sun*

"Reading Jonathan Rosen's new novel, *Joy Comes in the Morning*, is one way to celebrate American Jewry in its 350th year."

— *Hadassah Magazine*

"This novel is a pleasure. Rosen has in *Joy Comes in the Morning* penned a book filled with insight about human needs and passions, serious about Jewish faith and astute about Jewish life."

— *The Jerusalem Report*

"In shimmering prose and with uncommon empathy, Rosen creates a cast of characters plagued by profound spiritual crisis.... Not since Saul Bellow has an American novelist created characters so unabashedly determined to unleash their souls, to burst their spirit's sleep."

— *The Miami Herald*

"Marvelous . . . [a] book about family and faith, familial love and sexual love . . . it is also about human history and Jewish history, both in the particular sense . . . also in the larger sense.... Rosen is also at heart a writer with a comic point of view, who sees life in all its humor and absurdity, as well as its pathos. . . . There are scenes that are laugh-out-loud, side-splittingly funny. . . . This is a work to revel in, and truckloads of readers should do just that."

—*Jewish Exponent*

"[Rosen's] writing is crisp and elegant—perfectly suited to the book's elevated subject matter."

—*Time Out* New York

"Finally a novel about an American rabbi with sense and sensibility, written with felicity, extraordinary talent and full knowledge of Jewish life and learning. . . . Rosen is a superb writer and a serious explorer of Jewish American life today. . . . A wonderful read."

—*American Jewish World*

"A warm, generous, and often funny meditation on family and faith . . . An affecting and beautifully written book."

—Gary Shteyngart

"*Joy Comes in the Morning* is a novel that comes out of an all but eclipsed literary tradition of epic, morally infused storytelling. . . . The interweaving of the Friedmans' intense family life with a complex New York milieu brings to mind comparisons with the vaulting nineteenth-century narratives of George Eliot. . . . Rosen is one of those rare writers who not only sets his sights high but actually provides a good read on the way. This is a novel that is exuberantly alive with reflection; it dares to be serious in a compulsively ironic age."

—Daphne Merkin

"Exquisitely attuned to the vagaries of the inner self and the richness of Jewish spirituality, Rosen has created a marvelously accessible and touching novel that is at once profoundly philosophical and simply radiant."

—*Booklist*

"Jonathan Rosen's second novel—a spirited contemporary love story set on Manhattan's Upper West Side—is also a story about the meaning of faith in our times."

—*Reform Judaism Magazine*

ALSO BY JONATHAN ROSEN

The Talmud and the Internet

Eve's Apple

JOY

Comes in the

MORNING

Jonathan

Rosen

Picador
Farrar, Straus and Giroux
New York

www.picadorusa.com

Picador® is a U.S. registered trademark and is used by Farrar, Straus and Giroux under license from Pan Books Limited.

For information on Picador Reading Group Guides, as well as ordering, please contact the Trade Marketing department at St. Martin's Press.
Phone: 1-800-221-7945 extension 763
Fax: 212-253-9627
E-mail: readinggroupguides@picadorusa.com

Designed by Gretchen Achilles

Library of Congress Cataloging-in-Publication Data

Rosen, Jonathan, 1963–
    Joy comes in the morning / Jonathan Rosen.
        p. cm.
    ISBN 0-312-42427-2
    EAN 978-0-312-42427-5
    1. Women rabbis—Fiction. 2. Holocaust, Jewish, (1939–1945)—Fiction.
3. Loss (Psychology)—Fiction. 4. Holocaust survivors—Fiction. 5. Hospital
patients—Fiction. 6. Suicidal behavior—Fiction. 7. Jewish families—Fiction.
8. Single women—Fiction. 9. Jewish women—Fiction. I. Title.

PS3568.O767 J695 2004
813'.54—dc22   2004001742

First published in the United States by Farrar, Straus and Giroux

10 9 8 7 6 5 4 3 2

In memory of my father

ROBERT SAMUEL ROSEN

And for my daughters

ARIELLA ROSE *and* AVITAL LEAH

Weeping may endure for a night
But joy comes in the morning.

—PSALM 30

Book

One

SOMEONE WAS DYING.

Deborah felt it in her chest. She felt it along her spine. She felt it, though she could not have explained how, in her womb. The feeling stirred her out of half sleep. She opened her eyes. The shades were drawn but a blue light had begun to seep in around the edges. It was 6 a.m.

Now would be a good time to hear a voice. She would like to have been called. *Deborah! Deborah!* But it no longer happened that way, if it ever had. Deborah smiled at herself for a childhood fantasy that had never left her. The window glowed. She heard the flop of *The New York Times* against her front door. The newspaper delivery boy—actually a middle-aged black woman; Deborah had spied on her once through the peephole—stood in the open elevator and flung the papers, as if dealing a giant pack of cards. After a sleepless night Deborah found the sound reassuring, a town crier's reminder that the world was still there. Lately, there had been a lot of sleepless nights.

The strange sensation darkened her again, an inner shadow. Someone was dying. She tried to think who it might be. William who had emphysema and couldn't talk but whose hand she often held. The old woman on the eighth floor nobody came to see who had given her a recipe for sponge cake. Frank the trumpet player with AIDS for whom the complex cocktail no longer worked. That poor baby in the neonatal ICU, baby Emily the nurses called her, who had been born with a hole in her heart. Deborah shuddered at the memory of the tiny blue child. Angry Caroline with ovarian cancer, scarcely older than she herself was. That might explain the strange sympathetic sensation nestled in her own belly. She rested a hand there but her body told her nothing.

Somehow, she didn't think it was any of these. Of course, someone was always dying. It didn't have to be someone you knew. Visiting a hospital regularly you learned that pretty quickly.

She should make herself a cup of coffee and start the day. The newspaper was waiting for her. Reuben, when they had been together, all but heard the *Times* crying on the doorstep like an abandoned child. He would bring it into bed. Deborah could never look at the paper first thing in the morning. Though she was keenly attuned to the world's sorrows, internal matters always concerned her more.

Deborah decided to pray. She had promised herself that she would pray more regularly. She rose and stretched. She was wearing a T-shirt and nothing else. She stepped into a pair of underpants. It didn't seem right to stand bare-assed before God, though of course everyone was supposed to be naked before Him. Not that she thought of God as a seeing presence. Or a Him. Still, she slipped on a pair of red running shorts over the underpants. Barefoot, she padded across the wood floor and removed a large zippered velvet envelope from her top drawer. She left a smaller velvet envelope behind.

While she was up she shut off the air conditioner. It had been in the high eighties the past few days but Deborah hated the artificial cool. There was something dishonest about it, though this was the kind of observation that drove Reuben—who had bought the air conditioner for her—crazy. She always imagined that the heat was still lurking somewhere in the room, hidden behind an invisible veil of refrigerated air. If you exerted yourself only slightly you felt hot and realized that the whole thing was a kind of physical illusion. This belief was, in Reuben's words, a pantheistic delusion. But Reuben was gone, though his machine lived on, sucking life out of the room in his absence.

Deborah's grandfather had been surprisingly tall; she was reminded of this as she unfurled his large prayer shawl, ivory white with bold zebra stripes of black. Though she was five foot six inches tall, when she raised the shawl over her head she was completely shrouded. She loved the feeling of being wrapped, hidden away inside the soft armor of her grandfather's tallis. In the meditation she now recited, God was described as robed in light. Deborah held the ends of the prayer shawl together above her head and felt, for a moment, blissfully co-cooned.

When Reuben had seen her in her tallis for the first time he had called her a transvestite. Remembering it now, she burned with shame and indignation. He had pretended it was a joke and flashed her his gleaming, bearded smile, but she could see the disgust in his eyes. He had nothing against women praying, he told her, but why did they have to pray dressed like men?

Reuben was Orthodox. Of course he had slept with her anyway—not, she felt sure, the only one of the 613 commandments he had violated, but perhaps the one he most easily discounted. He had shown more anxiety about the state of her kitchen—the morning after, she'd found him sifting through the silverware to make sure that she indeed had a set for milk and a set for meat.

Deborah lowered the tallis so that the strip of gold embroidery lay behind her slender neck; she gathered up the extra material on either side and threw it over her shoulders, doubling the great square of striped cloth back on itself so that she wore it like a cape. The tassels hung down in front and behind.

It annoyed her to be thinking of Reuben now, in her moment of prayer, with his ortho-arrogant awkwardness, his air of entitlement and insecurity. Modern Orthodox men were macho sissies. He wasn't the first one she'd dated. They expected to inherit the earth but they had a nagging, inborn fear that they might be driven from it first. In this respect they weren't quite American, and Deborah supposed it was this mild foreignness, coupled with her own weakness for ritual rigor, that had drawn her to them in the first place. She had met Reuben in *his* synagogue, not hers. She herself must have held a certain exotic appeal for him—a Reform woman rabbi. She must not have seemed quite American either, or quite Jewish.

She resented terms like *Orthodox* and *Reform*—they seemed a substitute for the inner state. Did she have a Reform soul? She didn't feel that way, especially draped in her grandfather's tallis. Reuben can kiss my Reform rabbinical cross-dressing ass. She hurled herself into *Ma Tovu—How goodly are your tents, oh Jacob*—her heart pounding, trying to recapture the tented pleasure of the moment before. But it wasn't until she had blazed through *Adon Olam* and *Yigdal*—containing Maimonides's thirteen principles of Judaism, beginning with the existence of God and ending with the resurrection of the dead—that she settled down.

Deborah loved the praise part of prayer. In rabbinic school there had always been students who wrestled with praise and took a what-has-he-done-for-me-lately attitude toward God, an attitude of human entitlement and anger. Deborah had never understood this.

To praise God made her feel whole and she recited *Birkot Hashachar* with a schoolgirl's relish: *Blessed are you God who gives sight to the blind; blessed are you God who clothes the naked; blessed are you God who did not make me a slave.* She was using her grandmother's little prayer book, which made no apologies for *blessed are you God who did not make me a woman.* Deborah skipped that blessing and recited the female alternative, *Blessed are you God who made me according to his will.*

She found her groove and raced along, fast but focused, gathering the four tassels of her tallis in her right hand when she came to the "Shema and her Blessings" so that she could kiss them every time she uttered the word *tzitzit—And you shall look on them and remember the commandments, and not be seduced by the desires of the heart or of the eye . . .*

By the time she got to the *Amida* she had forgotten the distress of the morning and was moving smoothly along ancient verbal tracks of praise and petition. One of her liturgy professors had spoken of prayer in the language of sports. You break through the wall, he said, and you're no longer thinking, *I'm running, I'm running,* you're simply running. It's a beautiful state. She felt that way now. She entered the *Amida* almost before she knew it, bowing and bending and feeling the words alive inside her.

But then the persistent whisper in her blood distracted her. Again she thought, *Someone is dying.* Was it the hospital getting to her at last? Her sister, Rachel, had been telling her that she spent too much time there, which, considering the fact that Rachel was a doctor, was laughable. Though she *was* spending more and more of her time among the sick. She'd begun visiting congregants but had found herself spending time with other patients, too, Jews and non-Jews, old people and babies alike. Rabbi Zwieback, the senior rabbi, was only too happy to give her hospital detail, and for the past two years half her salary was paid by a grant that supported ministering to the sick.

Deborah had found in the hospital an air of truthfulness and, strange to say, vitality, that she could not account for. She sometimes felt the way she imagined a soldier might feel who discovers to his astonishment that he likes war. That in the thick of battle—bullets whizzing around his head, comrades falling, death undeniable, life its brightest and most immediate and most perishable—his inner state has finally found its outer expression. In the hospital Deborah found not fear but, oddly, a kind of peace.

Not that she had abandoned her other responsibilities. This very Sunday she would be performing a wedding. Now *that* was scary. Deborah had met with the couple twice and it seemed clear they weren't ready for marriage. Janet was only twenty-four and had already broken off the engagement once, during which time she had briefly returned to an earlier, non-Jewish boyfriend. Deborah felt this woman was still torn but, a pleaser by nature, she had reconciled because she could not bear to assert herself in a lasting way. Deborah had heard only a tiny piece of this story from Janet when they had spoken on the phone and had imagined she would learn more, but with her fiancé beside her the woman said almost nothing. The man, Rick, a tax attorney (Deborah tried not to hold his profession or his goatee against him) did most of the talking, and he did it in a controlling way Deborah resented.

"We've had some times," Rick had said, "but we've worked through them. We're ready to make the leap."

He kept on talking without pause, about what kind of service they wanted and about his father who had died and about how Janet's sister would be playing the flute. He left Deborah no opening so she had cut him off abruptly.

"Have the invitations already gone out?" she'd asked, more harshly than she'd intended. Tact was never her strong suit and when she was agitated or annoyed it went out the window. Man and wife-to-be had both looked at her in surprise. But she had persisted—she blushed at the memory of it. "I understand there have been some problems with . . . fidelity."

At last Rick, waking from his stupor, had snapped at her, "We both have therapists. We're not looking for another one."

No, dickhead, Deborah thought, *you want a spiritual caterer to hand you your wedding on a tray.* But she retreated. Janet had given her no support, saying only, "We're very comfortable now," several times. Comfortable? Deborah had wanted to scream: Do you love him? What about that other guy? Don't use religion as an excuse. Marry for love! But she had held her tongue. They did seem comfortable. It was she herself who wasn't comfortable these days. Weddings had become difficult. As a rule she loved them, standing at the center of the white ceremony, a figure of almost magical authority, braiding two lives together. The Talmud said the world was a wedding. But was it one for her? She was thirty and single. She felt more profoundly alone than she ever had in her life.

Deborah caught sight of herself in the full-length mirror on the back of her closet, a young woman wearing an old man's prayer shawl. Her bare legs came out the bottom. She should shave them before the wedding. Still, they were nice legs, though slightly knock-kneed. She adjusted her stance and almost turned to see her behind in the mirror but caught herself. She realized to her astonishment that she was still praying, her lips on automatic. She was impressed with herself and perturbed at the same time. So she knew the *Amida* by heart! Or at least her lips did. This did not altogether gratify her. When she swam laps she believed that if her mind wandered too much, she wasn't really exercising. It was one thing to break through the wall—it was another thing to leave the building. She drove her mind back to the prayers. *Oh Lord, guard my lips from speaking falsehood and my tongue from speaking guile . . . Let my soul be as dust before you.* She finished the *Amida*, took three steps backward, turned her body to the left and right, bowed, and stood straight again.

The room, in the absence of air-conditioning, had begun to grow warm. Deborah yawned. "Dear God, forgive my distractions," she murmured. More and more she was given to spontaneous prayer, something she had picked up in the hospital from a Baptist minister. There was no danger of your mind wandering when you spoke directly to God. The ice broken, she added, "Please don't let me be alone."

Was she praying for a man now? Or was it God she wanted?

She sensed the mysterious presence again in the room. A sort of tiptoeing shadow. She often felt her father, dead now fifteen years, with her, but that was a kind of inner glow. This felt different, stranger. God? The Angel of Death? Or only her overactive imagination?

She did not really believe in God as a physical being and yet she knew, too, that if a voice called out to her she would answer, without hesitation, "Here I am!" And she felt that mysterious things were always happening, and, what is more, on the verge of happening. She was constantly encountering, if not God, then at least the outer garment of God. A few days before, she had seen an elderly man on Broadway, copper bearded and stooped but neatly dressed in a seersucker suit, swaying over his own untied shoelaces. He was wearing running shoes, an incongruous but not uncommon fashion choice for Upper West Side elderly. The laces of both shoes were untied and he seemed incapable of bending over enough to get to them or of deciding which shoe to tie first. Without asking permission, Deborah had knelt down and tied them both. The humble gesture had flooded her with joy. It was the joy of kneeling down, erasing herself for a moment in an act of kindness. She'd felt astonishingly alive at that instant, as if she had been created for just such a purpose.

Deborah was no longer praying. Her mind was merely wandering. "Sorry," she said aloud. Her own voice startled her. *Talking to yourself?* she thought, and then quickly added, *Or are You there?*

Deborah smiled inwardly. *Are You There God? It's Me, Margaret* had been one of her favorite books when she was eleven. After four years of a very good college, five years of seminary, two and a half years as an assistant rabbi, after reading Maimonides and Kierkegaard and Heschel and Buber, had she come no further? But why be embarrassed—the psalmist himself asked such questions; he simply put them more gracefully. Oh Lord, how long will you turn your face from me? Oh Lord, answer me. Are you there, God? It's me, King David.

Deborah began to sing a verse of Psalm 116. It was not the prescribed psalm for that day but by this time she had given up on the prayer book. Psalm 116 was one of her favorites—she recited it often with patients in the hospital and the most stirring of its verses had been set to music.

Ana Adonai, Ana Adonai, kee ani avdecha. Deborah had a beautiful voice and loved to sing. She swayed as she sang, her soft, pure voice filling the room and soothing her. Her mind felt free again. Tears came to her eyes—not tears of sadness, precisely, but something deeper and at the same time less personal than ordinary sadness. They were tears of an unknown emotion, an unfathomable longing. They were tears of prayer. Deborah cried a lot, in many situations. It didn't bother her, though Rabbi Zwieback still looked at her in alarm when, midway through a service, she would stand up to announce a page number, her cheeks shining.

The prayer shawl slipped off one shoulder and hung over her like a toga, but Deborah didn't notice. She had shut her grandmother's little prayer book and held it against her breast as she sang, in Hebrew, her eyes closed, swaying. *Answer me, Lord, answer me, for I am your servant, the son of your handmaid.*

The psalm's male point of view did not bother her. She had never cared about making prayers gender neutral. The soul knew no gender. The words were intended for her. She wished to be God's servant. She felt a keen, delicious ache in her heart as she sang the verse over and over, lulling herself with the words and music. She stood in the warmth of the brightening room, swaying and singing.

Answer me, God. Answer me.

HENRY FRIEDMAN had taken to making lists. He no longer trusted his memory. He found the lists humiliating; old ones were always turning up and confusing him. He did not like the look of his handwriting since his stroke—it appeared to belong to an anxious child, making the lists a double reminder that he was no longer himself. But that morning's list was different. He sat at his desk and reviewed it with great care.

He had typed this list on his old manual typewriter weeks ago, and though he'd kept it in a locked drawer, it was written in cryptic shorthand. So cryptic that for a moment, Henry himself puzzled over the words. *Fst. Letts. JC. Ba. Pls. Bg. Sch.* Even the first line, *Fd Mph*, was in shorthand, though there was nothing about feeding his dachshund, Mephisto, that needed to be concealed. He did that every morning. Still, Henry had, by nature, a certain secretiveness. A child in Europe during the war, he had retained the furtive habits of someone fearful of discovery, even fifty years later. The lid of his rolltop desk had always been kept down, though after his stroke he'd had difficulty lifting it and now left it up. It seemed an emblem of his new state, the yawning contents of his life nakedly exposed for all to see, though only his wife lived at home at this point and she was not one to go through his papers.

Sadly, he wasn't really one to go through his papers either, though he'd done his best to make order. The legal documents—life insurance, pension, bank books, will—were clearly labeled in a shoe box on the shelf. The rest of his papers were more diffuse and, to Henry, more distressing. *Joy Comes in the Morning*, the memoir he had begun many years before, was far from complete.

As his wife often observed, Henry had great trouble finishing anything. He could not wash the dishes without leaving a glass or spoon behind in the sink. This had driven Helen crazy in the early years of their marriage. In analysis—terminated, of course, but who finished analysis?—he had dwelt endlessly with Dr. Prochnik on his unfinished childhood. There, at least, he could blame the war. The rest was his fault—his dissertation on Kafka, temporarily abandoned in favor of a slew of necessary jobs, lay half-written in a box somewhere—though Kafka hadn't been able to finish most of his own books either. His manuscript on trains that he had intended to publish at Ex Libris—the failed vanity press that he had named after his failed bookstore—was lost. His memoir was less than a third written, and when he had glanced at the sections he had considered done, they seemed a sketchy series of notes and dreams.

In the back of his mind he wondered if in fact he was really going to kill himself. Nevertheless, it was necessary to live with the assumption that one was going to do what one set out to do. The night before, while his wife slept, he had typed and sealed two letters, one for each of his sons. Now *there* was something he had accomplished. He had made a family. And though he had not given his sons everything he'd wished, he hoped he'd given them enough. It would have to be enough.

Henry considered the bundle he'd made of the first forty pages of *Joy Comes in the Morning*, along with the relevant notes and letters he'd hoped by now to have worked into the book. Briefly, he considered walking the pages out into the hall and dropping them down the trash chute. His heart sank again as he realized how little he'd written, how little he'd leave behind. Long ago he had abandoned dreams of literary success and thought only about leaving a record for his children and the few others who might care. But even this now seemed too much to have hoped for. Nevertheless, the idea of this book had comforted him for years and, at certain bleak moments, just saying the words *Joy Comes in the Morning* had the power to restore him to a kind of hopefulness. The phrase came from Psalm 30 and on the second page of the memoir he had typed the couplet as his epigraph:

Weeping may endure for a night
But joy comes in the morning.

Henry, who had wished once to become a professor of literature, had always loved a good line of poetry or liturgy, but lately the ratio of quotation to life, always high in him, had gotten even higher. He had retained a good head for the words of others even as his own words, particularly after the last stroke, sometimes eluded him. Goethe, Shakespeare, the Psalms had always spoken for him best. He wondered if that was why his memoir had become impossible. Walter Benjamin had wanted to write a book woven entirely out of quotations. But, in the first place, he hadn't. In the second place, Henry didn't really like Benjamin's work, which amounted to little more than fancy footnotes. And in the third place, he thought with sudden melancholy, Benjamin had killed himself. For good reason, of course. He feared the Nazis.

Henry hoped that would not be the reason given for his own suicide. It wasn't delayed sadness or despair. It wasn't because of his murdered parents or sister or friends. It was because of the stroke. And the heart attack. Because of depleted energy. Everything rested on a biological foundation. In the end, history walked on human legs. This was the problem with lofty ideas. Even a king on a throne sits on his own behind, as Montaigne said. Freud called us prosthetic gods, an ugly but apt phrase. We fly in airplanes and live in high-rise buildings but such technological achievements are strapped to our human frailties. We cannot conceal our mortality or the vast space between our lofty reach and our low animal limitations.

There would be some, Henry knew, who would tell themselves, Ah, his childhood overtook him at last. They had said it about Primo Levi, too. But he knew this was a lie. If it hadn't been for his fear of another stroke, and for the mysterious, lingering, widening effects of the last one, he would be in the park right now reading the newspaper, his dog tied to a green bench slat. Henry had never been one to think much about his body until it began to fail him.

onathan Rosen

Not that he looked bad. Even in his bathrobe he had a dignified demeanor. He had never lost his hair, but it had grown wispy and the red had faded and slowly mingled with white. His beard, neatly trimmed, gave him a kingly look, an appearance accentuated by the royal blue terry-cloth bathrobe, a gift from his wife. He had always been a careful dresser, but since his stroke his wife had taken to buying him expensive clothes; there was a compensatory luxuriousness to his wardrobe. He never went out now without a tie, carefully if loosely knotted. But he would die undressed. Naked we come into this world, naked we go out of it. *Hamlet? Lear.* Once, he would have had no doubt where this line came from.

Henry looked at his aborted memoir, the couplet from Psalm 30 typed in the anarchic letters of his old manual typewriter. It saddened him that the only thing about the book that continued to give him pleasure was the title, and that was not his own. But why shouldn't a quotation be his? While he had always imagined he would live in words of his own, in a book of his own devising, was it so terrible to live in the words of others? It required a measure of faith. What was a prayer book if not quotations that spoke for you? What was the Bible if not quotations that spoke to you? The emphasis on original words was part of the American obsession with the new. Originality, thought Henry, was overrated. He would leave his sons that psalm even if he would not leave them the shaped summation of his own life. He picked up a pencil and, in his wild hand, wrote "FOR MY SONS" across the title page.

He felt oddly exhausted after this action, as if it had required great exertion. His hand, he noticed, was trembling slightly. But he felt an inward calm, too, a stiffening of resolve. He had set himself irrevocably on his final course.

From the same locked drawer where he had kept the list he removed an Advil bottle that he had emptied and refilled with what he wryly thought was a far more effective painkiller. At least he hoped so. He had followed the advice in *Final Exit* and complained of insomnia to his doctor. It had required several visits and much complaining to work his way up the ladder of sleeping pills until he had been given Nembutal. The author of *Final Exit* recommended forty pills. He had amassed only twenty but he had supplemented these with other medications of his own and his wife's—a diazepam here, a Darvon there— hoarding the pills like a child putting pennies into a piggy bank.

The Hemlock Society, publishers of *Final Exit*, frowned on violent methods for what it called, in pleasant euphemism, "self-deliverance." Henry appreciated euphemisms. Poetry itself, read in a certain light, was really just a pleasant euphemism for death. The Hemlock Society had brought him more comfort through its name than through anything written in its literature. Until now.

Henry had read in *Final Exit* that alcohol doubled the effect of certain barbiturates and he had already filled a large tumbler with Scotch. He could smell it as he sat at his desk. It was too early in the morning to enjoy the smell, but the amber color comforted him and so did the memory it evoked. The Scotch had been purchased five years before on a trip to Scotland he had made with Helen. They weren't big drinkers, and at least half the bottle remained. The Scotch was from a distillery on the Isle of Skye where they had spent a week at the end of August in a little cottage they had rented. His wife had read aloud to him from *To the Lighthouse*. To the best of his recollection, the family in the novel never made it to Skye, where the lighthouse is, but he wasn't sure if he was remembering right. What he did remember was Helen in a yellow sundress, sitting with the book open on her lap, a wide-brimmed sun hat over her long, white, dramatic hair. Though slightly older than he was, she looked years younger, except for her hair, which had gone white when she was in her thirties. A photographer, Helen had a powerful sense of the picturesque, as if she were always regarding herself and the world with a framing eye.

Her photographs were everywhere in the apartment. They were beautiful, though photography didn't matter much to Henry. He had never really cared about the visual, sensible world. It was the invisible world that never could be photographed that mattered to him more.

Nevertheless, he admired her work in an abstract, dutiful way. His wife was proudest of the pictures she had taken as a young woman in Europe just after the war when she had talked her way overseas. It was a humorous irony of their lives that he had fought to get out of war-torn Europe and she, a well-to-do American girl, had fought to get in. The irony was even deeper, and more romantic. As a teenager, Helen kept a scrapbook of photographs—not, like most of her classmates, of movie stars, but of war photographs she clipped out of *Life* and *Look*. In 1945, when she was still in high school, she had snipped out photographs from a spread in the *Daily News* about Jewish refugees arriving at New York Harbor. Among them was Henry's picture—he was Heinrich then, fifteen years old. "An Orphan Hopes for Better Times," the caption read. A thick wool scarf framed a long, soulful face and dreamy eyes. Years later she met him at a cocktail party in Manhattan and, after hearing his story, felt she remembered his face. That night she dug out her high school scrapbook and found him, the man of her dreams.

That picture, framed, hung over Henry's desk. There were many pictures of Henry on the wall, taken by Helen at various stages of his life. Posing in front of Ex Libris, his ill-fated bookstore. Holding Jacob on his shoulders while Lev clung to his legs. In Central Park with a cigarette and beret and 1970s sideburns. Several that showed him as he looked now, bearded and bent over his desk. He recognized himself in none of them.

It was the pictures of his wife, the self-portraits, that Henry loved. These were not on display, though when he had first begun dating her, many years before, they had been. He had seen her naked in photographs on her wall before he saw her undressed in the flesh.

There were no photographs of the two of them together, because his wife was so often behind the camera, but nevertheless it was in photographs that they had come together. She had drawn him into the physical, visual world for a while. And he, perhaps, had drawn her into the world of unseen presences. They had met through the framed, shadowy portal of photography, though in recent years they had each retreated back toward the world they came from.

He had a sudden, deeply disturbing thought. Would she take his picture—afterward? A horrified shudder shook his heart. But he dismissed the fear. She wouldn't. Once, perhaps, in her early intrepid days, when she had lived for images, a young woman roving the graveyard of Europe. But not now. She didn't need another corpse for her collection. Not someone she loved.

There were also, on the walls, pictures of their sons as little boys, and Henry distracted himself by looking at several that hung on his study wall. Helen, who used only black-and-white film, took family pictures like a war photographer, the boys peering around corners, standing alone on the stairs of a vacation house, hunched under bushes. Was it his wife's camera style or something that had followed him to America that lent their lives an aura of tragedy even as they prospered? These pictures broke his heart and filled Henry with an ache of longing. He wished to reach back inside those pictures and comfort the frightened children there. Was he the one who had frightened them? He hoped to God he was not. But Jacob was thirty-six now and Lev was thirty-two. They had turned out all right, though Lev was in temporary freefall since the wedding disaster.

He had made a point of telling each of his sons that he loved him the last time he had called. Jacob had said, "I love you, too, Dad," which pleased Henry, not because he had doubted his son's love but because he wanted his son to look back on that conversation and feel he had expressed his feelings to his father. Lev, unfortunately, had not been home and Henry had simply left him a message. Lev had not called back and he knew that Lev would reproach himself for it later. Lev often went to science conferences for his magazine and no longer checked in as he once had. He needed privacy to get back on his feet. He was less practical and more emotional than Jacob. Henry made a point in his letter to Lev of reassuring him that he had been a very good son.

Each of these letters was in a sealed envelope on his desk, each with the name of one of his sons typed on the outside. The letter to his wife was handwritten and had been left on the dining room table so that she would find it before she found him.

"Dearest Helen, forgive me!" the note began. The hectic scrawl of his post-stroke handwriting gave the note the look of something written in great haste, though he had thought about it a long time before writing it. Sometimes, as his wife lay sleeping beside him, he whispered inaudibly, "Dearest Helen, forgive me."

Henry suddenly remembered that all this while the bath had been running. He picked up the tumbler of Scotch and, as quickly as he could, made his way to the bathroom. His left leg dragged slightly and he felt the familiar tipsy wobble of his walk. With the Scotch in his hand he might have been a morning drinker straining to maintain his composure. Parts of him felt oddly weightless, other parts drawn horribly downward. Gravity worked on him too weakly and too well. His orbit was decaying. Soon he would fall from the sky.

The bathtub was inches from overflowing. Moving with slow-motion haste, he set down the Scotch on the side of the sink and bent over the steaming tub. The heat of the bath hit him full force and he felt suddenly dizzy. He'd skipped breakfast—"Take care of the contents of your stomach," *Final Exit* counseled—and wondered if he was going to black out, but, holding onto the diagonal grip bar that had been installed after his stroke, he managed to shut off the tap. He was afraid of falling and noted the irony—the old physical fear still intact, even as he planned self-destruction. Self-deliverance, he hastily corrected himself as he settled himself carefully on the closed lid of the toilet seat.

He was breathing deeply. The steamy air was hard to ingest. Already the clean fantasy of a poetic departure was taking a more painful shape. The epigraph of *Final Exit* was a line from Keats: "To cease upon the midnight with no pain." Henry was a sucker for epigraphs; it was one of the things that made him trust the book. But nobody ceased without pain. Keats himself had coughed and cursed his way to the other side.

But he was doing the right thing. Three years before, he had suffered a stroke that had taken him a year to claw his way back from, physically and mentally. He knew—how, he could not say, but he knew—that there would be another stroke and that the next one would not be as forgiving. It was now, while he still had strength and clarity.

Henry had turned off the faucets imperfectly, so they dripped. He hoped this would not drive him crazy as he waited for the end. He'd had powerful hands once. When he hung his wife's pictures he pushed the nail in with his bare thumb, and there wasn't a jar he couldn't twist the lid off of; his grown sons, until the stroke, had handed him recalcitrant jars of pickles or jam.

He leaned forward and opened the drain so that the tub, when he got in, wouldn't overflow. Settling back on the closed lid of the toilet, he watched the water level slowly descend. The bath was his one addition to *Final Exit*'s prescription. The book said nothing about baths, but the idea of one had become fixed in his mind as a necessary part of his suicide. He had read about it originally in an obituary for the writer Jerzy Kosinski, who had followed the Hemlock Society instructions in 1991. The clipped obituary was in the locked desk drawer where he kept the pills and the list. Kosinski had used alcohol and pills and a plastic bag and had been found in his bathtub. Whether the warm water enhanced the effectiveness of the drugs and the alcohol, or whether it was simply Kosinski's private impulse to die in water, Henry could not remember and no longer cared. He, too, felt drawn to water, if only a bathtub's worth.

At first he had considered disguising his suicide. No notes to his wife or sons. Let it be a heart attack—that would hardly have surprised anyone, and the insurance company would have been more likely to pay out. But he would not be deprived of a chance to say good-bye, even if it would only be a word received after he was gone. He hoped his wife would declare it a heart attack anyway, though he did not wish to implicate her in any way.

He hoped the insurance company could be persuaded that his various illnesses would ultimately have proven fatal. They were old policies and might be honored—he had written his wife about this in a more detailed letter he had typed for her and placed inside the shoe box with his legal papers. But if not, he knew she would have enough. Her wedding portrait business was doing well; they had bought their apartment (over his objections) in the early eighties, and it had tripled in value. Helen also had bought the brownstone that housed her business, using money inherited from her father who, despite being a socialist, had been a shrewd investor. Henry's life insurance, if forfeited, was a price he was willing to pay for a chance to die a dignified death.

He hoped they would give him a Jewish burial. This mattered to him a great deal. His parents of blessed memory, reduced to ash, had not had Jewish burials. He wanted to lie with Hebrew on his gravestone alongside other Jews. "Bury me a Jew," he'd written in the note to his wife, and Helen, who was resourceful, would do that for him even if she had herself expressed the wish—God forbid—to be cremated.

Well, his sons would see to it that they were both buried. He could count on them—or on Lev at least—to disregard her wishes in the name of what was Jewish, what was right. They knew the restrictions and why cremation was abhorrent. Aboveground burial! Now there was a euphemism he loathed. No, his wife would lie next to him in death. In the twentieth century—perhaps not in America but in many other places—just to be buried was a luxury. He and Helen would stretch out together and enjoy the privilege. His sons would say Kaddish—or so he hoped. He had a certain anxiety on this score and had been explicit in his notes. His own fault; they were children of his ambivalence, not schooled as he would have schooled them now. But he hoped he had given them enough. As for suicide, Rabbi Hirsch would look the other way, or they'd find some obliging Reform rabbi who would interpret things favorably.

In any case, he was making no secret of his intentions. In addition to the pills and the alcohol and the bath, Henry planned to use a plastic bag. There was one already in the bathroom, its handle looped over the doorknob. The bag had been a problem. He had wanted to use a clear bag, and had found one, wadded up with the other bags in the kitchen drawer, but it had somehow gotten damp inside and was lined with fine yellow challah crumbs and tiny poppy seeds. He was willing to kill himself but not to get crumbs in his hair. *Vanity, vanity*, he thought with grim amusement. He'd been forced to settle for a Fairway bag, which he was planning to secure with a rubber band he had taken from that morning's *New York Times*. There was something undignified about the bag, which said "Like No Other Market" on the bottom. The notion that he would somehow be advertising a store in death unsettled him, as if even his suicide had a sponsor. He had been a reluctant and unsuccessful businessman all his life. But this was America after all.

Perhaps he wouldn't use the bag. It gave him a claustrophobic shudder to look at it. He had not followed the advice of *Final Exit*, which suggested trying it on beforehand. He thought he might be able to see through a portion of the thin, cheap, opaque plastic that was colored white and orange and black. The bag was to ensure that if the pills and the alcohol failed, and he merely fell asleep, his exhalations would slowly, quietly, painlessly finish him off.

Henry looked at his watch. He was running late. He was always forgetting how much longer everything took him now. His wife would be back at noon. He stood up slowly and realized that he had let out too much water from the tub. Carefully, hanging on once more to the bar, though with much more energy than before, he opened the faucets and let hot water cascade back into the tub until it was half full. He found he had greater strength in his arm, and this time when he shut off the faucet it didn't drip at all.

Proud of himself, he picked up his Scotch and carried it back into the study with him. It was only after he'd set it on the desk and sat down that he noticed it and realized the absurdity of his action. He had meant to leave the Scotch in the bathroom, but here he was carrying it around as if he were at a cocktail party.

From the bedroom he heard the scratches and whimpers of Mephisto, who did not like being shut up there. He felt sorry for the dog but he did not want him to be a witness, or to be found lapping his tub water afterward. He had an old-fashioned aversion to dogs, which he traced to his European Jewish childhood. Big dogs were set on little Jews. Or little dogs were primped and petted by Austrian ladies who treated their animals like people while human beings were carted away like animals.

But the dog had been a gift from his son Jacob and Jacob's wife, Penny, and dachshunds were scarcely dogs anyway. Henry's one act of rebellion had been in naming the dog Mephisto, short for Mephistopheles since—as he'd had to explain to both Jacob and Penny—the devil enters Faust's study in the form of a dog. He had grown fond of Mephisto in a way that had become a family joke. He insulted the dog and claimed to hate the animal, but he was the only one who was allowed to feed it or, until recently, walk it. It had been a reason to leave the apartment.

But lately it had become difficult to stoop down to clean up after the dog and Helen or Jack—a moody teenager who needed the pocket money and who lived on their floor—now did most of the walking. Sometimes Henry took the dog out anyway, against his better judgment, and against his own strict civic standards, furtively stalking away from Mephisto's modest but irrefutable excrement.

Henry had the sudden thought that after all the horrible impersonal upheavals of the century, and after a great deal of personal sorrow, he had decided to end his life because he could no longer walk his dog properly. This thought so overwhelmed him with shame that he immediately drove it out of his head. For a final time, he read over his list.

Fd Mph. Fst. Letts. JC. Ba. Pls. Bg. Sch. He had fed Mephisto. He had fasted. He had prepared his letters. Bundled up *Joy Comes in the Morning*. Drawn the bath. His pills were in front of him, the bag was in the bathroom. The Scotch was on the desk. He was ready but he thought everything through once more. He did not wish to discover, with his last gleam of consciousness, some key activity unperformed. "Leave nothing to chance," the author of *Final Exit* counseled, and Henry took the advice to heart. All four air conditioners were going full blast. It had been weirdly hot for April and he wished to be as considerate as possible. He took off his glasses and placed them on the desk. Somewhat improbably, his eyesight seemed to have improved.

He looked up at the photograph above his desk that his wife had clipped so many years before. She'd rephotographed it in her studio so that it looked like one of her own. The narrow dark eyes and wide, smooth cheeks. The scarf given to him by the JDC that gave him an inadvertently dapper look. The picture had grown painful to him—not because of how much he had changed, but how little. Fifty-four years later he still had the soul of a hopeful child, waiting for his parents to come and claim him. *An orphan hopes for better times.* Carefully and deliberately, he lifted the picture off the wall and placed it facedown on his desk, on top of the gathered pages of his memoir. The manuscript and its title seemed suddenly obscene to him. It occurred to him that he had never finished *Joy Comes in the Morning* because joy had never come. Was the title a lie? Was the very premise a lie? Was the psalm itself a lie?

He did not want to think it. He hoped his sons would not think it. A great deal had come to him. His wife and his children had come to him. The trouble wasn't joy. The trouble was simply that it was no longer morning. For so many, morning had never come.

What did his children believe? Henry hated to think that he had poisoned their faith in humanity. He himself was constantly surprised by sudden acts of kindness. Hadn't he been taken in by a Christian family? And just the other day, on Broadway, he had been unable to tie his own shoelaces, straining to reach them, when a beautiful young woman had appeared out of nowhere and wordlessly bent before him. She'd acted with such simplicity and directness that she made it impossible for him to feel shame. Afterward, he wanted to thank her but she had smiled and walked away before he had been able to get the words out. Speech had moved too slowly inside him and his inability to respond made him feel like a shy boy. Long after she was gone he had found himself moving down Broadway murmuring, "Thank you, miss. Thank you," over and over to himself. It was the sort of encounter he would like to have been able to capture in *Joy Comes in the*

Morning, but that he could never quite find the place for. Well, perhaps it would live in some other, invisible record.

He stood up slowly and slid the Advil jar into the large, square, soft pocket of his bathrobe. With an unsteady hand he picked up the Scotch. He looked around his study one final time to see that all was neat and ready for inspection. Should he return his picture to the wall? No, he would allow himself one dramatic gesture.

He stood for a moment in front of the vast bookshelf that formed one whole wall of his study. There were many books in several languages. Poetry. Novels. Histories. Prayer books. Somehow, they would have to speak for him. Part of him would live in those books much as part of him would live in the natural world that both his sons and his wife loved but that he had never had much feeling for. But he hoped that an undying element of his inner core would live on intact someplace other than this bookshelf or the grass around his grave. These of course were things one could not know beforehand, and to speak of them was to become not a philosopher but a child. All the big questions were a child's questions; he had always known that.

He would like to see his mother and father again. His sister, Esther. There were many friends from school who had not managed to get out. There were many cousins. An employee of his once remarked, when he turned sixty-five, that as you got older you had more and more friends on the other side of death and eventually, the balance tipped, you found yourself preparing to go there yourself. Henry, however, had always had more friends and relatives on the other side. And yet he had never felt prepared to go there himself.

Passing through the living room he paused in front of the stereo—they had never upgraded to a CD player, he couldn't imagine replacing fifty years of Bruno Walter and Toscanini and Heifetz or even that musical Nazi Furtwangler. He would have liked to listen to music but decided against it. That would be too dramatic and he did not wish to imagine his wife racing around the apartment while Beethoven, or perhaps the Verdi Requiem, thundered away. But perhaps Shlomo Carlebach. He had several albums by the singing rabbi that he loved.

When Carlebach was still alive, Henry had gone to his shul on Seventy-ninth Street. It evoked for him the Hasidic roots of his childhood, the psalms and liturgical couplets set to music that were at once deeply, Jewishly familiar and also melodious in a modern fashion that took him back to younger, more expansive days when he and Helen had gone to hear folk music in Greenwich Village and sat talking and smoking at the Limelight. He felt a momentary ache for Carlebach and for the music and for his sons and for his childhood and for his father and for the boy he had been when the war broke out. He had been called Chaim then.

He entered the bathroom solemnly and set his Scotch down on a porcelain corner of the tub. Unlooping the plastic bag, he let it float to the floor near where his head would be. He removed his bathrobe and hung it on a hook on the back of the bathroom door. Catching sight of himself in the mirror above the sink, he was shocked by his own nakedness, the bent back, the copper-white hair plunging like a waterfall from chest to belly. Unaccommodated man. A poor, bare, forked creature.

Well, he thought, we are all naked before God.

The sounds of the apartment came to him with great clarity. The persistent hum of the air conditioner. The faint scrabbling of his dog in the other room. The dim roar of the traffic below. He wished there was music. He stepped into the water—it had cooled considerably—and, hanging on to the grip bar, lowered himself slowly into the bath.

LEV FRIEDMAN raised his binoculars and brought into focus a tiny bird high above him, flitting in and out of view amid the leaves of a pin oak. For a blissful moment, Lev himself was lost among the leaves, unmindful of time.

He had spent the past few days at a conference at Princeton—the Ethics of Cloning. As a science reporter, Lev had a talent for explaining things he himself understood imperfectly, but he was happiest with the observable natural world. The conference had contained much drab public policy, a lot of nitty-gritty science and a few horrifying sci-fi scenarios. Someone had cited the ethicist Glenn McGee, warning about the creation of an "ape-human baby." Lev could not get the image out of his head. It was still early afternoon and he had gone straight from Grand Central to the Ramble, the wooded heart of Central Park. His overnight bag was between his feet; his blue blazer—a burden on such a hot day—was slung over his shoulder. A Yankees cap extinguished his red hair, except for a flaming tendril that crept out the back.

Lev had only recently reclaimed his old interest in bird-watching, having written a story about the hawks of Central Park for *Eureka*. He realized how much he enjoyed looking at life through a lens, though unlike his mother he never felt the urge to fix what he saw on film. The fact that it was fleeting was part of what attracted him.

It was mid-April—so far migration had been thin, but the weather was unnaturally warm and the wind had blown from the northwest for two days. Lev traveled with a pair of pocket binoculars. He peered upward, watching the bird snatch invisible bugs from the air. It could be a palm warbler (he looked for tail bobbing), but he saw neither the wings nor the tail clearly. There was definitely yellow on the tiny bird, somewhere. And black. Yellow-rumped? Magnolia? Lev paused only when the crunch of footsteps behind him became louder. In Central Park it paid to be mindful of men as well as birds.

The man Lev saw over his shoulder, clearly homeless, was staring down at the ground, muttering to himself. His unseasonably heavy coat and boots, his leaf-filled beard and gaunt face, gave him the quaint, antiquated look of a Matthew Brady photograph, a prospector or Confederate deserter. Milky sunlight filtered down through the trees and embroidered the man's coat with light and shadow. Lev knew better than to be fooled by picturesque effects and he waited for the man to pass.

Tall and slender, Lev drew himself up to his full height, took a step back from his bag, and unlooped his binoculars from around his neck in case he needed them as a weapon. If he turns on me, Lev thought, I'll kick him in the balls and swing these into his face. He had been taking Krav Maga with a group that met in the "combat room" of John Jay College of Criminal Justice, their mats a sea of sticky blue. The system, devised by a little Jew from Bratislava who had fought anti-Semitic hoodlums and even Nazis in his native country, and who had gone on to devise a new form of hand-to-hand combat for the Israeli army, had seized Lev's imagination.

Lev often found himself envisioning violent scenarios, despite the benign safety of Giuliani's New York and his own gentle nature. Twice a week he practiced various methods for breaking choke holds and fending off club-wielding assailants, along with the most effective ways to gouge eyes, snap windpipes, and knee someone in the groin. He had bought a plastic protective cup for his genitals. The course was supposed to instill self-confidence and well-being, but he found it feeding a sense of anticipatory dread that had lately taken hold of him. He fought off assailants in his dreams.

The homeless man's heavy, unlaced boots dragged as he passed. He seemed entirely unaware of Lev's existence. Lev thought inevitably of poor Neal, who also wore an overcoat in all weather, his pockets stuffed with notepaper and pens and odd talismanic items. Madness made some people tear off their clothes and run naked and wild like his father's beloved King Lear. For Neal it meant overdressing. Lev owed Neal a visit; he made a mental promise to go that week.

From behind, the homeless man was all rags and bad smell. Lev, though recoiling inwardly, took a few steps after him, half thinking he would give him some money and already reaching one hand into his pocket when the man suddenly spun around.

"Thief! Ghost in my pants!" he shouted, along with a phrase that sounded like, "Morgan! Morgan!" He then turned and stalked off through the bushes.

Lev stood, his heart pounding, his knees weak. He felt oddly embarrassed, though as far as he could tell no one had been around to witness the encounter. If he had been attacked, Lev realized, he would simply have stood there, despite his "training," without raising a hand.

"Face it," Jenny had said to him once, "you'd rather die than kill someone, even in self-defense."

They had been in bed at the time. It was said with affection, but there had been a vaguely taunting quality to it, too, though she was stroking him gently. Jenny was a lawyer with the D.A.'s office. Lev pictured her as she looked then, sitting astride him: her small freckled breasts; her auburn hair and green eyes; the underbite that gave her a sullen, aristocratic, sexy air.

Lev made a brief effort to return to his bird. Tipping his head back, he scanned the upper canopy with his binoculars, trying to recapture his earlier feeling of forgetful concentration. To his astonishment, his hands shook slightly, a vibration of fright, making it difficult to focus. He lowered his binoculars and looked with his naked eye. Both his father and his brother needed thick glasses but Lev, like his mother, had perfect vision.

Sticky new leaves unfurled against a blue background. Unfallen seed clusters and pods of the previous autumn mingled with new shoots so that for a moment it was hard to tell what season it was. He recognized the tiny, pointed leaves of a sweet gum, like animal footprints against the sky.

Lev smiled ruefully at himself, a thirty-two-year-old man happiest looking up—at birds, at trees, at the simple sky. No wonder Jenny had thought him a nice Jewish boy. But then he had ruined her wedding. That wasn't very nice, was it?

The thought of what he had done came back to him, as it did every day, like a remembrance of illness and made his face burn under the baseball cap. Four months later, Lev still reeled with astonishment and shame.

It was the photographs that had put him over the edge. He often thought that if they had waited till after the ceremony to take pictures he would be married. The morning of the wedding, Lev had arrived in his tuxedo and had posed dutifully with his family and Jenny's family, with Jenny in her resplendent dress. They had gambled on November but the weather was perfect for late fall—everyone kept talking about it. Lev smiled and tilted his head as directed and felt himself turning into a picture, an image of happiness he did not feel. He would wind up in an album of the sort his mother created for a living, sealed under plastic.

After the last picture was taken, Lev had excused himself and borrowed the keys to his brother's car. He told Jacob, who had driven him to Tappan Hill, that he had lost a tuxedo stud and that he wanted to look for it. Jacob handed over the keys to his rented Jaguar, only raising his eyebrows in an unspoken question to which Lev merely shrugged. The car had a phone and, a few moments later, Lev dialed his brother's cell phone and told him he couldn't go through with it.

"It's too late," were the first words out of his older brother's mouth. A businessman, Jacob had been doing the math all morning, commenting on the cost of everything. But his next response had been more human, and he told Lev that all grooms get scared, that he himself had panicked before marrying Penny, that this is human nature, and that he should be a man and come back and talk about it in person. But by then Lev was on the West Side Highway and there was no turning back.

Jake's cell phone was passed around. The rabbi. Lev's best man,

Bill. It was like a hostage negotiation. Lev was drenched in sweat. Cars were honking and shooting past him. Finally Jenny was fetched—it could not be avoided. The pain in her voice crushed and silenced him.

Jenny knew he was prone to panic—she had held his hand on airplanes, and once, when they were stuck between stations on the subway, had instructed him to close his eyes while she whispered erotic diversions in his ear until the train started again. Her gentle tone suggested she would understand if, despite all the planning, he wished to get married in a private room somewhere. But Lev could only blurt out, in a final spasm of truth compulsion, that he did not love her enough and did not wish to spend the rest of his life with her.

Jenny had seemed not to hear this. Her voice contracted and took on a cold prosecutorial cast. Was there someone else? There was no one else. Was he gay? He was not gay.

"Then," Jenny had shouted, "you're just an asshole, is that it? Or so cut off from your real feelings they can't be called feelings, can they? You're as crazy as your friend."

At the time he made no reply, though Lev, who reimagined this exchange daily, sometimes, belatedly, did try to answer these charges. Much later, he was forced to admit that if Neal had not gone mad a year and a half before the wedding, he might not have moved in with Jenny. No doubt that glimpse of chaos—along with his father's stroke, coming at the same time—had made life with Jenny seem a welcome refuge. And yet it was ultimately the specter of Neal's sickness and his father's frailty that had planted in Lev an urge to free himself from falsehood and compromise, to live a large and truthful life. The problem was that he did not know what this might mean, and when he formulated it, he did sound a little like his crazy friend. Certainly the day of his wedding he had behaved like a lunatic.

There were so many things to be ashamed of. He had cared enough about Jenny to want to spare her his wounding doubts, though this had turned out, of course, to be a coward's kindness, which is to say, cruelty. He had wanted to love her more than he did and his failure, as well as the ease with which he had hidden his feelings, shamed him. The feelings themselves shamed him—the craving for a deeper love seemed somehow unmanly. He was attracted to Jenny but his soul—a word that it embarrassed him to use (more shame!) but that he found impossible to avoid—felt oddly detached. And then of course there was his behavior itself.

Of all the many sources of shame, running away from his own wedding like a child on the first day of school was surely the greatest. Jenny would never have treated him that way. Decisive, forthright, she was, he often reflected, a better person than he was. It had been Jenny's idea to sponsor a child from Guatemala—when he moved out of their apartment, the one thing Lev had claimed custody of was the photograph of Rosita that the Save the Children agency had sent. He had neglected to put through a change of address form as he'd intended and the picture itself had soon vanished under a thatch of Post-its and party invitations and drawings sent to him by his niece, Margaret, stuck with magnets to his refrigerator in the tiny studio he now sublet. Occasionally he caught sight of Rosita's dark eyes, reproaching him.

The day of the wedding, Lev learned later from friends, Jenny had conducted herself heroically. She waited until all the guests were seated. The rabbi told the company that Jenny had something to say. The long train of her white dress gathered in one hand, she took the microphone and, with royal composure, thanked everyone for coming.

"It seems," she said, "my fiancé has run away."

She invited everyone to stay and enjoy themselves though she herself was going to go home with her parents.

Lev was by then cowering in their (soon to be Jenny's) apartment, unsuccessfully trying to anesthetize himself with Xanax while seriously contemplating jumping out the window—though from a safe distance, since even in despair he was afraid of heights. Perhaps it would have been better, as his unhelpful brother, Jacob, had advised, to have waited a year and then quietly gotten divorced.

Lev was still unsure four months later whether he had run toward life or away from it; whether he had doomed himself to loneliness and incompatibility or—with admittedly bad timing—set himself free. He still held out hope that he had done something sane, not crazy; something for love and not against it; something motivated by bravery and not cowardice.

Lev's therapist, Dr. Halpern, did not favor generous interpretations of Lev's aborted wedding and had gone so far as to suggest that Lev may have been re-creating, in a warped, misguided fashion, the disruptions of his father's refugee experience. But then Lev, a dutiful patient for many years—just as he had been a dutiful boyfriend and fiancé—had stopped showing up for his sessions. He had filled his time slot with Krav Maga.

It was still early in the season and Lev was too distracted for real birding. Still, he raised his binoculars whenever he felt the occult stirring of life above him or down in the scrub, where white-throated sparrows and the occasional towhee rooted for bugs and seeds amid the shrubs, leaf litter, and cast-off condoms.

The sound of drumming drifted toward him from across the lake. The drummers often gathered by Bethesda Fountain.

It was terribly hot and the edges of the lake were upholstered like a pool table with a thick layer of green algae. The lake gave off a boggy smell. A few rowboats plowed lackadaisically through the primordial pesto, but even with the greenhouse effect and the urban effluvia, Lev felt a kind of wild possibility as he scanned the trees and phragmities for birds. A few birders passed, dog walkers, the well-dressed men who headed off with discrete purposefulness into the bushes—the Ramble had its own complicated life.

Lev and Neal had spent many hours birding together in that very spot, though Lev's interest hadn't survived the conformist pressures of high school and he had given up his hobby for sports and girls and a different sort of hanging out. But Neal, who had clung to his interest with what always seemed to Lev a greater measure of integrity, had persuaded Lev when they were seventeen to spend a week at a bird banding station in Manomet, Massachusetts, where tiny transmitters were strapped to the backs of endangered birds—osprey and eagles and smaller birds as well. Years later Neal came to believe that he, too, had been banded like a bird; he had stopped wearing his watch for this reason, but that was insufficient to dispel his fear that his movements were being monitored by Nazis. After Neal had been institutionalized at Columbia Presbyterian, Lev had a recurring dream that Neal was flying over the city, darkening the apartment where Lev lived.

Lev could not help wondering if he wasn't looking for something connected to Neal as he wandered through the park. He wandered aimlessly but with a vague desire to move south and east, toward the Boathouse, where he would get a cup of coffee and organize his notes from the conference. It never ceased to amaze him that scientific accomplishments always contained the seeds of terrible things. The ape-human baby! *Eureka*, though a generally serious magazine, would want him to play that up though there was much potential good as well— the replacement of diseased organs and perhaps therapies for stroke or even schizophrenia. Lev's father did not really believe in progress. He often spoke about the way trains were the perfect symbol of the modern age—settling the countryside, knitting civilization together and allowing, at the same time, the mass movements of troops that made warfare an unimaginable slaughterhouse and mass deportations a matter of routine.

Lev suddenly saw a palm warbler sitting down low in a sweet gum, bobbing its tail, a little bird with a yellow eyebrow, a chestnut cap, and a cold black eye, a thrilling alien presence. Lev murmured a *Shehechiyanu*: "Thank you, God, for allowing me to reach this time." He did not consider himself religious but often, when he saw a "life bird"—a bird he had never seen before—or whenever he saw a "year bird"—a bird new to him that season—he recited the brief Hebrew prayer thanking God for the experience.

It gave Lev inexplicable pleasure to attach to the sighting of a new bird these few words of thanks, though it seemed to him simultaneously irrational and perhaps further evidence that he was losing his grip on reality. His father, even before he had returned to the religious observance of his childhood and come to regret the manner in which he had raised his sons, had often recited this blessing with Lev and his brother over a new fruit or a new activity, and the blessing brought with it a glimmer of childhood warmth.

Lev thought with a pang of his father. There had been a strange message on his machine before he went out of town. Lev had not merely neglected to return his father's call, he had failed to tell his parents where he was going or to take his cell phone. He was aware that in the last few months he was growing more isolated, almost against his will. And something in his father's tone had both alarmed and irritated him. His parents called him more since the wedding fiasco, and Lev suspected they feared for his mental health, as if they shared Jenny's judgment and believed that in some strange, doppelgangerish fashion, Lev was destined to share his friend's fate. They, too, had been shaken by Neal's schizophrenia—Lev had played with him so much as a boy that it must almost have seemed that a son of theirs had lost his mind.

And of course, Lev's father had his own mental fears.

"My mind isn't what it's cracked up to be," Henry Friedman sometimes joked after the aphasic moments that disturbed his speech. His father loved puns, and the stroke seemed to make his own sense of language even more self-conscious than his immigrant's awareness had made him in the first place.

Lev wished he had his cell phone with him. He felt a great surge of love mingled with guilt and protective concern. He owed his father a call.

He kept hearing his father's voice in his head—the studied absence of an accent constituting an accent of its own. The messages his father left often had the formality of letters read aloud. The last one in particular had a scripted quality. "Dearest Lev, it's Dad," his father had begun. "I need to talk to you. You must be roaming about. You've always remembered . . ." and here his father faltered and paused, saying only, "Call me when you can. I love you."

His father had always used somewhat formal locutions that were also attempts to sound colloquially American. He sometimes called

Lev "sonny" or "my boy"—phrases learned off the television in the late forties or from movies or from some long out-of-date textbook that, despite his father's literary sophistication, had lodged in his vocabulary.

When he became more religious—Lev by then was in college—his father often left pronouncements or calendric reminders on the answering machine: "Tuesday is Shavuos." Or, "This is just to say that Tisha b'Av is this Sunday. I don't know if you'll be fasting, but if you want to join me in shul . . ." Since his father's stroke, however, the reminders had grown less frequent. His father's own hold on the calendar seemed to grow more tenuous and Lev experienced a guilty sense of liberation from the reminders which, as much as the actual days, were how he had connected himself to Jewish time. At the same time, his father's growing silence had its own power.

All of which made his father's last phone call doubly disturbing. "You've always remembered . . ." what? What had Lev always remembered? The Jewish holidays? Hardly, he had always forgotten them. Inevitably, his mind supplied a phrase: "The restrictions."

"The restrictions" was his father's all-purpose term for Jewish law, specifically as applied to Jewish burial practices. This included getting the body in the ground on the day immediately after death. Whenever Lev or his brother went off on a school trip that lasted more than one day, or when they went traveling after college, his father would remind them to stay in touch by uttering the phrase, "You know the restrictions." It had become something of a joke between the brothers. When they were camping together, if one of them went into the woods to piss, he would say to the other, "If I'm not back in half an hour call Rabbi Markowitz. You know the restrictions."

Lev had by this time arrived at the Boathouse. He had lost his desire to sit at a table drinking iced coffee and reading. He had to call his father back—what had he been thinking? There were pay phones around the side of the restaurant. Lev dialed and to his surprise got the answering machine—his father was usually home by midday and his mother often came back for lunch.

"Mom, Dad," Lev said into the machine. "It's Lev. I would love to talk to you and to see you. Dad, I got your message but I've been away. Hope all's well." He wanted to leave more in the message, to say "I love you," as his father had, but he didn't. He would tell him when he saw him. He hung up and dialed his own machine. Lev had not checked his messages since Friday.

The first message was from his editor, Nick Henderson, who thought nothing of calling on the weekend to see how things were going. The second was from his friend Eric, confirming the next day's squash game. The third was from his mother, though her voice sounded like someone else's as it broke over the machine: "Lev, your father's in the hospital. Something very bad has happened."

Lev felt the air around him darken and his own body grow cold. His mother, though panicked, was always steady in the face of crisis and she was issuing directions. "Go straight to the hospital, ninth floor. It's on Fifty-eighth Street and Tenth Avenue. Enter on Tenth Avenue. Go straight there," she said again. "I've already left your brother a message."

Lev spun around in the vain realization that there were no cabs in the park. He shoved his binoculars into his overnight bag and began to run. He couldn't help the fleeting, wounded sense that his mother had called him second, though his older brother, Jacob, lived a thousand miles away and he was right there. He drove this resentment instantly from his heart. He was sure it was another stroke. A terrible wave of guilt that he had deferred returning his father's call came over him. *You know the restrictions.* Had his father had a premonition? Dear God, let him be all right.

Lev had chosen a bad path and was somehow running parallel to East Side Drive. He corrected himself and ran toward the closest exit, pained by an awareness that he was running east even though his father was west. But he needed to get out of the park as quickly as possible. He tore through a row of forsythia bushes and took off toward Fifth Avenue.

HELEN FRIEDMAN had felt something was wrong the moment she opened the door to her apartment. For one thing, Mephisto had not run out to greet her. It was unlikely that her husband had taken the dog for a walk; Henry was no longer able to clean up after the little dachshund. For another thing, the apartment was freezing cold, and though the day was hot it was unusual for her husband to keep the air-conditioning blasting, for reasons of frugality if not personal preference.

She let the door slam behind her and walked into the apartment holding a large bag of groceries from Fairway. In her agitation she did not set the bag down but called into the apartment. There was no answer. Waiting for a reply she heard the trapped scrabbling of Mephisto locked in the bedroom and all at once she felt afraid.

That morning her husband had seemed secretive and distracted. He had been very keen to know when she was planning to come back from her errands. He had suggested, uncharacteristically, that she take the dog. Lately, of course, he had been more and more preoccupied. He had recovered remarkably from the stroke, but it had scarred his mood and weakened him in many subtle ways that she knew he was constantly concealing. Once or twice he had addressed her in German without seeming to notice. But generally speaking she felt he was on the mend and she had dismissed her fears—although today she had decided against stopping by her photo studio. Something told her to come home.

She hurried into the apartment, still calling Henry's name. She ran to the bedroom and opened the door. Mephisto sprang out gratefully, pawing at her legs and sandaled feet. Helen ignored him. She called her husband's name again. He was not in the bedroom. She turned and ran back down the hall. She did not think to look in the bathroom though she was half aware that the carpeted hallway was wet. She was still clutching her groceries.

Everywhere she was confronted with her own photographs—Lev, Jacob, Henry. She understood immediately and as if for the first time how insignificant a photograph is. She kept calling his name.

In the dining room she saw a piece of paper leaning against a vase with the yellow freesia she had bought the day before. Her husband's frenetic handwriting leapt out at her. "Dearest Helen forgive me!" Her heart began to beat wildly and her vision darkened and for a moment she nearly blacked out. At the same instant she heard a great bang and into the dining room staggered a figure—white, naked, wet, and wearing on its head an orange-and-black Fairway bag. There was something so frightening and so absurd and so tragic about this vision that for a split second she simply stared. Then she screamed, dropped her groceries, and raced forward. In one swift motion she pulled the bag off her husband's head.

"Oh you foolish man, what have you done?" she demanded.

Henry looked at her in utter perplexity. Then he moved his mouth as if he wished to speak but no words came out. He gave an inappropriate little smile and staggered backward. She saw that he was about to fall and stepping forward threw her arms around him. She was off balance herself and he was much heavier than she had imagined but she hugged him with all her strength.

"I'm not letting you go," she said aloud. And together husband and wife fell to the ground.

DEBORAH SPENT SUNDAY MORNING at the synagogue in her small office. She met with Tyler Shapiro, whose bar mitzvah was in a few weeks. Tyler was tone deaf but sweet tempered and intelligent and she liked working with him. She had an effect on the teenage boys that she tried to be mindful of. For that matter, she had an effect on the teenage girls, who occasionally confided their chaotic secrets to her. There wasn't much you could teach these rich Manhattan kids about life, and yet there was an innocence at their core that Deborah recognized and loved. They intimidated Rabbi Zwieback and they intimidated each other but they did not intimidate her. She had been a rebellious teenager herself and their smoldering, needy, subversive energies were familiar to her.

In certain ways she was still rebellious. Not long ago, Zwieback had suggested, in his oblique, gentle, and thoroughly infuriating fashion, that her skirts were perhaps a little short for a "rabbinic role model." She did not wish to be one of those desexed rabbis who hung around the synagogue like neutered house cats. Or like so many of the women in her graduating class with their close-cropped Yentl-the-yeshiva-boy haircuts and frumpy clothes. You half-expected their voices to begin cracking. Deborah disliked being around them and hoped this aversion was not because her sister, Rachel, was gay, though Rachel, who was slender and elegant, wouldn't be caught dead dressing like the women of the golem brigade.

After leaving the synagogue Deborah had intended to go for a swim at the West Side Y but somehow found herself walking toward Roosevelt Hospital. There were several patients she wanted to check on, including Partha, a little Indian boy who had a brain tumor and spoke no English. He spent a great deal of time sitting on his bed, but if you began to play with him he leapt into impish, animated life. The week before, she had spent an hour sitting on the floor of the playroom setting up blocks, which Partha gleefully knocked down over and over again. Deborah tried to encourage him to build something but he wanted only to knock things down. Before he toppled blocks he would laugh and shout his own name. Who knew what complicated ritual of mastery he was enacting? Deborah didn't really feel the need to understand. It had been an exhilarating hour. Most of the adults brought only their tragic awareness into the rooms of these hairless, radiated, chemical-fed children. Deborah had a great capacity for play that allowed her not to forget they were dying, but to remember they were still alive.

But Partha, she learned when she got to the pediatric floor, had been abruptly taken home by his parents. The tumor was inoperable, the infection the boy had developed was not getting better, and his parents had decided to cease subjecting their son to hospital measures that were not in the long run going to make any difference. Deborah was told all this by Doreen, a sweet, plump Irish nurse who began to cry as she spoke to Deborah. Doreen couldn't get used to the children dying. She had worked in the ER before moving to the pediatric floor and felt she had seen everything, but somehow children with cancer was more than she bargained for. "I keep telling myself it's a good thing they're Hindu," Doreen said. "They think about life differently in India. But I know that's a crock. His parents will cry just as much when he's gone."

"Yes," Deborah agreed, "they will."

Somehow, perhaps because Doreen was crying, she herself felt oddly detached from the sadness of it. But she hugged Doreen and suggested they get coffee later.

Deborah made her rounds, looking in on congregants who were hospitalized and on the patients she'd developed a rapport with. In the ICU she noticed that a new patient had been admitted that day. The name on the door was Friedman. She assumed he was Jewish and stuck her head into the room.

There was a man lying in bed. He was not hooked up to a respirator but there was the steady whir and occasional beep of machines, the tubes for waste and fluid, discreetly but undeniably externalizing what should be hidden. He was alone and she stepped into the room. The man in bed had a neatly trimmed rust-colored beard. His eyes were closed. Deborah drew closer. There was something familiar about his face, as if she had seen him before in a dream. Was it her grandfather, who had died when she was five? She was aware of a greater emotional response toward him than she usually had to patients on first encounters, especially patients whose eyes were closed, who did not speak. She felt an impulse, which she did not indulge, to kiss him on the forehead.

"Excuse me, are you a doctor?" a voice demanded suddenly, calling Deborah out of her reverie.

Deborah turned around and saw a woman standing in the room.

"No," said Deborah, flustered.

"Are you a nurse?"

"I'm a rabbi."

The woman looked Deborah over from head to foot and smiled a complicated smile.

"Really," she said.

Deborah had by this time come over to the woman and put out her hand to shake but realized that the woman's right arm was in a sling. The woman kept staring at Deborah with weary, suspicious eyes. But she said, "I'm Helen Friedman. That's my husband, Henry."

Deborah liked the look of this strong woman. She wore sandals and a flowing dress of light patterned cotton that was tied around the waist with an elegant sash. A luminous jade pendant hung around her neck and there were several turquoise and silver bracelets on the wrist of her good arm. The other wrist, the one in the sling, was wrapped in an Ace bandage. She had surprising white hair, which she wore in a long braid like an aging Rapunzel.

"I'd like to be alone with my husband," the woman said.

"Of course," Deborah said, stung. "It's only if you want . . ."

"Who sent you?" the woman asked, before Deborah could leave.

"Well," she said, fingering the photo ID that hung around her neck, "I have a congregation on the West Side. This is part of my job. But, basically, I sent myself."

She was aware of wanting this woman's approval and of not quite receiving it. She reminded herself that this woman's husband was perhaps dying. What did her own vain needs and wishes matter?

The woman said nothing. On closer examination, she had the rumpled look of someone who had spent the night in vigil. Her eyes were ringed with darkness. She smelled of old perfume and cigarettes.

"Are you all right?" Deborah asked her. "Are you sure you don't feel like a visit?"

"You might have noticed," the woman said, "that it's my husband who's the patient."

Deborah nodded. This was part of it, absorbing their anger. She cleared her throat.

"Of course," she said. "I'm sorry to intrude. I only thought . . ."

The woman cut her off. "Forgive me. It's been a stressful twenty-four hours. My husband had a stroke. He wasn't planning to have a stroke," she said, rather strangely. "He was planning to . . . have something else. But that's what he had. He's woken up a few times. He's out of the worst danger, they say. He can't talk."

"I'm sorry," Deborah said. What was this woman trying to tell her? She did not wish to pry too much. She asked Mrs. Friedman if she wanted to say a prayer. At this suggestion the woman seemed to recoil slightly.

"Oh no," she said. "Not me. My husband is the one who likes to pray," Helen said.

"Would you mind?" Deborah asked, unable to resist, motioning to the man on the bed. The woman hesitated but at last she said, "No, go ahead."

Deborah moved to the side of the bed and laid her hand on Henry's. Before beginning she looked up to invite his wife to join her but the woman would not meet her gaze. Deborah did not push it. She shut her eyes and chanted a single verse of the Twenty-third Psalm softly in Hebrew, using the Shlomo Carlebach tune she loved. *Gam ki elech b'geh tzalmavet lo irah rah.* As always, the words and music stirred her deeply and in her mind she walked, with this man she did not know, who was yet so familiar, through the valley of the shadow of death. She had meant to sing the verse only once, mindful of the uncomfortable wife, but she found herself slipping from the last word back to the first word over and over. At last, she stopped singing and stood with her hand resting on the man's arm, her eyes still shut. Someone tapped her on the shoulder. It was Nick, the phlebotomist, who had come with his little kit to perform tests.

"Sorry, Rabbi," he said. "I've got a few things to do."

Helen was standing with her back to Deborah looking out the window. Deborah went over to the woman and saw that she was crying. She did not know what to do—she did not wish to interrupt the flow of tears—and simply stood nearby, looking down. The woman turned slowly.

"You pray very beautifully," she said.

"Thank you," Deborah said. "Would you like to talk a little?" But the woman shook her head no.

"Maybe I'll look in later if you don't mind."

The woman shrugged in a way that made it difficult to tell what she wanted.

"Good-bye for now," Deborah said. "I hope your husband has a speedy recovery."

It was not what she had wanted to say. What had she wanted to say?

"Good-bye for now," Helen said and, to Deborah's surprise, leaned over and kissed her on top of her head.

THE REALLY DEPRESSING THING ABOUT HOSPITALS, Lev thought as he rode up in the giant elevator, wasn't the odor of illness or of antiseptic, it was the smell of food. The entire building smelled like the lunchroom in his junior high school. It was a smell of despair from a time when a bad moment lasted forever and leaving was not an option.

They had told Lev in the lobby that his father was in the intensive care unit on 9-A West. The great automatic door of the unit swept open with mechanical violence. Lev scanned the names on the glass-fronted rooms, catching glimpses of inert and terrifying figures, wired and tubed, stretched out on display. He found the words "Friedman, H." scribbled on a little board and rushed inside but the room was empty. There was not even a bed.

Lev stood in the empty room and felt a surge of terror. For the first time it occurred to him that his father might be dead. His entire life seemed to him suddenly misspent. He had done nothing right, he did not honor or know his father properly and now he never would. He was entirely unprepared for this moment. The emptiness of the room, the whiteness, the silent standing monitors chilled his soul. Where was his father?

"Excuse me," said a voice behind him. "Are you looking for Friedman?"

"Yes," Lev cried. "I'm his son."

It was a Filipino nurse in baby blue hospital scrubs. She had a stern but kind face. "They moved him down to a floor. He's doing better."

She walked out of the unit toward the elevator with him.

"Did you come in from Atlanta?" the nurse asked. No doubt she had heard from his mother about Jacob. Lev burned with shame at this reminder that twenty-four hours had already passed since his mother's call and he was only now arriving.

"I was traveling," he said.

He tried to pump the nurse for information about his father. Was it a stroke? How was he? She seemed strangely reluctant to give straight answers. She confirmed it was a stroke and that his father was doing better but there seemed something more this woman knew.

"Your mama will tell you everything," she said. "She's a very strong woman," she added, admiringly.

"Yes," Lev agreed.

The nurse got in an elevator going up and Lev got in one going down. On the seventh floor he found his father. It was a double room but there was nobody else in it. Henry Friedman lay on the bed. The white sheet was drawn up right under his chin so that, despite his beard, he looked like a little boy. He looked like Little Bear in the children's book he had once read Lev. Lev bent over the sleeping form and gently put his hand to his father's cheek, the method his father had used to wake him every morning for school. Henry's eyes remained closed. Lev felt the soft hairs of his father's beard and a great wave of love overcame him.

Though his father appeared to be unconscious, the fact that he was there at all, that he was not dead, flooded Lev's heart with gratitude. He recited the *Shehechiyanu*, the prayer he said on seeing a bird for the first time. *Thank you God for letting me reach this time.* It was the only prayer he could summon to mind, though he imagined his father would have hoped for more.

Was it right to praise God before he knew what kind of shape his father was in, before he knew what time this was that he had reached? Lev wasn't sure, but he was so happy his father was still alive, so grateful seeing him there that he could not help himself. He wished he knew other things to recite. Instead, he spoke to his father in an inner whisper. *Oh Dad. Dad. It's me, Lev. I'm so sorry I didn't come sooner. I love you. I understand now. I understand.*

What did he understand? He didn't know. The mute confession surprised him.

Lev had visited his father in the hospital on past occasions—after his father's first stroke and, years before, after his mild heart attack. But somehow, almost because he was in those days closer to his parents, more attached to them, it had less of an effect on him. It had taken place inside the bubble of the family. Now his heart had to race back from some more distant place and the speed of the return journey left him dazed. He felt the intervening accumulations of his life—his job, his attitudes, his independence—accordion like a car in a crash. It was an unpleasant but irresistible movement.

Despite the fact that he had just arrived, Lev left the room again quickly to find a doctor who could tell him something. He knew his mother would be back soon but he could not wait to learn more. It was hard to find someone who knew his father's case, but Lev finally stopped a nurse, a tall, light-skinned black woman with gold-framed glasses who confirmed that, yes, his father had a stroke, though again Lev got the same odd sense of a secret being withheld.

Frustrated, he went back to the hospital room where, to his surprise, a woman was bending over his father. One hand was resting on his father's forehead, the other held his hand. Lev froze outside the open door. For a moment, he thought something had happened to his father and he was being resuscitated, but the woman wasn't in hospital dress. She had on a short gray skirt with dark stockings and a lemon-yellow blouse. Her thick, brown-blond hair was swept onto her head and held with a tortoiseshell clip. Her lips were moving but Lev could not hear any words. He did not need to. He understood everything in an instant.

"Hey!" he shouted, stepping into the room. "Please. Thank you, no. No thank you!"

He spoke as if to a foreigner who might not understand, or as if he were a foreigner himself.

Deborah looked up, startled.

"No laying on of hands, please. My f-father's soul doesn't need saving. We're J-Jews. We're . . ."

When agitated, Lev occasionally stuttered, though he had mastered what had in high school been a true affliction. Fearing he was about to become tongue-tied only made him more upset.

Deborah removed her hand from Henry's head. She lowered his hand back onto the bed and stepped away, smiling.

"Are you Henry's son?"

Her question was unnecessary. With his long, slender, mournful face, green eyes, and red hair, Lev was clearly the child of the man on the bed.

That this woman was already intimate with his father was strange and annoying, though she was quite attractive. She stared at him with rich brown eyes, arching her high, asymmetrical eyebrows a little condescendingly, he thought. Her smile had something of a smirk in it. She started to say something but he cut her off.

"The question is, who are you?" he asked, officiously pulling out the reporter's notebook he kept in his back pocket. "B-barging in here, giving my father last rites, or whatever the hell you're doing."

All the frustrations of his day overflowed in him.

Lev tried to read the ID tag hanging around Deborah's neck without appearing to stare at her breasts.

"I'm Rabbi Green," said Deborah.

She put out her hand, emphasizing the word *rabbi.*

Deborah noticed immediately that when he blushed, the freckles on Lev's face vanished. She'd wanted to embarrass him, but not that much, and she felt instantly regretful.

"I'm Lev Friedman," he said quietly, almost in a whisper, taking her warm, slender hand in his cool grip. "I'm sorry for shouting."

Lev glanced at his father. Henry's eyes remained closed, though Lev had a sudden sensation that his father was listening.

"I'm sorry I unsettled you," said Deborah.

She ought to have stayed; this was often how good visits began, but she had promised to meet Doreen in the cafeteria and somehow she had an impulse to flee. She felt simultaneously vindictive and ashamed. Lev's intensity reminded her of someone, though she could not say whom.

"I'll leave you alone with your father."

Deborah bent briefly over Henry's face and murmured words Lev did not catch, though it was clear to him that they were in Hebrew. He smelled something lemony as Deborah bent over and a hint of something warmer and more intimate. There were pale stains under her arms.

His embarrassment, and his fear of stuttering, was too intense to allow him to do more than nod at the departing woman as he took a seat beside his father. He placed his hand in his father's and felt disappointment in the hand, as if his father wanted the rabbi to come back, too. He would like to have put his hand on his father's forehead, as Deborah had done, but he didn't.

His father's eyes were suddenly open.

"Dad, it's me, Lev!" he cried. "I'm so glad you're awake."

But his father's eyes were shut once more.

What an idiot I am, thought Lev.

He looked around the room and noticed for the first time that there were photographs of his father everywhere, including the photograph of his father as a young refugee that his mother had snipped out of a newspaper before they met and that usually hung in his father's study. The others were all hers. She had wasted no time. He knew it had been done to humanize the place, but he couldn't help feeling a little disdainful as he imagined his mother explaining to the nurses, "I'm a photographer. Now I run a wedding photography business. Let me give you a card."

But just then his mother walked in and as soon as he saw her he repented his feelings. She looked shattered by grief and strain, her face drawn and sleepless. He jumped out of his chair, threw his arms around her, and, to his surprise, began to cry. She was crying, too.

But he felt her wince as he hugged her and when he stood back and looked at her he realized that her arm was in a sling. It was a stylish sling she'd made out of a scarf that matched her dress. A large jade pendant that she had acquired on one of her travels hung around her neck.

"I sprained my wrist," she explained, drying her eyes and blowing her nose with a single deft hand. "It's nothing."

She told her son an edited version of what had happened. Henry had been in the bath. He had become disoriented. He had wandered into the living room and collapsed in her arms.

She did not tell him about the note she had found. About the Scotch and the pills and the plastic bag. She did not tell him that although he appeared not to have followed through on his plans, it was necessary to inform the ambulance drivers and the attending Emergency Room doctors and they had pumped his father's stomach, though they found nothing there at all and blood tests had since shown neither drugs nor alcohol in his body. She did not tell him that with the irony her husband so savored in literature and noted in life he had very likely induced the stroke he was fearing. Or that his failure to finish whatever it was he had set out to do, which had exasperated her for years, had this time very likely saved his life—though it had also impaired him in a way they would have to wait to understand and that was tearing her apart with grief and anger.

She did not tell her son any of this. Instead, she told him that his father's neurologist, Dr. Barton, had already been by. So had several intensivists as well as a host of interns whom his mother referred to as "the usual children." She gave him the medical picture as best she could and Lev absorbed it all, briefly putting on a journalist's information-gathering face.

"They gave him this new drug right away," she said. "You have a few hours and it prevents damage."

"Tissue plasminogen activator," said Lev automatically. He had written about it.

"I don't know," his mother said.

"It's called tPA."

"Yes," she said. "That sounds right."

"Will he be OK?" Lev asked in a child's whisper. His mother had already been over everything once. They spoke in urgent undertones as far from the bed as they could.

"As I said, he can't talk. They don't know what he may have lost. Also . . . well, I'll tell you later."

Lev noticed that his father's eyes were open again and he hurried to the bedside.

"Dad, it's me, Lev. I'm here. I love you."

His father raised his eyebrows slightly in a kind of facial shrug. It was amazing to Lev how much of his father was present in that tiny gesture.

"Do you understand what I'm saying? Blink yes if you do." His father blinked—or rather shut his eyes so that for a moment Lev thought he had dropped back to sleep but then they opened and Lev understood that this was a long affirmative blink. His father held his eyes open on the other side of the blink so that they seemed round and bright.

His mother stood beside Lev, her good hand on his shoulder.

"Henry, Lev's here," she said loudly. "He was at a conference when I called. I should have tracked him down through the magazine but I wasn't thinking."

Lev's father blinked again. Lev felt himself descending into an unprotected, emotional freefall. The fish-tank hum and smothered silence of the room weakened his brain. He would like to have curled up on the floor and gone to sleep.

"Jake's here," Helen explained to both of them. "You were sleeping when he came. He's home now walking Mephisto." His father blinked again slowly. "He'll be back soon."

Lev was glad Jacob had arrived but wasn't sorry he had gone to walk the dog. It gave Lev a few hours to be beside his father and mother before his older brother arrived and took over.

Lev bent over and took his father's hand.

"Sit," his mother told him, pushing him into the chair beside the bed.

"Mom, you take it," Lev said. But she wouldn't, so he sat and held his father's hand.

Dr. Barton had promised to come again at 3:00 but it was 4:30 and still there was no sign of him, though a parade of nurses and residents came and went. Lev, using the reporter's pad that still had interviews from his weekend, jotted down whatever information he could.

Helen watched him with touched, scrutinizing concern. He seemed very grown-up and competent, asking informed questions and yet, at the same time, he scribbled in his little notebook like someone only pretending to be a reporter, the way, as a child, he had followed her around taking hundreds of imaginary photographs on a pretend camera.

Lev looked thinner than usual. His freckled pallor and pale lashes had always exaggerated the delicacy of his face, but Helen feared he wasn't eating enough. It had been a difficult year and a half for Lev. Several times during a lull in the medical traffic she wanted to tell him the full story of Henry's suicide attempt but, though she had already shared it with Jacob, something held her back. Neal's crackup had hit him hard—he had a way of internalizing other people's pain and she had frankly worried about his own mental health. Then came the fiasco with Jenny.

Lev communicated less about himself than before. There was something secretive about him that reminded Helen of his adolescence; perhaps he himself did not know what he was hiding. He'd always had something of his father's furtive, melancholic manner, as if he'd inherited it along with his red hair. Perhaps he had—Lev was always talking about the "genetic legacy" that was more and more evident—and yet Helen felt it was far more likely Lev had developed his shy, empathic, self-conscious habits living with a wounded, loving, mercurial man.

She often wondered if she had protected the children enough, though Jacob certainly had a hearty manner. Despite a far less intuitive personality than Lev, he was shrewder and had immediately divined what Henry had done. Lev seemed clueless, though he was always picking up slight disturbances in the family atmosphere. The summer in college when Lev had gone to Israel to work on a kibbutz and had suddenly turned up in an Orthodox yeshiva, for example—Helen had often wondered if he had done it for Henry, who was just then turning back to his own religious childhood. Trying to please an unpleasable man was, Helen knew from experience, a heartbreaking activity.

She knew that Henry wasn't an easy father to have. He wasn't, for that matter, an easy husband. But she was bound to him at the deepest level, and when her son Jacob arrived, she had run home not merely to change clothes but also to gather up the photographs that bore witness to their past. Next to Henry's bed she'd placed the picture she had clipped once from the *Daily News*, a face full of poetry and sorrow. She'd found the framed photo lying facedown in his study. He had, in younger, crueler days, accused her of marrying him the way a sculptor might marry a model, because his face inspired her. It held out the promise of future work and the reminder of past accomplishments.

It was true that he was a link to a world she needed. Nothing had been so fruitful for her—a sheltered American girl—as the wasteland of Europe. The ragged men and the strong desperate women, the faces against the wire. The fighters. The victims. The pits and smoke still settling. Trees, buildings, people pulled out of life by the roots. It had answered some chaotic need of her own, but also offered an anchoring force in her unmoored life. She was drawn, too, to the life that had been there before the calamity, still wafting through the wreckage, still visible in the faces and the voices and the stories she heard. She had never felt so alive and had never worked so well. She had sold pictures to everyone in those days.

And this man had stepped out from one of the pictures. Only for him it was more than a picture. She was always forgetting and always discovering that the cruel world she had visited and then quit still clung to him. When he cried out in the night or raged in the day, when he had struck his children and a kind of bottomless outrage and grief darkened his voice like an accent, she felt that world and the loss of that world still working in him. Once, in Amsterdam, she had visited a Jewish orphanage for boys. It had been in use since the early nineteenth century, though during the war all its residents had been shipped to Sobibor. When Helen visited in 1950 it had been turned into a way station for orphaned boys hoping to immigrate to Israel. She photographed boys kicking a ball in the old stone courtyard but was so affected by the faces that she simply began handing out what she had, chocolate and coins and even—most were teenagers—cigarettes. A crowd gathered around her and soon they were sticking their hands into her pockets, into her dress, their skinny arms surprisingly forceful. She had torn herself away but still shuddered at the recollection of it, and sometimes she felt that grim indecipherable force in Henry, in his rages and in his needs. Even now, in his inscrutable silence, the open asking eyes.

At the same time she always felt lurking in him that young man she had seen in the *Daily News*, an innocent openness in his face. It helped protect him—she saw the way even that woman rabbi who had never met him responded to some vulnerable childlike quality in him, something ineluctably lovable, detectable even in sleep. The nurses seemed to feel it and treated him with motherly solicitude. And Lev, too, sitting here bewildered, wanting to give his father something and not knowing what.

She sighed and stirred. Lev stood up and insisted that his mother sit down.

"Then find a chair for yourself," his mother told him.

But Lev needed a walk. He went downstairs to the cafeteria to get them each a yogurt, which his mother reluctantly admitted she would eat.

There were young interns in scrubs and clogs, with stethoscopes tucked into their breast pockets, and nurses and family members dotting the tables. Everyone looked tired and in possession of some kind of dark, secret knowledge. He cradled his two yogurts and his two cans of tomato juice, preparing to go back upstairs, when he recognized at a distant table the woman rabbi. He blushed again at the memory of their encounter.

Deborah was talking to a plump woman in white who looked like a nurse. The woman in white was crying softly and Deborah was handing her tissues from a little plastic packet and stroking her arm. The nurse looked at her watch and the two of them rose and walked toward the elevator.

Deborah kept on talking to the nurse in a low, intimate voice. Lev allowed himself to stare, taking in her body. She was taller than the portly nurse, her shoulders surprisingly broad. There was the dangling badge and the soft bulge of her breasts behind it. Her knees nearly touched as she walked, undermining the sturdy impression her upper body made.

The women were headed in his direction. Lev had an impulse to walk away but he remained stuck to his spot, half thinking he would apologize more fully to the rabbi for his behavior. He hoped she would glance his way but she did not. Her cheekbones were wide, almost Navaho. Now that he studied her, she looked Jewish, with the slightly Asiatic cast of some Russian Jews, but he forgave himself for his mistake. Who prays like that? Recalling their exchange, it seemed to him she had been mocking him a little. He felt a renewed wave of indignation.

Deborah was close enough to touch. She and the woman beside her seemed deep in conversation, though neither was saying a word. Lev noticed that there were tears in the rabbi's eyes. He found himself unable to speak. He stood dumbly cradling his food, watching the women pass.

DEBORAH WAS LATE FOR THE WEDDING. Since she was performing it she was not panicked, because, after all, they could not start without her. On the other hand *she was performing it* and everyone would be waiting for her.

She zoomed down the Henry Hudson Parkway in stocking feet, her high heels on the seat beside her. The wedding was at Wave Hill in the Bronx. Deborah had performed weddings there before but in her distracted state had failed to turn off the Major Deegen and lost time turning around.

The bizarre April heat wave had broken, which was a relief, but it was a gray day, threatening rain. Deborah knew this would only increase the stress of the wedding, which was supposed to be outside. Anxious eyes would be looking out the window, watching the weather and waiting for the rabbi. There was already a certain amount of built-in awkwardness—Janet's parents were divorced and her father had reneged on his promise to pay for the wedding, though he had been talked back into it at the last minute. Janet's parents were both going to walk Janet down the aisle, but then they were going to go their separate ways. "I'm not standing near another wedding canopy with that bastard," was how Janet had reported her mother's words to Deborah. Deborah tried to detach herself from this and all other worries. The pooled anxiety of multiple families would strike her like lightning when she arrived and if she was floating in fears of her own the sheer force of unsettled feelings would burn her up.

She tried to compose her remarks in her head. Deborah never knew what she was going to say until the morning of the wedding, but today she had cut it a little close, particularly because she had not felt the usual connection with this couple and didn't like the idea of lying.

She couldn't say, "I knew the moment I met Rick and Janet that this was meant to happen" because as far as she was concerned they should have pushed the whole thing off for a year at least.

She paused in her thinking. Rick and Janet. Was that right? Rick? Was Rick really his name? Or was it Eric? No, it was Rick. Like Rick's Place in *Casablanca*. Like Ricky Ricardo. Like the funk rocker Rick James. *Rick Rick Rick*. The big fear was blanking out on a name—people seldom knew enough to notice other types of errors. She could butcher the Hebrew, omit a whole chunk of the ceremony, she could bless them all in pig Latin, but the names of the bride and groom were sacred. *The first time I met Rick and Janet* . . . She tried to fix them in her head. Not that she'd ever flubbed a name, but it was always possible. Still, she was a natural performer and things tended to clarify themselves while she was under the chuppah. She was often at a loss for words in private, but in public a kind of cool control descended and the words materialized.

That was what she loved about a wedding. It could never truly be rehearsed. And yet, if it went well, it also had the quality of something foreordained, inevitable. Everything, for half an hour, was symbolic. The way your parents escorted you down the aisle but left you to take the final step alone. The shared cup of wine, the wedding canopy, the ring. The kiss. It was a prescribed ritual and yet it was concocted out of the moment. It was a play that happened only once in the lives of the couple and that changed them forever, even though it had happened thousands of times with other players, in countless other ages and places. *Behold, with this ring I consecrate you to me according to the laws of Moses and Israel.* Deborah had acted in college productions (she'd been Ariel in *The Tempest* and Masha in *The Seagull*), but she had never experienced the thrill she felt when presiding over a wedding. It was at once ancient and live in the truest sense of the word. Which was also of course what made it frightening.

The first time I met Rick and Janet . . . Then what? *I realized what an arrogant dickhead Rick was and tried to warn off Janet* . . .

The sky seemed to be clearing, which had a calming effect on

Deborah as she turned off the highway. She could see the mansion, the yellow and white striped tent, the Hudson snaking slow and gray behind it. It was 11:30. The wedding was called for noon. Not terrible. Not great. She parked at a bad angle and slipped on her shoes. The air was cool and fresh and soothing.

She was wearing a long pale silk dress with large green and auburn roses. It was important to look good but not too good. The bride needed to shine. Some reform rabbis wore their black robe when they performed a wedding. Deborah did wear her robe in synagogue, but at a wedding it seemed pompous, funereal, inappropriate. Still, it made dressing easier. She tried to catch her reflection in the window of her car. She should have brought static guard.

The grounds were sumptuous and elaborate—there were gardens and greenhouses and a sort of sloping park with wood pagodas. Deborah decided that she would like to be married outside, though these big estates had a country club quality, a sense of rented splendor she didn't quite like.

But the Hudson glittered beautifully in the newly emerged sunlight. She wondered if she might not work it into her talk. There was a river in Eden. There were the rivers of Babylon. There was the Hudson. She liked to think that things were linked through the ages, river to river, soul to soul, a golden thread of meaning. Perhaps marriage made us whole and brought us home. Perhaps.

Deborah found Rick, patrolling the grounds like a maître d'. He was wearing a tuxedo with a gold-and-black paisley vest and a yellow bow tie. He ignored her outstretched hand and gave her a bear hug. She apologized for being late but he was surprisingly calm. His only concern seemed to be for Janet, whose dress had torn up the side—it was being mended right now. Deborah began to have the feeling she had judged him too harshly. She told him to assemble his close relatives and friends for the ketubah signing. There was a round table under some trees near the main building and she thought they could do it there. Rick ran off to round up his family and Deborah went to check on the bride, whom she found in a state of mild hysteria, surrounded like a queen by anxious courtiers. It was a relief when she detached herself and went back outside.

The Jersey Palisades, clay-colored cliffs with green and brown and yellow trees massed above, looked pristine, wild. You expected to see mountain goats skipping down to the water to drink. Most of the guests—the men in tuxedos, the women stylishly dressed—had staked out seats. There was something surreal and elegant about the rows of chairs set up outside, facing the river.

"Hello, Rabbi," said an intimate, ironic voice as Deborah was walking across the grass. Deborah turned and recognized the photographer, Bill Patterson.

Bill wore two cameras around his neck, several lenses dangling from his belt, and double straps of film like one of Pancho Villa's men. He had a slender goatee but no mustache and the dashing good looks and reckless attitude of a war photographer, which he had once been. She was not sure what made him give it up. He smiled at her as if they shared a secret.

There was something derisive about Bill's manner but she didn't really mind and there *was* an odd, unspoken bond that existed between the rabbi and the photographer and the caterer and the band. They were all help, Deborah thought—though of course they were elevated help and she was perhaps the most elevated of all. Still, she was not there as a friend or a relative or a guest. She was paid to do something divine, a strange job.

"Hi, Bill," Deborah said.

"Aren't we scheduled for noon?" the photographer asked.

"We're running a little late," Deborah said.

"Everything all right? I hope we're not going to have a repeat of the Milstein affair," Bill said, grinning.

Deborah laughed, though at the time the Milstein wedding—her very first—had not been funny. During the ceremony, just after the blessing over the first cup of wine, Adam Milstein had fainted. One minute there had been two of them, the next minute the groom lay at her feet like a gunned-down mobster, red wine pooling around him.

Many doctors had rushed forward—it was, after all, a Jewish wedding—but everyone knew it was nerves. The rest of the service was completed with the couple sitting down. Deborah was shaken up, but even that wedding had turned out all right—Deborah had run into the couple on Columbus Avenue just the other week and Abby (she was Abby Cutler-Milstein now) was eight months pregnant.

"They ought to pad the area under the wedding canopy, like under a jungle gym," said Bill.

Deborah smiled but started to move away.

Bill detained her for one more moment.

"I'm not supposed to freelance—I work for an agency now—but if anyone's looking for a photographer . . ." he handed Deborah a business card. It said "Helen Friedman Portraits" at the top but Bill had written his own number on the bottom. He smiled at her again. Was he flirting? Of course. But he was also looking for business. He was rakishly attractive, totally unsuitable. Was he Jewish? He'd told her a story once—a Jewish grandmother, she couldn't remember exactly now. She looked at the business card again. Helen Friedman was a familiar name but she couldn't place it. She slipped the card between the pages of her rabbi's manual.

By way of good-bye, Bill raised his camera and snapped her picture.

It was noon. The wedding was officially in overtime and Deborah began moving as quickly as possible. She smiled at familiar faces—there were several congregants in the crowd—but she moved purposefully.

DEBORAH WAS JUST FINISHING UP HER EXPLANATION of what the ketubah was when Rick's grandfather, a lean, white-bearded man whom Deborah liked instantly, stepped forward.

"Rabbi, I'd like to ask you something," the old man said, leaning close.

"Of course," said Deborah.

"Is it necessary to mention God in the service?"

"Well," said Deborah, surprised and a little flustered. "Actually, it is. Yes."

"Grandpa Dave," said Rick, in a warning tone. "She's a rabbi. Of course she has to mention God. And I want her to."

The old man glowered.

"Is there a problem?" Deborah asked.

"Bullshit!" the old man muttered suddenly. "It's all bullshit!"

Deborah stared at him.

"Grandpa!" said Rick. "You promised."

"I'm sorry, Ricky, I can't help it. It's the truth. I raised your father to be a rational man. If he was here he'd say the same thing."

"Your son's not here?" Deborah said.

"Not unless the dead attend weddings."

Deborah realized with horror that she had forgotten Rick's father had died; she'd mistaken an uncle for the father. Strange that nobody had brought him up. She was glad they were thinking of him now.

"The tradition tells us that they do attend," she said softly.

The old man laughed bitterly, baring bad teeth.

"I can imagine how hard it is, in the face of loss like that . . ." Deborah began.

"Nonsense! I didn't believe in God before my son got cancer. I certainly don't believe in God now. God can kiss my ass. How about that? He can kiss my bony ass! Only he doesn't exist. So he can't. He can't do anything."

Suddenly the old man began to weep. Rick put his arm around him and looked apologetically at Deborah.

"I feel the same way myself sometimes," Deborah started to say but somehow nobody was listening to her. The old man's outburst cast a pall over the ketubah signing but also added an emotional urgency. Deborah wanted to speak more to him but Rick's brother led him away and someone else whispered to her, "He's not right since his stroke."

Well, she would try to find him later. But right now it was very late. Deborah, having remembered about Rick's father, sang "*El Maleh Rachamim*," the prayer for the soul of the dead. She asked Rick the name of his father so she could insert it into the prayer. He didn't know his father's Hebrew name but his English name was Morris. Does Mordechai sound right? Deborah asked.

"He didn't have a Hebrew name," said Rick's mother.

"What about his father?" Deborah asked.

"I wouldn't ask him," said Rick, glancing at his grandfather who was sitting in a chair nearby, under a tree.

"Pinchas!" the old man, who had been listening, suddenly burst out. He said it like an expletive. Deborah tried to catch his eye but he was glowering at the ground. She began chanting in a soft, low voice, " '*El Maleh Rachamim, shochen bamromim.* Dear God, exalted and full of compassion, grant perfect peace in Your sheltering presence, among the holy and pure to Morris, the son of Pinchas who has gone to his eternal home . . .' "

Deborah finished the chant and when she was done she saw that everyone had tears in his eyes, except for the old man, whose eyes were closed. Then Deborah began a *niggun*. To her surprise, Rick's family, stirred by the prayer for the dead, took up the tune. Deborah scrolled up the ketubah like a diploma and left the family to take her place under the chuppah.

DEBORAH SURVEYED THE CROWD, a conductor standing before an orchestra, except that nobody had brought his instrument. This was a solo performance. She was there to remember for them what a Jewish wedding was, in 1999, in this spot along the Hudson. She was there to remind them of the eternal rivers of Eden. She saw the white gleam of the bride's veil like a sail on the horizon as Janet and her entourage came into view. Deborah nodded to the flute player and the violinist who were standing off to one side of the chuppah and who began their stately rendition of "Dodi Li."

Deborah nodded again and the members of the wedding began

their slow march toward her, smiles frozen on their faces. The colored mass of pale green chiffon that had surrounded the bride broke away and the three bridesmaids came toward her, paired with three tuxedoed friends of Rick.

As she watched them all walk toward her, Deborah felt suddenly, unbearably alone, cut off for a moment not merely from the bride and groom but from God. Who was *she* to be presiding over this day? What was her power? She heard the old man's voice, unwelcome, in her head: *It's all nonsense.* What if the old man was right?

Finally the bride came, floating between her parents. (It was remarkable how the bride, no matter how nervous or ungainly, always floated. No doubt this had to do with the architecture of those gowns but still Deborah loved to see it.) Janet's mother was on her right, clutching her daughter with a sort of grim sorrow. Janet's father walked down the runway like a candidate at a political function, smiling and nodding. He forgot to kiss his daughter when he let her go but she reached up and kissed him and then, as if for the first time, he seemed to realize what was happening and embraced her.

Anxiety and emotion, formality and self-forgetting, Deborah recognized all the weird contradictory energies of a wedding in the crowd and in herself. The flute and the fiddle, those ancient instruments of Jewish hope and sorrow, cast a delicate spell, though Deborah was a little sick of the tune, which was really a folk dance that had been slowed into a wedding march. When they stopped playing, everything was quiet except for the muffled roar of an airplane and the faintest murmur of distant highway traffic.

Deborah smiled at the bride and groom and then noticed that somehow Rick had wound up on the right side of the bride. Deborah reached over and rearranged the bride and groom, like giant chess pieces, so that Janet was on Rick's right. People chuckled. Janet blushed behind her veil. Bill Patterson had already begun to prowl discreetly in the background, camera raised.

Deborah paused for one more moment and looked over the seated assembly. She was not afraid of silence, not afraid to use it in a ceremony, and felt that it had as much place as music and prayer. Rabbi Zwieback, she had noticed, tended to enter talking and to conduct services like a grand filibuster, as if he feared that to fall silent would be to court chaos, doubt, defection. But Deborah enjoyed standing under the chuppah as the tension mounted. Perhaps because she knew she could hold them for a while with her face, her body, her presence before them. But today she was unsettled, her pause grew longer and longer until it took on a life of its own. It seemed to her a palpable expression of her loneliness. The longer she waited the harder it would be to shatter the silence and she felt momentary panic flutter in her heart. But finally, when both the bride and the groom were staring at her in increasingly anxious anticipation, she lifted her head and sang, in a loud, clear voice, "*Baruch Ha Bah, B'shem Adonai.*"

And as soon as she began chanting the Hebrew she felt a sense of calm descend on her. Everything would be fine. She translated, chanting, in English: "Welcome, in the name of God." And then continued, in Hebrew and English: "O most awesome, glorious and blessed God, grant your blessing to the bride and groom."

As she sang she scanned the seats. There, in front of her, was the old man, sitting impassively with his head bowed. She wondered what he was thinking and hoped he would not jump up and shout, "Bullshit!"

Deborah finished the blessing over the wine and the betrothal blessing that followed. She watched as Janet lifted her veil and sipped the wine and then passed it to Rick, who also took a sip. She saw the way Janet, with trembling hands, kept her veil lifted for an extra moment to look at Rick as he drank and that Rick did not take his eyes off her even as he lifted the cup to his lips. She saw that indeed they did love each other and that they were right to get married. This filled her—to her surprise—with a whisper of jealous melancholy but it also calmed her and pleased her. She was genuinely happy for them and she knew now that this wedding was important and that it was right that she was performing it.

Bill Patterson's camera clicked behind her. She looked up and saw a bird fly over the heads of the gathered family and friends.

When Rick had finished slipping his ring over Janet's finger and reciting the formula—"Behold, with this ring I consecrate you to me according to the laws of Moses and Israel"—Janet slipped a ring over Rick's finger. It was a miracle, Deborah thought, that Rick was marrying Janet, that they were making a Jewish family. Did it matter that Jews married Jews? Somehow to her it did, just as it mattered, in a larger sense, that the species as a whole continued. To what end one generation succeeded to the next, endlessly into an unknown future, she did not know. But she knew that an earth without human beings would be an empty earth. And an earth without Jews? For Deborah, that, too, would be a terrible emptiness. Her sister called her tribal. Perhaps she was.

Janet's friend, a shy girl with a diamond stud in her nose, then stepped forward and read, in a voice barely above a whisper, a Sioux Indian fertility prayer. It was pure paganism, but Deborah found herself stirred by the words: "The wind will bless you, the fire will bless you, the water will bless you, the earth will bless you, the sea will bless you, the stars will bless you, the sand will bless you . . ."

When she was done it was Deborah's turn to speak. She cleared her throat, thinking, *Janet and Rick, Janet and Rick.*

"It says in the Talmud," Deborah began, "that the world is a wedding. The world is a wedding . . .

"It says in the Talmud that even God spends His spare time making matches, fixing people up." She paused, waiting for the old man to object, but all was silent except for an airplane overhead. A child began to cry and was carried swiftly down the aisle. "One would imagine from those rabbinic observations that marriage is easy, that we have only to open our eyes and our perfect mate will be there . . ." (*Mate's a bad word,* she thought, too late.)

"When I first met Rick and Janet . . . When I first met Rick and Janet I told them that marriage isn't easy. But they didn't want to hear about this . . ." She felt the divorced Mrs. Shapiro staring at her. The bride and groom were watching her cautiously, smiles frozen on their faces. "Marriage is fragile," she continued. "It's why the wedding canopy, the chuppah, is so fragile. It is blown by every passing wind, but it is also supported by friends. It is open to the elements but it is also open to family, to community. Sickness and illness and restlessness and sorrow are hard to keep out and it is an illusion to pretend that we can. We should never forget how much help we need to hold up a marriage." *Enough with the fragility. Circle back now.* "But I can see," she said, "looking at Rick and Janet as they stand here before me, that they know their own hearts well.

"I can see, looking at Janet and Rick, how brightly love burns in them." The truth was, she *could* see it. They loved each other! It struck her again, and again she felt an exalted happiness and a dark, unwelcome undercurrent of longing.

"It says in the Song of Songs that love is . . ." She glanced down at the rabbi's manual where the verse was printed. "It says, 'Love is strong as death, and passion as unquenchable. Its flashes are flashes of fire; a divine flame. Many waters cannot quench love, neither can floods drown it.' That is the kind of love I see in the faces of the bride and groom, in the faces of Rick and Janet."

Was it? Or was it merely the kind of love she craved?

"Rick and Janet are a great couple," she said, carried away now by the momentum of her speaking. "Rick is a tax attorney and we know he will take seriously the contract that Janet's mother is holding, the ketubah. But he also has a creative side and when he proposed to Janet I'm told he sang her a song that put new words to 'You're the Top,' and that during dinner we might hear a little of that song." People chuckled in amused anticipation. "And Janet, who works in the world of television and who would like to be a producer, has a creative soul but also knows what goes into making a show successful. It isn't only passion but also discipline and hard work and attention to practical things." (*Careful Deborah! It was time to wrap up. There was no time to talk about the river.*)

"Not only are all of us present here today as witnesses but also those who are no longer here on earth" (she felt the silence intensify at this allusion to the supernatural). We think in particular of Rick's father, Morris, who died of prostate cancer seven years ago." She heard soft murmured sounds of acknowledgment, a kind of sighing, from the seats. How, she wondered, had it been possible to forget his death when her own father had died? "We think of him and we know that he is here, under the chuppah with his son on this day. Because at a wedding the living and the dead are both present.

"Love is as strong as death. We are enjoined to remember this. It is a custom that we go to the cemetery and invite the dead to the ceremony" (she wished she had mentioned this to Rick whose eyes had filled with tears). "We know that they are present, just as all the Jewish generations are present. And we anticipate future Jewish generations, the children that this union will produce and all that will follow from them." *It was time to wrap up.*

"The world is a wedding. And what Janet and Rick, with their love and devotion, are doing, is making a world. May God bless them."

When she was finished, Deborah lifted the kiddush cup and sang the *sheva brachot* in Hebrew. Her voice was clear and pure and she looked at the bride and groom in turn, feeling protective and strangely close to them. Several of the seven blessings began with "*Baruch Atah Adonai*, blessed are you God, king of the world," and every time Deborah sang that phrase she felt that God *was* the source of all blessings and this calmed her. She sang with growing ardor, and gratitude for the very feeling the prayer induced in her. *Oh God*, she thought, *bless this couple, give them the things that will make them happy, give them love and children and good health.*

She handed the cup of wine first to Janet and then to Rick. She felt again a great inner silence, a profound aloneness as she stood facing the bride and groom and all of their family and friends. When they were done drinking she placed the cup back on its tray. She announced that there was one piece of the wedding remaining but she refrained from offering any explanation. Sometimes, she thought, ritual should just be performed.

She took the wineglass wrapped beforehand in a linen napkin, put it on the ground, and nodded to Rick, who stomped on it with violent joy. And then it was over. The violin and flute player, joined suddenly by a trumpet, broke into an up-tempo rendition of "*Siman tov u'mazel tov*" as the bride and groom kissed.

The married couple walked quickly down the aisle. Deborah could see that Janet's dress had opened up again slightly along the seam but it was clear that Janet no longer cared about her dress. Her mother and father forgot their pledge and walked off side by side; Rick's mother walked accompanied by Rick's brother. There were tears in her eyes and she held her son's hand. Then the bridesmaids and the aunt and uncle who had stood the whole time half in and half out of the ceremony. Finally Deborah, alone, walked behind them.

Somehow it always came together and Deborah knew she had done a good job, despite her own misgivings about her words. People were still drying their eyes. It was a triumph. Many congratulated her as she walked. Several wanted to detain her, she felt the need in their touch, pressed behind their smiles and in their eyes. She overheard muttered comments. "So beautiful." "Such a voice!" "Pretty. A pretty rabbi." The comments were patronizing but heartfelt, too. *Heartfelt* was a word she hated, but it had begun to sneak into her vocabulary. She was becoming a rabbi in a way she found frightening. "The day I wish someone a 'hearty mazel tov,' " she had once told her sister, "shoot me," and Rachel had looked at her and said, "Bang."

A middle-aged man had taken hold of her arm. She thought she recognized him from somewhere. Was he a congregant? There were so many and most did not attend regularly. In her three years she thought she'd gotten to know them all, but she was always being surprised by new faces. This man clearly had a question in his eyes. Perhaps he was planning a bar mitzvah for himself after having been too poor for one forty years ago. Or his daughter was inter-marrying, or his son. Someone was gay. Someone close to him was sick or dying. He needed a rabbi for a wedding or a funeral. His wife wanted a divorce. He had found a letter written in Yiddish from a great granduncle and wondered if she could translate it for him. The letter was in his car.

Usually she loved such questions, but right now she needed to collect her thoughts. She was worn out by the service.

"Let's talk later," she said. "There's something I've got to do."

She was sure the man would find her again. But he would not let go of her arm.

"Rabbi, you dropped this," he finally said, pressing something into her hand. It was Bill the photographer's business card, with the words "Helen Friedman Portraits" at the top. And suddenly she realized that the name Helen Friedman was the same name as the woman she had met in the hospital the month before and visited several times—the one whose husband had had a stroke. And hadn't she been a photographer?

She thought fleetingly about that family. The mute husband, ill but oddly expressive. The mother, from whom Deborah was conscious of wanting something she could not identify. The two sons, one breezy and self-confident, the other intense and shy, who had confronted her so awkwardly in the hospital room.

She thanked the man and made her way across the terrace, now filling with people and waiters carrying trays of hors d'oeuvres. She entered the cool silence of the marble-floored main building and found the ladies room. "That was so beautiful," said the ladies' room attendant, a black woman whose praise Deborah found moving, important. "I was outside listening. You've got God in your voice, do you know that?"

"Thank you so much," said Deborah. She would like to have hugged this woman but she only smiled at her, still in her professional mode, still contained.

Deborah entered a stall and locked the door. Then, making as little noise as possible, she began to cry.

THE FIRST THING HENRY FRIEDMAN SAW when he opened his eyes was the photograph of himself as a young man that his wife had clipped out of a newspaper years before. For a moment he thought he was back in his study and he felt perplexed but relieved because he had a vague sense that many bad things had been happening to him. But then he noticed, beside the small side table, the standing metal pole and the clear bag of liquid dripping down through a plastic tube that fed into the back of his hand, though he could not see his hand or lift his head to look. He understood that he was in the hospital. He shifted his eyes and looked once more at the surprisingly optimistic young man in the photograph.

"You again," he thought.

He did not know how long he had been in the hospital. He called for Helen and then for a nurse but nobody came and he realized that in fact he had not cried out and that he could not speak. This discovery did not cause panic but only a sort of childlike resignation. It was like being inside a dream. His mind drifted, he was no doubt drugged, but he groped for clarity. The last really clear memory he had was of sitting in the bathtub.

Henry, in his hospital bed, remembered only scattered details of all that had happened to him. He could see himself sitting in the bathtub but he did not know how he had gotten out of the tub or what had happened after he had. He remembered being wheeled outside on a stretcher and that the sky had been blue streaked with blackness that kept intruding into everything. He reawakened briefly under very bright lights with some unspeakable invasion of his body in progress, though, mercifully, it seemed at that moment no longer to be his body. After that he slept, if it could be called sleep. He remembered nothing until that moment when he opened his eyes and saw the photo of himself that he distinctly remembered taking off the wall.

His wife had wept the first time she had told him what had happened and he had listened with an odd detachment. He seemed to view everything from a hovering height, once removed from the sort of intimate habitation of himself that made life so painful.

There were still many things he did not recall and that had only been half-communicated to him or that he had been told and instantly forgotten. He had a sense that it wasn't his wife who had pulled him out of the tub, as he had originally believed, but someone else, some strong unknown hand he was afraid to inquire after. In any case, he did not have the means to ask.

He had the sketchiest recall of his suicide plans—more as things he had once written down than anything he had actually carried out. He understood that he had not followed through with this plan but that it had somehow been aborted, and that the very violence of his unremembered actions, his leap back into life, had torn the fabric of his health further than anything that had happened to him before. Though he was aware of the irony of this discovery, and the pain and regret it would once have induced in him, his feelings of self-reproach were blunted.

He understood, too, that it might also be the seminarcotic hospital torpor that lent itself to rich and hallucinatory imaginings. Perhaps his wife's explanations were themselves a dream. None of this really troubled him.

Henry had had his appendix out when he was seven and that time kept coming back to him with unexpected pleasure. His parents were still alive then and despite the emergency nature of the surgery he felt a clean, soft safety in his memories. These belonged to the Time Before, and therefore lived in a kind of hallowed light. He had been rushed to a Catholic hospital and had, during his recovery, refused to eat the food, but his mother had told him he had to, even if the food was not kosher. He remembered the swishing sound made by the white-clad nuns when they walked into the room, their hats shaped like origami swans. There was a crucifix over his bed that had terrified him, but there was something forbidden and sweet, too, in the hospital and in the nuns; he encountered these feelings again when the May-banks took him in—good Christians, though of course they were paid.

Some space between past and present had been collapsed. He felt like a child, swaddled. The past felt very near. He kept drifting off to sleep and every time he woke up he saw himself as a young man.

One time when he opened his eyes his wife was there, holding his hand, and his eyes filled with tears of gratitude that his wife was there beside him, and tears of frustration as he tried to speak to her. He understood every word Helen said and wished she had spoken more than she did, but the next thing he knew he was waking up and she was gone and the nurse was there fussing over the tubes he could not see but that he knew were plugged into some invisible vein, just as he knew there was a tube that carried waste out of his body and into the plastic bag hung from the side of the bed.

The periods of sustained consciousness grew longer and he established a sort of routine of communication with his wife, blinking once for yes and twice rapidly for no. This of course had severe limitations, and when Helen asked one day in a fierce whisper, "Why, Henry? Were things so bad?" he could only stare up before blinking yes—no—yes—no in confused succession.

Later, when he could move his right hand but still not speak, they brought him a kind of Ouija board with the alphabet on it and he pointed tremblingly to one letter then another to spell out simple words. The first sentence he spelled out, with his wife holding the board for him and bending anxiously over the side of the bed was, "N-O-T Y-E-T."

Helen had immediately tried to decipher the meaning of this phrase. Not ready to die yet? Not ready to go home? Finally, she asked, "Don't tell the children yet? Is that it?"

Henry had blinked yes though he was no longer at all sure what he had meant since what it was the children might be told, what he had actually done or intended to do, kept vanishing from view.

He liked having the boys around. Jacob had already gone back to Atlanta but Lev spent part of each day working in a corner of the hospital room. Lev had been dutiful, typing away on his laptop and reading to his father from *The New York Times*. Henry could not bring himself to tell his son that he did not care to hear the news. It seemed abstract and irrelevant to him, though he knew Lev was trying to bring him back into the world and was grateful for that.

Far more in keeping with his hospital mood were the mysterious moments of prayer he had with the young woman he had first heard singing while he was asleep. For several days he felt quite sure that he had been visited in his dreams by a figure who had sung to him a verse of the Twenty-third Psalm. It was only when he was awake and more alert and she had come again that he understood that it had not been a dream or angelic visitation. But seeing this young woman was even more unsettling than dreaming her because Henry felt quite certain that she was the young woman who had tied his shoes for him on Broadway and whom he had found himself unable to thank. As she stood beside his bed, resting her hand on his shoulder, he experienced that same mute frustration he had felt on the sidewalk when the words had simply not come out. And he began to wonder if that encounter, too, had been a dream, though it stood out vividly in the fog of his other recollections.

She sang the Twenty-third Psalm and she recited Psalm 91, which happened to be one of his favorites. She chanted it in Hebrew but read it in English as well. Henry wished she had used the King James Version, but her translation had glimmers of it. *He will cover you with his pinions, and under his wings will you find refuge: His truth will be your shield and buckler. You will not be afraid of the terror by night; nor of the arrow that flies by day; nor of the pestilence that walks in darkness; nor of the destruction that wastes at noonday. A thousand will fall at your side and ten thousand at your right hand; but it will not come near you.* This last verse had always troubled him, but in the sweet assurance of her voice did not seem triumphalist or self-serving. He wished he could speak to her about this, but he contented himself with her voice and felt as if he himself were praying aloud.

Hers was the voice he wished he had been able to send out of his body, up to God. His own was too often off-key and had, besides, too much doubt in it. He felt, listening to her, that nothing bad had ever happened to her and he was glad of that and found in it an aspect of his own innocence that did not seem to require qualification or understanding. Before she left the room she would ask, shyly, if he wished to be blessed and he found himself, to his surprise, blinking in the affirmative. His assent surprised him because it had never been his style of prayer before, this laying on of hands. But when she put her hands carefully on his head and recited the priestly benediction—*May God bless you and guard you. May God show you favor and be gracious to you. May God show you kindness and grant you peace*—he had felt tears, over which, since his hospitalization, he seemed to have no control, rush down his face.

But despite those tears, Henry continued to be aware of a sort of disconnection that seemed to him not the cold remote sensation he had felt during times of depression but what, if he had put it into words, he might have called a warm detachment. It was soothing to have his wife by his side, to have his son working in the room, to have this lovely young woman sing to him and bless him. But it was a little as though some small piece of himself had in fact died and he was alive now without a certain desperate urgency. It was a kind of peace though it was a little like the paralysis that afflicted parts of his body and silenced his vocal chords. It was as if some invisible part of himself were mute, too.

Nevertheless, he often felt a deep sense of shame because of what Helen had told him—that he had tried to commit suicide. And he felt a more mysterious, deeper sense of shame that he was still alive, surrounded by tokens of his lucky life.

The Brahms that his thoughtful wife played for him on the little portable tape player that had miraculously appeared one day on the table beside the photograph of himself as a teenager. The photograph itself, that he hated and longed for like a childhood friend. That sweet woman's voice he heard first in a dream, singing a verse of the Twenty-third Psalm over and over again. Why should these things embarrass him?

More life. Is this not what the psalms themselves constantly demanded? Even this, to be here in bed thinking. To hear the voice of his wife and of his sons. Was it better than death? He asked himself this question with the same detachment with which, at that moment, he viewed everything. He was not sure of the answer. Still, here he was.

Book
Two

DEBORAH SAT SMOKING A CIGARETTE in the far corner of the garden where the old people did not go. Most were in wheelchairs and they tended to cluster near the upper deck where the transport aides could find them easily. If they ventured down the ramp to the lower level they stopped at the stone pond with the fat orange and white goldfish.

Breathing in the soft smoke, inhaling, as she usually did not, Deborah felt a measure of calm returning to her. She was trying to get the smell out of her nose, to fumigate her soul and cleanse it of the odor of decay. Deborah hardly smoked anymore, but she had bummed a single cigarette from a nurse's aide and sat on a slatted wooden chair, her legs crossed, far from the oxygen tanks and imploring looks of the elderly inmates—there was no other word for them—of the Sinai Center.

The nursing home was hard for Deborah—much harder than the hospital, where the atmosphere of crisis kept things moving, where everything had a purpose and her spiritual interventions often absorbed the urgency of medical procedures. The hospital was a sort of battlefield. Death was the dark backdrop that threw life and God and prayer and Deborah herself into sparkling relief. Nothing in the nursing home was black or white. It was a gray place, however brightly lit the hallways. It was a holding pen for departing souls whose flights had been mysteriously canceled. Many seemed to have passed through death already and come out the other side, breathing only through accident, oversight.

Sometimes, it was true, Deborah liked being there. There were a few patients in particular she had grown close to—Minnie Adelson, on the fourth floor, Rose Marx on six. And there were days when she felt each soul glowing, however dimly, inside its ravaged vessel. There was no predicting these moments. They were like those unexpected occasions when she wandered into the Metropolitan Museum of Art and everything—the Ming vases along the hall that she had never noticed before, the African carvings, the geometric Islamic mosaics—*everything*, no matter where she looked, burned with beauty as if lit from within.

This was not one of those days. Deborah had spent the morning with sick children and she found it suddenly impossible to feel much for the very old. Some of these human husks you just wanted to smother with a pillow. Deborah recoiled from her own dark fantasy. But it was almost as if they had stolen from the children, misers breathing out their life a penny at a time, while the children spent all they had in one openhanded instant. She would like to have effected a redistribution of health.

God of course was anything but a socialist—some had and some had not, and as a rule she accepted it all as an insoluble mystery. Finding the infinity inside every inch of life was a religious necessity, and she liked to recite to herself the verse from Psalms, *Teach me so to number my days that I might have a heart of wisdom.* But this afternoon the Sinai Center pissed her off.

She had been up on Jacobson Eight—the Alzheimer's unit—and the experience had worn her out. The reek of urine, the babbling and random cries, the blaring televisions, the low perpetual moans that lent the whole place a hellish aura, like a Victorian madhouse. She had no patience, no room for the experience. She had wanted to flee.

Deborah stubbed out her cigarette on the flagstones with deliberate care. She did not wish to ignite the oxygenated elderly. Several had clear plastic tubes passing under their noses and stretching up behind their ears. This made them look vandalized—as if someone had painted Salvador Dalí mustaches on their cracked, delicate faces. Even without oxygen, they looked combustible.

She ought to be getting back to her office. She was giving the sermon for Shabbat Hazon—a grim portion devoted to an enumeration of Israel's sins in preparation for Tisha b'Av, the upcoming commemoration of the destruction of the Temple for which the wayward Jews were, according to tradition, responsible.

Deborah utterly rejected this notion and wondered if she should say as much in her sermon. Nobody in her congregation would dispute her interpretation, but she would like to come up with a meaning she could pass on, not a mere rejection of traditional interpretation. Something about blame and responsibility—if Jews were to blame then they were not powerless, even against the might of the Babylonians who destroyed the first Temple or the Romans who burned the second one. And so maybe feeling guilty was a form of control, a form of power. You felt bad but you felt powerful. That was a trap to be avoided. Too pop psychological?

Deborah was a little lightheaded—she should not have smoked, and she should have eaten more for lunch besides the yogurt and roll she had grabbed in the hospital cafeteria. But even as she regretted this she suspected with a sickening feeling that she should not have eaten anything at all. To confirm this she fished her little Hebrew calendar out of her bag and thumbed quickly through it until she found the day's date. On the left side of the page it was July 11. On the right-hand side, it was *Shiva Asar b'Tammuz*. The seventeenth day of the month of Tammuz. The day the walls of the Temple were breached. A fast day. Shit!

How had she forgotten? Usually Deborah had a good sense of the Jewish calendar. It was hardly a requirement for Reform Jews, even rabbis, to keep the minor fasts. Still, she felt a sense of failure that deepened her gloom. She knew that Reuben—why did she still think of him?—would be in his office, dressed, despite the summer heat, in a jacket and tie, briskly fasting, the date somehow engraved in a part of his brain that she seemed not to possess.

Deborah raised the cigarette in her hand toward her lips before she realized that she had extinguished it. She smiled at herself and glanced out over the garden to see if anybody had noticed her, but the old people sat in their chairs staring off in fixed positions. Again she felt a pang of guilt for her earlier irritation. The residents were mostly women, and they sat in their old-lady housedresses with giant faded flower prints, their legs—if they still had both of them—spread wide, square shoes resting on the footrests of their wheelchairs. On their laps were loose-holed quilts the women might have crocheted themselves in nimbler days. They were always cold, even in summer. On a bench, three private aides, black women in white outfits, sat chatting together like nannies on a park bench, glancing from time to time at their elderly charges.

Perhaps there was an idea for a sermon in the Sinai Center, Deborah thought. The inmates of Jacobson Eight. Their mental walls were breached; their bodies broken. Could she speak about that, about the nursing home? Or was that too New Age—the body as God's temple. And what did it mean? She remembered a passage of Talmud, from tractate Brachot, about the first set of tablets that Moses had smashed on coming down from Mount Sinai. According to tradition, these tablets were gathered up and kept in the ark along with the new set. The talmudic passage went on to say that a mind that has lost its understanding is like those broken tablets, possessing hidden value, a thing to be treasured with mystical regard.

She was thinking about this, looking out at the old men and women, when she saw him. It was the man from the hospital, the man with the beard and all the photographs in his room she had sung psalms to. Friedman. So this is where he had gone! She had imagined that he had been sent home, but no, he would need too much rehab for that.

Why the rush of excitement at the sight of the inert old man here in the garden? He sat, dreamily staring at nothing in particular, a purple polar fleece pullover draped over his shoulders despite the hot weather. This gave him a regal look, and even the upright, stiff way he perched in the wheelchair made him seem enthroned. He was wearing an incongruous Yankees cap, which had slipped back on his head so that the bill pointed up at the sky.

Deborah decided to go over to him. She rose—at the very least she should fix his cap—but before she took a step, she noticed his son coming out of the main building, carrying a cup of coffee and a wrapped piece of cake. She sat back down to watch for a moment.

The son—Dov? Gil? *Lev!*—settled himself in a garden chair, lowered the brim of his father's hat, and unwrapped the cake. He broke a piece off and put it in his father's hands and when his father failed to do anything with it he took it and placed it carefully in his mouth. His father chewed in a sort of mechanical, absentminded but wholly absorbed way and when he was done, Lev lifted the coffee to his father's lips.

There was a tenderness to the way Lev ministered to his father that belied the anger she had encountered in the hospital. Lev repeated the procedure patiently, wiping his father's mouth from time to time with a napkin. When the cake was gone, Lev took up the Sunday *Times* from the little table, plucked out a section, and began reading aloud. Deborah strained to hear but she could not. She stood up again. She didn't want to disturb them but she ought to say hello. Let them know that this was also a place she visited.

"Rabbi! Rabbi!"

Deborah looked down. It was Ida Horne, a tiny woman in a pink cardigan looking up from the depths of her wheelchair, her sharp, skinny shins wrapped in Ace bandages like New York City saplings. She was rolling herself, an inch at a time, in Deborah's direction.

"Are you going inside, Rabbi? Would you take me to the elevator?"

Deborah was familiar with the pleading sweet, bossy, vulnerable tone adopted by the elderly sick, many of them tough as nails, who spent the day being pushed and pulled and dressed and changed and wiped and washed by hired help. They had gotten good at angling for a little extra attention.

"Of course," said Deborah. "How are you, Ida?"

Ida's dim, unadorned face, the hairs sprouting in tiny clumps on her cheek and chin, the damp open eyes moved her. You could even see a little glimmer of what Deborah thought must have been Ida's teenage self. A sort of flirtatious crinkle around the mouth.

On the Alzheimer's unit they posted old photographs—sometimes yearbook pictures from the 1930s or 1940s—on the doors of patients' rooms. Those eager black-and-white faces could make you cry. Sometimes Deborah would spend her visit privately trying to fathom the space between the photograph and the person before her, a humbling enterprise. What kind of old lady would Deborah become? Would she be alone then, too?

"Oh, not too bad," said Ida, eventually. "My daughter's coming tomorrow."

"That's nice," murmured Deborah, bending to release the brakes on Ida's wheelchair and encountering a braided plume of urine and tea rose perfume she recognized from her own grandmother. The little flourishes of lingering vanity, of persistent human effort undone by dissolution, moved her and at the same time, bending over, she felt lightheaded all over again so that she steadied herself on the handles of the wheelchair as she rose.

She knew from Claire, the social worker, that Ida's daughter was in fact dying of breast cancer and never came.

Deborah pushed Ida's wheelchair slowly past Henry and Lev. She heard Lev reading headlines from the *Times* in a low voice, the open paper flapping and half concealing him. "Moynihan Said to Back Bid by Bradley." "Congo Rivals Sign Cease-fire Without 2 Rebel Groups." "Barak Takes Charge in Israel." Lev seemed to be waiting for a signal from his father to read a story in full, but Henry looked unmoved by the words he was hearing. Neither looked up as she passed.

It was cooler in the main building but Deborah was still feeling a little weak and she stopped in the hallway by the water fountain.

"One second," she said to Ida.

"Take your time, dear."

Deborah bent into the porcelain hood of the fountain, like a niche for a saint. She held her hair back with one hand and let the water play over her face. She wasn't sure if she ought to drink or not—it was, after all, a fast day—but the water felt good on her face, restorative. She pulled away from the fountain dripping and realized she had nothing to dry off with. She contemplated her shirt front, already dappled with water, when a voice said,

"Would you like to use this? It's clean."

Deborah raised her wet face and saw Lev holding out a handkerchief. She took it gratefully and blotted her face.

"Thanks," she said, a little breathless.

"I'm sorry, I've forgotten your name. Although I know you're a rabbi."

"Deborah," Deborah said, disliking the sound of her own name more than usual.

"I'm Lev. We met in Roosevelt Hospital."

"I know. I remember your father. I'm sorry they moved him here."

And then, correcting that comment, she said, "I mean, I'm sorry he couldn't just go home."

Lev nodded. There was something he wanted to say that he had practiced in his mind as he followed her down the hall.

"You know, I was hoping I'd find you after that time in the hospital. I feel I owe you an apology."

"Oh don't worry about it. You had every right to kick me out."

She was taller than Lev remembered; she seemed to tower above Ida's wheelchair. She was wearing three-quarter-length pants, which made her seem even taller, as if she had suddenly shot out of her clothes, like Alice after eating the cake.

Deborah was wondering if she should introduce Ida. But Ida had shut her eyes.

"Well," said Deborah. "Thank you." She held out the damp handkerchief.

"Keep it," he said. "I've got plenty."

"Thanks," said Deborah. "So how is your father doing? I saw him in the garden."

Lev was silent for so long Deborah thought for a moment that he hadn't heard her.

He touched his face as if he was used to having a beard and was surprised to find himself clean shaven. His green eyes had the same faraway look as his father. Deborah had assumed it was the look of a man who'd had a stroke—seeing it now in Lev she realized it was simply a hereditary attribute. She found the resemblance touching, a glimpse of the old man Lev might become, or the young man Henry had been, that filled her with unexpected tenderness toward Lev.

At last he said, "It's hard for him. He can't really speak and he still has bouts of confusion. But he can use his body much better. He's here for physical therapy. We wanted Rusk but the insurance company decides where you go . . ."

"How's your mother holding up?" Deborah remembered the dramatic woman with the jade pendant and white braid.

"Oh, my mother's pretty strong," Lev said. "But of course it's hard for her, too. Seeing him here. It's a hard place to get used to, even though he's in the rehab unit."

"You don't get used to it," Deborah said with unexpected vehemence.

Lev looked at Deborah with mild surprise. Her spontaneous self kept skipping out from behind her rabbinical self. Like the stately way she pushed the old woman's wheelchair down the hall and then stopped to stick her whole face in the water fountain. He liked the way she smelled. She smelled like shampoo and, if he was not mistaken, cigarettes. A welcome whiff of the outside world—although something was rising from Ida that was not wholly pleasant.

"Listen, can I buy you a cup of coffee?" He asked. "The coffee shop's right here. We could drink it in the garden."

"I can't," Deborah said. "It's *Shiva Asar b'Tammuz*."

Lev looked at her without comprehension.

"It's a fast day," Deborah explained. "The seventeenth day of Tammuz. The day the walls were breached. Of the Temple. The Babylonians broke through the walls of the Temple in Jerusalem."

"Really?" Said Lev. "How come I don't know about this? Was it in the *Times*?"

Deborah laughed. "It's kind of an obscure day. But . . ."

She assumed a formal, rabbinical tone of explanation as she elaborated on the meaning of the day. A shadow of irritation fell across Lev's face. Suddenly, two thousand years of Jewish history stood between them and a cup of coffee.

Deborah, in fact, felt like a hypocrite explaining to Lev about fast days when she herself had completely forgotten. She wanted to get off the Temple, but Lev actually seemed interested. She heard the word Nebuchadnezzar come out of her mouth as if she were speaking in a dream. She shuddered inwardly.

"Maybe another time," Lev said. "I should be getting back to my dad anyway."

He seemed vaguely insulted.

"Is your father a Yankees fan?" Deborah said abruptly, to prolong the conversation a little and banish the Babylonians.

Lev stared at her curiously.

"The hat," Deborah explained.

"Oh," said Lev. "The hat's mine. He shouldn't be in the sun. But we do go to a few games a year. We pick them at the beginning of the season. He's not what you'd call a fan, but he used to go to games when he was new to the country, sit in the bleachers. We were supposed to go this Sunday, in fact. I had even thought, maybe . . ."

His voice trailed off.

"Who are they playing?" asked Deborah. An inane response. Clearly he wanted to talk about his father.

"Oakland," said Lev.

"They've got no pitching," said Deborah, unable to help herself. She watched *SportsCenter* and she was from the Bay Area.

Lev smiled. "You follow baseball?"

"All rabbis are baseball fans," said Deborah. "You know, like the Bible says: In the big inning."

More inanity. This was Rabbi Zwieback's joke. Might as well grow a beard and be done with it.

Her laugh was a sort of musical shout. Hah!

"I never heard that one," said Lev, unsmiling.

"And you never should have." After a pause, Deborah added, incongruously, "Actually, I forgot, too."

"Forgot? . . ."

"I forgot to fast. I ate breakfast. In fact I ate lunch, too. I forgot it was *Shiva Asar b'Tammuz*. It's just, once I remembered, coffee seemed wrong . . ."

Deborah felt freer, forcing out the confession. It felt good to tell him, to clarify, so as not to be mistaken for . . . what?

Here she came again, skipping out from behind the pulpit. Her brown eyes sparkled.

"Well," he said, "I won't tell."

She smiled at him and arched her dark eyebrows comically. She looked, Lev thought, like an opera singer, not the old-fashioned fat ones but the new breed, the attractive women who actually had acting talent. There was an appealing fullness around her throat.

"You know," he said, "I still have my dad's ticket for Sunday's game. If you'd like to go with me . . ."

"Really?" she said.

"I mean if you want to. I feel I owe you something."

Was he so intent on reparations? Was it a date? Or did he need pastoral care for his father? It was difficult to read his body language. He was really very shy. She thought he might be blushing. His freckles had suddenly vanished and his face seemed darker.

"Sure," she said, giving her little musical laugh. "But I warn you, I'm from California. I'll root for Oakland."

"That's OK." He had a good-humored but melancholy smile.

"Wait a minute," said Deborah. She pulled her little Jewish calendar out of her bag. "What time's the game?"

"Noon," said Lev. "Is it another fast day?"

"No, but I'm doing a memorial service in the morning. Do you mind meeting me at Roosevelt Hospital? I'll have a car. I can drive us. I'll be downstairs by the front desk. Say, 11:15?"

"Perfect," said Lev.

And then he said, "I really should get back to my father."

"Say hello for me," said Deborah. "I'll visit him, if you think he'd like that."

"I'm sure he would," said Lev, before hurrying down the hall. He had left his father roasting in the garden.

Ida's eyes were still shut. Had she been listening? Or was she dead! Deborah put a hand gently on the old woman's shoulder. Ida's eyes popped open. She lifted her small, birdlike head and looked at Deborah.

"My daughter's coming tomorrow."

"That's wonderful," said Deborah.

IT WAS STRANGE for Lev to be back in Roosevelt Hospital. When his father was there he had always hurried in and out of the lobby, but now he was stuck in the vast, vaulted, impersonal space, waiting for Deborah, who was already twenty minutes late.

He was beginning to regret his invitation. What had he been thinking? A rabbi!

Lev had liked watching her drink from the fountain, the way she stooped into the gleaming white hollow and then pulled away with her face and hair all spangled with water; the way she stood laughing at herself. But the professional air of concern put him off. The hand on the shoulder—had she put a hand on his shoulder? There was something a little preachy about her. As if she was always up on the dais. Of course that might have been the platform shoes. But she seemed to be looking down from some remote moral perch. *I can't. It's a fast day.*

He would be justified in leaving because she was now half an hour late.

He was considering doing just that when the security guard manning the front desk, who had been eyeing him for the last ten minutes, beckoned.

"You waiting for the lady rabbi?" he asked.

Lev said he was and the man gave him a folded piece of paper. He opened the note quickly and read:

Dear Lev,

I am so sorry. Somebody died and I didn't have your number! I have to do the funeral—I'm pinch-hitting for another rabbi. I'll understand if you just go to the game, but if you want to find me, I'll be at Riverside Chapel on Seventy-sixth and Amsterdam. The funeral starts at noon.

With apologies—
Deborah

Well there it was. He had a feeling that death was never far from this woman, even though she herself had such a lively air.

Lev did not feel like going to Yankee Stadium alone but he was pretty sure he did not want to attend a stranger's funeral. Still, he found himself heading uptown to Riverside Chapel. He was wearing jeans and sneakers and a black polo shirt, hardly funeral-wear, but he figured he could slip in and find Deborah before things began, say a quick hello and a quick good-bye. It would be only polite to let her know that he had gotten her note.

He had been to Riverside Chapel before. He had grown up near it on the Upper West Side and had often walked through clustered mourners out on the sidewalk. The upper windows were all blotted out with a milky white film. He had been fascinated since childhood by the side entrance with its wide, riveted steel doors, cryptically lacking handles, like the doors of a bank vault—through which, one imagined, corpses came and went in the dead of night. He sometimes stopped to stare through the ground-floor window at the ominous display of tombstones provided by "Sprung Monuments." There was always the creepy, unarticulated expectation that one of the tombstones would bear his own name.

A dark-suited "greeter," stationed in the lobby, nodded impersonally at Lev as he entered the funeral parlor.

"Corngold?" The man asked.

Lev did not know what funeral he was going to but he said yes.

"Second floor."

Lev took the stairs. He was claustrophobic at the best of times and there was something about a funeral home that made him more eager than ever to avoid the enclosed space of the waiting elevator. The second floor was filled with mourners milling around like guests at a lugubrious cocktail party. The atmosphere was muted but there were odd, merry outbursts—"Cindy, you made it!"—a reunion atmosphere of hugs and kisses amid the murmured comments—"It's better this way, she won't suffer"—and the unrelated chitchat. "The stock was doing gangbusters a week ago," a man said ruefully behind him.

There was an ethnic familiarity in the air, a sort of genetic overlap. Everyone's face seemed once-removed from faces he knew. These might have been his relatives. There was a Jewish undertow pulling everyone at some occult level toward a shared past—or was it a common future? Someone flashed him a big familial smile and then, looking closer, took it back.

Lev spotted Deborah in a far corner of the room. She was dressed in a lavender business suit and her hair was pulled back tight and twisted into a bun. She was talking to a little man in a dark suit who Lev presumed was a funeral director. The funeral director nodded discreetly, like a hit man receiving instructions, and then disappeared into a side room.

Deborah straightened up and surveyed the crowd. She saw Lev and broke into a big smile, moving toward him immediately. She seemed uncowed by the crowd or the occasion.

"You must hate me," she said, a little breathlessly. "Rabbi Zwieback has a stomach bug. He was supposed to do this one. If you want to just take off I'll totally understand."

"Would you mind if I stayed?" Lev hadn't expected to but he was suddenly curious. The idea of watching her perform appealed in an odd, almost perverse way.

"Sure," she said. She seemed pleased, a little flattered. "It should take about half an hour. You can skip the burial—but if you want, I've got my car and we can drive straight to the stadium from the cemetery."

She laughed a little nervously at the absurdity of it all.

"Or you can see how you feel after the service. This must be kind of weird."

"Kind of," said Lev.

Deborah smiled at him but her eyes were already darting around the room nervously. She was looking for the funeral director.

Lev noticed that in her left ear, along with a simple pearl earring, there were several tiny, unused holes, not merely in the lobe but perforating the delicate outer rim of her ear.

"Who died?" Lev asked.

"Irma Corngold."

Ah, Jewish names, thought Lev. Depriving even the dead of dignity.

"She was ninety," said Deborah. "I have to interview her family to get a little info for the eulogy. I've never met her."

The little man in the dark suit had come back. He was holding several black ribbons attached to safety pins. Deborah took them and counted them out.

"We're short," she said reproachfully, as if to a dishonest merchant.

"There are six," the man said.

"There should be seven," Deborah said. "Four children, three sisters."

"I was told six," the man said defensively.

"Well we need one more."

Deborah seemed exasperated all of a sudden.

"Bring them to the Rabbi's Room," she said as the man went off.

"This guy is such a nitwit," she muttered to Lev under her breath. A change had come over her. But then she smiled, a little sheepishly. Lev had a slightly detached, scrutinizing way of staring that made her self-conscious.

"Does it matter that I'm not dressed right?" he asked.

"Oh don't worry about that," said Deborah. "You look great. But you might want a *kippah*." She patted her own head demonstratively. Several stray strands of hair had come loose from her bun and hung curling over her ears like the payos of Hasidic Jews. It exaggerated the exotic aura of her face, the high, wide cheekbones and Asiatic shape of her eyes.

"Will you be OK if I go do some things?" she asked. Lev assured her that he would be fine and Deborah went off to the Rabbi's Room where the sisters, children, and grandchildren were waiting in seclusion from the others. Lev helped himself to a black nylon kippah from a wicker basket and, head covered, felt calmer, camouflaged. He considered signing the guest book but thought better of it, and, to avoid the crowd, opened a side door and entered the room where the funeral itself would take place.

Except for an elderly couple sitting in the back row, the room was empty. It was a religiously neutral chapel with a rounded ceiling painted blue with gold stars. Lev took a seat a few rows from the front. There was a podium and flowers and, on one wall, stained-glass windows of indecipherable images in blue and purple—purposely blurred, Lev decided, for ecumenical use. It was only after he had sat in the cool silence for a few moments that he realized there was also a coffin in the room.

The coffin stood at the front, resting on a stand with wheels. How had he overlooked it? It was of pale polished wood and there was a Jewish star in a circle carved neatly on top. The fact that there was a body in the box, that someone who had been alive was now dead, struck Lev with unexpected force. He felt the narrow sides of the coffin confining his own breath, shrinking the boundaries of his body. He inhaled deeply.

But it wasn't him. Irma Corngold, or what had been Irma Corngold, was in there. He tried to figure out where the head was and where the feet. Probably the Jewish star was over the head.

"Where are you now?" he thought. As soon as he thought this he imagined the whispering presence of Irma Corngold's soul still hovering. He shivered away this superstitious inkling—he was prone to them—and was grateful when the doors were propped open and people began to drift into the chapel.

When the chapel was full and everyone had sat in murmuring, uncomfortable silence for what seemed a long time, the little funeral director came in and asked everyone to rise, like the bailiff at a trial when the judge is about to enter. Lev stood with the others as the immediate family, wearing their little black ribbons on their lapels, filed somberly in and took their seats in the front row of the chapel. Deborah was in the lead and, instead of sitting down, she went immediately up the few stairs and stood behind the lectern, looking out calmly over the crowd.

Behind him somebody said, in a harsh whisper, "A woman rabbi!"

"Why not?" said her companion. "We have one in Florida."

"She's a doll," said somebody else. Lev felt an unexpected flush of pride that he was . . . what? Her date? He stared at her—everyone was staring at her—and she made fleeting eye contact with him. Unless he was mistaken, Deborah had winked speedily in his direction.

The gesture was charming and disconcerting. It suggested that the whole funeral was a performance; that the wood coffin and the flowers and the mourners were all just props and extras in a play. He tried to renew eye contact but Deborah stared implacably out over the seats, her gaze everywhere and nowhere, the way a lifeguard scans the ocean. She had tucked the few curling strands back into her bun and was now wearing a black rabbinical robe over her lavender suit. She kept gazing out over the assembled mourners, even after the few stragglers who came in through a rear door had found their seats and a deep hush had fallen on the room.

Then, out of the deepening silence, she began to speak:

"A voice says: 'Cry out!' And I say: 'What shall I cry?'

" 'All flesh is grass, and all its beauty is like the flower of the field. The grass withers, the flower fades, when a wind of the Lord blows upon it. Surely the people are grass. The grass withers, the flower fades; but the word of our God shall endure forever.' "

She had begun barely above a whisper, so that the old people shifted and strained forward and the hush in the room became even deeper, a layered silence. But as she spoke Deborah's voice grew clearer and louder so that by the time she finished reading the paragraph of

Isaiah aloud, people had again settled back in their seats. Now she was chanting the Twenty-third Psalm in Hebrew. Deborah had the same rhapsodic look she wore when praying with his father. His own rude outburst, "Are you here to give him last rites?" came back to him and he cringed with embarrassment. Well, she didn't seem to hold it against him.

Her voice rose and fell in gentle waves. Her eyes had a faraway look. Lev was close enough to see that she was on the brink of tears, but her voice did not falter. She invited members of the family to come up and speak. Little by little, an image of Irma took shape in Lev's mind. Her mother had died in the influenza epidemic of 1918. She had been only nine but she had helped raise her siblings, all of whom, except sister Sophie, sick with arrhythmia in Florida, were gratefully present. She had married Max, who sold pharmaceutical supplies. He had died twenty-four years ago of a brain tumor. It had not been easy. It had been a hard life and a good life and a prosperous life and a sad life. And now she was in a box with a star on it.

Deborah, back at the lectern, was reading, in her sonorous voice, a passage out of her rabbi's manual. Her broad face, above the black robe, was luminous.

" 'Fear not death; we are destined to die. We share it with all who ever lived, with all who ever will be. Bewail the dead, hide not your grief, do not restrain your mourning. But remember that continuing sorrow is worse than death. When the dead are at rest, let their memory rest, and be consoled when the soul departs.

" 'Death is better than a life of pain, and eternal rest than constant sickness.' "

People nodded at this but others shifted uncomfortably. How many here, Lev wondered, believed in "eternal rest"? What did the word *eternal* mean? It was a child's question but one he realized he wanted to know the answer to. He would like to have raised his hand and asked.

But then, as if in answer to his thought, Deborah declaimed:

" 'Seek not to understand what is too difficult for you, search not for what is hidden from you. Be not overoccupied with what is beyond you, for you have been shown more than you can understand . . .' "

Lev drifted off with this. He found the formulation oddly comforting, though it was no answer at all. When he tuned back in Deborah was thanking the family members and friends for their beautiful words. She added a few observations she had gleaned in her interview. But Lev was scarcely listening. He was looking at Deborah's bright eyes, her full lips forming words he could scarcely focus on. He was thinking, suddenly, "She's beautiful."

He wondered vaguely what she looked like under her robe and if she would sleep with him. Unlikely on a first date. And of course, he'd have to go to the cemetery first. There'd been nobody serious since the Jenny debacle and he realized he must be getting desperate.

Deborah was chanting, in a soft, rich voice, *El Maleh Rachamim*, the prayer for the dead. This time she did cry—her high cheekbones were shining and it was as if she were somehow linked to each body in the chapel; Lev felt her little sob release an echoing sob in the throats around him. And he understood that in some way, everybody in the chapel had fallen in love with her.

And then it was over and people were again standing as the box with Irma's body was wheeled slowly down the aisle. People were weeping. The realization that this was final, that this was death, filled the room. The immediate family followed behind the coffin and people were reaching out to them.

Deborah brought up the rear. People hugged the mourners and several pulled at Deborah's sleeve as well.

"Beautiful," someone murmured.

"Thank you, Rabbi," someone else said.

She looked suddenly small. The towering apparition chanting *El Maleh Rachamim* was gone. In her black robe, Deborah looked like a college student at graduation. She caught Lev's eye and flashed him a half smile. Like the wink, Lev found it a little disconcerting and also oddly thrilling.

When the mourners had passed and his turn came he left his pew and moved out the door. Separating himself quickly from the crowd he took the stairs and went outside where the limousines were already idling their engines. Lev felt a sense of release in the bright sunshine. The coffin would be taken down in its own elevator and loaded unobtrusively into a hearse. But Lev was free, and he had an impulse to just keep going, down the bright sidewalk.

But he stayed put and soon Deborah was standing beside him. She was no longer wearing the black robe and she looked transformed yet again. She was a real person in a lavender suit that buttoned over breasts, with a skirt that seemed slightly crooked and white stockings that had a run in one leg, moving like a zipper toward the inner thigh.

"Hi."

"That was great," Lev said, with genuine enthusiasm.

Deborah shook her head. "I called one daughter Ellen but her name's Elena. I forgot to give the address for shivah."

She seemed uncomfortable. Lev said nothing. He stood squinting in the bright light, trying to regain his bearings.

"Listen, I don't want to pressure you," Deborah said suddenly, "but I've got to get into the procession."

They walked in silence to the corner.

"Somebody took my car when I got here. Let's see if I can get it back—last time they lost it."

She again had the unexpected, imperious tone that seemed to say, "I'm surrounded by idiots," though she laughed disarmingly at herself right after. Her car was fetched without difficulty and when she opened the door of the little red Honda, Lev found himself climbing in beside her.

"Follow that car," he said, pointing to the hearse that was just now emerging from the parking garage underneath the funeral home. He glanced at Deborah to see if she was offended but she was busy nosing into traffic, taking her place behind the hearse and two black limousines.

Lev could not help noticing that Deborah had on only a bra under the lavender blazer. He thought the V of naked flesh a little daring for a funeral, though he remembered the short skirt at the hospital and, after all, she'd worn a robe for the service. There was a chain around her neck suspending a small gold star of David. Judaic icons seemed kitchy to Lev, as a rule, but this small sharp star had a delicate beauty—a tiny echo of the star on Irma Corngold's coffin, nestling above Deborah's breasts.

"Not a bad turnout for an old lady," Deborah said.

Lev was looking around the car trying to learn what he could about its owner. There were a number of cassettes on the dashboard: Shlomo Carlebach, Ray Charles, Guided by Voices, Melissa Etheridge, k.d. lang (was she a lesbian? he wondered suddenly), Lauryn Hill, and—most surprising—Marian Anderson singing gospel.

"Do you do a lot of funerals?" he asked.

"Too many. It's weird when you don't know the person who died. *Shit!*"

A cab had darted between her and the procession. Deborah swerved around it and cut off another car pulling out of a parking spot. The driver gave her the finger.

"It's a funeral, asshole!" she shouted back. Lev was glad the windows were closed and the air-conditioning was on.

"Sorry," Deborah said, scrunching up her face amusingly. "I don't like city driving. I'll be fine when we get on the highway."

Lev checked to make sure his seat belt was on.

"Anyway, funerals can be strange."

"I thought you did a beautiful job."

"Well, thank you. I'm mostly an emcee. That's my main job. To facilitate, to create a ritual framework for other people's grief, for their stories."

"It's quite a job. You're really at the heart of things."

"I suppose so. Funerals aren't so different from the rest of life," she said. She was talking without turning her head, keeping her eye on the car in front of her, which had pulled over to the side to let other members of the cortege catch up.

Deborah pulled over as well and took the opportunity to reach back and grab a plastic bag from the back seat.

"It's time you learn the most important lesson about funerals," she said.

"What's that?" Lev asked, genuinely curious.

"Food!" Deborah said. "Always bring your own."

Lev laughed in surprise.

"Seriously," said Deborah. "The funeral *started* at noon. Then you go to the cemetery—which is always out in Long Island or New Jersey or a part of Queens you've never heard of. It'll be three or more likely four before anyone makes it back to shivah, which is in the Village at her daughter's place. Then you have to attack the lox like a starved hyena, which is really humiliating for everyone. You expect Jews to know better than that."

Deborah had opened the bag on her lap and was rummaging through it. She removed a box of raisins, a bag of baby carrots, and two sandwich-shaped squares of tinfoil.

"I have tuna and egg salad."

"Tuna," said Lev.

He took the sandwich she handed him gratefully. He was, he realized, starving.

THE GRAVESIDE CEREMONY WAS SHORT, as Deborah had promised, but the burial itself took a long time. Deborah believed in a "full burial," and she explained to the mourners that this was a powerful custom, a chance for the community to do something for the dead that the dead could not do for themselves. And so she held off the grave diggers, who waited impatiently in the background, while beckoning the mourners, who lined up awkwardly beside the heaped mound of red earth.

The family itself seemed divided about this practice. Irma's youngest daughter, Doris, loved the idea of burying her mother and was first in line, but two of Irma's sisters stalked away from the grave, weeping and angry. Lev himself escorted the third, tottering in heels, up to the edge of the pit so that she could throw in her token shovelful. The falling earth hit the coffin with a hollow thud, as if the body inside had already vanished.

Deborah was tireless, hurling herself into the physical work with gusto when volunteers dropped off, shaming a few younger cousins into removing their blazers, rolling up their shirtsleeves, and joining her. Lev, dressed for labor more than the others, had taken a long turn. But the crowd got antsy and Deborah, looking defeated, waved in the jumpsuited grave diggers to finish the job. They shoveled with indifferent ferocity.

When they had completed the job, Deborah recited a few phrases from her rabbi's manual: "The dust returns to the earth, as it was, but the spirit returns to God, who gave it. May the soul of Irma Corngold, *Rochel bat Shimon v'Netti*, be bound up in the bond of eternal life . . ."

There was something strained and anticlimactic to the funeral's end. Deborah tried to line up the crowd in two rows so that the mourners could walk between them and receive condolences on their way back to the car. But the mourners walked too quickly and nobody knew the Hebrew formula Deborah coached them to say. The two angry sisters, who had refused to come out of their limousine even for Kaddish, glowered through the tinted glass of a waiting limousine.

Lev understood their anger. Why should old people be forced to stare into the loamy pit where they soon would be; forced to hear dirt thud on a wooden box hiding what was left of their beloved sister? Why should they have to shovel her under with their own weak hands?

Deborah, on the other hand, had no patience for them at all.

"It was something they could have done for their dead sister, instead of preserving their old-lady vanity, or denial, or whatever it was," she said with surprising vehemence once they were in the car. "They may be in their eighties, but they've absorbed the worst of modern America."

She was in a bad mood. Grave dust still powdered her ankles and streaked up toward the hem of her skirt.

And then, either to change the subject or to continue it—Lev wasn't sure which—Deborah said, "So what do you do?"

They were waiting for the car in front of them to start moving along the narrow car-path inside the cemetery.

"I write about science for a magazine called *Eureka*."

Deborah did not give any sign of recognition.

"It's science for the general reader. I don't write about the hard stuff," Lev added, for some reason. "I leave nanotechnology and string theory to the experts. I do more feature-type reporting."

"You mean like, 'Fat People Weigh More Than Thin People, Study Shows'—or, 'Depressed People Are Often Sad'?"

"I see you have the proper respect for my profession," he said.

"I don't mean to be snide," said Deborah.

"It just comes out that way?"

"Sort of," said Deborah, apologetically.

"There are a lot of amazing things going on in science," Lev said.

"Who knows, in a few years it might be possible to extend our life expectancy by twenty years. Irma could still be alive."

Deborah shuddered.

"What a revolting notion," she said.

"Why shouldn't people live longer?" Lev asked. And then he added, somewhat irrelevantly, "Francis Collins calls DNA the language of God."

"Who's Francis Collins?"

"He's leading the government effort to map the genome," said Lev. "He found the gene for cystic fibrosis and Huntington's disease. And he's a religious Christian."

Lev was rooting for Collins to decode the genome before his rival, the capitalist and presumably godless Craig Venter, but he felt he was pandering a little to Deborah, in spite of himself. But Deborah said nothing and a moment later Irma's daughter Doris came up to the open car window waving an envelope.

"Rabbi, I just want to thank you. It was beautiful. I light the candle when I get home, right?"

"That's right," Deborah said.

"I want to give you this," Doris said, thrusting an envelope through the window.

"Thank you," said Deborah.

She took the envelope and put it on the seat beside her.

"Do you have a card or something?" Doris asked.

Lev could feel the longing in her, the need. She wanted something, some intimacy, some answer. She wanted, Lev thought, to get into the car with them. As if she needed Deborah to pilot her through the valley of the shadow of death. Lev felt that way a little himself.

"I'm sorry, I didn't bring any cards," Deborah said. "You can always find me through the temple."

She reached through the car window and took Doris's hand. She looked her right in the eyes and said something in Hebrew that neither Lev nor Doris understood. But Doris looked very moved, said, "Thank you," and reluctantly walked away.

"What did you say?" Lev asked.

"It's the standard phrase of comfort for a mourner. It means, 'God will comfort you along with the other mourners of Zion and Jerusalem.' It's a reference to the destruction of the Temple. Whenever we lose someone we love, it's as if the Temple were destroyed."

"Ah," said Lev. "There's that Temple again."

But Deborah didn't smile. She didn't say anything. The car in front of them had started moving and Deborah began inching along the narrow road. She was tired, lost in thought. Off in the distance, amid the sea of tombstones, Lev saw that another funeral was in progress.

Irma Corngold's solitary grave had affected him deeply. Was it because his father was ill? The hole in the Long Island earth, where Irma lay, quietly annihilated hope and faith—though Lev was already aware of both these things creeping back, like a weed he could not kill.

When they were about to drive through the cemetery gate, Deborah stopped the car. She took a water bottle from under the seat, leaned out the car door, and poured water first over her right hand then over her left. She did this three times, alternating hands each time.

"You're supposed to wash after contact with the dead," she explained. "It's one of those ancient beliefs, that the dead make us impure. We're going back to the world of the living."

She offered the bottle to Lev but he declined. It seemed like an insult to Irma Corngold, but he only said, "No thank you," as if Deborah had offered him a drink.

Deborah shrugged nonjudgmentally and recapped the water.

"It must be hard to perform a funeral and then just have a normal day," Lev said, as Deborah restarted the car.

"What's a normal day?" she asked, swinging into traffic.

THEY GOT TO YANKEE STADIUM just as the seventh-inning stretch was ending.

The outfield sparkled greenly. It had the enriched, darkened look of a meadow just before a rainstorm, but in fact the sky was free of clouds and the sun was strong. The lively crowd restored Lev, though it was impossible for him to see the red infield dirt of Yankee Stadium and not to think of the earth falling on Irma's grave. Indeed it was hard for him to look at the brilliant grass of the outfield without thinking of the cemetery, as if there were bodies lurking under the spot where Paul O'Neal was whipping a ball to Bernie Williams. Yankee Stadium held fifty thousand men, women, and children and all of them would wind up under the ground. The empty seats in the right-field bleachers had the look of row upon row of tombstones.

Deborah, however, seemed to have left the cemetery, and her bad mood, far behind.

"This is great!" she said, looking around with satisfaction. "Just what I needed."

As she had promised, she rooted for Oakland, which had taken a three-run lead by the time they arrived. "Come on!" she yelled encouragingly to every A's batter. She razzed the Yankee pitcher—David Cone—with the same look of intensity with which she had shouted, "This is a funeral, asshole." Lev felt she took pleasure in rooting for the opposite team.

She booed Scott Brosius because he had gone to the Yankees from the A's. "Traitor!" she yelled.

She was letting off steam. The funeral had been stressful—the tension at the grave over the burial in particular had worn her out. Contradicting the roar of the crowd was stressful, too, but invigorating. She did not mind the dirty looks or the occasional insults she was receiving from the Yankee fans around her. They were by and large good-natured. There was even something flirtatious about it. She would toss a gloating look at the men who had been jeering at her three rows back, pointing a triumphant finger at the scoreboard. This made Lev, who did not like to stand out, vaguely uncomfortable, but he was fascinated by Deborah's bravado. When she went to buy herself and Lev a beer at the bottom of the eighth (she insisted on treating him—after all, he had been a good sport and gone to a funeral), she came back wearing an Oakland A's hat that she had bought off the head of another embattled fan she met at the concession stand. It touched off a whole new exchange of insults.

Deborah had also removed her stockings and stuffed them into her bag. It was hot at the stadium and Lev had noticed earlier that the run in her left leg had gotten longer during the burial. But he couldn't help wondering if there wasn't some secondary meaning to their sudden disappearance. On the other hand, she was a *rabbi*. Lev was not sure what this said about her physical life. What would it mean if they wound up alone? *I can't, it's a fast day.*

Lev studied Deborah in stolen glances. She was wearing her Oakland hat, clutching her beer in both hands as if it were a steaming mug of cocoa; he tried to reconcile the image with the woman in the chapel in the black robe, commending the soul of Irma Corngold to heaven.

It was hard to make casual chatter. The stadium was loud and the Yankees had tied the score in the ninth off a double by Tino Martinez so that the game stretched into a tenth and then an eleventh inning. But at one point, Lev, shouting over the noise—and yet pulling back his voice, too, so that he wouldn't quite be screaming in her ear—said, "Shouldn't we have gone to shivah?"

It was as if he wanted to call Deborah back to her rabbinical role, even though he had been eager, earlier in the day, for her to shed it. Now he wanted her to reclaim a little of it. She had taken on the whole section and kept shouting instructions to the players. He wondered if it was to prove to him—or herself—that she was not just a rabbi. This in itself seemed somehow rabbinical—the wish, maybe even the need, to be in control of every situation. As if Yankee Stadium were one big shul to her and she needed to be the center of its attention. He felt inexplicable resentment surging, a sort of anticlerical feeling, which was odd, given Deborah's ball-game demeanor. He felt like the pious one and didn't like the feeling.

"I only go to the shivah if it's someone I know. For a last-minute job, this was plenty," Deborah roared back.

The Yankees won it six-five in the twelfth.

Deborah drove him home. She was double-parked, there was no chance of her coming inside. Lev felt disappointment mingled with relief. He kept seeing Deborah standing at the podium of Riverside Chapel.

"Thanks for the ball game," Deborah said.

"Thanks for the funeral."

Deborah laughed. "Any time."

They sat for a moment in silence. It was awkward in the little car now that they were no longer moving. A boy on a tricycle pedaled down the street. A maternal voice called after him. "Stop, Jonah!"

The sun had set but the street was bathed in peach-colored light. Deborah was studying his face with great tenderness. He had long, pale lashes that made his face look naked, like the Jewish faces you saw in black-and-white photographs taken in Europe before the war.

Lev looked back at her. The glow of the street had somehow ignited her hair. Her hands were on the wheel, as if she were still driving. A streak of dirt—from the grave?—traveled along one pale naked leg, just above the knee. Lev, surprised at himself, reached over and brushed it with his fingers. He was barely touching her but Deborah felt a warm thrill run through her. She kept her hands incongruously on the steering wheel but shifted her body toward him and turned to face him more fully. Her leg slid into Lev's touch. He flattened his palm and allowed his hand to move slowly along her thigh. His fingers were just beneath the hem of her skirt.

It had been easier to begin at the bottom, away from her yearning eyes. He smelled the faint exhalation of ball-game beer and something sweet, as if her body had released perfume. A strange confidence propelled by desire had taken hold of him. But when he leaned forward to kiss her he was suddenly restrained by the harness of his shoulder strap. Deborah's open lips broke into a smile. Lev swore and leaned back, fumbling with the seat belt. He was suddenly self-conscious. The car was ridiculous. He felt like someone trying unsuccessfully to remove his pants. Deborah watched as he jabbed his thumb into the stuck square button of the buckle. There was something touching about his helplessness and she thought suddenly of Henry Friedman. She'd been meaning to ask about him all evening.

"How is your father doing?"

"Much better," said Lev, distractedly. "He'll be coming home soon."

He was finally free and hoped to recapture the earlier mood. He glanced down the street to see if there was a parking space, but Deborah was still talking about his father.

"Are you afraid he'll try again?"

Even as Deborah finished her sentence she realized she had blundered. Lev looked at her strangely.

"Try what?"

Deborah considered making something up, lying. Or pretending she hadn't said anything. But there was no taking it back. Was it really possible that nobody had told him?

"Do you know why your father wound up in the hospital?" Deborah asked, as if speaking to a small child.

"He had a stroke," said Lev.

The statement sounded like a question. A powerful intimation was rising up his spine. Deborah's face frightened him, as though she were about to say that his father wasn't alive anymore. Her expression contained the response to a reaction he hadn't had yet.

Deborah took his hand but it seemed to Lev a condescending gesture. All the electricity had gone out of their touch. His own hand was suddenly cold.

"Tell me what you know," Lev said.

"Your father did have a stroke," Deborah said softly. "But it seems, just before that, he was about to swallow a lot of pills. He planned to kill himself. Your mother never told you?"

"No," said Lev.

He pulled his hand away from Deborah's and opened the thin car door, though he did not get out. There was suddenly no air. He had an impulse to run somewhere. He felt foolish and angry and somehow ashamed.

"I'm sorry, Lev," said Deborah. "I thought you knew. It must be . . ."

"I have to go," Lev said, cutting her off.

The strangeness of responding so long after the fact to something he had just learned was disorienting. He felt a weird disjunction, a sense of urgent immediacy no longer right for the situation. But he needed to get out.

The car door bumped into the car at the curb, a looming black SUV. Lev didn't care and shoved his way through with violence. Once on the sidewalk, he did not go into his apartment but started walking briskly toward Amsterdam.

"Lev!" shouted Deborah. "Wait."

Lev did not turn around. Deborah started her car and lurched after him. She pulled parallel with Lev, driving slowly.

"Please get in," she called out. "I can take you where you want to go."

"No," he shouted. "I'm sorry. No."

There was a van behind her. She was forced to turn uptown at Amsterdam. Lev turned the other way and broke into a run.

LEV'S FIRST THOUGHT had been to go to the Sinai Center, as if what he'd heard about his father hadn't happened yet and it was in Lev's power to prevent it. But he cut over to Columbus and hailed a taxi going downtown. He needed to see his mother.

Helen Friedman answered the door. Her long white hair had been liberated from its heavy braid and fanned out loose over her shoulders and down her back. She was in a bathrobe, though it was only 8:30. She kissed her son and greeted him with concealed concern—he seldom stopped by without calling and she wondered what had brought him.

There was something off-kilter about Lev. He seemed anxious, breathless. He looked ill and she felt a pang of maternal panic. But she decided to wait for him to speak.

Mephisto came out yapping and started untying Lev's shoelaces with his teeth. Lev picked up the little chocolate-colored dog and carried him into the living room where he sat down on the sofa and onto a chew toy, a rubber bone that let out a squeal. Lev flung the toy down the hall and Mephisto ran after it.

Lev's mother had been paying bills and listening to a Schubert quartet, she wasn't sure which one. She found it almost an obligation to play Henry's records, as if, like walking the dog, Mozart and Beethoven and Brahms needed to be exercised in her husband's absence. And it made her feel that Henry was home, in the next room, reading or translating or working on one of his obscure writing projects.

She offered Lev tea; she'd already made a pot for herself. The fat yellow teapot rested on the coffee table surrounded by five little cups, like a hen surrounded by chicks. She had bought the set in Kyoto—or

rather Henry had bought it for her one day while she was out photographing schoolchildren. They'd laughed at the tiny teacups, more for
a child's tea party than for grown-up drinking, but Helen loved the
pale yellow glaze on the outside and the splash of black at the heart of
each cup. It was like drinking out of a tulip.

"Lev, are you all right?"

"We have to talk about Dad."

"Did something happen?" Mrs. Friedman asked with sudden
alarm. "Are you coming from Sinai?"

Lev realized his mistake.

"Mom, you saw him today after I did. That's not what I mean."

His mother's tired face relaxed again. She was, despite her forceful
optimism, afraid that something terrible would happen to Henry
while he was living out of the apartment.

"He's coming home a week from Tuesday," Helen said with a weary
smile, as she poured herself a thimbleful of pale green tea. "They told
me today. He'll need assistance; I've hired someone from an agency
part-time. But he's doing well. Didn't you think so?"

"Did Dad try to kill himself?" Lev blurted out.

Helen Friedman froze; her hand was still stretched toward the
teapot. Lev heard in her silence absolute confirmation. He had hoped
on his way downtown that Deborah was wrong. That she had picked
something up in the hospital, some misinformation, and passed it
along as truth. That she had confused Lev's father with somebody else.
But in fact what she'd told him answered to some unspoken intuition.
Why then was he so angry at Deborah? Did it humiliate him that she
knew something about his own father he did not?

"Who told you that?" his mother asked at last.

"Never mind who told me," said Lev, standing up. "Is it true?"

Mephisto had come back and was once again nibbling at Lev's
sneakers. Lev lifted the little dog on his sneaker and tossed him a short
distance, harder than he'd intended. Mephisto landed not on his feet
but on his side, whimpered and ran under the couch. The dog was fine
but Lev felt sick, as if he had kicked his father.

"Sit down," his mother said, in a gentle but firm voice.

She looked at Lev with a mixture of apology, pity, and affection hardened by something that might only have been exhaustion but was perhaps irritation—one more inept man in her family needing something from her.

"I wanted to tell you right away. But then, for Dad's sake, I suppose, I held off. Because I knew he was going to get better. And it had to do with his health, it really was his health."

"Does Jacob know?"

Lev was embarrassed to ask this question but it had gnawed at him the moment he'd heard from Deborah. Somehow the fact that his older brother might have been told, when he was not, upset him almost as much as the fact itself.

"Yes," said Helen. "But he was at the hospital that first night. The doctors were all talking about it. They had to pump his stomach."

"And you told Jake not to tell me."

"I was going to tell you myself. Every day I was going to tell you. But you've been through so much yourself."

She meant, presumably, the smashed wedding. But also Neal's crackup. Was she afraid one more trauma would tip him over the edge into the crazy company of his friend?

"I don't need special treatment!" Lev shouted, the break in his voice making him sound to his own ears like a child, which only made him more upset. *This is how people are driven crazy*, he thought.

"I know you don't," said his mother softly. "I'm sorry. I was wrong."

They were silent for a while. The dog had emerged but was now curled up in its little basket lined with its red pillow. Mephisto eyed Lev warily.

"How could he?" said Lev.

And then, to steer away from that: "Is it possible that it was an accident?"

"It wasn't an accident," Helen said. "But he didn't go through with it. It was a kind of trial run, I think, to see if he could do it. If he still had control over his life. He loves you very much. He loves us all very much. He didn't want to leave us."

"What happened?" Lev asked in a trembling voice. "I want to hear from the beginning."

Helen told Lev what had happened, leaving out only the plastic bag she had found over her husband's head. She did not want her son to picture his father as she had seen him.

Lev's head was spinning. He still thought perhaps the whole thing had been a misunderstanding. Perhaps his father had been in great pain. Perhaps the bath was connected to his aching body.

"Was there a note?" he asked.

Helen rose and went over to her desk, which was in the living room and could be closed to look like a small, freestanding cabinet. She opened a drawer and took out an envelope that she handed to Lev. It wasn't sealed—the flap was merely tucked in.

"I don't know if I should give this to you. Technically, it still belongs to your father. I was going to destroy it but I couldn't bring myself to. There was also a note for me, making things pretty plain. And a letter for Jake."

"Did you give Jake his letter?" Lev asked, in spite of himself.

"No," said his mother. "I still have it. I haven't mentioned it."

Lev realized he was being asked not to mention it either and felt that delicious, uncomfortable collusion left over from childhood when his mother had managed to make each of her boys feel chosen at the expense of the other.

Lev looked at his name printed on the envelope. Three scratchy letters were enough to evoke his father's peculiar, slanting European handwriting. Suddenly his father's whole mysterious presence filled the room. The Schubert recording had ended but Henry Friedman's music was reverberating everywhere.

He would have liked to open the envelope on the spot but something prevented him. His mother was watching him intently. Lev sat down holding the letter in both hands. It felt like a letter from beyond the grave.

"Do you think Dad will mind?" he asked.

Helen sighed.

"I'm not sure he'll know. Your father's mind has cleared in many ways. I think he remembers a lot and he knows, because I told him, what happened. But he doesn't seem to remember the details of the day at all. I don't know if he's repressed them because of trauma or if the stroke that followed has something to do with it."

"Or if he's pretending," said Lev, suddenly feeling that his father was even more of a riddle than he had realized.

Helen shrugged, though she did not think it was likely. Her hands were in the pockets of her bathrobe; in one pocket, she discovered her empty teacup and rolled it between her fingers. She herself was trying to figure out who could possibly have told Lev. She had intended to tell him herself but then found she was glad he didn't know. It wasn't only because she felt the information would devastate him. She wanted Henry to have a chance to go back to being the way he was. She knew she did not need to mold her sons' opinions of their father, though she had done it so much in her life, explaining him to people because he did not bother, or seem able to, explain himself. And she wanted the world to understand him as she did. She believed in explanations more than her husband.

Lev folded the envelope his mother had given him and put it in his back pocket. He was not going to read it in her presence, though the envelope wasn't sealed and he assumed she had read it already.

Mephisto, holding no grudge, trotted across the room.

"Has he already been walked?" Lev asked, stooping down to scratch the dog.

"Would you mind?" his mother asked. "I was just going to take him when you came by. But I'm not dressed . . ."

"Sure," said Lev, lifting the leash from the umbrella stand where his mother had draped it and taking a plastic bag from a box that rested beside the stand. He hesitated by the door.

"Mom," he said. "Is it safe to leave Dad there alone? I mean, isn't it possible that he'd try to do something again? Shouldn't we be watching him?"

His mother sighed.

"Your father has promised me. I know that sounds strange but he wouldn't lie to me. And he seems to have lost the desire. And . . . he doesn't have the strength. But that's not why. He just isn't going to."

"You didn't know he was planning to last time," Lev said. His mother flinched, wounded, even though Lev quickly added, "None of us did."

"No," she said. "We didn't know."

Lev put his arms around his mother and hugged her. She embraced him back and to his surprise began to weep. He felt her body shaking before he heard a sound. For a brief moment her crying was uncontrollable; she sobbed on Lev's shoulder and gripped him tightly. Mephisto, meanwhile, attached to the leash Lev was holding, became part of the embrace, racing around their feet and tangling them up. Helen, still crying, lifted her head and laughed, wiping at her tears with the sleeve of her bathrobe.

"You goddamn dog," she said.

She looked at Lev, who was pale with concern.

"I'm sorry," she said. "Don't worry about me."

"Of course not," said Lev, sarcastically, "who cares about you?"

It was a family that often—with the exception of Lev's father—showed affection through sarcasm.

"No, I'm fine," Helen said, producing a rumpled Kleenex from her bathrobe pocket, like a sick person, and dabbing her eyes with it. "And I think Daddy will be, too. I know it seems extreme. It *was* extreme. But he wanted to spare us—and himself—something very hard. I wish he hadn't thought about it that way. But he did."

LEV FOUND A PARK BENCH on Riverside Drive, just inside the park, and took out his father's note. It was typed; the flying letters of the manual typewriter were as direct and personal as his father's handwriting. They reminded Lev at once of letters he had received in camp and notes to his teachers, always typed, excusing him from a test or from gym class because of one or another of his many childhood illnesses, real and imagined. Lev ran out a long length of leash and trapped the holder under his thigh so he could use both hands. Then, by the yellow light of a streetlamp, he began to read.

My beloved son Lev,

By the time you read this I will no longer be alive. Hard words to write! But what I have done is painless and necessary. Necessary not because the world is a terrible place—it can be, of course, but it is also full of wonderful things and I wish them all for you. Necessary because my body is failing me and I do not wish to burden you and Jacob and most especially your mother if I should have another stroke—which I believe is not far off.

I know this will be hard for all of you but I know you will rally together and help each other and I pray most of all that you will understand and forgive me. You are a wonderful young man. Don't worry about your wedding. Yeats wrote: "Nothing can be sole or whole that has not first been rent." Sometimes it is the breaks that build us up. You will find someone who is right for you. I am so sorry I will not be there when you do but I will be there I hope in other ways.

Lev, dear boy, I want you to say Kaddish for me. You should start the day of the funeral and continue for eleven months. (I do not expect you to do this three times a day but I'm sure you can find a morning minyan. There is B'nai Jeshurun, not far from where you live and also the Jewish Center and the SAJ. Lincoln Square will also have one.)

I was never able to say Kaddish properly for my own father (or mother) because they had already been dead too long when I was told about their being gone . . . In any case I was too young to be obligated at the time. And there were historical circumstances making it difficult. But I've felt bad about my failure to do so and I would like to believe that I have raised a son who will fulfill that obligation. In saying it for me you will in some sense be say-

ing it for them, too. And for all Jews who had nobody to say Kaddish for them.

I could and should have taught you a great deal more than I did. But I hope I gave you something that will carry you through this and will make you feel attached to the generations that came before you of whom I am just a brief but loving representative. I know that I failed terribly to educate you properly. I am so sorry.

I want you to know that I love you very much and have always loved you very much. Having you and Jake, and of course marrying your mother, has made my life worthwhile. But there are things larger than ourselves that we must all submit to. I know that you will come to understand this.

Our obligations sustain us. Yours is to continue on, to be kind to yourself and to others and not to give in to despair. Choose life.

Yours forever,
Dad

Lev was trembling when he finished the letter. He had tears in his eyes, despite the fact that he was hoping in some strange way for something more. What did he want to hear? What mystery unfolded? What declaration of love and pride and faith? He read the letter several times. His father was giving him an assignment. It wounded Lev's feelings to think that his father did not trust him to say Kaddish for him unasked. He had always intended to. But Lev understood that it was himself Henry was doubting. What had he given his son?

There were a few things in the letter Lev wasn't sure how to interpret. What did his father mean by "things larger than ourselves that we must all submit to"? Was he referring to his own intended suicide, to death itself? To the inevitability of illness and decline? Was he talking about God? Or was he simply making sure that Lev was really going to say Kaddish for him, that he was going to submit himself to a tradition larger than himself?

Choose life! Only his father could write a suicide note and end it with those words. They came from the Bible and his father often quoted them. Did he think Lev, too, wanted to kill himself?

Lev did not think so. For his father, "choose life" meant something else. Not merely living but living a certain way. A life of obligation inside of which one might find freedom. There was the paradox at the heart of everything and it filled Lev with conflicting emotions.

Mephisto, despite the long leash, wanted to be walking and wanted Lev to be walking, too. While Lev was reading, the dog had untied Lev's sneakers again. Moreover he'd crapped over by a little strip of grass and seemed to want to tell Lev about it. Lev debated ignoring it but stooped to pick up the warm turd, his hand gloved in the plastic bag that he turned inside out and tossed into a mesh garbage can.

Lev looked down at his father's little dachshund, trapped in the anatomical folly of its breed. The tiny legs, refashioned by human whim, were the result of genetic engineering of an ancient sort. Lev began walking back to his parents' apartment. The dog scurried along with an unself-conscious awkwardness that gave it, like its pale eyebrows, an oddly human pathos.

Had his father composed his note on this stretch of Riverside Drive, moving absentmindedly from hydrant to hydrant? Lev had a powerful desire to go and see his father but he knew that they would never let him in so late and, in any case, his father was probably asleep at this hour.

A tremendous loneliness overtook Lev. He felt for a moment that he had lost his father. He leaned against a lamppost and read the letter one more time, just to hear "My beloved son, Lev" in his head and to see the word *Dad* handwritten at the bottom.

DEBORAH CALLED LEV when she got home and left him a message.

"Call anytime," she said, but Lev did not call that night. The next day she tried him again and still he did not call her back. She considered stopping by his apartment but something held her back. He would find her when he wanted to.

That weekend, Deborah went out of town to visit her friend Terri at a time-share in the Hamptons. Deborah didn't like the Hamptons, she didn't even like Terri all that much, but she loved the ocean and she had hardly been away all summer. But on Saturday morning, when Terri and another friend had driven to the beach and Deborah, who wouldn't ride in a car on Shabbat, stayed back, she experienced a loneliness she had not felt in a long time. She walked to a local beach—if Terri had been a different kind of friend, she'd have gone there, too— and went swimming alone.

The ocean always restored Deborah. There was no lifeguard and Deborah felt a small thrill of danger as she swam out beyond the breaking waves. She was a strong swimmer and felt confident; she felt she might swim as far out as she liked. There were a few families on the shore, children running up the beach to avoid the cold waves, shrieking as they ran. A man and a woman bobbed in waist-high water behind her. She was the only person so far out. She turned her back to the shore and faced the horizon. There was a prayer said on seeing the ocean although she couldn't remember if it was just the Mediterranean or if it was any ocean. She said it anyway.

Stirred by a sudden impulse she slipped the top of her one-piece off her shoulders. No one could see—she was up to her neck in water. She wanted to feel the ocean on her breasts. She rode up on a swell.

That was a secret of the ocean, that the waves that broke so fiercely on the shore never lifted their heads farther out.

Deborah felt deep invisible currents tug at her. She shut her eyes for a moment, riding her wave in red darkness as if she were literally floating inside her own bloodstream. Sunlight penetrated her mass of wet hair and her scalp tingled and glowed. She felt attached to the sun. Her soul felt stretched and alive.

Then, quite unexpectedly, a wave broke over her head. She sank under it, swallowed a little water and felt with it a taste of acid. Her balance was thrown off and when she resurfaced, coughing, she wasn't sure what direction she was facing. It must have been out to sea because another wave suddenly broke on top of her, like a punch in the face.

She felt astonishment and outrage and a brief surge of fear. Water ran up her nose and down her throat. She remained upright but she had slipped in the water, fallen deeper into it. She felt crushed back against the kernel of herself, all helpless body. But she managed to keep her head above the water. Her eyes stung but she could see; the sky was very blue and she fixed on the horizon, where the spidery arms of a fishing boat crawled across the ocean. A cold vibration of ocean entered her bloodstream and she shivered. There was a machine oil taste in her throat. Panic? Pollution? She realized another wave was traveling toward her, bulging the surface of the water like an animal under a bedspread. Would it break or could she ride it?

It broke and this time Deborah went under completely. Somehow she did not panic but dove down deeper; it was like driving into a skid. She was a strong swimmer and she was not going to retreat. Reuben, her mother, and even her therapist had all accused her of taking the universe personally. The water was ice cold but she felt defiant as she powered herself forward and down, her body rocking. Time stopped for a moment and she felt encased in black ice; her lungs felt empty, her legs had lost their kick. She felt the chill absence of everything, not just sun. For a split second she felt she would simply sink to the bottom, but even as she thought this her body was fighting and she popped up gasping beyond the breaking waves.

She was still coughing but she quickly caught her breath and her balance. She was farther out now. A swell lifted her, foaming around her, but it did not break. She remembered her suit and for a moment thought she had lost it but found it clinging to her waist and hauled it back in place, coughing and laughing in a strange voice. She felt triumphant. The breaking waves had been an aberration. She was again floating on swells. Her heart was pounding. She looked back at the shore and saw the same children, the couple holding hands, a dog running on the beach with a Frisbee in its teeth. Nothing had changed.

Could she really have drowned? Her father, dead now fifteen years, would not have let her. She'd felt him lurking in the water, though not in that second of darkness. But he was there now. She felt him, a childhood reassurance she had never lost.

Back at the beach house the loneliness returned. You could not love—or hate—the universe for long. Her friends had not returned. And if they had, she would not have told them about her day, though something of deep importance had happened to her in the water. Precisely what she could not have said, though it involved her and her father and the strangeness of being alive. It was nothing and it was everything.

She thought of Lev and wished she could talk to him. She wondered what had happened after he had left her. Undoubtedly he had spoken to his mother but what then? She kept picturing him running down the sidewalk, away from her.

She liked the intelligent benevolence of his face, something he shared with his father. He was handsome in a pale, old-fashioned way, except for the surprising red of his hair that kinked up suddenly in a flaming wave above his forehead. She did not quite believe in his quietness. He was a torch who was trying to be a candle. He was tall, though he seemed uncomfortable taking up space.

Deborah disliked short men—Reuben had been a shrimp, though

he had the ego of a whale—but there was a gloomy diffidence Lev seemed to sink into at unwatched moments that made her leery. He had eaten her raisins as if he were taking Advil, sprinkling a few onto his palm and then tossing them into his mouth with furtive, hypochondriacal haste. She'd have preferred a man who stuck his hand into the box, and yet when he touched her she had felt an electric thrill.

She did not want to talk about Lev with Terri and the others. She could hear them saying, "A funeral? You took him to a funeral?" It would fit every stereotype they had about her.

Deborah had been a rabbi long enough to know that nobody re-acted neutrally to her. She had friends who apologized when they swore—despite her own foul-mouthed proclivities; who deleted sexual details they'd have included in other conversations. Who assumed she did not see stupid movies or watch stupid television shows so that she would sometimes take pains to prove just how frivolous she could be, which only falsified her in the opposite direction. Her own mother could be full of snide asides and odd innuendoes. "*You're* the rabbi," Laura would say. "God doesn't talk to *me*."

Laura—Deborah had called her mother by her first name since childhood—was a psychoanalyst and an atheist and if Deborah had be-come a voodoo priestess her mother could not have been more mystified or irritated. Her father, an oncologist who never spoke about religion one way or the other but who had loved everything she did and seemed to have secret reserves of unarticulated faith, would have approved, Deborah believed, of her career choice. But her father had been dead a long time.

Deborah showered and washed out her red one-piece. Dark sand fell from the lining of the suit onto the tiled shower floor—along with a small shell that suddenly sprouted legs and dragged itself a few inches across the tiles. Before she had time to think Deborah had picked it up and thrown it in the toilet with a shiver of disgust. Noth-ing to do now but flush. She sighed, disappointed in herself.

Really, she might have drowned. She ought to say a prayer of thanks. She was not sure what that might be—it seemed melodramatic to "bench gomel," and recite the prayer one said in synagogue after a dangerous illness—or after childbirth. Instead, as she toweled off, she recited the morning prayer thanking God for giving her back her soul.

On impulse, Deborah broke Shabbat by calling in to her machine at home, checking, she realized, for a message from Lev. Instead she found a message from Rabbi Zwieback, who had recovered from his stomach bug and gone on vacation in Florida. He was calling to make a special request. A woman was sick, a member of the board of trustees, would Deborah please visit her? His careful midwestern speech depressed her, he overenunciated in the old style of the Reform movement so that her name sounded like "Deb-Oh-Rah." Deborah favored a speedy two-syllable pronunciation. It embarrassed her to be hearing his voice on Shabbat, though Rabbi Zwieback in fact used the phone on the Sabbath, as did most Reform rabbis. He also drove, used money, and was careless about kashrut. Deborah, like a handful of her Hebrew Union College graduating class, had gotten more observant while she was a rabbinic student and was far more traditional than many of her teachers, though she still embraced the spirit of Reform.

Lev did not seem like the kind of person who would get stuck on her profession. If anything, the fact that he had been so rude to her the first time they met seemed oddly promising—a total disregard for any sort of clerical authority. Of course he had not yet known what she did. Deborah also considered the possibility that it might simply be *her*, and not her profession or the odd circumstances of their first date or even the revelation about his father that sent Lev away. It might be that she was not in fact his type, though Deborah didn't believe in types. She did believe in souls predestined for each other, but that was different.

And yet, when she looked in the mirror after stepping out of her shower, her hair washed and drying in ringlets that had lightened in the summer sun, her cheeks flushed, her grandmother's little star hanging between her breasts, she could not help thinking, "I'm beautiful." This wasn't really vanity, just a quiet sense of her own luster.

But she wasn't often visible to others as she was to herself at that moment—delivered from the rough ocean, soothed by prayer, naked and unself-conscious.

Lev had said that in the nursing home he felt like the Flash, vibrating to the point of invisibility while all the patients and doctors and aides and spouses were stuck in a kind of concrete stasis. She often felt that way even when she was not in the nursing home.

Lev had turned out to be different from what she had imagined. Far shyer and yet he had an inward, unspoken self-confidence that was unsettling. A kind of muted arrogance. An ambiguous smile that was hard to read.

Still, she was touched by what she had seen of him in the nursing home, reading aloud to his father. That moment had captured something that she felt in him later on, a kernel of compassion at the core of his scrutinizing glance. He was very different from her and yet—was she just a big narcissist?—he reminded her of herself. Or at least she had sensed an unexpected aura of compatibility.

Deborah could not rid herself of the suspicion that she had dropped her bomb on Lev for a reason. Hadn't she suspected deep down that he was ignorant of his father's suicide attempt? She wanted him to know. But did she also suspect she would propel him out of the car and, seemingly, out of her life? She felt suddenly unable to determine if she had been trying to draw him closer or send him away.

THE NIGHT LEV READ HIS FATHER'S SUICIDE NOTE he dreamed about Deborah. He saw her lying in bed, wearing her black rabbinical robe. Her hair was loose and spangled with water. Lev knew in the dream that Deborah had nothing on under her robe, the robe was a sort of nightgown, and her bare feet were visible. He lay down next to her—she opened her eyes slowly and smiled at him invitingly. He put his arms around her, only to realize that they were in fact lying together in a grave. Damp earth was sifting into his collar and seeping under his shirt. Dirt was falling on them. Deborah did not seem to mind but Lev cried out in terror. He was being crushed! He woke bathed in sweat, his heart pounding.

Lev did not say to himself that it was because of that dream that he neglected to call Deborah the next day, as he had planned, or the day after that. He told himself that he intended to find her again—she of all people could help him fulfill the wishes expressed in his father's note. But every day he found a reason not to call, though she had left several messages.

He did visit his father the next day, having decided, despite his mother's warning, to communicate with him about the note he had read. Lev's mother was in the room when Lev arrived and looked at him with concern. When she ran out to do a few errands and asked Lev to take his father in to lunch, she threw him a look that seemed to Lev a warning.

Lev wheeled his father into the dining room, filled with other stroke victims, rehab patients, and some of the heartier long-term residents. They all wore large white napkins that fitted over their heads like ponchos. The room smelled like a high school lunchroom, and the food—salisbury steak or fish sticks—had the same heart-shrinking look.

Lev's father had gotten much more adept at using his fork but there were several occasions when Lev took over, cutting and lifting the food to his father's mouth. Henry, who did not speak, ate with focused, sloppy dignity. He had always been careful and refined in his habits and that aura still clung to him, even as the food began spattering his bib and collecting in his beard.

When Lev was sixteen, he and Neal had gotten into a fight with two Hispanic kids while playing in a pickup basketball game in the playground on West Seventy-sixth Street. Neal had held his own—his father had taught him to box when he was a kid—but Lev had gone down fast and came home with a black eye and battered ribs. A few days later, he bought a weight bench and free weights so he could work out in his room. He needed someone to spot him during bench presses; his brother, Jacob, had already gone off to college. His father reluctantly agreed, though the whole thing seemed to embarrass him.

Henry would come into the room in the evening wearing his bathrobe over his shirt and tie and carrying a record from his own collection. He put Schubert or Bach on Lev's stereo—he refused to listen to the Rolling Stones or anything else from Lev's high school collection and Lev was certainly not going to impose The Ramones or even Elvis Costello on his father—he was ashamed enough as it was. And so, with violins weaving intricate patterns in the air, Lev lay on the bench and looked up into his father's mild, abstract face. Henry peered down at his son, cupping his surprisingly large hands under the bar of the barbell as Lev had taught him, following it up without interfering until he was needed. But some inner current of the music along with his father's brainwaves undercut all his efforts at becoming a brute. To this day he could not go into a gym without thinking of the Brandenburg Concertos.

Sitting with his father, smelling the high school lunchroom smells and seeing the here-but-not-here look on his father's face, Lev felt again that sense of frustration and pity, humiliation and outrage he'd felt lying on the weight bench. But he felt touched by his memory, too, and a smile actually came to his lips. Love for his father welled up inside him. He was spotting Henry as delicately as he could, muttering little phrases like, "Come on Dad, good" and "Almost there," helping him raise his large hand and the fisted fork that, loaded with a small piece of meat, seemed almost too heavy for his father to lift.

But when they were back in Henry's room, Lev was overtaken by silence, as if he were the one who had lost the power of speech. Words kept forming in his mind and then floating away. He had discovered that he could in fact recite the Kaddish—he had said it in his room that night, trembling with a sense of sacrilege since his father still lived. But he could not shake the feeling that he knew nothing at all of what his father wanted him to know.

"Dad, what do you want from me?" he almost shouted. But in the end he said nothing, unable even to muster the strength to read the *Times* aloud. He took his father's hand. Henry looked at him with tender abstraction, and the two men sat engulfed in silence.

SINCE RETURNING TO THE CITY, Deborah had been busy. She performed a second funeral on Wednesday, this one much harder than the one Lev had attended—it was for a teenage boy with cystic fibrosis named Billy whom Deborah had visited several times in the hospital. She paid a shivah call to Mrs. Corngold's daughter, met with two bar mitzvah students, counseled a couple she was marrying in October, worked on her sermons for the high holidays—which were bearing down on her with alarming speed—and made her rounds as usual at the hospital.

Deborah also visited the Sinai Center several times. She was too busy to go during the day but she managed to get there after supper, when a peaceful, abandoned dimness fell over the corridors of the nursing home. The aides always washed Henry for bed but it was Helen Friedman who combed his rust-streaked hair neatly against his head like folded wings before she left for the night, planting a kiss on his high forehead and then on his silent lips. He sat in his wheelchair in his bathrobe and slippers, a king under house arrest.

Deborah sat with Henry in his room, holding his hand and singing to him.

One time Deborah came in and saw that one slipper had fallen off his foot onto the floor. There was something about that bare foot that overwhelmed her. He hadn't been able to call for help or to bend over and retrieve it himself. His naked foot seemed frozen in its whiteness, though the room was heated and the weather was warm. She resisted the impulse, as she bent before him, to rub it between her hands.

Deborah could feel how glad he was that she was there. His eyes lit up when she sang, especially a verse from the psalms. She sang "*Min*

Hametzar"—"from the straits I call to you"—and *"Ana Adonai"*—"answer me, God, for I am your servant."

Or she sang *"Eli, Eli,"* by Hannah Senesh. She had loved that song as a teenager and had loved Hannah Senesh, the heroine who had given her life for the Jewish people, parachuting at the age of twenty-one into Nazi-occupied Hungary. Tortured, she had refused to give up her secrets, to turn in her fellow paratroopers. Senesh had died fighting. And she had written a handful of beautiful poems before she died.

There had been something unhealthy, Deborah thought now, in her teenage death-obsessed infatuation with Hannah Senesh, but she still loved the songs.

Henry had learned *"Eli, Eli"* in the days when he still went to Zionist gatherings. He always preferred the song to the other Hannah Senesh classic, about the blessed match consumed in the flame, a sort of suicidal paean to self-sacrifice. *"Eli Eli"* suited his temperament better; it praised things that will never end: the sand and the sea, the thunder and the sky, the crash of the waves, the prayer of man.

Deborah shut her eyes as she sang but Henry's stayed open, watching her in the dim light. She seemed to him like a dream. Or rather, it was as though the rest of his time in the nursing home was a dream; when Deborah came he felt awake at last. Watching her sing was a physical pleasure.

Deborah's eyes seemed to Henry to be shut out of necessity, as if her broad face, filled with song and emotion, had run out of room. Henry liked the way she smelled and noticed the white silk blouse, open at the throat to reveal a Jewish star. He felt like a teenager, smelling the lemony, perfumed air around her and furtively feeling with his sight the contours of her body beneath the blouse. Her throat thickened as she sang, a blanket of soft tissue lay over her whole body, traveling upward from her breasts.

Deborah felt peaceful and unself-conscious in Henry's presence. Because he could not speak she treated him almost like a blind man. Henry wanted at that moment simply to be that song, rising out of that soft throat, nesting inside her breasts and belly. The tears, that since the stroke came with obscene ease, ran down his face so that when Deborah stopped singing and opened her eyes she cried "Oh!" with quiet surprise, pulled a tissue out of the box on the night table, and dabbed his face with gentle care. She saw in it an older echo of Lev's. She wished that Lev would show up unexpectedly, though he seldom came at night and in fact visiting hours were over. But she felt in some inexplicable way that she was caring for Lev and drawing closer to him even in his absence. She decided she would go to the home in the afternoon, when she knew Lev paid his visits.

But Deborah was too swamped with synagogue work to make it the following afternoon. She wound up meeting with a young woman named Lenora who had been studying with Rabbi Zwieback and who was scheduled for conversion at the beginning of September, just before Rosh Hashanah. Lenora had called in a panic and Deborah had invited her to come by the synagogue for a chat.

"Thank you so much, Rabbi," Lenora said breathlessly as she settled herself across from Deborah and clasped her hands nervously over her knees.

She had a long neck and short hair and a clean no-nonsense athletic appearance that Deborah liked. She wore a blue denim skirt that came down to just above the knee and dark blue espadrilles. She had clean-shaven legs but somehow they did not look like they needed shaving, they seemed ivory smooth by nature, as were her arms. She was not especially pretty but neat, stylized, and trim—hearty enough for field hockey, slender enough for a two-piece bathing suit. Deborah could see why this woman's fiancé, some brooding hairy medical student, had chosen her. Didn't opposites attract?

"You told me on the phone," Deborah said, after they had chatted a little, "that something was troubling you. Are you starting to have doubts about converting?"

It was her obligation to ask this as a rabbi. Zwieback was known to be a pushover when it came to conversion. Come on in, the water's fine! He gave preaching to the converted a whole new meaning.

"Oh no," Lenora said, with determination. "I stood at Sinai. My soul was *there*. I feel I belong in temple. Conversion is . . ." she hesitated, looking for the right words, "coming home for me."

Deborah had to suppress a smile but she was touched. She suspected most converts of converting for spouses. It was rare when someone just fell in love with Judaism, though in a sense that is what had happened to Deborah. Of course she had already been Jewish. It was harder for Deborah to imagine loving someone so much that you would take on his religion. But perhaps that's what it meant to be in love—to be a convert of some sort.

"Is your fiancé supportive?" Deborah asked.

Lenora shrugged.

"I suppose so. Steve doesn't really care one way or the other. I mean he doesn't want me to do it if it isn't for me. His parents care . . ."

"How about *your* parents?"

"They'll miss us at Christmas. But they don't think I'm going to hell or anything. At least I don't think they think that. They're pretty liberal . . ."

"Then what?" Deborah pressed. She was curious.

Lenora was looking up at the books lining the walls, the forbidding volumes of Talmud and Mishnah, the multivolume histories of the Jews, the multiple editions of prayer books and Bibles.

"Will you miss him?" Deborah asked suddenly, taking a chance.

"Who?" asked Lenora, startled.

"Jesus."

Lenora was silent a long time. She gazed up at the Talmud above Deborah's head, as if she were looking for an answer there.

"Yes," she said. "I will. I mean, I'll miss that way of thinking about God, that sense of somebody there for you who cares. I'll miss that. But," she hesitated and looked at Deborah. "Jews have that, too, don't they?"

"Some do," said Deborah, "some don't."

"Steve told me that Jews don't need God." Lenora said this in an anxious, wounded voice.

"Bullshit!" Deborah burst out. "You cannot wake up in the morning, if you are a religious Jew, without thanking God. You cannot eat a piece of bread, drink a glass of water, or lie down at night without God. You cannot have sex, you cannot have a baby, you cannot go to the bathroom. You cannot be a Jew without God," Deborah said. "It's all about serving God."

Why was she so angry? Why had she taken Lenora's boyfriend so personally?

Lenora looked startled but relieved. Rabbi Zwieback didn't talk this way.

"This doesn't mean," Deborah added, "that we know what God is. But we know that God is the cornerstone of everything and is everywhere, like the air. Maybe God's more abstract than Jesus, that's true, that's a change. But we are told that Moses talked to God face-to-face, as a man talks to a man," she said. "Do you ever pray?"

"I used to pray a lot," said Lenora. "But my Hebrew is awful. I can bless the bread and bless the Shabbat candles."

Deborah wanted to correct Lenora and explain that you don't bless the bread or the candles, you bless God, but she didn't. She said instead, "Do you think if you're Jewish you can only speak to God in Hebrew?"

Lenora smiled sheepishly. Deborah felt a sudden resentment of the books lining Rabbi Zwieback's wall. They were the glory of Judaism, but what about the language of the heart that the tradition also spoke of? Deborah reached out impulsively and took hold of Lenora's left hand. It was cool and smooth and dry. Lenora flinched, as if she wanted to draw away, but Deborah held on to the hand and squeezed it tight.

"We could pray right now," said Deborah. "In our own words."

Lenora stared at her like a frightened child.

"Would you like to?" Deborah persisted.

Lenora nodded.

Deborah shut her eyes and took a deep yoga breath. She did not bow her head but tilted it back, as if listening. She sat for a long moment, gathering up the silence.

"Dear God," Deborah began at last. "Dear God, Elohim, creator of all things. Help us find words to talk to You with. Help us find You. Help Lenora find peace in her soul, peace in Judaism. Peace with her fiancé. Peace with herself. Peace with her family. Help make this time leading up to her marriage a fruitful time. A time of discovery and understanding. Help her feel Your presence. Help her find her own path that is also the path of community. Help her, God . . ." Deborah ran out of things to say and fell silent, but it was as though she kept talking; there was a thickness of thought and feeling in the air.

Deborah opened her eyes and saw Lenora staring at her with wide-eyed reverence, even a sort of love.

"Thank you, Rabbi," she whispered, emotionally. Her eyes were moist.

Before leaving she embraced Deborah warmly. She seemed buoyed and, at the same time, almost somber with relief and renewed purpose.

Deborah, however, was exhausted. She felt emptier than she had before Lenora had come into her office. And when Lenora left, Deborah lay down on Rabbi Zwieback's leather couch, closed her eyes, and fell asleep at once.

DEBORAH WAS AWAKENED half an hour later by a knock on the office door. She opened her eyes, startled, and saw Lev peering down at her.

"I'm here for my bar mitzvah lesson," he said.

Deborah sat up, laughing self-consciously. She touched her cheek. Had she drooled? She would like to have looked in a mirror.

"Aren't you a little late?" she said.

"You're supposed to tell me it's never too late."

"It's never too late," said Deborah. "Sit down."

"The door was open," Lev said, suddenly apologetic. "And the secretary's gone. I knocked before I saw you."

This wasn't true; he had watched her for a moment as she slept, her untucked blouse revealing the merest triangle of belly, her hair fanned out behind her. One arm trailed onto the carpet. He'd felt the mortal weight of her hand and had a sudden urge to lift it up and kiss the fingertips. He felt pulled toward her as if *he* were dreaming; he had knocked as much to awaken himself as Deborah.

Deborah was very good at waiting until other people spoke; in a hospital room she could sit for an hour without saying anything. But her silence was a learned skill and Lev's came naturally to him. He seemed almost to be by himself, which conferred a feeling of awkward voyeurism on the person beside him. Deborah wasn't sure if this was self-assurance on Lev's part or shyness but she found it disconcerting.

"So?" she said at last. "The last time I saw you, you were pretty upset . . ." She sounded to herself regrettably like Sheryl Cooper, her therapist.

"You were right, of course," said Lev.

He had already retrieved an envelope from his knapsack, holding it out to Deborah like a boy offering a note to a teacher. Deborah took the letter. When she realized what it was she shivered slightly. She read it carefully, slowly.

"Wow," she said. "It's a beautiful letter."

"I'm trying to figure out why my father didn't teach me the things he wanted me to know."

Deborah shrugged.

"People don't always articulate the things they care most about," she said at last. "Even to themselves. At least you know now. In that sense your father's letter is a kind of gift."

She would love to have had some sort of final word from her own father who took off unannounced, without any sort of good-bye at all.

"But I can't pray," Lev said. "I can't do anything."

He was sitting where Lenora had sat. All of a sudden, another seeker. Deborah felt vague disappointment. He wanted a rabbi after all. What had she imagined he wanted? A kiss? A touch? She felt overwhelmed with loneliness. But of course, she had to help him.

"Can you say Kaddish?" she asked Lev.

"Yes," said Lev. "I read Hebrew. But I don't think that's what my father meant. I don't *know* anything. I'm not attached to tradition at all. And I don't know where to begin."

"Find yourself a teacher and get yourself a friend," she said, quoting a rabbinic precept.

"I thought you could teach me," Lev said softly.

Deborah had often imagined how nice it would be for a man she was interested in to wish to learn from her and for her to teach him all she cared about. And yet she felt herself somehow erased by Lev's need. If he offers to pay me, thought Deborah, I'll throw him out. But he did not offer and Deborah did not give him a chance. She invited Lev to dinner for the following week; they could eat and then study. Lev wanted to start right there but Deborah was late for the hospital. She had already risen and was gathering up her things.

"Do you ever feel," he asked suddenly, "that although you know you're sane, and intelligent—you don't hear voices or think the houseplants are talking to you—that you're living in a dream? That people come and go out of the darkness and you don't know why or where?"

"All the time," said Deborah. "You know, when people get sick, or when they are in mourning, or when they face death, they often feel crazy when in fact they're seeing reality very clearly, it's just a different reality from the one they're used to focusing on. Suddenly the routine of denial and habit doesn't help them, it isn't available anymore. Jewish tradition, for me, creates a kind of counter-routine that doesn't dissolve in a crisis. So that you're not suddenly looking down and discovering in a shocked way that you're walking on a narrow bridge. Tradition is kind of like the railing of the bridge. The bridge is still narrow and it's still suspended over darkness. But there's something to hold onto that lots of other people have held onto."

While she was speaking, Deborah pulled down a prayer book from the shelf. She stood next to Lev and opened to the very first page. Lev, she noticed, was staring not at the book but at her. She felt herself being discovered as a woman again and, strangely, this freed her to act unself-consciously like a rabbi.

"Here's your homework. I want you to learn this prayer and say it when you wake up. It's three sentences. Take it."

Lev took the book from her hands.

"I'll see you next week," she said.

DEBORAH TOOK A TAXI ACROSS TOWN to New York Hospital, feeling lighthearted. She often felt like a bright object falling through space alone. But here was Lev spinning into her galaxy, hurtling suddenly beside her.

Most of the people Rabbi Zwieback asked her to visit were rich. He had a special obligation to keep board members happy and Shirley Fink was a trustee of the synagogue. Much as she loved her time in the hospital, Deborah did not like being dispatched in this way. And yet she was singing softly to herself as she walked through the hospital corridors.

Deborah found the old woman in one of those private rooms that look almost like hotel accommodations. There was real furniture and the television was not mounted high on the wall with steel bolts but hidden inside an armoire that could be closed. A large sealed window looked out over the slow-moving East River.

A small woman lay sleeping stiffly in bed, her upper half propped up on pillows in just the way that Deborah used to put her dolls to bed when she was a little girl. Deborah stood quietly by the bed, listening to the fish tank hum of the hospital room. She had a strong feeling that Lev had seen her sleeping before he knocked. How had she looked to him? Better, she hoped, than Mrs. Fink, whose face had more wrinkles than any face Deborah had ever seen. These were not mere deepening crows' feet and spreading frown lines; they ran vertically as well as horizontally, creating little boxes, like lizard scales enlarged. It was tempting to touch them.

In truth Deborah felt there was great beauty to Mrs. Fink's face, you just had to adapt yourself to it, like the desert. She was glad the woman was sleeping, if only because it allowed her to stare. She crept a little closer to the bed. Deborah found that she was synchronizing her breathing with the slow rise and fall of Mrs. Fink's blankets. She felt as though she were watching herself sleep at some point in the far future. She thought again of Lev peering down at her—she was used to being looked at, and liked it, but she felt awkward at the thought of his judgmental eye on her when she was unconscious.

Deborah had just decided that she would come back in the morning when the old woman's eyes popped open, so abruptly that Deborah let out a little gasp. She wondered if the old lady had been playing possum.

"Who are you?" Mrs. Fink demanded in a stern, suspicious voice.

"I'm the rabbi from Temple Emunah," said Deborah. "The *assistant* rabbi . . ."

"Ah," said Mrs. Fink. "Elliott sent you." Elliott was Rabbi Zwieback. "I'm sorry—for your sake. Don't they have anything better for you to do than spend time with old *kockers*?"

"I like visiting the sick," said Deborah. "I'd have come anyway."

"How flattering," said Mrs. Fink.

"Can I sit down?" asked Deborah, uncowed.

Mrs. Fink didn't answer and Deborah remained standing.

"Sick people. Old people," said Mrs. Fink. "A pain in the ass. I don't see why you'd like visiting them. And I am old and sick."

Deborah smiled. "I've learned a lot from sick people."

"Yeah?" Mrs. Fink said, sarcastically. "What have you learned?"

Deborah was about to answer when Mrs. Fink said, "You're staring at my face."

"Your face is beautiful," said Deborah.

"Oh please! My mother looked the same way when she got old."

Awake, Mrs. Fink took on an iguana toughness; when she narrowed her eyes you half expected a long tongue to shoot out and taste the air. But Deborah did not allow herself to be driven away. Many of the cranky old were like mythical creatures—if you hung on tightly enough and didn't let them throw you then they calmed down and even gave you something, a gift, a blessing. Of course there were some who simply threw things. Deborah wondered if there was a bedpan under the covers.

But no, the woman had a Foley catheter—Deborah noticed the grim tube emptying into the plastic bag hanging from the side of the bed, half-concealed by blankets, collecting its amber liquid.

Deborah was determined to win her over. It was a matter of pride as much as compassion.

"How come I don't recognize you?" the old woman asked, peering up. "How long have you been at Emunah?"

"Almost three years," said Deborah.

"You're very pretty. Elliott must enjoy having you around."

Deborah felt herself blushing.

"I haven't been to temple in a long time," the old woman said regretfully. "Otherwise I'd remember you."

"It's nice we can meet now," said Deborah.

The old woman gave her a sarcastic look.

"You don't like being here," Deborah said.

"No I don't. But you were going to tell me why you like being with sick people."

"They're real," said Deborah.

She felt, as soon as she said it, that it was a stupid thing to say and not what she had meant.

"And you're not?" Mrs. Fink asked. "Am I wasting my time with you? Are you a dream?"

What had Deborah meant to say? *God* was what she wanted to say. Too late to change her answer? Deborah was feeling, in the presence of Mrs. Fink, that verbal formulations were a trap and beside the point and it would be better to stay away from them. Let the old lady air her anger—like the piss siphoning into its little bag, Deborah was there to collect it. She felt a sudden bitterness but fought it down.

"We're both real," Deborah said with a shrug.

"You know," Mrs. Fink said. "I would like to have been a rabbi myself. It wasn't possible in my day. My father wanted me to be a bookkeeper, just until I got married. You women today are lucky, you can be anything you want. Except of course happy," she added. "Are you married?"

Deborah ignored the question.

"Did you really want to be a rabbi?"

"I really did. Of course I didn't know enough. Not that they'd have let me if I did. But I always thought it would be nice to study."

"Would you like to study with me?" Deborah asked. "We could read Tanach, even a little Talmud if you wanted. There are English translations of everything."

Mrs. Fink looked touched by this offer but she shook her head.

"It's too late for me."

She said this matter-of-factly, not regretfully. And then, looking up at Deborah, she said, "So what do they say about me? That I'm going to die?"

"I don't know what they say," Deborah told her truthfully. She didn't know what was wrong with Mrs. Fink. Rabbi Zwieback hadn't told her and she seldom tried to find out. She believed that everything she needed to know would come from the person she visited.

"Are you frightened?" Deborah asked.

"You want to know the truth? I'm not. I'm really not."

"I believe you," said Deborah, feeling an uncanny power in the old woman.

"It's true," said Mrs. Fink. "I can't talk to Elliott about this, of course. Religion's not his thing."

Deborah laughed but Mrs. Fink held up her hand—an IV was stuck into the back of it, which made her look like a marionette.

"You shouldn't laugh—Elliott's a wonderful man, he does great things for many people. But he is who he is. Now you young people aren't scared of God, are you?"

"I can't speak for other people," said Deborah.

"I thought that's all rabbis did."

But Mrs. Fink was smiling. She didn't mean to be so rude. Deborah laughed. She did not have a very high opinion of her colleagues either.

"Do you want to hear a secret?" the old lady said mischievously.

"Yes," said Deborah, sitting down slowly on the bed. Mrs. Fink did not make room for her but she did not seem to mind the new intimacy. She was a tiny woman and did not take up much of the bed.

"I'm not alone."

Mrs. Fink spoke softly and very clearly.

Deborah waited for the old woman to go on.

"My children and grandchildren don't understand. They're always trying to lure me to the country or somewhere. Last year they rented a house in France. *France!*" She laughed at the absurdity of it. "But I don't have to go anywhere. I still have my husband."

"He lives with you?" Deborah asked.

"He died eighteen years ago."

She paused and looked at Deborah for a reaction. The thought flashed through Deborah's mind that this woman might have gone soft in the head. It happened a lot to the elderly—they kept the habits of sanity, the intonations of reason, but they started saying impossible things. But Mrs. Fink did not seem in any way demented.

"We were married for forty-seven years," said Mrs. Fink. "And he is still with me."

Deborah felt a ghoulish thrill, as if Mrs. Fink had her husband's head in a hatbox under the bed. But it was nothing so gothic.

"I talk to him every day," she said. "He's with me all the time. Does that seem strange?"

"It seems wonderful."

"You'd have liked him," Mrs. Fink said. "He was a lot nicer than I am. He'd have asked you to sit down right away . . ."

"Is he with you now?" Deborah asked, shivering inside slightly.

The old woman paused and then said, softly but with conviction, "Yes."

"What do you talk about?" Deborah asked.

"I tell him about my life."

"Does he tell you about his?"

Mrs. Fink looked up with quick, shrewd eyes to see if she was being mocked, but it was clear from Deborah's open, curious face that this was not the case. Deborah had asked because she wanted to know.

"No," she said. "Not exactly. It's more a feeling of companionship. He's just *there*."

Deborah thought of her father, hovering like a secret shadow, but decided against mentioning him.

"The liturgy speaks of a *y'did nefesh*," said Deborah. "A soul companion."

"That's exactly right," said the old woman, brightening. "He is my soul companion."

Deborah did not add that this description was for God.

The old woman was chuckling softly to herself and Deborah wondered again fleetingly if the woman had Alzheimer's or perhaps some milder form of dementia. But she seemed lucid, and that was the sort of thing Zwieback would have told her. He'd said only she was "difficult." Of course she could be getting some sort of painkiller. Who knew what was in that IV fluid?

Mrs. Fink had shut her eyes.

"I'm going to take a nap," she said. "Visit me again."

She had returned to her earlier, imperious tone.

Deborah touched her hand—the near one, not the hand with the IV line—and found it cool and surprisingly smooth, hardly wrinkled at all, though speckled with brown, like the first drops of rain on dry pavement. Mrs. Fink did not stir. She let out a loud, unexpected snore. Deborah tucked her hand under the blanket.

Then, as quietly as possible, she stood up and left the room.

LEV KEPT THE PRAYER BOOK Deborah had given him, with its brown faux-leather binding and gilt pseudoarchaic lettering, on the little table next to his bed. It joined back issues of *Science* and *Nature*, a copy of *Brave New World* that Lev had never managed to read in college but had alluded to in several articles he'd written about human cloning and felt at last he should actually finish, and a half-concealed issue of *Penthouse* that he had bought one lonely night, a purchase that like everything else he had done since breaking up with Jenny made him feel not freedom and autonomy and easy bachelorhood but an uncomfortable return to shameful adolescence, even though he was thirty-two and a grown-up in every way.

The prayer Deborah had assigned him was incredibly simple: "I give thanks to you, living and everlasting God, for you have restored my soul with mercy. Great is Your faithfulness." Lev was familiar with the prayer from his stay in the Yeshiva but in those days he had tried so hard to embrace so much that there was a sense of anxiety and obligation about the whole thing. Encountering the prayer in isolation gave it a singular beauty, like a poem. Lev particularly liked the instructions that preceded it: "A Jew should wake up with gratitude to God for having restored his faculties and with a lionlike resolve to serve his creator. Before getting off the bed or commencing any other conversation or activity, he declares his gratitude."

Lev did not as a rule wake up with a lionlike resolve to do anything. He was not lazy—he enjoyed his work and had always been an early riser—but there was a muffled uncertainty about a lot of what he did. It is what allowed his relationship with Jenny to hover without wind for so many years. Reading the directive energized him, though more in the realm of inner expansion. He was not sure what it would mean to serve his creator outwardly.

He wondered about the word *restored*. Did that mean that your soul isn't in your body when you sleep but that it is given back to you—restored—when you wake up? Or just that your soul is refreshed in the morning, fluffed up like a pillow? And what was the soul? The book, the prayer, took its existence for granted, which was part of the prayer's appeal. Despite the fact that he wrote about science, and believed wholeheartedly in evolution, Lev had never felt that chemical explanations were sufficient to describe his experience of being alive. He had a category, an unnamed sensation in his being, that attached itself to the word *soul*.

But he realized how rudimentary his religious thoughts and feelings were; he had ignored them for so long. He had once written an article about art therapy for the elderly and one of the therapists had explained that you only draw as well as the last time you drew. For most people, this was in childhood, so most adults draw like ten-year-olds. Perhaps his religious life was like that, undeveloped and childish.

It would be wrong to say that the prayer transformed Lev, but it opened a little channel to a feeling he had always had without addressing directly. When Jacob's wife—Lev's sister-in-law, Penny—was pregnant, she told Lev that she could not walk down the street without thinking about how every person she passed had once been a fetus inside a mother's womb, and that experience changed her for life. Lev felt something similar in the morning thinking that everyone he passed had a soul. The very old man creeping along with his aluminum walker; the tattooed woman with stringy hair sitting on the sidewalk in front of a cardboard sign that said "No Home," the baby girl sleeping in the stroller pushed by the enormous black woman wearing a tube top, the enormous woman herself, the Sikh cab driver stopped at a traffic light, staring fixedly ahead. Thinking this simple thought, that they all had souls, made Lev feel drunk, queasy, uncomfortable, excited, and unaccountably calm. Though the effects of such thinking had mostly worn off by the time he got to his office, where it evaporated in the face of artificial intelligence and new galaxies discovered at the far edge of the universe, a small glint of unarticulated belief lingered on in him.

And in the morning he felt again the renewed sense of possibility, as, still groggy, he recited his prayer. To be sure, the *Penthouse* sometimes wound up on top of the prayer book. But Lev did not expect animal instincts to disappear in the face of spiritual discovery—he'd have panicked if they had.

He did not think Deborah expected it either; at least he hoped not. He imagined her lying in bed, reciting the same prayer.

DEBORAH LIVED IN A DOORMAN BUILDING on the Upper East Side between York and East End, near the river. The Reform movement did not care if she took a bus or taxi to synagogue on the Sabbath but she preferred to walk, even on rainy days. She liked having Central Park between her and her congregants, a buffer of green that made her feel at night she was back in her own world, though of course the congregants drifted after her, telephoning her at home and entering her dreams.

When Lev smelled the roasting, garlic-laden chicken halfway down the hall from Deborah's apartment he felt a sudden desire to bolt. He half expected his grandmother or some pious old lady in a faded housedress to meet him at the door. But it was Deborah, in a sleeveless white turtleneck and capri pants with retro paisley swirls, vented at the bottom with inverted Vs that revealed the tan skin of her strong calves. Her hair was twisted back and held between the teeth of a giant tortoiseshell hair clip. No wobbly upper arms, no false teeth.

She was wearing open-back clogs that made her tall, though not as tall as Lev who bent down to kiss Deborah's cheek in greeting—it was flushed and slightly damp from the hot stove. Should he have kissed her? Was this a date or a study session? The ambiguity was stressful. He was coming to learn how to pray, but he had changed his underwear before leaving home.

He had brought a bottle of wine and the prayer book she had given him, tucked under his arm like a box of chocolates. They sat on an overstuffed velvet sofa and crunched carrot sticks and ate olives, depositing the pits in a little empty china dish. Lev was wearing black jeans and a pale blue Oxford shirt with the sleeves rolled up. He had made an effort to comb his uncombable hair and he had the slight powdery smell of someone who had just stepped out of the shower. His pale speckled skin was very smooth—Deborah suspected he could go a day without shaving without anyone noticing. "I've got more hair on my arms than he does," she realized when Lev reached for an olive.

The prayer book was open on the table, beside the olives, and they began talking about the prayer Deborah had given him.

"Why," he asked, "after you thank God for giving you back your soul, do you say, 'Great is Your faithfulness'? What does that mean?"

"It's interesting, isn't it," Deborah said. "I think it means just what it says—God has faith in people. God has reason to lose faith, same as us, but so far it hasn't happened. God keeps giving us back our souls every morning. God goes on creating us. But it recognizes that God requires faith in us just the way we need faith in God."

In Deborah's presence religious assertions and the metaphors that communicated them seemed to work—he found that he did not wish to break them down. Lev was not sure if this required suspension of his critical faculties or the application of some new faculty he was not much in the habit of employing. She spoke of creation without irony and yet it did not imply a storybook creation but something real, something he could believe in. It was a tone more than anything else, a sort of sophisticated simplicity. No, sophisticated was the wrong word. It was just simplicity—but intelligent simplicity. Perhaps a different kind of intelligence from the sort Lev typically encountered. It occurred to him that perhaps his father had it, too, though his father was neither direct nor simple in anything he said—except, perhaps, in the suicide letter he had written Lev, where he had appeared like the ghost in *Hamlet*, pointing an admonitory finger.

"Do you ever find those words," Lev asked, "*God* and *soul* and *create*—a little . . . embarrassing?"

He was asking not the way Deborah's mother or her sister might have asked, with a hint of derision, but with genuine curiosity. "I mean, God *doesn't* create us each morning. He didn't even create us in the past. *Maybe* he created some blue-green algae or a few specks of possible RNA or the particles they came from that slowly slowly

slowly, millennia after millennia after millennia, morphed into us. But only in the face of infinite random variations in the environment. Darwin didn't even think evolution meant progress—we're the result of blind chance."

"But here we are," said Deborah, shrugging her bare shoulders.

"Yes," said Lev. "Here we are."

THEY KEPT TALKING THROUGH DINNER and into coffee. Lev was surprised to learn that Deborah hadn't been raised religiously at all.

"Did you have a sudden conversion?"

"Oh, no," said Deborah. "Just a friend in junior high school. We all thought we were so rebellious, but Tamara didn't use the phone on Saturday and she didn't care what anybody thought. I used to spend Shabbat there—her family would sing at the table after meals. They were very accepting. I started going to synagogue and studying. One thing just led to another. Really it was a matter of finding a vocabulary for what I'd always felt intuitively. Although a lot of it wasn't about me at all. It was about reconnecting to what had been there not long before—my grandfather, for example, whom I really loved, had been observant. It was my parents who were the aberration."

"Judaism was everything and nothing in our house when I was growing up," said Lev.

"What does that mean?"

"I'm not sure," said Lev. "I suppose it was a kind of ubiquitous presence that never got converted into anything tangible. It was like wind blowing through the house, but there were no windmills to catch it. Maybe my father had no way to harness the wind . . ."

"Maybe he *was* the wind," said Deborah.

"Maybe," said Lev.

They had finished the wine and Lev's head was cloudy. They sat in silence for a moment and Lev was just thinking that perhaps the study portion of the evening was over when Deborah rose and said, "Time to get serious."

Was she going into the bedroom? She was. Should he follow? He did.

Lev looked in and saw the large, half-made double bed. Crumpled clothing danced in the corners of the room. Deborah was squatting in front of the large bookshelf that stood opposite the bed. She had removed her clogs somewhere in the course of the evening and Lev noted the way her chafed, naked heels met the rounded bottom of her paisley pants.

"Which do you prefer," she called over her shoulder, " 'marriage contracts' or 'blessings'?"

Lev did not know how to answer.

"Let's go with *ketubot*," said Deborah. "That's marriage contracts. Traditionally that's a good place to start. It's got a little of everything."

Lev had told her a little about Jenny, but it was only after she had pulled the large brown volume from the shelf that she realized a man who had called off his own wedding might prefer to study "blessings." But it was too late.

"Don't look so scared," she said, settling in next to Lev on the sofa, when they had returned to the living room. "Have you ever studied Talmud?"

"I tried a few times on my own after I came back from Israel," Lev said. "The college library had a complete set of the Soncino Talmud. It was too much for me."

"You're not supposed to do it alone," Deborah said.

She opened the book carefully and with a sense of ceremony. One panel of the book rested on her thigh, the other on Lev's.

"This big word, *betulah*, is where the Mishnah starts," she said, pointing to a single, gigantic word in a filigreed black box at the top of the page. "That's the oldest part of the Talmud. It was codified about the year 200 but is much older than that. The rabbis were basically establishing laws people could live by. The text that begins under it is the Gemarah. That's the conversation later rabbis had about the Mishnah. There's a lot more Gemarah than Mishnah—the rabbis were taking the laws in the Mishnah and trying to bring them into line with the

Bible, which isn't always easy. The Gemarah's where you get all that rabbinic acrobatics where something suddenly becomes its opposite. It was codified about the year 500. This is Rashi, the medieval commentator. These are his grandchildren, the *tosefists* . . ."

Deborah sounded as if she were pointing out faces in a family photograph. Her own face had grown serious, intent. Lev's father, a book lover, could gaze at a page with the same face of longing; sitting there next to Deborah he felt closer to his father, though his father, to his knowledge, did not even own a Talmud. But perhaps this was what his father meant—an education, a familiarity with his people and culture. Mending the broken thread. Deborah's earnest delight enticed him.

Lev contemplated the dazzle of alien letters. He actually read Hebrew quite well, though without much comprehension, and the letters and words seemed to spin apart like the fragments of a kaleidoscope. He examined the long seam dividing the two pages, the parted waves of paper falling on either side, an unexpectedly sensual image that brought, unbidden, a physical memory of Deborah's backside. Blaspheming already and they hadn't even begun.

Deborah looked up at him suddenly. "Do you want to cover your head?" she asked.

Lev hesitated.

"You don't have to," said Deborah. "It's custom, really. A sign of respect. To the text. To God . . ."

"Do you cover your head?"

"If I were a man I would."

"But you don't?" he asked.

"No. Traditionally, women don't have to. I'm not a parity freak."

Lev felt an odd relief.

"Sure," he said.

"I'll go find you a kippah."

She slid the big book over to Lev.

"Oh, look at that!"

She began brushing off her thighs, which were covered with dusky streaks of book pollen. "I have to get Ludmila to vacuum more. They don't get as much use as they should."

In fact, Deborah could not remember the last time she had studied Talmud. She had promised herself when she graduated that she would study every day but, like morning prayer, it was a vow she had broken.

She went out of the room and Lev sat staring down awkwardly at the book, as if he had been left with a child on his lap. He was afraid to drop it.

Without Deborah, the magic had gone out of the page. Lev felt, rising up from the tarnished paper, a whiff of decay and dislocation, of disembodied, ink-bound existence. The old bone color of the paper, frayed slightly at the edges, depressed him. He felt an impulse to shut the book and run. Out of the valley of words. Away, away! The same impulse he felt in the Sinai Center, visiting his father. The same impulse he'd felt in the hall smelling garlic chicken. Jews. Death.

Deborah came back into the room holding up a kippah. It was a small black, tightly knit thing, the kind worn by modern Orthodox men—more like a coaster than religious headgear. Somehow, Lev knew that it had belonged to a former boyfriend. There were a few dark hairs clinging to the bobby pin stuck through the center. He didn't want to put it on but he did.

Deborah lifted half the book like a gate and slid under it. She turned a few pages and stopped.

"This Talmud was my grandfather's," she explained. "He had it in Poland before the war. It belonged to his grandfather who was a rabbi. I think it was the only thing he brought to this country. He kept it in his jewelry store and when things were quiet, which they were most of the time, he would study behind the counter."

It was clear that Deborah had none of Lev's gloomy associations— huddled Yeshiva boys in dank study houses waiting like seeds in a pod to be blown away by Nazi winds. Pencil-necked little boys poring over giant books instead of looking out the window at the natural world.

And because her fine silver bangles jingled on her wrist, and because she had a ring on her thumb, her hand persuaded him to pay attention as she ran her fingers lovingly over the columns of type. She stared at the page with the same look of eager anticipation she'd had at Yankee Stadium, as if the page were not a large drab black-and-white puzzle but a green field. And because she was there with him, he felt that the book was somehow a living thing. Or was it because her lap was under it?

She began reading aloud, first in Hebrew and then in English, beginning with the giant word *betulah*.

"Betulah means virgin," she said.

Lev nodded, thinking suddenly, *Are you?* But no, of course not. A rabbi wasn't a nun. And she hadn't been a rabbi in high school or college. Or even in rabbinical school.

"A virgin is married on Wednesday, a widow on Thursday. Because twice a week the courts sit in the towns, on Monday and Thursday."

That was what the first *Mishnah* said. But this simple statement spawned pages and pages of commentary that they began slowly to make their way through, Deborah explaining as she went. The general gist was that a man had to inspect the sheets the night of his wedding if he married a virgin. That meant that if he discovered on Wednesday night that there was no blood, which is to say if he discovered he had not in fact slept with a virgin, then the next day he could go to court and lodge a complaint against his bride. If he married a widow, it wouldn't matter if the courts were open or not, because there'd be no blood in any case.

That was the gist, though the gist was not what the rabbis seemed to be after, and whatever little frisson came from talk of sheets and virgins vanished in the welter of voices speaking out of the darkness, agreeing and disagreeing and quoting things from places Lev had never heard of.

"Got it?" Deborah asked. She had been untangling the threads of thought for Lev and had lost her look of transcendent rapture; she wore, instead, the face of an accountant at tax season.

"I've lost track of who's speaking," said Lev. "Which rabbi's speaking?"

"Good question," said Deborah. "Actually, right here"—she pointed to a line of text—"a rabbi isn't speaking. The Talmud itself is speaking. The *stammah d'Gemarah*, as he's sometimes called. He's the editor, or one of the editors. A kind of ghostly narrator who appears from time to time. He's like the webmaster in a chat room. He's managing the conversation—which isn't easy because, as I'm sure you've noticed, the participants all lived at different times. Some of them are dead but are still included."

"They're all dead," said Lev.

"Not while you're studying Talmud, mister!"

They plunged back in and the rabbis suddenly switched direction and someone—Lev didn't quite follow who, was it the Talmud itself again?—suggested that a virgin gets married on Wednesday because if she got married on Sunday—which, like Wednesday, also falls a day before market day (and therefore a court day)—her bridegroom wouldn't have time to prepare a nice feast, since he wouldn't be able to do any preparations on the Sabbath. This rabbi was promptly attacked by the others but Lev wasn't precisely sure why, because by then he was only half paying attention and hoping, like a sleepy student, that he would not be called on.

He wondered if Yeshiva boys sat this close, so that they could smell each other as they studied. He supposed they had. He had seen Roman Vishniac photographs of shtetl study houses: a long table in a dark room, two boys to a book, pressed close. It had seemed like shtetl thrift but he realized it wasn't that at all—it wasn't about reading alone, it was about something else. Deborah herself was quite physically involved in the text—occasionally wrenching the book completely onto her lap when she was trying to figure something out, tilting the book toward her with both hands but then looking up at the ceiling, like a woman at the beach trying to tan under her chin. From time to time she ran to her book shelf to fetch a supplementary book—Jastrow's *Dictionary*, a Tanach, a book of rabbinic terms and concepts. Soon there was a little pile beside her.

She gave Lev a demonstration of rabbinic singsong and the accompanying hand gestures—a thumbs up as a question is asked and a thumbs down as the rhetorical question is answered: "*Whyyyyy* (thumb up) is a virgin married on Wednesday????? Be-*cause* (switching to thumbs down) the rabbis were patriarchal *pigs*."

"Were they?" Lev asked.

"Sometimes," said Deborah. "Most of the time they're pretty impressively humanistic. But occasionally it's hard to ignore, like when they say that a woman is a vessel full of blood and shit."

"Youch!" said Lev. "That's awful."

"Yes," said Deborah. "But then someone comes along and says the opposite. It's the back and forth that matters. Not just the forth, if you know what I mean."

He felt it would not be right to kiss her over a volume of the Talmud. Her lap was underneath the book—she had pulled it over to her side again, like a woman hogging the blankets in winter. An hour passed and yet pages and pages of discussion lay ahead, all commenting on the opening statement that a virgin is married on Wednesday and a widow on Thursday. He realized that he still had no idea what the answer was.

"We hardly got anywhere," Lev said after an hour had passed. "And we skipped most of the commentary."

"I told you," said Deborah. "It's not about forward progress."

"Not just the forth but the back?"

"Exactly. That's why the rabbis felt studying Talmud was a form of prayer. *Is* a form of prayer." (Lev was glad he hadn't kissed her mid-explication.) "And really it's more than that. It's like you were telling me how every cell in the body contains the whole genome and the map for making a whole person. Every page of Talmud's like that. I mean think about it," Deborah said. "Just trying to answer this one question about what day you marry a virgin involves thinking about the nature of the Sabbath and what can and can't be done on that day. It involves knowing about market days (which incidentally are the days the Torah was read aloud). It requires having a definition of marriage. Of who's responsible for a canceled wedding. Of what you can and can't do when a woman has her period."

"It doesn't bother you that this is all about trying to determine if the woman is pure? I mean the whole thing is about making sure you have a virgin."

"Well at some level, sure," said Deborah. "You could say we're back to blood and shit. But it's really about so many other things—it's not that there isn't a literal point at the heart of this. It's just that the argument is the point as much as anything else—that's why this is still a relevant text. I mean, even if you're Orthodox and you want to know the law, this isn't where you have to look. There's a book of simple answers for that: The Codes. But you miss the context. It's not the meat, it's the motion. It's the way they reason. The way a rabbi quotes something in the name of another rabbi. It's a lesson in how to think. Our whole culture comes out of the book like a genie out of a bottle. You can't get married on Thursday because the court won't meet on Friday because that's the eve of the Sabbath. And they're afraid a man's anger will cool if he doesn't go to court right away—you could say that means that they want him to be angry and prosecute the law. But you could also say they're offering a little definition of what is normal for a man—and it's normal for his anger to cool. It's normal for him to be taken with his bride or allow her to explain away the situation. It's normal to not want to go to court. It's normal to want to avoid conflict. Or maybe even it's normal to fall in love with your bride and not want to give her up. Or to find her so attractive you can't turn her in."

Deborah suddenly wondered what precisely had happened between Lev and his fiancée. It occurred to her that this entire study session had rubbed salt into his wounds.

"The main point," said Deborah "is that nothing is left alone. Everything's open."

"I'd say the opposite is true," said Lev. "Everything's figured out."

"Yes, you're right, too. The opposite is correct also."

"You're talking like the Talmud," said Lev.

"Thank you."

Lev shook his head. He was thinking, "Can this possibly be what my father meant?"

"You have to start somewhere," said Deborah, as if she had heard him.

She felt drawn to Lev. He had an attractive vulnerability as he stood there. His hazel eyes, and even, she realized, his freckles, suggested tears. But she felt he had his own sort of strength, hidden like a rock under moss. He had the air of somebody working out something important. The busted wedding was both a sign of strength and a wound; he would need to be nursed back. *I'll let him stay the night*, she thought, surprising herself.

"You know," she said, "the mystics used to look at your forehead before they would teach you. As a way of examining your soul."

She put her hands up to his face and brushed back the red hair, exposing his high forehead. Her touch was warm and confident. She traced his pale eyebrows with her fingertips. Her brown eyes pored over him.

"What do you see?" asked Lev.

"Intelligence," said Deborah. "Gentleness. You have a great capacity for understanding. A kind of old-world quality. A real Jewish face. It's in your eyes."

Lev winced. He stepped back from Deborah's touch.

"You're sure it's not in the nose?" he asked.

"That's not what I meant," Deborah said.

Lev's own reaction surprised him. He'd been feeling so pleasant, but something in him flared in resentment. A gentle soul! A Jewish face! He put his hand to his forehead, as if to expunge whatever Deborah had seen.

"It's not the mark of Cain," said Deborah.

"I don't want the mark of Abel either."

They stood in awkward silence for a few moments.

It's because I'm a rabbi, Deborah thought. *He can't take it.*

She felt disgusted all of a sudden. Angry. She walked away from him and sat down on an ottoman. Lev remained standing. He felt inexplicable sadness.

After a moment, Deborah rose and walked over to Lev.

"I'm sorry if I insulted you by saying you had a Jewish face," she said softly. "You know, I meant it as a compliment."

"I know," Lev said.

She was very close. He bent down and kissed the smooth dome of her forehead, the spot where she had searched for evidence of his soul. Deborah felt doomed by the kiss. He was punishing her with gentleness. Or perhaps behaving like the pious rabbi he feared her to be. A few minutes later he was gone.

IT WAS TOO LATE to walk through Central Park but Lev was reluctant to get on a bus or hail a cab. He always felt lonely on the East Side and he felt lonely now; his life felt lonely to him. There was a suggestion of fall in the cool air.

He did not try to imagine if the people passing him had souls and if he had, it would not have consoled him. He walked into and quickly out of a Barnes & Noble—he could not think of a single book or magazine that would contain the things he wanted to know, though he could not have said what those things were precisely. He stepped into the street and looked up just in time to see the broad, whalelike forehead of a crosstown bus bearing down on him. He barely retreated in time.

On Madison he stopped into a Greek coffee shop. It was the kind of old-fashioned pre-Starbucks place his father loved. Donuts under a plastic dome. A large metal bowl of eggs on the counter, no matter what time of day or night, and, high up, cans of Campbell's soup, tiny boxes of cereal, and tilted tins with corn muffins and bran muffins waiting to be pried out for customers. It was never early or late in a place like this. Lev watched as the man who brought him his coffee dropped an English muffin into a toaster that had six slots for toast, as if it were in the kitchen of a giant family.

Lev wasn't so much thinking about Deborah as he was feeling her. Did he fear falling into the folds of her rabbinic world? He had a memory of what she smelled like, the mingled odor of cooking and perfume. The way she looked fetching the volume of Talmud and how she tugged a stray curl when she puzzled over a passage.

He knew that he did in fact have a throwback face and old-world longings. Just as he knew, despite the winks and nudges of his friends, that when he left Jenny what he wanted, more than the chance to sow wild oats, was somebody he would want to spend his life with. Why that desire should embarrass him was a mystery to him, but it did embarrass him. It seemed . . . unmanly. It seemed Jewish.

As if in confirmation of all Lev's fears, he noticed, looking in the mirror above the cash register as he stood waiting to pay, that he was still wearing the little kippah that Deborah had given him. He felt as if he had been walking around with his fly open.

Lev could often tell from the front who would have a kippah on the back of his head. There was a certain style, or lack of it. A certain waddle: the pregnant man! A certain look, intelligent but simultaneously retarded, like the kids in advanced physics in high school.

There were exceptions, of course—swaggering Sephardic Jews, the sons of rich Iranian or Syrian exiles, in their thuggish leather jackets and sharp shoes and macho black leather *kippot*. Cocky Upper East Side day school students, their yarmulkes askew like berets. But on Lev, the little knit bull's-eye target seemed a virtual "Kick Me" sign.

He snatched the kippah off his head and stuffed it in his pocket, along with the change he received.

DEBORAH LOADED THE DISHWASHER listening to a Lucinda Williams CD, the mournful, mooning, sexy southern voice lifting her spirits.

Let him go, Deborah told herself. *You don't want a man who's always running.*

She tried making a few notes for a class she was teaching on repentance in preparation for Yom Kippur, but her heart wasn't in it. Better to work on her sermons for the holidays. Meanwhile she took a bubble bath, with a notebook and the portable phone on the tiled floor beside the tub.

One sermon was going to be about Hannah, the barren woman in the *haftorah* reading for Rosh Hashanah. Deborah's congregation was full of women who could not have children or who had waited so long they feared they could not have children. She wanted to tell them that in Hebrew the word *womb* and the word *mercy* have the same root.

In the Book of Samuel, Eli the high priest sees Hannah praying for a child and thinks she's drunk because her lips move but no words come out. What is so threatening about female spirituality that it seems like drunkenness? Deborah would raise that question, but just in passing. It's possible that a man praying like that would have gotten the same response. In any event, Eli realizes his mistake and God has mercy on Hannah and she gets pregnant and gives birth to Samuel, who becomes a man of God. It had always seemed a little cruel that having had a child at last Hannah has to give him up. But it is her pledge; worse for poor little Samuel who, as soon as he's weaned, has to go live with the old priest Eli. What kind of childhood could that have been? On the other hand, Deborah's favorite moment in the entire Bible was when God calls little Samuel by name and he thinks it's Eli calling him. He asks the high priest what he wants and Eli, misunderstanding as usual, sends the boy back to bed. It happens again and only then does Eli realize that God is talking to the little boy.

Deborah! She had called her own name in the bathroom, startling herself. She sat listening to the bubble-clouds crinkle and collapse.

When the bubbles died she drained the water, sat on the edge of the tub, and shaved her legs. She was about to get into bed with the Book of Samuel and the latest issue of *Vanity Fair*, with Julia Roberts on the cover, when the downstairs buzzer rang. Louis, the night doorman, announced Lev Feldman.

"Friedman" she heard Lev say in the background.

"Should I let him up?" Louis asked, neutral but insinuating. The doormen all knew she was a rabbi.

"Yes, Louis, please," said Deborah.

She debated whether or not to change. She was wearing shorts and a T-shirt that said "Seven Ways to Love Israel" that she had been given while chaperoning a teen tour to Israel the summer before. At the last minute she changed tops, pulling on a "Target Breast Cancer" T-shirt and rolling up the sleeves to give it a little style. Breast cancer, she realized, was sexier than Israel, a notion too depressing to think about now.

Lev seemed strangely disheveled as he stood in the shadow of the doorway; she wondered for a moment if he'd been mugged. But then she saw that he was holding out the kippah she had lent him, one of Reuben's. Deborah reached for it without a word. Their fingers touched.

He was kissing her before he had finished crossing the threshold.

Book

Three

NEAL MARCUS lay on his bed, listening to the voice of Henry Kissinger rumble through his brain like a truck driving over gravel.

Sometimes Kissinger spoke to him through the dayroom television or via the clock radio he kept beside his bed. Unplugging the radio made no difference. Kissinger's voice traveled directly along the earpieces of Neal's eyeglasses, which acted like tiny transmitters. He had broken three pairs of eyeglasses and his mother had stopped bringing new ones, but still the voice sought out Neal's brain. It was cheaper to tell yourself that the voice wasn't real, which, thanks to Risperdal, he now realized, though it paid to listen just in case the doctors were wrong, which wouldn't be the first time.

"The danger is very great," Kissinger warned. "But we must be patient and prudent. Your moment will come. Everyone is counting on you. But patience is paramount."

Neal groaned and shifted on the bed as the voice droned on. The Countering Voice talked over Kissinger, but the Prompter, who made dangerous suggestions, had gotten very loud. A kind of summit was taking place.

If there are enemies everywhere, said the Countering Voice, then there are enemies nowhere and you should just relax and live your life. But, said Kissinger, the Nazi next door is closer than the Nazi across the street. And the Nazi across the street is closer than the Nazi in Germany. And the fire inside is louder than the fire outside.

The Prompter spoke loudest of all.

Go to the window. Go to the window now.

But Neal did not go to the window. He lay on his bed and shuddered.

There was too much noise. Too much noise! So take the horse out of the house and the chicken and the rooster and the cow and the dog and the cat and the bird. It will just be the old man with the wind and his wife and the door and the hinges and the leaves on the window. *Swish swish swish.* But the Nazis remain and the fire on the wall and on the carpet and the spies in the house. Who gets rid of the spies? You have to kill them and cut their heads off and then damp it down with dirt and it won't grow back. But patience is paramount. And prudence.

Neal shivered again though he was not cold. He should get up off the bed and go somewhere. Not the window. Or perhaps the window. Not the dayroom. Or perhaps the dayroom.

The dayroom was full of smoke and where there's smoke there's fire. And where there's fire there's death. God doesn't want death he wants life. But death has a mind of its own. And a loud voice. And a German accent. So pray it away. Pray it away now!

Baruch ata!

Neal's lips moved.

Baruch ata! Like a spell. The other words could burn your mouth but if you said the beginning with the proper feeling it would work anyway. That's what Rabbi Feffer said. *Baruch ata baruchatabaruch-atabaruchata.* Too much noise! Get rid of the cow and the horse. *Baruch ata. Baruch ata. Baruch ata.*

Neal looked up and saw Lev standing by the bed. How had he gotten past the fire?

Lev looked down at his friend, stretched out on the bed sweating, so that his dark hair was plastered against his forehead. His lips had been moving.

Lev felt a familiar mixture of sadness, revulsion, affection, and fear. Lately, encouraged by Deborah, he had been visiting more often. He knew from Neal's mother that Neal was going through a bad patch, though they were trying new medicine and it seemed to be taking hold. She was hopeful he'd be going back to the group home soon.

Neal's face was pale and drawn—it sometimes looked swollen—though his upper body was still powerful looking in the T-shirt visible above the covers. His glasses were taped on both sides.

There were two other beds in the room but they were empty. Lev was glad they were alone.

"I brought you what you asked for," said Lev.

"Thank you."

Neal worked hard to push words to the surface—every one had to be guided like a small child through a crowd. The voices receded— they never vanished completely—and so did his energy.

"They're giving me new medicine," said Neal. "And medicine for the medicine."

Neal held up his hands and Lev saw them trembling. They were large hands. Neal had been able to palm a basketball in seventh grade. Lev never could.

"What are they giving you?" Lev asked.

Neal listed about six medications. He always knew what they were giving him. In the group home in Brooklyn where he lived when not in the hospital, Neal had named all the tropical fish after medications he had taken: Trilafon, Stelazine, Clozapine, Navane. Lev was familiar with the drugs from his reporting. Neal pronounced the names with a sort of pride—there was something astral, scientific and ethereal about them, like the names of galaxies or kingdoms in a science fiction saga.

Neal seemed to take pleasure in mastering the technical aspects of his illness. He would engage Lev in conversations about the way neuro- imaging of the thalamus had shown that it was smaller in schizophren- ics, and he was informed about the race to locate the gene that controlled it. There'd always been a boasting quality to Neal and it sometimes seemed he was showing off about his illness, though Lev re- alized that Neal had nothing to be smart about now except the very thing that had destroyed his intelligence. He was making the most of what he had.

Lev reached his hand into a plastic Barnes & Noble bag he had brought with him. Neal raised a hand to cover his face, not wanting to see the severed head, but it was only a book. He grew calmer at the sight of it. The book was *Basics of Biblical Hebrew Grammar*, by Miles V. Van Pelt. He hefted it in his hands, turning the pages with careful, trembling fingers. He had been studying with a Lubavitcher rabbi who came by to visit him.

"Barnes & Noble didn't have it and neither did West Side Judaica," said Lev. "I borrowed it from . . . someone."

Deborah had insisted on lending her copy, though Lev told her she might never get it back. She didn't care. Lev had been careful to white-out Deborah's name and telephone number from the inside cover, but Neal immediately asked who owned the book, and Lev felt unable to lie.

"Her name is Deborah. She's a rabbi."

Neal looked up, fascinated. Lev had told him, in a general way, about his breakup with Jenny. He was never sure how much Neal had absorbed.

Neal raised himself up in the bed as if forcing his head through inner clouds.

"Is she your girlfriend?" he asked.

It seemed cruel to tell Neal about his relationship, so he merely shrugged.

"Fear of commitment is a terrible thing," said Neal, adding, with a wry smile, "I mean, I've got a fear of commitment but that's because I've been committed."

Lev laughed. For a moment, despite the slow staccato speech, Neal seemed his old self.

"You should bring her here," Neal said. "I'd like to meet her."

Lev again regretted mentioning Deborah's name. Jenny had been afraid of Neal and sometimes had bad dreams about him. She had prosecuted a homeless man who pushed a woman onto the subway tracks at Union Square.

That's not the norm, Lev had told her. And that's not Neal.

But he heard himself say, "Deborah's very busy."

"Oh no, she'll see me," said Neal.

Lev knew it was true. On several occasions she had wanted to come with him.

"Well," said Lev. "I'll ask her."

"I have a lot of questions," said Neal.

Lev did not answer. He reached into the bag again and brought out another book, David Sibley's *Guide to the Birds*.

"I thought you might like this," said Lev. "Perhaps when you're better . . ."

His voice trailed off.

Neal took the big book and examined it carefully.

"You remembered," said Neal. "You remembered."

He said this as if he had explicitly ordered the book. He thumbed through it, admiring the illustrations and paying particular attention to the range maps at the bottom of the page. Neal stopped on a page of tanagers, orange and black and red birds.

"Teenagers," said Neal.

Lev laughed and then realized it wasn't a joke. Or maybe it was. Neal was unsmiling, gazing at the brightly colored birds. Messengers from another world. He shut the book and handed it back to Lev.

"Put it in my drawer, please. I don't want them flying out."

There was a minute, unnatural separation between every word Neal uttered, like the spliced-together numbers on an operator's message.

"That's a joke," he said, unsmiling. "I'm not as bad as all that."

"I didn't think you were," said Lev, though he had believed him. The strange braid of sanity and madness always shook Lev more than anything. If Neal had been a stark raving lunatic it would have been easier.

Lev put the book back in the bag and placed it in Neal's night table drawer. There were notebooks in the drawer, a nylon kippah, a Bible and prayer book, and several wadded-up tissues. Lev shut the drawer.

Neal had flipped onto his stomach and was gripping his pillow in both hands in a manner that reminded Lev of the way Neal piloted his flexible flyer when they were kids. Neal was fearless and would run alongside his sled to pick up speed before jumping on. Their preferred place was the hill in Central Park that had since become the enclosure housing the Temple of Dendur at the Metropolitan Museum of Art.

Looking at Neal, the blankets plowed up around him, it was possible for Lev to summon the feeling of ice and sweat and reckless exertion. His mind still held the vast expanse of the white slope, buried now by glass and steel and stone, like the island in the Nile that, drowned by the Aswan dam, had given up its treasure to a museum in Manhattan.

Before he left, Lev reset Neal's clock, which had been flashing at 0:00.

"Take care of yourself," he said.

"The servants do that for me," said Neal. "And God."

Lev again checked Neal's face for irony or laughter but his face was a mask, impossible to read. He seemed to be descending back into the state in which Lev found him.

"I'll come again."

"Don't forget to bring Deborah."

Neal's memory had always been phenomenally good. Lev forgot people's names as they mentioned them, a liability for a journalist. But Neal had a quickness visible still under the occluding atmosphere of illness and medication.

To Lev's surprise, Neal got up off the bed and walked him to the end of the hall. Before he left his room he put on a fleece jacket, which he zipped up to his chin, and slippers. He walked slowly and carried himself with great care, as if he were a full cup of water he was afraid of spilling.

"I think I'll stop here," he said, as they came to the locked door. A key was required to get out as well as in. Lev rang for the attendant.

"Good-bye," he said, taking Neal's large trembling damp hand.

Neal said nothing but hurried back to check on the birds.

LEV DREAMED he was carrying his father in his arms down Broadway. His father was not his present self but the younger more vigorous man Lev remembered from childhood. His father had a thermometer in his mouth, but it was dangling like an unlit cigarette, giving him a rakish look. Lev arrived at a supermarket with tilted wooden tables set up out front. These tables were loaded with produce—boxes filled with oranges and apples and bananas. He was going to put his father down in a bin heaped with cherries, but suddenly the cigarette-thermometer dropped from his father's mouth; Lev tried to catch it and all of a sudden his father became too heavy for him. To his surprise, his father did not fall but simply stood up and said to Lev, "I'm going to take a nap. Don't let me sleep more than fifteen minutes." Then he walked off. Lev found himself standing alone in front of the supermarket.

When he woke up Lev was in Deborah's queen-size bed. This was still a novel and pleasant sensation. He had only recently begun sleeping over. The High Holy Days had been chaotic for Deborah—she had been rabbinically "on" more than usual, reworking her sermons, teaching class on repentance, and spending long days at Temple Emunah, where the tide of human need rose with the season. Deborah also took the "Days of Awe," the ten penitential days from Rosh Hashanah to Yom Kippur, with great seriousness. Her policy on premarital sex with a man she cared about and felt she might have a future with was lenient, but the *Yamim Noraim* were not the most propitious time for launching a relationship. She was her most authoritative as a rabbi and her most insecure as a person, and the result was that she felt anxious and bitchy and slightly depressed. She was also very busy. In general, the Jewish holidays were a setback, intensifying Lev's apprehensions about getting involved with a rabbi.

Even the night he had come back to return Deborah's kippah had been fraught with awkwardness. The sheer fact that Deborah was a rabbi had almost paralyzed him. Lev could tell from the way Deborah dressed and how she carried herself and from the perfume she wore behind her neck and who knew where else that she did not believe being a rabbi was at odds with being a sexual creature. This, however, did not make grabbing her ass a religious activity. Finally, Deborah had led him into the bedroom.

"I'm a rabbi," she whispered, "not a nun."

After that things went more smoothly, though Lev, who had spent so long living with another woman, felt weirdly virginal. Deborah, more bodily in many ways than Jenny had been, gently persuaded Lev it was all right to touch her. Even there. And there. Her spiritual authority gave her physical authority. It was a power that had driven several men away.

Lev felt happy waking up in her bed. He knew her now in a different way, the human animal all alive, and her rabbinic identity was losing its power to unsettle him, though he was still slightly afraid of it. He wanted to tell Deborah his dream but she was not beside him. He heard stirrings in the next room.

He said his own modest prayer, *modeh ani l'fanecha*, thank you, God, for giving me back my soul, and really did feel gratitude for being alive, at that moment, in Deborah's big bed, with winter light filtering through the half-closed blinds. He had a vague qualm he was perverting the meaning of things—thanking God for letting him get laid and not for giving him back his soul. But at the same time he felt a sort of redefinition going on inside himself, an incorporation of God into his actual daily life, not as a form of bleak renunciation but something that filled him with excitement. This seemed like Deborah's special gift to him.

He looked at the heap of clothes at the base of her closet, and the pile of *Vanity Fair* and *People* and *Reform Judaism*. At the reproduction of Klimt's *The Kiss* hanging crookedly on the wall. It constantly surprised Lev that so many of the artifacts of Deborah's life, her public expressions and formulations—the posters and magazines, the clothes she wore and the television shows she watched, even the sermons she gave and the rituals she performed—were not unique but drawn from the culture around her. One day, flipping through her rabbi's manual, he realized how much the funeral she had performed that had so impressed him had in fact been formulaic readings. At some level he expected her to have her own religion.

But Deborah kept reminding him that religion was a communal cloak that fit individuals, too. It wasn't a smothering blanket. It was old but alive. You could lie in the bed of a woman you weren't married to and recite a prayer without feeling like a hypocrite. Was God—in the midst of famine and war and daily degradation, the death of children that defied comprehension, the suffering of the poor, the executions and abductions and murders and rapes—peering down and disapproving of premarital sex between people who cared about each other and didn't hurt anyone? What kind of God would *that* be? Of course, one could wonder as much about anything—keeping kosher, observing the Sabbath. Praying regularly. Why do anything—why abstain from anything—as long as you caused no harm? You could only update a religion so far. Deborah, who loved Jewish ritual and loved binding herself to tradition, seemed to have found her balance. Lev was still bemused by it all.

He recognized how easily the little puritanical voice that perhaps had its origin in parental control or fear or Western culture or maybe even genetic imperative of some sort—the caution that kept you alive—could be pinned on divine will. *You must do this. It is forbidden to do that.* A responsiveness to order. He knew even from his brief yeshiva stint how soothing it was to give in to the simplicity of rules rather than the negotiated truce that Deborah seemed to have achieved.

Deborah recognized that the rules she lived by—and the rules she ignored—had been devised by humans, though she saw them as divinely inspired and therefore worth maintaining. As a Reform Jew she was not obliged to see Jewish law as immutable and binding and yet she chose to observe a great deal. Something in the tradition transcended the individual and became a living embodiment of God for her, even if the pieces were all man-made. But it was not her only conduit to religious life. Always, outside the system, she felt God lurking, gleaming around the patches of law and tradition and improvisation she had half inherited and half stitched together, so that she had a sense of spiritual well-being that lived beyond her traditional life. Lev recognized this in her and admired it intensely.

"You're like a plant," Lev told her.

Deborah had not understood the compliment until Lev explained that only plants convert the sun's light directly into energy. When we eat plants, he said, we are eating stored energy. Sometimes we eat the animals that eat the plants that store the energy. We don't have the ability to turn the sun into energy ourselves so we need something to do it for us. But you're different.

Deborah seemed capable, even though she embraced tradition, of nourishing herself directly from the source.

"You're like a plant, Rabbi Green."

Lev found Deborah's faith deeply consoling; being around her gave him a strange sense of getting closer to Judaism without being annihilated by it. He felt in an almost primitive way that God was with her and that therefore God was with him. The dry, rigid renunciations of his yeshiva days had both intoxicated him and made him feel cut off, as if Judaism were a monkish pursuit, abstract and intellectual. A form of self-righteous masochism. With Deborah the opposite seemed true.

Lev dressed, went into the living room, and was astonished to discover a strange ghostly man swaying and muttering by the window. But no, not a ghost and not a man at all, but Deborah, wearing her grandfather's tallis, robed in white, only bare calves visible below, which made her look a little like an otherworldly flasher.

She was just at the end of her prayers. Lev studied her in the mirror above the dresser. He could not help noticing that her face in prayer bore an uncanny resemblance to her face during sex—the eyes squeezed shut, her mouth half open, the jaw rigid, the throat webbed—a look that bordered on suffering.

She took three paces backward, bent left and then right, bowed in the middle, and then stood, still swaying. The tallis was draped over her head like a hood, gathered at the throat in one hand. She was singing softly now, a wordless song. He felt her body gradually unclench, she released the fabric in her hand, and the tallis drooped and sloped back over her shoulders. Her hair was loose underneath though it was encircled at the top by the black band of her tefillin. Between her eyes, like a blunt horn, sat a little black box, held in place by the leather band around her head. Scrolled invisibly inside was the biblical declaration that God is one, along with a list of the blessings that come from serving God and the terrible punishments that follow from forgetting Him.

There was a black box on her left arm as well, jutting off her naked bicep and held in place by a loop of leather. Her plump flesh bulged through the spaces made by the leather thong as it circled her upper arm and wound round her forearm, seven times, before forming an intricate pattern on the back of her hand, where it spelled out the word *Shadai*, a name for God.

Lev wanted to call out to her, to approach, but he felt nailed to his spot, watching in silence as Deborah began unwinding the long leather thong that was bound around her hand and around two fingers, stiffening them like a splint. When she had unwound the name of God she wrapped the strap around her hand again and took off the headpiece, carefully capping it with a little silver square before wrapping its straps around the box and tucking it into a little velvet pouch. Then she began unwinding the arm strap. Lev saw how tightly she'd wrapped the strap, which left pale stripes on her arm.

He whispered her name and Deborah let out a little cry.

"You scared the shit out of me!"

"Well, you scared me, too," said Lev, smiling.

Deborah scowled.

She did not always put on tefillin when she prayed—she did not always pray in the morning—but since the holidays she had been trying to do both and when she did put on tefillin she felt she owed them her attention. Putting away her tefillin was part of the ritual for her; they had belonged to her grandfather and she liked thinking about the way those strange talismanic boxes had rested on his head and near his heart. A jeweler, he had made the little protective silver cases himself.

She did not want at that moment even to be reminded that Lev was in the apartment. Lev was barefoot, though looking very tall nevertheless. He was wearing jeans and a white undershirt, his bright hair still flattened from sleep. One fair cheek was whiskered with lines from the creases of his pillow. He was staring at her with that anthropological air that registered as disapproval. Perhaps disgust.

He's going to leave me, she thought.

Deborah grew suddenly self-conscious. Under her tallis she was wearing red shorts and her "Seven Ways to Love Israel" T-shirt. In spite of herself, Deborah glanced in the mirror. There was something defeminizing about the whole getup, something bar mitzvah boyish that dismayed her.

"If you call me a transvestite you're dead meat," said Deborah, who was monitoring Lev's expression out of the corner of her eye as she continued wrapping up her tefillin.

"Dead meat? What are you, a Teamster?"

Deborah laughed but she continued to monitor Lev's face.

The pale hair on her arm had been flattened by the leather strap, like beach grass after a storm.

"No bondage jokes either," she said. "Let me finish."

She zipped the wrapped tefillin into the wine-colored velvet pouch and dropped it onto the coffee table. She still had not taken off her tallis. She turned and faced Lev, who was staring at her intently.

"What are you thinking?" she asked.

"You look like an angel," he said, drawing closer.

Deborah broke into a girlish smile.

"Come here," she said, lifting up her wings.

AT FIRST Lev did not join Deborah in synagogue. Gradually, though, he began showing up on Friday nights. He sat in the last row, feeling like the illicit lover of an actress in the nineteenth century, waiting for her to finish the performance.

Temple Emunah was a grand and beautiful building on a side street off Amsterdam Avenue, with a towering facade of smooth stone that had been built in the 1920s. Carved above the entrance were the words: "Do Justly, Love Mercy and Walk Humbly with Thy God." Lev loved the outside of the building, but he found the sanctuary numbing. When he had gone to services with his father it was never to a Reform synagogue. The interior of Temple Emunah seemed oddly ersatz to him—the perfunctory stained-glass windows of the twelve tribes, the pseudo-Moorish arches, the blue carpeting decorated with triangles that suggested Jewish stars but weren't. The optional yarmulkes in their basket out front. The narrow nylon prayer shawls for Saturday services, more like scarves than the great tasseled tablecloths of the kind Deborah wrapped herself in at home. Cut off from tradition as he was, Lev could not help viewing the whole thing as vaguely goyish.

The Israeli flag at one end of the bimah and the American flag at the other, the giant brass candelabra at center stage, made him feel as though he was in a high school assembly. The organ, hidden behind an ornate wooden grill, and the arrangements of flowers in front of each of the lecterns, gave the air a funereal cast, despite occasionally spirited singing from the congregation and Deborah's sweet voice filling in gaps when the congregation fell silent and Cantor Baumwald was saving up for his next solo. The warmth and immediacy Lev felt praying with Deborah alone eluded him in the big antiseptic space. He tried to remind himself of what Deborah said, that God was present in a different way when you prayed in a group, but much of the time he felt the trapped distraction of an airline passenger.

He stood and sat when commanded, mumbled the responsive readings, learned the songs, drifted in and out of the service, diverting himself with whatever stray literature was stuck into the shelf on the back of the pew in front of him or by watching how Rabbi Zwieback and Cantor Baumwald, who, he knew from Deborah, were trying to get each other fired, avoided eye contact. Occasionally he would wake himself up by imagining Deborah naked under her black robe.

Did men in the congregation fantasize about her? It suddenly irritated him that they might. Once, a man in front of him murmured something to another man and chuckled. Were they talking about Deborah? She was facing the ark, which looked like a giant box of Godiva chocolates. The Torahs stood inside on their peg legs, dressed richly in blue and crimson velvet, crowned with filigreed silver cones. Deborah was deeply moved by the presence of these Torahs, the books at the center of everything. No body on a cross, no statue of Mary, no image of God. Just words, handwritten on parchment, scrolled on wood and lovingly dressed in velvet. Around each armless Torah-torso hung a breastplate of silver—for two thousand years this was the only army Jews had and the sight of it stirred mixed emotions in Lev, who felt awe and mild revulsion. For Deborah, however, it was nothing but inspiring. Returning the Torah to the ark after the weekly reading, she often wept as she sang, "It is a tree of life to all who hold fast to it."

Deborah's back was to the congregation during the moment of silent meditation that followed the Amida. He knew that her face, though hidden, would be wearing its intense, almost sexual expression. Was the laughter of the men in front of him directed at her? Lev wanted to smack the man in the back of the head and drag him out of his seat. He leaned forward and hissed.

Deborah did not conceal Lev from the congregation but she did not go out of her way to introduce him either. Lev had the feeling she would not have minded if he had not been there at all, though she had encouraged him to start coming. She needed her energy to focus on the congregation; afterward she stood at the foot of the bimah next to Rabbi Zwieback as congregants filed past to shake their hands and exchange a few words. Deborah looked like the vice president after the State of the Union address.

The rabbis had to have a few words for everyone—comfort for the bereaved, congratulations for weddings or the births of grandchildren, inquiries and encouragement for upcoming bar or bat mitzvahs. He and Deborah knew all the secrets and adjusted their body language when wordless communications were called for.

It was a prosperous congregation and Lev marveled at the complexity of the rabbi's relationship to his flock—a servant who was nevertheless expected to lead the people who paid his salary. Rabbi Zwieback's contract was up soon and it was rumored he would not be renewed. He earned a quarter of a million dollars, Deborah had told Lev, and there were many in the congregation who felt he wasn't worth it. A learned man with a Ph.D. in Bible who had taught at Brandeis before entering the rabbinate, he wore a permanent passive-aggressive smile and was beginning to resemble the crumbly cookie his name suggested. He had two daughters in college and a four-bedroom apartment in the Apthorp. He could not go back to teaching and would have to take a pulpit in Phoenix or Houston or one of the other growing centers of American Judaism. Back to the desert.

At the far end of the bimah, Cantor Baumwald, who despite being a nitwit was extremely popular with parents, was puffed up like the lord mayor, still wearing the high black cantor's hat that made him appear even taller than his six-foot frame. Cantors, Deborah had explained, were like anchormen in broadcast journalism. It was a pretty voice, not a brain, for which they were employed. Rabbis actually knew what they were reporting. She didn't respect Baumwald but at least he had charisma, while Zwieback was a burned-out case and she had little patience for him.

While the congregation was filing past the rabbis or heading for the exits, Lev would slip out and wait for Deborah in her study upstairs, where she went to change out of her black robe, or, if it was a mild night, he'd meet her out on the street. He refrained from kissing her until they had rounded the corner.

"WHERE'S THE RABBI?"

Lev cringed inwardly at Jacob's question but embraced his brother, who had answered the door to his parents' apartment.

"Deborah's at the Brooklyn Botanical Garden," Lev said. "Performing a wedding."

"Wow!" said Penny, Jacob's wife, who had also come to the door. A convert to Judaism, Penny had an enthusiasm that lacked the teasing humor of Jacob but it embarrassed Lev. It was for just this reason that he had hesitated telling them about Deborah. He did not fear disapproval, just the implication that he was suddenly part of a novelty act, as if he had eloped with the sword swallower or the bearded lady. Nobody he knew reacted neutrally—and why should they? Rabbis, as Deborah herself had told him, were the religious equivalent of strippers. Everyone has a private spiritual core but only a few people exhibit it in public.

Lev's two-year-old niece, Margaret, ran over and hugged his shins. She wore only a shirt and was diaperless down below. He scooped her up. He had not seen her in several months and was amazed at how she had changed. She looked like her mother, golden hair and green eyes with an oddly adult composure—until she started squealing and saying "bunny doodie" over and over and giggling wildly as Lev made farting noises by blowing against her belly.

As he put her down Lev saw his father, sitting in a wheelchair, immobile as a lawn ornament. He did not look Lev's way or show signs of getting up. *The New York Times* was on his lap but it was just a prop, positioned at an unreadable angle.

Lev knelt down beside his father and kissed his cheek above the beard. His father's eyes were closed but they popped open and he smiled faintly.

"Lev!" said his father. "Forgive me."

He had at last begun to speak, though at times the words were jumbled. His voice had a faraway, tinny tone and his jaw seemed, since the stroke, frozen shut so that you wanted to get the oilcan.

"Were you sleeping?" Lev asked.

"Resting. Are you first?"

Lev wasn't sure *first* was the word his father wanted.

"Deborah's working," he said. He kissed his father's cheek again. "That's from her."

He had explained that Deborah would be performing a wedding back when Jacob had announced that he and Penny were coming in for a few days. But nobody in the family seemed to remember anything. Since his father's stroke, they had all lost their short-term memory.

Despite his exhaustion, Henry was doing much better. He was getting around on his own in the apartment, though he still used a walker or wheelchair for going out. One arm was still partially paralyzed and Lev found no sight more heartbreaking than his father lifting his left hand in his right and positioning it on the table.

Helen Friedman came into the living room. She had been in the kitchen, getting brunch ready, and smelled of onion bagels and smoked fish and perfume.

"Where's Deborah?" she asked, kissing her son.

"Making a golem."

"I thought she was performing a wedding."

"Then why did you ask?"

"I was just wondering where the wedding was. I have someone in Brooklyn today." Her photographers worked weddings all over New York. They might even have been covering this one. But no, she didn't think she had anyone shooting at the Botanic Garden.

Lev's parents already knew Deborah, of course—they had met her at the hospital, which vaguely embarrassed Lev, who was afraid it would appear that in the midst of a family crisis he had been courting a caregiver. He suspected his mother knew that Deborah had been the one to tell Lev about his father's suicide attempt and resented the fact, though she had never mentioned it.

Helen had been extremely cordial to Deborah at dinner the one time Deborah had come over, despite the awkwardness of Deborah refusing—politely of course—to eat the unkosher chicken Lev's mother had prepared. Pork and shellfish were not served in the Friedman home, though when Lev was younger they had been. His father had gradually banned them as he returned to religion, but there was still an open admissions policy for chickens. Lev had neglected to vet the menu or brief his mother beforehand and, had Deborah not noticed the Perdue packages in the kitchen garbage and shared her discovery with Lev, he would probably not have thought twice about it.

Deborah had a hard time believing it was mere oversight—surely Lev's mother should have known a rabbi did not eat supermarket chicken—but she had reminded herself that everyone had different standards and degrees of knowledge. Her own mother once bought a kosher turkey for Thanksgiving for Deborah's sake and then rubbed the skin with butter before cooking it, which made the whole thing *tref.* Her mother had been defensive but Helen had seemed genuinely embarrassed by her error and Deborah had explained, in an effort to minimize the awkwardness, that the rabbis of the Talmud had once considered declaring chicken to be like fish—a neutral food that could be eaten with either milk or meat. A feathered vegetable.

But chicken, alas, was not a vegetable, and Deborah understood that she emitted, despite her best wishes, a sort of rabbinical radiation that contaminated the food on other people's plates and made them squirm. She had heaped up her own plate with salad and bread and potatoes, despite her suspicion that the potatoes had been cooked in the same pan as the chicken. This concession went unappreciated and a shadow of disapproval settled over Lev's mother.

The dinner was marred for another reason. Lev's father had seemed not to recognize Deborah, though it was hard to tell these days what was exhaustion, what was depression, and what were the blurring effects of his stroke. When Deborah herself explained that she was a rabbi, Henry had shocked his son by recalling Dr. Johnson's comment that a female preacher was like a dog walking on its hind legs—remarkable simply because she was doing it at all. He did not mean it as an insult: He was happy to have discovered, in the great archive of his memory, a quotation that seemed suitable to the occasion. But Deborah found it hard to reconcile the observation with the man who rested his large hand in hers as she chanted psalms aloud, tears running down his face.

But something had happened to the way Henry thought. In some respects his mind had never been so clear. He could recall and even hear whole pieces of music in his head with such intensity that he sometimes forgot the stereo wasn't on and he was merely imagining the Jupiter Symphony or the Egmont Overture. He once asked Lev to turn the stereo down when the two were sitting in complete silence. Poems he had memorized years before came to him unbidden; names and events and faces from the past rose up before him with great vividness. But the organizing framework of his intellect was somehow damaged so that the files became jumbled. His sense of time was disturbed. Whenever they took him to the doctor, someone would ask him what he had eaten for breakfast and who was president, questions that always startled him with their blunt irrelevance.

There was a slight otherworldly quality to Henry now that Helen found disturbing. He had taken catnaps even when he was well, and Helen had always found the sight of a grown man unconscious on the couch disconcerting, but now he slept even in the morning after breakfast, often without bothering to lie down. A quality of sleep seemed to have lodged permanently inside him so that even when he was awake she felt that sense of uncanny stillness in the room, a sense of being turned herself into a dream. It frightened her. She still spoke to Henry in detail about her business and her day and their children and what was in the paper, but Henry often failed to respond. Or he commented in a gnomic, irrelevant way that Helen could shape into a response only with effort.

She was glad that Jacob and Penny had come to stay with them. She wanted Jacob's opinion of his father, even though she feared it.

Jacob's opinion had already been given. He felt that Henry's mind was damaged and that it would not come back. He had read a great deal about stroke victims, as had Lev, but Lev had managed to find stories about unexpected recoveries that took place six months or a year or even more after damage was sustained; Jacob tended to emphasize what the doctors themselves often said, which was that what you got back in a week you kept; after that the odds of real recovery went down. You could exercise an arm back into use but if a mind was damaged there was nothing to be done. Still, Henry had been speaking, though in a limited way, and that in itself was a sort of miracle.

Jacob and Lev sat side by side on the sofa, talking in an undertone. Helen and Penny were in the kitchen, stacking dishes and wrapping up the ragged remains of lox and whitefish. Henry was still at the dining room table, a napkin tucked into his shirt. *The New York Times* was once more on the table in front of him but his thoughts were elsewhere.

Henry had been imagining himself back in Ex Libris, the failed bookstore that he and his friend Walter Sonnenschine had owned for two years in the early sixties, a crammed second-story space on Fourth Avenue that had lost money from the day it opened but that Henry still visited in his mind and viewed with the deepest nostalgia. He spent a great deal of time imagining himself back in the bookstore, though imagining himself back was not the right way to describe the experience. It was as if the bookstore was imagining itself back in him, coming up unbidden as the music and the old conversations did. The thin but indestructible industrial carpeting, the green tin-print roof, Helen's black-and-white photographs on the wall, and the sweet, mulchy smell of used books with something slightly poisonous, the spray of the exterminator, underneath. Henry shut his eyes and gave himself over to the vision.

"I think when I got here he didn't know who I was," Jacob was whispering vehemently. "There are times he just seems to wink out. He naps all the time; it drives Mom crazy."

Jacob had his mother's energy. Lev was, like his father, a napper, and did not like the association of daytime dozing and disability.

Jacob was built on a different plan from Lev—short, stocky, dark, and balding, he resembled their mother's father, a union organizer and socialist from Minsk who had worked as a furrier in Brooklyn and come home after a twelve-hour day of manual labor to drink tea and read Tolstoy in Russian and who had died before either of them had been born. Lev resembled his father's father—a tall, wraithlike pharmacist, from whom Lev had inherited his red hair and who had died in Buchenwald concentration camp.

Jacob had been wondering from the first days of Henry's stroke if his father recognized him, and Lev could not help feeling there was a psychological component to Jacob's uncertainty, a feeling of invisibility he'd always had around his father. After Henry's first stroke, Jacob had peered at their father in the hospital and demanded, "Who am I?" and Henry, in a quiet, ironic voice, had responded, "Don't you know who you are?"

Lev had laughed about it for days afterward.

Jacob and Lev had already had it out on the phone about Jacob's failure to tell Lev that his father had attempted suicide. To his credit, Jacob had apologized, though in a blunt, preemptive way—"You're right, I was a bonehead, no excuse"—that squelched conversation but not resentment and that Lev found deeply unsatisfying. Jacob spoke with the superior tone, the air of authority and rationality and vague condescension that no doubt went with being a management consultant. Even his apologies seemed triumphalist. Lev could not help feeling pleased, as he looked at his brother's muscular frame and round face, to note that Jacob's hairline had receded to the point of virtual baldness, leaving only a little island of hair, like a sandbar at low tide, surrounded by glossy scalp, a fate Lev had avoided and that he viewed as compensation for having red hair.

"Mom thinks it's depression," Lev was saying in a low whisper. "Depression can mask a lot."

Jacob shrugged, unconvinced.

Henry opened his eyes. Could he hear them? Lev worried suddenly. But Henry was smiling at Margaret, who was bringing Henry "presents"—fallen leaves from the houseplants, coasters wrapped in toilet paper, and stray pieces of mail that she had found lying on the coffee table or had retrieved from the wastepaper basket. By the time Henry had marshaled himself physically to reach out and take what she offered she had vanished, the present deposited at Henry's feet. He did not dare reach over to pick it up, fearful as he was of tumbling out of his chair, but merely stared down at the brown shoes with Velcro fasteners that Helen had bought him, thinking "my feet?" and watching the growing pile of random objects as he sank lower and lower and grew more and more lopsided in his seat.

Occasionally Penny would call out from the kitchen, above the rushing water, "Greta—do you need the potty?" and Margaret would yell, "No no no no no," reaching behind to pinch her own bottom shut as she scampered off down the hall in search of more treasure. She was often distracted by the dog, who followed her through the apartment, waiting until the inevitable pretzel, cheddar goldfish, or cookie fragment fell from her hands.

"He's not himself," said Jacob. "He's just not there."

"I disagree," Lev whispered vehemently. "I think in some ways he's there more than ever. Even when he's quiet, I can't help feeling that his soul is present, maybe even intensified . . ."

Jacob did not let him finish.

"His soul? You sound like Penny."

It was classic that his brother could insult him by likening him to his wife.

It had always seemed unfair to Lev that Penny was the one who had converted to Jacob's religion, since she actually had a religious temperament and Jacob seemed to lack one entirely. But perhaps she felt something in Lev's brother that he could not see. When Jacob teased Penny as she lit Friday night candles or blundered through the blessing over the bread, she did not seem to mind, and perhaps she knew that Jacob was secretly pleased and grateful to her for becoming a Jew, if only because it mattered to his father.

"Remember when you came back from that yeshiva and threw out all the Baco-Bits and then it turned out they weren't bacon anyway . . ."

His brother laughed at a joke that was no longer funny to either of them but that had once been amusing and that Jacob mechanically used to torment his brother. Lev smiled but he did not like to be teased—he felt a surge of anger toward his brother and rehearsed several Krav Maga moves in his mind, jabbing and throttling and throwing imaginary elbows.

"That was before you became Mr. Genome," his brother said. "I guess now you're back the other way. I guess the rabbi . . ."

"Her name is Deborah!" Lev hissed, loudly and full of anger. He wanted to pound his brother into the couch.

"I'm sorry," Jacob said quickly.

He seemed genuinely regretful. Teasing Lev was a hard habit to break. But he looked at Lev with fraternal affection.

"Is it hard being with someone religious?"

The question was asked seriously.

"Is it hard for you?" Lev asked.

Jacob smiled.

"Penny doesn't ask me to do anything. It's just the way she is. She just believes."

"And what about you?" Lev asked.

The question sounded juvenile and stupid to him. Believe in what? He didn't even know what he was asking. But at the same time, he wanted to know.

"Did you ever read 'Big Two-Hearted River'?" Jacob asked.

"It's a Hemingway story, isn't it?"

"Yes. The narrator comes home from World War I and he goes trout fishing."

"Uh-huh," said Lev.

"The whole story's really about keeping it together. You pitch your tent. You take out your rod. And you catch a bunch of grasshoppers to use for bait and put them in a can."

"Then what?" Lev asked.

"Then you go fishing. The point is, you just do your thing. It's about living your life. Not thinking too much about painful things or unanswerable things. Or about emptiness. Just scanning the grass for grasshoppers."

Lev felt very close suddenly to his brother, but his warm feeling was tinged with pity.

"Is that really what you think life's about?" Lev asked. "Distracting yourself from ultimate emptiness? That's your philosophy—a story you read in high school. Who explained that to you, Mr. Capazelli?"

"Well, obviously it's more than fishing." Jacob looked insulted. "It's being with my family. It's looking at nature. Doing a good job."

Lev waited but there was no more coming. A feeling of sadness overcame him.

The brothers sat in silence until a small voice declared, "Greta make peepee!"

Both Lev and Jacob looked and recognized the great dark circle that had bloomed on the pale rug and saw Mephisto sniffing the edge of the stain with animal curiosity.

"Oh Margaret!" said Penny, coming out of the kitchen, "you said you'd tell me."

"Greta make peepee!" Margaret said again, without a hint of shame. Helen, who wandered out of the kitchen with a roll of paper towels that she handed to Jacob, went over to Henry, hauling him higher in his chair.

"Henry!" she said, as if Henry were responsible for the big spot on the carpet. "Didn't you see what she was doing?"

Henry said nothing. There was no point blaming him. She felt instantly remorseful and began massaging his shoulders. But then she noticed the pile at his feet, supplemented by living leaves plucked by Margaret from the ficus that a quick check told her was now nearly leafless below.

"Greta darling, we don't pull leaves off houseplants," she said gently to her granddaughter—she wasn't angry at Margaret, who was only two and a half, but how could Henry have let her do it? He was staring helplessly down at the pile of green as if noticing it for the first time. Helen was still massaging Henry's shoulders but felt suddenly like throttling him. Had he just given up?

Jacob, treating the carpet with the Nature's Miracle that Helen kept under the sink for Mephisto's accidents, gave Lev a knowing look.

Helen, still massaging her husband's neck, could feel how unnaturally stiff Henry's muscles were in places, while in others they were weirdly soft and lax; she felt a wave of pity for him. He was shifting uncomfortably, gripping the armrests, trying to get out of the chair. Helen bent over, smoothed his hair and asked, in a whisper, "Do you need the bathroom?"

Lev watched his father stiffen with shame and try to shrug away Helen as best as he was able with his lopsided shoulders. The apartment was very quiet, except for Margaret who continued to chatter and who, pointlessly diapered now, had joined Jacob as he blotted the excess Nature's Miracle off the carpet. Finished with his work, Jacob picked Margaret up and spun her around, slinging her over his shoulder like a sack of potatoes as he sang "Hi Ho, Hi Ho," carrying the used paper towels into the kitchen, his daughter squealing and laughing and kicking her bare feet.

Jacob was, Lev had to admit, a wonderful father. Lev could not believe, watching his brother clutching his daughter, that she was a mere grasshopper to him, a distraction from the void. When Margaret was born, Penny had said to Lev, in the surreptitious earnest way she always shared her religious feelings, that she felt very close to God. Lev had felt that way, too, holding his newborn niece. And though his brother may have teased his wife for saying so, he saw the same acknowledgment in Jacob's face. Margaret still seemed dipped in something divine. Lev knew her cuteness was a matter of adaptive advantage, that you would not wish to take care of such a helpless creature if there wasn't some inborn response activated by big eyes and round cheeks and tiny hands and feet. But that did not make her arrival from nowhere any less mysterious.

WHEN JACOB AND PENNY went to the Museum of Modern Art to see the Brancusi retrospective, Lev volunteered to stay back and put Margaret down for her nap, allowing his mother, who did not get out as much as she used to, to join them. It was also a way to stay home with his father, whom he hoped to have a chance to talk to.

Henry did not like being pushed in his wheelchair, loathed his walker and, in any case, could not keep up on foot. He seldom went out these days. Helen left him home in the mornings but she did not like doing it and knew that soon she would have to hire someone full-time to be with him. Henry was too unsteady on his feet, too slow in his reactions. He refused to have a Medic Alert pendant and Helen was afraid he would fall. She never said she was afraid he would try to kill himself again and indeed he seemed truly to have lost the will, or at least the strength, to do himself harm. But that did not mean she did not race home after her mornings out, her heart pounding as she drove the key into the lock.

"Ask him if he needs help getting to the bathroom," Helen told her son in an undertone at the door. "He can't always stand up when he needs to and his . . . control isn't perfect. He hates being asked, but you have to. You can just leave him at the door," she added, seeing Lev's anxious expression.

PUTTING MARGARET TO BED took longer than he'd anticipated. She sat on his lap in the spare bedroom, where her Pack n' Play was set up. Lev read her story after story, *Good Night Moon*, *The Carrot Seed*, *In the Night Kitchen*. Several of these books had once belonged to him and he felt the ache of time collapsing. That was his green crayon that had scribbled on the snow in *The Snowy Day*, the child he had once been passing a note to his future self, though the note said nothing at all, merely made him aware that his hands had once been as small as Margaret's, his brain as undeveloped, his soul as fresh.

Margaret was clutching a tiny, frazzled stuffed dog that she called simply "Dog-Dog," and a "sippy cup" filled with milk. She burrowed into Lev, getting sleepy, so that her few interruptions and announcements sounded almost drunken: "That Mama, that Dada, that Greta, that cow" or, more awkwardly, "Greta have penis!" a declaration, made on seeing the naked boy in *In the Night Kitchen*, that Lev did not bother to refute.

When Lev thought it was time for her to go into her portable crib, Margaret insisted that she needed another diaper and indeed her diaper was heavy and warm, so he transferred her to the carpet and she very dutifully lay back and put her legs in the air and there was something so touching and guileless about her lying on the carpet that Lev almost wanted to weep. She was a beautiful girl and her hair was somehow grown-up hair, long and full, and Penny styled it with little clips or braids in a way that made Margaret look sometimes in a homuncular way like a tiny woman and not a two-year-old. But Lev, bending over the naked bottom half of his niece, the chubby thighs and bald fleshy vulva with its simple line, more dimple than vagina, felt no desire, he was happy to discover, but only a sort of paternal warmth and protectiveness, stirring him deeply as he ministered to her, talking softly to distract her as he slid out the old diaper and slid the new one under her.

She looked a great deal like Penny but there was also something in her eyes that belonged to Jacob, and, Lev imagined, belonged to himself as well.

"A river out of Eden," the biologist Richard Dawkins called the genetic stream that linked the generations. Dawkins fascinated Lev because he was a die-hard atheist, and yet the poetry of that phrase always stirred Lev deeply and he felt something transcendent in his genetic bond to his niece, though he could not articulate exactly what.

The new diaper gave Margaret her second wind and she demanded more stories. Several times, Lev tried to shift her into the crib but she squirmed and fought and said, "Lev read 'nother story!" or asked for juice or a rice cake so that Lev, who knew he was being snookered but wanted to be loved, left her alone and zipped into the kitchen to get her a rice cake, passing his father dozing over the paper. He was hoping his father would be awake when he was finished so they could talk.

The rice cake was for "Dog-Dog," who did not want it, so Lev slid it into his breast pocket. At last, when the comments stopped, the sippy cup fell from her hand and she did not ask for it back, when she was sucking her thumb in a sort of trance, Margaret allowed Lev to lower her into the crib and cover her with a small yellow fleece blanket. She then put her hands over her eyes in a hide-and-seek manner and waited, and when Lev began to walk out of the room she yelled "Ma!" and Lev came back thinking she had called for her mother, but she peeked at him expectantly from between her fingers. She kept covering her eyes and waiting and Lev tried to play a game of peekaboo with her that only made her angry. He offered her the sippy cup but she threw it down and she kept saying "Ma!" and covering her eyes and Lev, in growing frustration, explained for the last time that her mama was out but would be back when she woke up. He was about to leave despite Margaret's tears when, in a moment of inspiration and surprise, he realized that Penny, the dutiful convert, must pray with Margaret at bedtime.

"Does your mother say the Sh'ma with you?" he asked.

Margaret stopped crying almost immediately and laughed in relief at being understood at last.

"Dada Mama do it," said Margaret. "Dada say 'Ma and Mama say Ma,' " and she began to chant a gibberish approximation of the Sh'ma, covering her eyes like a traditional Jew. *Sha yo adna hats* . . .

Lev brushed the tears from her face with the back of his hand and then, directed by Margaret, covered his own eyes while Margaret covered hers. It was only naptime, not evening, but he chanted, in Hebrew, "*Sh'ma Yisrael Adonai Elohainu Adonai Ehad*—Hear O Israel, the Lord our God, the Lord is one." He had only recently begun saying it in bed himself. As if a magic spell had been uttered, Margaret curled up under the blanket, gripping Dog-Dog, her blond hair covering her shut eyes.

Sneaky bastard, Lev thought, with great affection for his brother as he walked softly out of the room, turned off the light, and closed the door.

"JACOB SAYS the Sh'ma with Margaret," Lev said, sitting down next to his father at last. His father was no longer dozing but staring straight ahead with a look of surprising alertness. Lev expected the news to make an impression, but his father merely turned his head, slowly, almost robotically, and blinked at Lev.

Henry was back in the bookstore, going through estate boxes in the back room, remembering a single shipment from a Columbia professor of religion: Marcuse, Marx, Luther, *The Lives of the Saints* in scaling brown and gilt, spooky books he did not open. *The Decline and Fall of the Roman Empire*. Romain Rolland, Thomas Wolfe, John Dos Passos, those fallen giants. Joseph Campbell, Mircea Eliade, anti-Semites, he'd since learned, but in those days clean bricks to build a house with. And for some reason, Carl Sandburg's biography of Abraham Lincoln, though there were only two volumes, not three. The dust from the books pollinated his fingertips. Who said that?

"Dad!" Lev called, louder than he intended.

Henry looked at Lev for a moment in confusion. Lev had an impulse to say to his father, as Jacob once had, "Who am I?" but then Henry said, in a slow voice that seemed to have gotten higher since his stroke, "Jacob is full of surprises."

Henry remembered vividly the words of Walter Schneiderman, a neighbor in Vienna, a gambler and ne'er-do-well who sometimes came home drunk and slept at the foot of the stairwell until someone helped him up, and who occasionally joined the family for Shabbas dinner at his father's urging though his mother he knew did not like Walter: "Jews will be saying *Sh'ma Yisrael* long after Germans have stopped saying Heil Hitler." He might have been a gambler but he'd had a traditional upbringing and often chanted snatches of liturgy when drunk. If Henry remembered correctly—and who knew, he'd only been a child at the time, but some memories were indelible—there were tears in Walter's eyes as he made his pronouncement to little Henry. It's possible of course that he had been drunk. He had said this just days before Henry was put on a train with a big number printed on a placard around his neck and sent to England with other boys and girls. And it was true, too, thought Henry—though Walter, as he learned much later, had been beaten to death in the street and though Henry himself had stopped praying altogether almost immediately after arriving in England . . .

"I've started saying it," said Lev, feeling embarrassed, like a little boy showing something to his father.

His father smiled without opening his mouth, a cryptic smile, almost a reflex, almost ironic, though perhaps merely affectionate.

"How's Jennifer?" his father asked.

Had he forgotten about the canceled wedding? Had he meant to say Deborah but used the wrong name? Perhaps he imagined that Lev was in touch with Jenny and was simply asking about a woman he had known for many years and made a place for in his family and heart.

"I don't know, Dad. I don't talk to her anymore. Not since I moved out."

His father nodded slightly.

Henry had forgotten. He was realizing this and correcting it, recalling now, though in a muffled way, the commotion and distress. He felt a stab of embarrassment that he had said the wrong thing. It would be good to get back to the bookstore where Carl Sandburg was waiting for him.

"Dad," Lev said, after waiting for more words. "Do you remember that I've been seeing Deborah Green, the rabbi who used to sing with you sometimes? Do you remember her? I've been studying with her. I've been . . ."

His voice trailed off. It seemed a pathetic description of his relationship but he left it.

"I've been studying Talmud."

He waited for a response. Henry's face was impassive, but then Henry put his hand slowly on Lev's leg. Lev felt tacit approval. Of course his father knew. He had known, Lev thought, even before he had brought Deborah home. There'd always been something omniscient about his father, for all his seeming distraction. And he liked Deborah.

But then his father began moving his hand—it was the good hand, the right—slowly up and down Lev's thigh, digging his fingers in. Scratching. Henry had an absentminded look on his face. Did he think he was scratching his own leg? Or was this merely affection made awkward by motor difficulties?

"We've been studying Talmud," Lev said again. "And some prayers. I thought you'd like to know."

He said this with delicate insinuation, studying his father's face for a response. He didn't know if he should bring up the suicide letter directly. He never had. Henry's hand had stopped moving, though it remained on Lev's leg. Should Lev simply say, "I'll be able to say Kaddish for you"?

"I've started saying *modeh ani* every morning," Lev ventured.

Henry smiled, in his slightly ironic way. His smile, at any rate, was still intact, in all its indeterminacy. Lev suddenly felt that his little morning prayer was a paltry offering. He would never know what his father wished him to know. The smile spoke to the inadequacy of his efforts.

His father shifted in his chair and seemed to notice for the first time that his hand was on his son's leg. He patted Lev's thigh carefully and restored his hand to the armrest of his own chair.

Perhaps the smile was not mocking but pleased. Maybe it had to do with Deborah, a happy memory of her presence. His father's smiles had spin on them, like English on a squash ball that sends it jumping in the opposite direction. Perhaps, if it was mocking, it was mocking not about Lev but about the prayer itself. How would a man who had wished to die recite a prayer thanking God for giving him back his soul?

But Henry was saying something and Lev strained to hear what it was. His father was speaking very softly, with a swallowed restraint, frozen-jawed, the tin man after rain. It sounded like Hebrew. Lev thought for a moment it was the name of a prayer. But then his father repeated himself more clearly and Lev heard the word *bathroom*.

It was Lev's turn to stare blinking into his father's face for a moment before absorbing the request. His father had to go to the bathroom! Lev stood up and offered his father his arm. But his father, in a surprisingly fluid motion, stood up on his own, pushing off on the armrests of the chair, and walking slowly across the carpet in his stooped fashion, leading with one shoulder like a man who wanted to knock down a door. He was wearing shoes but he walked as if in bedroom slippers, his feet low to the ground. One leg lagged behind the other. Lev did not want to insult his father by taking his arm so he merely hovered nearby, ready to catch him if he should go over, his arms slightly spread in an embrace that did not touch.

I will lead him to the door and wait for him outside, thought Lev. *Everything will be fine.*

As they were moving together across the carpet, his father suddenly stopped and it became clear to Lev that something dreadful had happened. There were sounds Lev had been ignoring. There was a smell. His father's eyes widened with panic and mortification and Lev felt his own heart begin to race.

"Dad," he said, "we have to get you to the bathroom."

Henry nodded slowly without speaking. He had retreated completely inside himself; his body was like the abandoned casing of a cicada, light and irrelevant. His mind went back to the books in Ex Libris but he found, to his horror, that the books had shit on them. He closed his eyes, not outwardly but inwardly; some inner lid blocked out the light and he tried to disappear. Lev took his arm now and moved him forcefully across the carpet, his father clenched in discomfort and shame but following Lev's lead. He had lost the ability to navigate on his own.

Lev steeled himself and decided that the best thing to do was to get Henry into the shower. He would help him undress and assess the damage. Perhaps nothing much had happened. They would get him into the shower. That was his focus. The shower.

Lev parked his father in the middle of the bathroom. His father gripped the sink with his good hand while Lev stepped over to the tub, reached in, and turned on the faucet. Water immediately rained down on him. But Lev felt better now that the water was running. He had begun talking aloud in a voice of assurance, trying to make his father feel that everything was all right.

"I'm just getting the water going, Dad, we need to get you in there."

His father said nothing. Lev did not expect a response. His face had a fixed, almost frozen expression, grim but remote.

Lev had to pry his father's fingers off the sink. Half hugging him, he waltzed his father over to the tub, holding him up but keeping his distance, too. He parted the curtains and then tried to lift his father's leg over the side. The tub was not high, he knew his father used it because there was some kind of chair contraption inside, but either from stress or because Lev was doing it wrong, or because Henry did not wish to be doused like a drunken sailor, he would not or could not lift his leg up over the side of the bathtub. Perhaps Oleg, a strapping Russian who helped his father shower, simply picked him up and plunked him down in that chair. But Lev couldn't do it. His father was shaking his head, like a frightened child, no no no.

And so Lev led him back to the sink, already realizing how idiotic it was to try to push his father, fully clothed, into a running shower. He ought to have undressed him first. Moron! Still, he left the water running; perhaps they would use it later. It was important not to panic.

"We have to get these off. Mind if I undo the belt?"

His father nodded, slightly but enough. Lev was saying to himself, *This is normal, this is normal.* He undid his father's belt. Undid the button and the zipper. He kept talking, asking, narrating.

"Just pull these down, all right?"

Lev's father was a proud and discreet man. Lev remembered vividly how his father had taught him how to use a public restroom, the two of them standing, father and son, inside a metal stall of the cavernous bathroom in the Museum of Natural History. His father putting the black horseshoe-shaped seat down with the toe of his shoe, a balletic act, and then laying a length of toilet paper on each of three sides, as if he were setting the table. When Lev had finished his business, his father showed him how to flush with his shoe. All a little excessively cautious, Lev came to feel in later years, contemplating his own hypersensitivity to germs, but it was one of those father-son moments that took the place of learning how to throw a football or how to field a grounder; it had a tenderness that came to Lev with great unexpected force at this horrible moment.

The water in the shower had gotten too hot, Lev realized, because the bathroom was filling with steam. Thank God he had not pushed his father under there. Lev wished, frankly, that the steam was thicker, that nothing could be seen, certainly not the tragic mask of his father's face, and not what was to come—the discovery that his father was wearing some sort of diaper, a complicated contraption, half cloth and half disposable liner, with an elastic belt holding everything up. Why had nobody told him? But then he could not imagine his mother simply announcing the fact. He tried to pretend that it was the most normal thing in the world, that he wore one, too.

"Lucky you had this on," he said.

His father's expression did not change.

The diaper was full, and its contents had traveled. The smell went like a nail into his nose, his sinuses, his brain. The steam seemed to pack it in around him like cotton. He thought for a second he was going to black out or be sick. He breathed through his mouth.

"Dad, we're going to have to get this off."

His father didn't answer. His lips were moving, he was muttering something, but Lev felt that it was not an answer. A prayer perhaps. Impossible to tell.

Lev got down on the white tiled floor. Safer to be at his father's feet. He stared at his father's ruddy, wrinkled knees, which he imagined he would inherit someday along with the freckles that had enlarged and merged into penny-sized spots and gave his father an almost leopardlike pattern.

He took off his father's shoes, lifting each foot like a blacksmith shodding a horse. Ripping open the Velcro tabs, he tossed the shoes into the hall. The pants, already bunched around Henry's ankles, slid off easily after. Those, not wholly clean, went into the bathroom garbage; he would deal with them later.

Lev stood up a little too fast and felt wobbly for a moment. He was drenched in sweat and steam. But he recovered his balance and gingerly, gripping clean corners, he managed to work the diaper off over his father's feet. Shit stained his father's pale thighs and buttocks but at least the heavy diaper was off. He got his father to step up again with each foot in turn and slid the diaper out and rolled it up in the little round bath mat without thinking, folding it over on itself to make a tight package. Lev stood holding the stinking package like a quarterback looking for an open man. His father was not looking at him, was not looking at anything. Merely staring at a spot on the wall, still gripping the edge of the sink so that he would not fall, murmuring his strange sounds.

"Do you want to try the shower again?" Lev asked softly.

Lev's father shook his head again, no.

"Fine, that's fine," Lev said. "I'll just get some paper towels."

Don't fall, don't fall, don't fall, he thought, as he raced to the kitchen for a roll of paper towels. His father was still standing where Lev had left him. Lev maneuvered his father away from the sink and toward the toilet; Henry managed to lean forward so that he was leaning against the wall, the good hand bearing his weight, the left hand hanging down at his side, his legs spread like a suspect about to be frisked. His back was turned. His shirttail hung over his buttocks but his naked legs were visible below.

Lev set about cleaning his father, tearing off a large bunch of paper towels, running them under the faucet, and, holding up his father's shirttails, daubing his father's backside.

Henry winced with every touch like a man receiving lashes. Lev assumed it was the general ordeal but in fact the water in the sink was boiling hot, though Lev, in his desire to clean and in his distraction and because he had so many paper towels wadded in his hand at once had not noticed. And all the while he was doing this he heard sounds coming from his father and tried to make out what they were. Henry's lips were moving. Lev felt sure that his father was praying and he tried to grasp the words but he could not, especially with the shower thundering into the tub and the faucet of the sink open all the way. What prayer, Lev wondered. What prayer?

In fact, Henry was reciting the Gettysburg Address, which he had memorized years before for his naturalization hearing—it hadn't been asked of him, and there was no opportunity then to recite it, but he had wanted to have it under his belt just in case some extenuating circumstance came up, as a way of proving his devotion, and it had popped into his head, the way poems sometimes did at stressful times, particularly Shakespeare sonnets—"Shall I compare thee to a summer's day?" for example, and "My mistress' eyes are nothing like the sun"—along with Andrew Marvell's "To His Coy Mistress" and Lord Byron's "She Walks in Beauty Like the Night." But it was the Gettysburg Address that at this terrible moment he found himself reciting softly, inwardly, over and over again.

So while the shower—which for some reason his son had forgotten to turn off—hissed into the very bathtub that Henry had planned to end his life in, or so Helen had explained to him, though the exact details of that day had fled his mind, and while Lev spoke aloud in an attempted voice of authority and normalization—I'm just going to flush a few of these, there we go, all right—Henry was declaiming, at some inner imaginary podium in the dark, *The brave men, living and dead, who struggled here, have consecrated it, far above our poor power to add or detract* . . . saying it inside to drown the shame, and haltingly, mutely aloud through involuntarily gritted teeth into the tainted steamy air of the bathroom.

Lev was not satisfied with how he had cleaned his father, but he could not do much better, careful as he was to avoid the genitals, hanging humbly in a thicket of graying copper hair, or to dwell too long on the stained region behind. He began toweling his father's legs, losing himself a little in the work.

"Are you doing all right?" He asked his father, who nodded distractedly.

We are met on a great battlefield of that war. We have come to dedicate a portion . . .

When Lev was done toweling he left his father still standing and raced into his parents' bedroom, past the closed door of sleeping Margaret, hoping she would not wake up. He quickly found his father's dresser, all the black socks neatly folded into themselves like sleeping birds, the white V-neck T-shirts giving off their special laundered smell that for some reason nobody else's clothes had, and grabbed a pair of underpants, though he noticed on the floor next to the dresser, half concealed, adult "Incontinent Garments" and grabbed one of those, too, and, back in the bathroom, trying to use an utterly normal voice, asked his father, which of these goes on first? And his father, still moving his lips, *that from these honored dead we take increased devotion to that cause*, nodded almost without looking toward the diaper that Lev, literally holding his breath, strapped on badly before having his father step into a pair of underpants that did not in fact fit over the diaper and that Lev abandoned. He crouched down to help his father's foot over the opening and felt something wet land on his arm and glanced up fearing the worst only to realize that tears were streaming down his father's face, past the strangely working mouth, *that this nation, under God, shall have a new birth of freedom*, and Lev wished that he could, like Deborah, sing his father a song that would comfort him but he only continued dressing his father who was utterly exhausted though still reciting, lost, trancelike and weeping, beginning over when he had reached the end and drooping slowly toward the floor like a sinking ship.

Lev led Henry to his bed where he helped him lie down and then covered him with the blanket and kissed him on the forehead and said, "I love you Dad," and found he was crying himself—his father's tears had not stopped, they were simply there in a stream, not like tears at all, and perhaps they weren't.

His father shut his eyes and Lev left him to sleep. Or so he hoped, though Henry's mouth was still moving slightly while Lev went back to the bathroom where he sprayed with Lysol and at last turned off the shower and threw the soiled clothes into a plastic bag and then another bag around that and for a moment considered throwing the whole thing down the incinerator but instead carried it into the kitchen where he put it next to the garbage and then washed his hands again and again in the kitchen sink. His clothes were drenched and his hands were shaking slightly and there was a smell inside his nose he could not expunge.

He fed the dog and welcomed the intentional stink of the canned food. He straightened up again, checked on his father who this time really was sleeping, and returned to the living room where he stood staring out the window at the cars flowing down Broadway, tiny taxis the size of toys.

Lev found himself thinking of an article he was writing, about a spacecraft launched to study an asteroid called "433 EROS." The asteroid was a slice of the same primordial rock that had made the earth, and was perhaps as old—four and a half billion years, an unfathomable number. The asteroid might have become part of the earth but was instead shot out for eternity in a blind, mindless journey. The little spacecraft had spent four years sailing after it, like a whaling ship, pursuing it through black, empty, bottomless space. And even though the ship was unmanned, Lev felt a kind of comfort knowing it was up there, with human observers down on the ground monitoring its progress, making the black void a little less void, though still terrifying and blank so that your lungs contracted at the mere thought of it, cold beyond imagining and big beyond imagining and black beyond imagining, not a place for people to be at all. No wonder some scientist had named the asteroid Eros.

Already he was comforting himself, distracting himself, putting things back in place. Collecting grasshoppers, as his brother would have said.

But his hands were still trembling and the image of his father broke through, standing like a humiliated child with his pants down at his ankles, and tears sprang to Lev's eyes all over again. He wanted to shout aloud, but Margaret was sleeping and his father was sleeping, and even Mephisto was curled up on his little pillow-lined basket.

Lev watched the cars crawl along Broadway far down below. And he understood that God, however much He might or might not exist, played no role whatsoever in human affairs.

DEBORAH CONTINUED TO VISIT MRS. FINK, who lived on in her luxury room at the top of the hospital without being discharged. Deborah liked to stop by the old woman's room, sit on her bed, and hold her hand. She called her Shirley now. Sometimes the tiny woman would shut her eyes and nap. Sometimes she chatted idly. She was very interested in Monica Lewinsky, the stained dress. It distressed her that Monica was Jewish, and from a good family, too. She was interested in celebrity gossip. In poor Elizabeth Taylor, who had a brain tumor and had gotten so fat, but then she hadn't taken care of herself. She admired Judge Judy and always watched her program, chuckling at the television adjudicator's tough humor.

Occasionally, she reminisced about her life with her husband who had died so many years ago but whose soul she felt around her every day. They did not discuss his lingering presence much, but Deborah was keenly aware of its effect on Mrs. Fink who, though she lay in bed like a pebble, had the anchored weight of a boulder.

It never failed to impress Deborah that the keeper of a divine mystery should read *People* magazine and not the Bible. Her refined presence, almost aristocratic, was hard to square with her diet of concerns. One of her aides brought her back issues of the *National Enquirer*, though she also read *The Wall Street Journal* in great detail.

She was less like a patient and more like a long-term resident in a hotel. Strange that she hadn't been sent home. She must have been sicker than she looked. She was also rich and may simply have preferred the bustle of the hospital to the loneliness of her apartment. She would not hear of a nursing home.

One day, shortly before Passover, which was the anniversary of her father's death, Deborah went to visit Mrs. Fink. Deborah had been feeling a vague, incipient depression despite warm weather and longer days. It had been over fifteen years since her father died but she still felt the same tingling awareness as the date of his death arrived, an even greater propensity for tears than usual, and a great desire, which she countered with sheer will, to stay in bed. She kept the Hebrew anniversary of her father's death, the fourteenth of Nisan, unlike her mother and sister, who kept April 8, the date on the Christian calendar when her father had, without warning, suffered his heart attack. This made her commemoration of the loss an even lonelier time, since the Hebrew calendar often diverged by several weeks from the Christian calendar. This year the date had already passed for her mother and sister, whom she dutifully called though she knew in advance that they would not know when the fourteenth of Nisan fell and, eager to put the date of death behind them, would not care to mark a second date of death on the calendar. Deborah was the only one who lit a Yahrzeit candle for her father, though while she was alive Deborah's grandmother, who had outlived her son by several years, had lit one, too, and Deborah found herself missing her grandmother along with her father when she decided to visit Mrs. Fink.

She had not seen the old lady in several weeks and Deborah thought it would lift her spirits to spend a little time there. The door was open and Deborah walked in, knocking on the open door and calling hello in a soft voice. For a moment Deborah thought she must be on the wrong floor. The room was empty, the bed stripped.

Deborah stood in the middle of the room, unable to move. She did not think that Mrs. Fink had been sent home. The words *baruch dayan ha'emet*—blessed be the true judge, the formulaic phrase recited on learning of a death—rose to her lips, but she could not say them aloud, in part because she hoped that Shirley was still alive but also because she did not feel like praising God. Mrs. Fink was an old woman and Deborah had seen children die, but somehow she felt bereft in a deep and personal and paralyzing way. She felt like a child herself.

She stood in the middle of the large room. She tried to conjure

Mrs. Fink but found herself unable to. The room smelled of disinfectant. She ought to have gone to the nurse's station to inquire but she felt rooted to the spot. She shut her eyes and simply stood still, hugging herself.

Deborah felt a heavy hand on her shoulder and jumped. Maribel, a kind, enormous nurse's aide, was standing beside her. She smelled like sweat and cookies and perfume. Her chin had many folds, her hair was very black. A tiny gold crucifix rode the ripples of her throat.

"It's OK, honey," Maribel said softly, standing close. "She came back."

Deborah did not know what this cryptic comment meant.

"The old lady. She had a heart attack. She coded, but she came back. We thought she was gone, everything was flat, but they shocked her and things started up again. Jesus must love that woman. She's in the ICU."

Deborah smiled and gave Maribel a kiss.

She went at once to the seventh floor. It seemed fitting that Shirley should have had such an experience. She was, after all, watched over, though it pained Deborah to think of that tiny body shocked into responsiveness by paddles. It was her understanding that Mrs. Fink had signed a do-not-resuscitate form—she had often spoken of her wish to join her husband in his world, rather than keeping him in her own. Deborah suspected the old woman would be enraged at her revival.

But Shirley had no strength for anger. Despite Maribel's description of her recovery as a miracle, Shirley looked terrible. Her teeth were beside her in a glass and her contracted mouth reminded Deborah of the little drawstring bag of jacks she had carried around as a child. Mrs. Fink was hooked up to more than one IV bag and her inner arms were bruised and patched with little Band-Aids. A light at the tip of one finger, measuring oxygen flow, made it glow like E.T.'s extraterrestrial touch. Her tiny legs, which Deborah had never seen but which were exposed now, were sheathed in rubber casings, like the "floaties" little children wore in swimming pools; they inflated at odd moments to promote circulation, filling with an alarming hiss. But this was not the reason for Shirley's transformation. Deborah could see at once that something terrible had happened to her inside as well as out.

Shirley simply shook her head no at Deborah's approach. Her eyes looked frightened.

Mrs. Fink's daughter, Nancy, was in the room. A handsome middle-aged woman, Nancy had a face that looked like the unlined version of her mother's. Deborah suspected that Nancy had had a face-lift. They had met once or twice before and Deborah had found her cold and suspicious. Once, early on, Nancy had asked Deborah to leave so she could be alone with her mother. When Deborah returned later that day, Shirley had said, "I'm not leaving you any money, you know." It was like Shirley to say something blunt and rude, and ordinarily Deborah would have laughed, but she blamed the daughter for the comment and felt stung for weeks.

Nancy scarcely acknowledged Deborah but, bending low over her mother to hear the mouthed, murmured words, straightened up and said, "My mother would like you to come back in an hour."

Shirley's voice sounded hoarse, whispery. No doubt she had been intubated; she was now breathing on her own but the breathing machine was pushed ominously close to her bed, a threatening presence.

Deborah pressed her hand on Shirley's forehead in lieu of the kiss she would like to have given her, but Shirley cringed as if she expected a blow and shut her eyes. It was terrible to see.

Deborah did not have the heart to visit other patients and killed half an hour wandering the floors. At a pay phone she called Lev at his office but got only his curt, recorded voice: "This is Lev Friedman at *Eureka* magazine—please leave a message." Deborah hung up. She called him again, this time at home, where he sometimes worked, and where a slightly warmer message told her that nobody was there to answer the phone. Deborah wanted to hang up but found herself talking into the machine—"I'm thinking about you . . . I'm here at the hospital so no point calling back but I just wanted to say—" What? She paused, hating the needy sound of her voice, as if perhaps he were there and would pick up the phone after all. The same wish, she realized, that came over her when she prayed—Pick up the phone! Pick up the phone! The machine beeped. Lev's machine didn't tolerate long messages. She had been cut off before. She did not bother calling back.

Instead she sat, wasting time she did not have, in the visitors' room, watching the *Jerry Springer* show with the stupefied relatives of a man dying of emphysema. They ate McDonald's takeout, their children playing glumly with action-adventure figures while on the television two sisters accused each other of sleeping with the same man. The man, with the inevitable earring, tattoos, and mustache, looked boastful and abashed and mildly retarded. The sisters looked slutty, depraved. They made Deborah think of high school, which only deepened her gloom, as did the penetrating odor of french fries and ketchup.

When Deborah returned to the ICU, Shirley's teeth were back in her mouth. Her hair had been brushed out of her eyes and clipped by a barrette at the top of her head the way you clip a child's hair. But the same look of adult despair was in her eyes. Her daughter was no longer in the room.

Deborah pulled up a chair alongside Shirley's bed and took her hand. She felt, despite the look in Shirley's eyes, a thrill of excitement. She was curious, more than curious, to find out what had happened.

But Shirley remained silent and Deborah sat in silence, too, holding the old woman's hand. At last Deborah couldn't keep quiet any longer.

"Well," she said. "It sounds like you've really had a miracle."

But Shirley made a face, as if pained or offended by Deborah's remark. She was wearing an oxygen collar; they must have given her a tracheostomy. Somehow Deborah hadn't noticed it before. It meant that Shirley could speak only in a whisper, since air otherwise leaked out the hole in her throat. And in a whisper, Shirley told Deborah what had happened. Or rather, what hadn't.

"I was unconscious," she said. "They tell me I was gone . . ."

She hesitated and fell silent. Deborah thought perhaps she had fallen asleep. But her eyes were open wide as if reliving some unspeakable horror.

"Shirley," said Deborah softly, "what happened?"

For a few moments more the old woman lay mute. Then she mouthed a word that Deborah could not quite make out. She leaned close and the old woman moved her lips again.

"I'm sorry," said Deborah, "I'm just not sure . . ,"

"Nothing!" Shirley hissed, air leaking from her throat and giving the word a ghastly overtone. She craned her head forward slightly from the pillow, like someone who had seen an awful apparition and was seeing it again: "There was nothing."

Something inside Deborah went cold.

Deborah did not believe in bright white lights beckoning to the other side and yet she had thought, perhaps, that Shirley might have encountered *something*. She had been halfway there already.

"I expected to find him," Shirley whispered, and Deborah knew she did not mean God but Seymour Fink, her husband of forty-seven years, whose presence she had felt so consistently and powerfully since his death.

"You didn't feel anything?" Deborah asked.

"Nothing," Shirley repeated, in her otherworldly whisper. "They tell me I was dead. But if I was dead I should have found him. Or at least felt him. But there was nothing there. A dark place, full of nothing." She shuddered.

No God. No Seymour. Nothing. She was ready to die and yet less ready than ever because now there was no place to go. She'd been had. Fooled. It was as if Seymour had put a pillow in the bed beneath the covers and slipped out. Betrayed in the end by the man she loved. Betrayed by life. Betrayed by death. She didn't say any of those things. She said only, "nothing there, nothing there."

She seemed half mad. But she wasn't.

The old woman was weeping. Deborah was not prepared. She realized how much she had counted on Shirley's unarticulated assurance of immortality. Deborah had come—what seemed like days ago—to cheer herself up, even if it was in the guise of a visit to a sick old lady. There was always something uplifting about Shirley, and Deborah always hoped a little of her calm conviction would rub off. She had been secretly thrilled when she heard from Maribel what had happened to Shirley.

It was clear that some awful change had taken place.

Deborah felt it as a change in herself, as if she, too, had lost something precious. She tried to ignite a sensation inside herself to counter Mrs. Fink, despite her own belief that feelings should never be forced. She called to her father but he did not come. Her own pilot light had blown out and she smelled nothing but gas. She literally found it difficult to breathe.

But Deborah forced a smile and squeezed Shirley's hand as she watched the creases in the old woman's face rout her tears in crazy directions.

Deborah was talking almost before she knew what she was saying. She was, she felt, violating her own practice of allowing a patient to simply talk no matter how painful the feelings. Deborah wanted to expunge the bad feelings in Shirley and herself.

"The rabbis have a category for what became of you," Deborah said. "They call it a *goses*. A person who isn't alive and isn't dead. It is a special category. It's a kind of suspended animation. You shouldn't expect to see God, or anyone else, in such a state."

"I shouldn't?"

"No," Deborah said firmly.

She always carried her little book of Psalms and she took it out of her bag.

"The psalmist talks a lot about what happened to you and about where you have been."

The old woman looked at her with interested eyes. She never wanted psalms recited aloud for her but she did not stop Deborah who, as much for her own sake as Mrs. Fink's, was chanting from Psalm 30: "You have raised my soul from the Lower World. You have kept me alive, lest I descend to the Pit . . ."

She paused at these lines. "Nobody really knows what 'the Pit' is," said Deborah. "Is it death or is it someplace worse than death, a place we all get stuck from time to time. Is it a place we go when we are still alive?"

"You think that's where I was?" Shirley asked.

"Yes," said Deborah. "And now you are back. And you know, if you had seen God, and if you had seen Seymour, you would not have come back. You would not have wished to live. And life, being on earth, is a great and mysterious and overriding virtue. You have children and grandchildren and things to do here you may not know the reason for. In some hidden way what happened," Deborah paused, incredulous at her own formulation but speaking nevertheless with force, as if she were trying to hypnotize Shirley, "what happened to you may have allowed you to remain alive, to keep living and wondering and hoping. To be on earth a little longer. And you will find, I think, the old feeling coming back."

Shirley turned her head away from Deborah, but Deborah could tell that she was listening intently and that she wanted Deborah to continue. Deborah returned to the book: " *'Weeping may endure for a night, but joy comes in the morning.'* " She paused and looked at Shirley, who was still facing the machine on the far side of the bed. "It was nighttime for you," Deborah said, "maybe for the first time. I think it is still nighttime right now for you. For a lot of people, this struggle, this darkness, is the way of things. You've been so blessed to have known a different reality."

Shirley didn't move and Deborah read on: " 'You hid Your face and I was terrified. I cried to you Adonai; and to You I made supplication. What profit is there in my blood when I go down to the pit? Shall dust praise you? Shall it declare Your truth? Hear, O Lord and be gracious to me: Lord, be my helper. You have turned my mourning into dancing: you have loosed my sackcloth and girded me with gladness.' "

Here Deborah looked again at Shirley. "That was definitely true for you. Your mourning for your husband, for Seymour, was turned into comfort. And it will happen again. I believe that it will."

She returned to her little book: " 'To the end that my glory may sing praise to you, and not be silent. O Lord my God, I will give thanks to you forever.' "

Shirley had rolled her head back toward Deborah. She said simply, whispering the words, "Read another one."

Deborah read more. She read Psalm 27, dwelling on the words, " 'Conceal not Your presence from me, do not turn your servant away in anger. You have been my help; neither cast me off nor abandon me.' "

She read aloud the favorite parts of her favorite psalms, the verses she sang to herself for comfort and recited with patients to give them strength. But the words were absorbing something of Shirley's dread experience and had a bitter taste in Deborah's mouth. It seemed an irony when she read, from Psalm 139, " 'Where could I go from Your spirit, or where could I flee from your presence. If I would ascend to heaven, You are there, and if I were to make my bed in the grave, You are there . . .' "

"So you think," Shirley asked, almost shyly, mouthing the words more than saying them, "just because I didn't feel him doesn't mean he wasn't there?"

"Of course not," said Deborah. "Have you ever been under anesthesia for surgery?"

"Yes," said Shirley. "I had a triple bypass nine years ago."

"Did you feel him then?"

"No," Shirley acknowledged. She had felt nothing. She had been awake one moment and the next moment she was awake again and what had happened in between was a blank.

"But that didn't mean you were gone. You were suspended. That's what we call it. Suspended animation. Neither here nor there."

Shirley seemed doubtful but a look of peace crept back into her features.

Deborah knew she was restoring to Shirley something she had lost. And all the while she hated herself because she felt—no, she knew!—that she was faking it. That Seymour was not waiting on the other side for Shirley but that he had in fact crumbled to dust long ago in the cemetery in Queens or New Jersey or wherever the hell it was, someplace like the cemeteries where numerous relatives of her own lay moldering, though her father—excruciating memory—had been cremated and his ashes scattered at Point Reyes National Seashore.

This time, when Deborah asked Shirley if she wanted to pray, the old woman said yes. Deborah was almost sorry she had asked. The psalms at least had already been written. But she took Shirley's hand and cleared her throat.

"Dear God, Source of Life," she began—but she felt, even as she spoke, that God was not there—"we pray that Shirley is healed in body and in mind. In soul and in spirit. We pray that she . . . We pray that Seymour . . ." Deborah groped for words. "We hope that the door that was opened between this world and the next, the door that let Shirley and Seymour find each other, doesn't remain shut. But if, for some reason, that door is closed, because Shirley came so close to dying that it looked like she would not need a door anymore at all—if that door is closed, we pray that Shirley will have the strength to be patient for that time when it opens again to receive her and reunite her with her beloved husband . . ."

"*Faker!*" a voice inside Deborah cried. "*There's nothing!*" But she kept talking, kept formulating words and thoughts. Tears ran down her face, not because, as sometimes happened, she felt how near God was, but because she felt God was not there at all and that she was speaking aloud in a cold white room, for the benefit of an old lady. She shut her eyes and kept talking—what was she saying? She didn't even know, the words came out and then a song of some sort. Her voice caught and she was silent, afraid to open her eyes again.

But when she opened her eyes she saw that Shirley was smiling faintly, through her exhaustion.

"God bless you, dear," she mouthed weakly, as if Deborah were deaf. A nurse had entered the room and begun drawing the curtains around Shirley's bed. She was going to get a sponge bath.

"God bless you, too," said Deborah. She felt weak, depleted. But she laid her hands on Shirley's head, the dry white hair, and this time Shirley did not flinch at all. Deborah recited the priestly benediction:

May God bless you and keep you,
May God's presence shine upon you, and be gracious to you,
May God's presence be with you and give you peace.

The ministering motion, the laying on of hands, always gave Deborah a kind of nameless calm, as if she were being blessed in the act of blessing. It restored her a little to do it now, but she wished someone were laying hands on her. She could almost feel her spirit passing out of her body, into the frail form of the old woman.

She had no strength left when she pressed the metal square that mechanically opened the ICU doors. The double doors swept open and Deborah almost banged into Nancy, who was walking with a man Deborah did not recognize, her husband, perhaps, or a friend. He had a solid, benevolent presence. Nancy hesitated for a moment and looked at Deborah expectantly but Deborah only nodded and walked past, down the quiet hospital corridor. How was it possible for her to remain upright? She felt an overwhelming urge to sink down against the wall, or to clamber onto one of the empty gurneys lined up in the corridor.

Nothing had changed. Mrs. Fink was still alive. A miracle, really, when you thought about it. Only it did not feel that way.

THE VISIT TO MRS. FINK left Deborah feeling blank and anxious. Though in general her work at the hospital buoyed her, she'd had, in the course of the past few years, several hospital encounters that had challenged her faith and left her exhausted. Ultimately, she'd always rebounded, even when—the memory still haunted her—a newborn was given only twenty-four hours to live and the parents, horrified by the verdict and their malformed child, had left her alone in the neonatal ICU so that it was Deborah who sat up with the unnamed infant, reciting psalms and prayers of her own devising.

But that child had not been able to speak to Deborah. Its mute suffering reduced her to tears, but she could imagine its young soul returning to God, no memories or attachments to surrender. Mrs. Fink, with her whispered report of nothingness, had opened a door onto darkness. The glue seemed gone from the world. Deborah was aware of an old fear that everything would fly into a million meaningless pieces.

That night was Shabbat. Deborah felt almost drugged as she stood up on the bimah of Temple Emunah in front of the congregation. The peaceful blue rug and the giant vases of white and yellow flowers, the rainbow light from the stained-glass windows as the sun set through the western exposure, the organ tones rising from their high, hidden pipes, the congregants dressed and expectant and spread out like a sea before her, usually filled Deborah with peaceful joy. But she felt like someone in a dream, naked and conspicuous and out of place. What was she doing up there? What was anyone doing there?

But that was her voice singing, "You shall love the Lord your God," and that was her head bowed, adoring the "ever-living God." And now Rabbi Zwieback was blessing the congregation, his stubby hands, cloven like hooves, raised in benediction. She lifted her own hands mechanically. Cantor Baumwald sang "Shabbat Shalom" and it was over.

Deborah and Lev had been invited to Shabbat dinner but Deborah said she thought she was coming down with something and wanted to eat at home. Lev felt a surprise of disappointment. He had gotten used to Sabbath gatherings: the candles; the ordered table with its twin loaves of bread, like husband and wife, lying under the silk cover; the glasses of wine and the little booklets containing blessings and songs that had been swiped from Jewish weddings and bore the names of bride and groom and the date of the wedding embossed on the cover; babies, dangling off-center from front-carriers like badly hung paintings, worn to the table by egalitarian fathers.

Back in her apartment, Deborah stood at the little table where she kept her grandmother's candlesticks and struck a match. Lev encircled her from behind. Deborah gathered the light toward herself with a beckoning gesture of both hands, repeated three times. Then she covered her eyes, chanted the blessing in a faint, almost inaudible voice, and remained silent, head bowed.

Usually Deborah included a prayer for her family and for whoever it was in the hospital or in her congregation who was sick or suffering. She always prayed for herself as well, believing it was important to ask for blessings. She tried to let her mind range out into the hurt world and then come back into the safety and sanctity of Shabbat. She shut her eyes more tightly and saw Mrs. Fink, lying shrunken in her hospital bed.

Dear God, she whispered in her heart at last. *Please restore her faith in You.*

Lev felt the intensity of her petition, whatever it was. He knew her father's Yahrzeit was coming up. Perhaps she was communing with her father. When Deborah removed her hands from over her eyes there were tears.

Despite the Sabbath, Deborah wanted to watch television and they sat on the couch and watched one quarter of a Knicks game and two-thirds of *The Postman Always Rings Twice*, with Lana Turner and John Garfield (whom Lev's father had always referred to by his given name, Julius Garfinkle). It was the sort of "normal" Friday night Lev used to crave. He often felt a pang of exclusion as they walked past crowded restaurants and bars, the lines outside of movie theaters, on their way to Shabbat dinner. But again he found himself missing the communal spirit of the evening they had given up, the song welcoming the Sabbath angels that preceded the meal.

Lev felt strangely unsettled though Deborah kept assuring him she was fine, just a little under the weather. They went to bed early and made love, Deborah with an abandon that thrilled Lev until he saw in her face that flickering moment of transport and torment he recognized from her prayers—something alien and unreachable.

Afterward they held each other for a long time.

A WEEK BEFORE PASSOVER, Lenora, the woman Deborah had counseled in her office, officially became a Jew. Deborah was on the *bet dín* that approved her conversion and afterward she accompanied Lenora to the mikvah. Certainly Rabbi Zwieback wasn't going to watch her jump naked into a pool of water, much as he might have liked to. He conducted his conversions in front of the open ark in the synagogue's main sanctuary. It was Deborah who had persuaded Lenora to seal her conversion with a ritual dunking, despite the optional status the Reform movement gave actual immersion.

Lenora had loved the idea—it was, after all, a kind of rebaptism into her new faith. She would have done it anyway, just because Deborah had suggested it. Since her first visit, when Rabbi Zwieback had been out of town, Lenora had come back several times. She admired Deborah with schoolgirl intensity.

Deborah had developed a real affection for the earnest Lenora. Once upon a time, in junior high school, Deborah would have resented Lenora just for being named Lenora and having such fine hair and for serving as a shiksa magnet for smart, athletic, self-confident Jews of the sort she was now going to marry and on whom Deborah had wasted an untold amount of adolescent angst and energy. But that was a long time ago. The smart, athletic, self-confident Jews had grown up and become members of her congregation and she would not have wanted to marry any of them. She had, however, made her peace with them. Though many had fulfilled the promise of their early arrogance, many more had suffered humanizing adversity—failure in business or in marriage, an autistic child, the death of parents or siblings, the pain and humiliation of unexpected illness. It wasn't that she needed them wounded in order to like them so much as that their wounds exposed a part of themselves that had previously been hidden. Becoming a rabbi had given her new eyes. She now saw women like Lenora as yearning souls who, if anything, craved Deborah's exotic intensity as much as Deborah had once envied their cool detachment. The old categories had ceased to exist.

A kind of friendship had sprung up between Deborah and Lenora, though Deborah did not share much about her own life and was feeling a little worn out by Lenora's spiritual hunger. When she came to the customary reading from the Book of Ruth, Lenora glanced not at her fidgety fiancé, who had arrived late from his office, but at Deborah, as if she were reading it for her:

" 'Entreat me not to leave you, or to return from following after you. For wherever you go, I will go. Wherever you lodge, I will lodge. Your people shall be my people, and your God my God. Where you die, I will die, and there will I be buried.' "

Deborah smiled at Lenora but she felt embarrassed. She stifled an inner qualm of unworthiness that mutated into resentment at being made somehow emblematic, though she knew it was her role to be an emblem, one she had in the past accepted and cultivated and enjoyed. Confusion and fear stirred in her.

Her bad mood got worse. She was impatient with the ceremony—which she usually loved—and with the slow, pompous way Zwieback ran it. Lenora declaimed the next reading in a proud, tremulous voice, like a child in a school play:

I am a Jew because my faith demands of me no abdication of the mind.
I am a Jew because my faith requires of me all the devotion of my heart.
I am a Jew because in every place where suffering weeps I weep.
I am a Jew because at every time when despair cries out, I hope.
I am a Jew because the word of the people Israel is the oldest and the newest.
I am a Jew because the promise of Israel is the universal promise . . .

Deborah could not help thinking, *But you're not a Jew, Lenora. You're a Christian who's marrying a Jew and who wants to be a Jew but who never will be.*

When I asked you about Christmas at the bet din you said you'd have a small tree. A small tree! Hadn't Zwieback ever mentioned that?

It was true that poor Lenora had turned beet red when she realized it was the wrong answer. Remembering that, Deborah softened toward her. Who was she to say what kind of Jew Lenora would be, or what kind of children she would raise? Or what Dave, her fiancé, with his set jaw and anxious bearing, was really thinking as he sat up on the bimah in one of the high-backed chairs usually reserved for officers of the temple, seemingly consulting his Palm Pilot? It was she herself Deborah was thinking about. *If I had to convert right now*, she wondered, *would I do it?* Nothing in that long litany had provided the reason she craved.

Deborah stumbled particularly over *no abdication of the mind*. A fine sentiment, rational and sane. But what kind of religion would that be? Judaism seemed suddenly like a course in civics.

After the ceremony in the synagogue ended, and Lenora had received from the president of the congregation a pair of candlesticks, and wept, and hugged Rabbi Zwieback and Deborah and the two witnesses, and kissed her fiancé who had to get back to work, Deborah and Lenora walked to the ritual bath in the West Seventies.

It was a cool, moist, windy day. Pink blossoms rained down on West Seventieth Street from a cherry tree blooming in the front courtyard of a brownstone. Gingko trees waved tiny, new-grown leaves like infant hands. Lev, who went birding with increasing zeal as spring approached, and who always stopped to check on the progress of leafing trees, had made Deborah more aware than ever of the unfolding of spring. She enjoyed his enthusiasm but spring gave her a great nameless ache, a longing she could not quite identify that verged on pain. She understood why the Jewish New Year began in fall, when everything was beginning to die.

She felt herself becoming morbid and she did not like it. She was also aware of Lenora looking at her as they walked along, glancing at her with shy concern. She *is* like Ruth, Deborah thought with affection, walking a new path, even if she isn't quite sure where it will lead.

"Are you all right?" Lenora asked Deborah, putting her arm around her when they had stopped at a light.

"I should be asking you that," said Deborah. "You've just done a very big thing."

"I'm fine," said Lenora. "My family's been very good about the whole thing. I haven't lost my family, just certain things. I'm sorry about the Christmas tree comment—that was really stupid. I know we can't have one. But there'll be other things. And we'll have our own family, too."

They had talked about all this before. She and Lenora walked in silence for a moment until Lenora said, "But what about you?"

"What makes you ask in that way?"

"You don't seem yourself," said Lenora. "You seem distracted and . . . sad. I hope you don't mind my saying something."

"I appreciate your concern," said Deborah, a little stiffly. "I suppose I am a little distracted."

Too many things were on Deborah's mind and she did not feel she could share any of them. Since her visit to Mrs. Fink she had felt a deepening gloom. Outwardly she did her work, observing the social and professional and religious forms, but inwardly she felt that a bottomless darkness had opened up and that she was constantly tiptoeing around the rim.

She had found herself incapable of sharing this with Lev and as a result she both wanted him around and feared him at the same time. He rented his studio apartment from a journalist friend posted to Africa named Bill McGovern and their deal was that Lev would vacate when Bill came home. Bill was coming home the second night of Passover, and though Lev could have gone to his parents' or to another friend's, Deborah had recently invited him to move in for the month. Her position at the temple would be compromised if it was discovered that a man she wasn't married to was living in her apartment. But the chances of this were small and something reckless, defiant in Deborah made her not care. It would be pure hypocrisy not to invite Lev—he often spent the night with her. What real difference would this make?

And she wanted him around. She found his presence deeply comforting and she knew that eventually she would talk to him openly. But she had always prided herself on a certain self-sufficiency.

She felt on the verge of pouring out everything to Lenora, but it would be unseemly and unprofessional. Friendly as they were, Deborah was in some sense her rabbi.

"If you don't mind my asking," Lenora said, fixing her bright, intuitive blue eyes on Deborah, "are you with someone? I've seen you with that tall man with red hair."

"Yes," said Deborah. "Lev."

"He's your husband?"

"My boyfriend," said Deborah, thinking, what a silly term, but then wondering if the term didn't suit Lev, who had a certain boyish quality alongside a certain quality of being prematurely old.

"Is he a rabbi, too?" Lenora asked.

"Oh no," said Deborah with a little laugh. "He writes about science."

"But he's religious," said Lenora. She said this more as a statement than a question, but it hung in the air like a question.

"What makes you say that?" asked Deborah. "Is it because I'm a rabbi?"

"Well, yes. And because he looks religious."

"It's the red hair," said Deborah.

"And something in the face. He has a lot of quietness."

Deborah smiled.

"In some ways he is religious," she said. "Temperamentally, I think. And . . . in other ways, too. I think he's religious without knowing it, if that's possible. But he doesn't observe very much. Sometimes I feel it isn't me he loves—it's my . . . faith. It's like he's worshiping by proxy. He doesn't realize . . ."

Deborah cut herself off. How could she have said so much? But Lenora was merely nodding, taking it in.

"Do you think you'll get married?"

"He called off his first marriage," Deborah said. "He has a lot of fears."

"Is he afraid of *you*?"

Deborah thought for a moment. "I don't think so. No. I think he's much more afraid of himself."

She was appalled at the ease with which she had betrayed Lev's secrets to a virtual stranger. After so much withholding she was suddenly afraid she would spill everything and she made an effort to rein herself in.

"I think all men would call off their weddings," Lenora said, "if they could do it without consequences."

"Oh I don't know," said Deborah. "I think men need attachment as much as women. They just might not like to admit it."

"My therapist told me that all marriages are mixed marriages," said Lenora. "Even if both people have the same religion. Everybody really comes from a different world and sees things in a different way."

Deborah nodded but didn't answer.

They had arrived at the unassuming building where the mikvah lady lived on an upper floor; the tiled pools, one for men and several for women, were down below.

"Here we are," Deborah said.

Deborah loved the ritual bath and the old Eastern European woman who ran it, whom everyone referred to simply as "the mikvah lady," though in fact her name was Fruma Lubkin. Her name was written in ink in a little slot above the buzzer.

They were buzzed in and trudged up the stairs to Mrs. Lubkin's apartment. She opened the door a crack, the chain still in place. She wore a faded flowered housedress. Her prune-colored wig, like something an abandoned doll would wear, was slightly crooked. Like a lot of Orthodox women of a certain age, she had the look of an aging drag queen or—Deborah always felt guilty about the association—an old madam. You paid her first and Lenora had brought cash, as instructed, and handed the bills over to Mrs. Lubkin who, though she had removed the chain, kept the door only partly open, counted the money, and then said to Deborah, "You know where is. I come."

Deborah led Lenora to the changing room several floors below. Only once had she been invited into Mrs. Lubkin's apartment, which was heavy with the smell of roasting chicken and candy and something ranker—herring? Deborah had come alone to inquire about using the facility for Reform converts. She'd anticipated opposition, but Mrs. Lubkin had said only, "Jew is Jew." Deborah had sat on a plastic-covered couch, which had clung to her exposed thighs, and learned that Mrs. Lubkin's entire family had been gassed at Auschwitz, not merely her parents but three sisters and two brothers. Her youngest sister, Chaya, was only three years old. Fruma had run away the day before deportation with a friend from her town and together they had hidden in the woods and had learned English—this was the part that amazed Deborah the most—by reading *The Sun Also Rises*, which somehow had made its way into the Polish forest. There was a certain Hemingwayesque curtness to her manner. She told her terrible story with a resigned shrug. How she had pieced her life back together, met and married Mr. Lubkin, who had since died, rediscovered her faith, these were all unanswered. And perhaps Mrs. Lubkin could not have answered them. Deborah had always anticipated a follow-up visit but she was never again invited back inside and no opportunity presented itself.

Deborah smelled the mikvah water while still on the stairs. It had the chlorinated odor of a swimming pool. The chemical smell, the echoing slap of water in an enclosed space, gave Deborah the same tang of excitement and nostalgia and anticipated competition she always felt around pools, having been on the swim team in high school.

A young woman was using a hair dryer in the waiting room while a middle-aged woman who could only be the mother looked on. They were clearly Orthodox. The mother had a very stylish wig and, though their skirts were ankle-length, the daughter had on Manolo Blahnik open-toe sling-backs that Deborah herself had passed up as too expensive and too outré for temple. Deborah assumed that the daughter was going to be married and had gone to the bath in preparation.

Ordinarily she would have inquired, wished them mazel tov, chatted a little. She loved this ethnic, locker-room intimacy, a little glimpse of what real community might be. But she did not speak to the Orthodox women. She left Lenora to change and shower, and went into the tiled area overlooking the water where she could watch the proceedings.

Deborah herself had never been in the water, though she often imagined she would go before getting married. How nice it would be to have a mother who would take you, who had been herself. She did not go, though Reuben had asked her to. The hypocrisy of his wishing to honor ritual purity while sleeping with her out of wedlock—and after having explained to her why he could never marry her—had astonished and depressed her. The memory of it brought up buried bitterness.

But it hadn't diminished her affection for the place itself. Or for the mikvah lady and the brusque way she instructed brides-to-be and would-be converts how to immerse themselves for the first time. "Everything off—the clothes, the jewels, the Band-Aids." Deborah had already explained that every inch of skin must touch the water. Lenora had listened like a dutiful, nervous schoolgirl.

There was always a kind of poignant strangeness about standing in the humid subterranean room. Deborah had been to Auschwitz and seen the tiled rooms of artificial showers, which, she reflected, had not looked so different. But of course that space was for killing. Lenora was becoming a Jew. Here was life. Here was a victory, an undoing of death. But Deborah could not keep the other associations at bay. She felt the tiny ghost of Mrs. Lubkin's littlest sister, only three, and felt her eyes grow full. Lev's grandmother had walked into such a place. Is that why every enclosed space made him gasp for air? Lev would have recognized her reaction to the space; it was almost as if she was having his association. He saw ghosts everywhere.

Is he too Jewish for me? she thought suddenly, with grim amusement. And then wondered if it was true that all marriages are intermarriages. Deborah herself felt like a mismarriage, a weird amalgam of conflicting feelings. She wished Lev was with her at that very moment and felt in a mysterious way that he was. She was glad he was going to be moving in.

Mrs. Lubkin was suddenly standing beside her. Despite the warmth, she was wearing a cardigan over her housedress. She seemed to be about a foot shorter than Deborah but she had a stolid authority as she stood next to a puddle in her worn shoes, the sides slit to accommodate her swollen feet. She nodded at Deborah and Deborah smiled back.

Lenora emerged from the changing room in a short white bathrobe. She slid the robe off and handed it to Deborah with a shy smile. She left her little pink flip-flops by the edge of the steps leading down to the pool, then folded her towel and set it down on top of the flip-flops. Lenora's naked, pale body gleamed, her hair, darkened by the shower, hung close against her skull. She descended the tiled steps. Her body seemed tapered as if already distorted by water; she had wide hips, narrow shoulders and small breasts. Women's bodies were never what you expected, Deborah reflected.

And then, with Deborah and the mikvah lady looking on, Lenora jumped in awkwardly, her fingers spread like a pouncing cat so that the water would reach even in the spaces between her fingers, as she had been instructed. Deborah had in the past wept at this moment, but watching Lenora flop froglike into the water and then dunk herself she felt instead a detached impatience.

She experienced, almost simultaneously, an unexpected jealousy. She would like to have jumped in the pool, too, and swum away. Lenora came up for air as if she had just crossed the channel, though the tiny tiled area was just for dunking; you swam only in your mind. But Deborah had lost the ability to see it as bottomless, a mystical well. Or rather, her mind refused to allow her the flights and plunges that had come so naturally to her in the past. *My faith demands of me no abdication of mind . . .*

Lenora had to do the whole thing twice. The first time she had left a crown of hair above the water and the mikvah lady was a stickler for total immersion. Lenora looked sheepishly at Deborah. She listened to the verdict, dripping and disappointed, like a camper who had failed a diving test, then dunked herself a final time.

This time there were no complaints. The mikvah lady yelled "Kosher!" in her sweet, strident voice, and Lenora became a Jew.

THERE WAS A MESSAGE from Neal on the answering machine.

Deborah heard it first and played it to Lev. There was no mistaking the awkward, urgent voice that lurched forward like a car with the brake and the gas pedal depressed simultaneously. The words were spoken to Lev but were really for Deborah.

"Bring your friend," Neal said. "I have some . . . very important . . . questions. I have some . . . information."

Lev had heard that voice many times before. In the early months of his illness, Neal had called urgently requesting a camera so that he could document hospital abuses, and admonishing Lev to keep it hidden so that "they" didn't confiscate it. Lev had rushed over to Columbia Presbyterian with a disposable camera concealed in a sweater, realizing only when he got a good look at Neal and heard him speak about laser beams and mental vasectomies that he had stepped inside a delusion. Lev's very susceptibility had unsettled him more than Neal's madness.

The message stirred Deborah. It called to her out of a buried darkness; Jonah praying from the belly of the whale.

"We have to go," she said.

Lev resented the thrill in her voice and felt an unwelcome pang of jealousy. He was annoyed at himself for leaving Deborah's number on the answering machine of Bill's apartment. But he heard himself say, "Of course we have to."

Neal was back at the group home. Carol Marcus answered the door of the dilapidated but tidy brick townhouse in Brooklyn where her son lived with thirteen other voluntary patients. The vestibule smelled strongly of cigarette smoke and exterminator poison and the meat sauce two of the residents had cooked in a large vat. Deborah was touched by a little needlepoint sign that said simply, "Bless Our Home," framed and hanging slightly off center.

Mrs. Marcus embraced Lev warmly.

"Oh, Lev!" she said. "Neal will be so happy you came."

There was none of the resentment Lev usually experienced when he ran into her on the street, only warmth and resignation. Carol had once said to Lev, "Neal was better adjusted than you, wasn't he?" It was during Neal's first hospitalization and Lev had let the comment go. Besides, it had been true. Neal *had* been better adjusted, or at least more self-confident. He had more friends. He was a better student, a better talker, a better musician, a better athlete. But as it turned out, he was also crazy.

Carol seemed unusually exhausted.

"How is he?" Lev asked.

Mrs. Marcus started to cry. She pulled a crumpled tissue out of the sleeve of her beige cardigan; she expected to cry in the course of her day.

Deborah hugged her as if she had known her all her life.

Lev could see down the hallway into the dining room. A few residents were still sitting over their meal but most had dispersed. Someone was playing show tunes on an upright piano.

Lev was never sure of the rules of the place, but his understanding was that people could come and go as they pleased, as long as they checked in with the counselors each morning for medicine and signed in every evening by ten. Lev had visited Neal at the home before, though he seldom recognized anyone besides Mildred, the spry social worker who ran the place. Residents often vanished into hospitals for long stretches. Some never came back.

Lev wrote about mental illness for *Eureka*. He had written about drugs like Zyprexa and had visited other homes besides Neal's. Several had been far drearier, with patients beached on their beds in stifling rooms. This was comfortable by comparison, with a sense of actual community. There was a "chore wheel" on the wall of the sort Lev recalled from his bunk in sleepaway camp—where Neal had slept on the bed above him. Still, the home could not escape its aura of quiet devastation.

"He's upstairs," Carol said. "I'm afraid he may have to go back."

Back meant to the hospital.

They found Neal lying fully dressed on his bed. He was wearing one of his business suits from the days when he had worked, dark blue with pinstripes, a white wrinkled shirt, and no tie. There were obscure streaks of brown on one lapel.

Deborah was surprised at how handsome Neal looked, with his head of dark curls and brown, almond eyes. His face, though bloated from whatever medications he was taking, had, in its roundness, the ethereal aspect of a Byzantine mosaic that survived even the silliness of the nylon yarmulke rising up awkwardly on his head like a dunce cap.

Seeing Neal overwhelmed Lev with guilt. He knew better than to embrace his friend—Neal had recoiled from that sort of contact in the past. He bowed his head in greeting. But Neal did not stop staring at Deborah.

"It's so nice to meet you finally," Deborah said, with complete ease, shaking Neal's hand. "Thank you so much for inviting me."

Henry Kissinger had told him that there would be spies. He had recognized Lev but he knew, too, that there were clever dolls that only looked like people you knew who did not wish him to solve the riddles that lay before him. Could he be sure Deborah was someone to trust?

"Thank you for coming," Neal brought out at last.

Lev was ashamed that he had tried to talk Deborah out of joining him. What reason did he have for keeping her away beyond the usual unspecified superstitious dread surrounding his interactions with Neal? Unless it was something in the way Neal had begun asking about Deborah. His thoughts were tangled up with religious fantasies, and with other sorts of fantasies, too. Did she go to the ritual bath? What prayers did she say before bed? Lev did not like the questions he asked.

Deborah's insistence made Lev feel that it was Deborah who had questions for Neal. Lev believed that her hospital visits were making her soul-sick and he did not see how Neal could help her. And yet she did seem more peaceful in his presence.

Deborah had a way, Lev had noticed, of thanking the people for whom she was doing a kindness. She was persuasive, often because she really was grateful for a chance to feel herself of use. Just being there, shedding her human light, made the dim room less gloomy and made Neal seem less a castaway. His single bed no longer seemed an island now that Deborah sat beside it.

Lev felt his own irrelevance and drifted away from Neal's bedside. He and Carol sat on folding chairs near the unmade bed of Neal's roommate. On the floor beside the bed was a Bible with a filled ashtray on top of it. It seemed everyone reached for the same supports. Above the bed were neatly cut out images of naked women snipped from *Playboy* and *Penthouse* and stuck to the wall with Scotch tape.

When Lev was sixteen, he and Neal had gone to Show World, the pornographic emporium in Times Square. Neal had doctored their student IDs, though they were never even asked their age—Neal was already shaving and Lev kept the hood of his sweatshirt up. They were each sold a handful of octagonal tokens by an indifferent man behind a glass window. The tokens, tattooed with the silhouette of a naked showgirl, were in themselves exciting, if you didn't think about who had handled them. They'd walked trembling down a long red corridor lined with tiny, red-doored rooms, like phone booths in hell. Lev, always claustrophobic, still remembered the click of the door behind him. Neal was next door. They had anticipated a woman dancing, but it was hard-core porn on multiple channels, arousing and vaguely sickening—anal sex, group sex, blow jobs—and every minute the screen went black and asked for another token. Lev's head was spinning from claustrophobia and desire and fear. Better not to look at the floor.

They each burst out of their booths at the same moment. There had been grand plans of staying for a live show but there was no discussion in the corridor as they all but ran from the place, laughing uproariously and taunting each other as they walked home—"Did you?" "Did you?" "Did you?" Neal was convinced—shades of his later illness?—that everyone was secretly filmed, and Lev, aroused as he was, would as soon have shot himself as unzipped his pants in that place.

Lev chatted with Carol, filling her in on some of Neal's old friends whom he was still in touch with. Carol's curiosity was tinged with impatience and suppressed outrage. None of them came to visit, she informed him. Only Lev. And of course Lev did not come often.

While they were speaking, Lev strained to catch what Neal was saying; each swaddled word seemed to hang in the air before Deborah gently gathered it in. Neal had been studying Jewish texts with a local Lubavitcher rabbi and there was a passage of Talmud Neal had puzzled over with Lev on several occasions. It was the parable of the four sages who entered *Pardes*—a kind of orchard or garden or maybe even Paradise. There the rabbis looked on God. One went mad, one became a convert, one died. Only Rabbi Akiva, the greatest of the sages, entered in peace and left in peace. The parable held great mystical fascination for Neal.

Lev had discussed this parable with Deborah, who explained that *Pardes* was also an acronym of the four types of talmudic interpretation—*pshat, remez, drasha,* and *sod. Pshat* meant the simple meaning, *sod* meant the secret meaning. Lev could never remember what the intermediate terms meant but it didn't matter—Neal was fixed only on *sod*, the secret meaning. Why did God kill you? Why did God make you mad? What was Akiva's secret—was it something he did or just who he was?

But Neal was unable to formulate these questions now that Deborah was here to ask. He'd had something to tell her but he could not remember what it was. Someone was jamming his thoughts.

"Focus on the real and now," he thought, repeating the phrase he had been given by Dr. Emannuel. But that smell of lemon permeating his brain was eating his memory. He tried hard to ignore the voices thrumming in his head, but the effort was too great. He began to shift uncomfortably in bed. A great weight seemed to be pinning him down.

Deborah saw what was happening.

"Neal," she said, "you look tired. If you ever have anything you'd like to ask me . . ."

Deborah printed her address on one of the scraps of paper Neal kept beside the bed for the urgent scribbling he did when seized by voices requiring transcription. Neal held the scrap in his trembling hand and studied it as if it was rich with "*sod*," secret meaning. Neal held the paper close. He was not wearing his glasses and he squinted, as if studying a foreign script. A shadow seemed to darken his face and he said, in a low husky voice, "I know who you are."

Deborah had visited enough people with mental illness to know that Neal's brain, wadded as it was with medication, was shading into paranoia. But she could not help herself. She leaned closer and asked softly, "Who am I?"

Lev, watching this encounter, strained unsuccessfully to hear what they were saying. Neal had always had a questioning intensity that Lev admired. At the Friedman family dinner table, Neal, when he was a guest, would ask Lev's father questions that Lev himself never dared ask. What had happened to his parents? Had he ever seen a Nazi rally? Lev had learned more about his father from those dinners than he had in his entire conversational life with his father. Later, after he was already sick, Neal's obsession with the Holocaust and those touched by it grew and he often spoke of Lev's father as an "emissary" or a "messenger" in a way that made Lev deeply uncomfortable, precisely because he had sometimes felt that way himself.

There was something parodic about the world Neal lived in that made Lev feel implicated in the general off-kilter aura of the home. Neal once told him that mentally, he had to keep himself in the basement. He wanted to lift the lid and let himself out but then he wouldn't be himself anymore; he'd be crazy. His trap was that his medicated mask was closer to his "real" self than the demons that lurked behind it, but giving in to the mask meant giving up the most alive part of himself—which explained why Neal sometimes stopped taking his medication. But who hadn't felt he had a truer, sleeping self hidden beneath the face given to the world? Hadn't Lev hoped to abandon a false version of himself at the altar as much as he'd fled Jenny? The problem was figuring out what self or selves replaced it.

Carol was telling him, in a desperate undertone, how bad things had gotten. The medicine was failing, she was at her wit's end. There had been an "incident" the week before, she said, lowering her voice even more. Neal had tried to choke one of the counselors. They wanted to send him back to the hospital but she had begged Mildred, and the group home staff agreed it was an aberration. They adjusted his medication instead.

"He's an angel," said Carol, shaking her head sadly.

Lev agreed, though he remembered stories of Neal patrolling the living room of his mother's house with a kitchen knife. Fearing aliens. Spies. The cartoon clichés of psychosis. Neal's mother had shut herself in the bathroom and called 911 on the cell phone.

"It's not his fault," said Lev. "It's an accident of chemistry."

"Screw chemistry," she hissed, with whispered fury. But then began apologizing for her outburst. She was afraid of driving people away. Her husband, a Columbia math professor—Lev had used his textbook in ninth-grade algebra—had not been able to deal with Neal's illness, and her reaction to Neal's illness, and had left.

Lev heard Deborah singing *"Gesher Tzar"*—*"the whole world is a narrow bridge, and the main thing is not to be afraid at all."* Neal's eyes were closed; she had sung him to sleep. Or whatever he was taking had knocked him out. The nylon kippah had drifted onto the mattress.

Neal's big pale hand was still holding the piece of paper Deborah had given him. He seemed more drugged than usual, just an outline of himself.

"Be kind," Lev's father had often said, quoting someone from somewhere, "for everyone you meet is fighting a great battle."

Lev forced his attention back to Carol. He felt sorry for her but he wanted desperately for her to stop talking. Involuntarily, he glanced at the naked figures dancing above the bed. Carol's voice went on and on, feeding on itself. From time to time she let out a mirthless burst of laughter. Then she went back to her story, filling in the dreary details against the backdrop of Deborah's song.

LEV'S PARENTS went to Atlanta to join Jacob and Penny and Margaret for Passover. Penny was pregnant and feeling too ill to travel. It was the first trip his father had taken since getting out of the hospital—a large undertaking, and Lev felt guilty for not joining them. But he had a powerful desire to be with Deborah, who had to remain in New York to conduct services.

Clearly something was happening to her. She had become moody and withdrawn. She hurled herself into Passover preparations, hauling out her grandmother's dishes from the storage room in the basement of her apartment, boiling the silverware and purging her apartment of *chometz*, the leavening associated with bread that was forbidden during the holiday.

Passover had always brought out in Deborah an Orthodox impulse beyond anything she'd learned in rabbinic school. This year Deborah felt an added intensity, a kind of desperation as she mopped and scrubbed and boxed and boiled and sorted. Her scrubbing was an almost atavistic attempt, more vigorous than usual, at self-renewal. An urge, unspoken even to herself, to recapture something she had lost. Lev helped Deborah conduct the ritual search for chometz the night before Passover, moving through the darkened apartment with a lit candle, a feather, and a wooden spoon, sweeping up the little disks of symbolic bread that Deborah had wrapped in tinfoil.

A few minutes later, standing in her darkened kitchen, reading by the glow of the little candle, Deborah chanted from a page of the Passover Haggadah proclaiming all the chometz in the house that had been overlooked—"*k'afra d'ara*"—as the dust of the field. Deborah recited the Aramaic formula as if driving a demon out of her home. The light flickered in her dark eyes and the shadows played on her broad, illuminated face. The Yahrzeit candle she had lit earlier in the evening for her father burned on the counter, the two flames answering each other. And Lev, for reasons he could not identify, looked into Deborah's face and felt a flicker of fear.

They went to a seder hosted by a friend of Deborah, a Conservative rabbi named Wendy about whom Deborah, with the blunt ill-humor she could not restrain, observed, "She'd be a better rabbi if her ass wasn't so big."

All evening she felt detached, critical. What a pretentious way to make kiddush, she thought, as Wendy chanted the blessing over the wine in her pseudocantorial voice. Wendy had a nervous blink, her eyelids fluttering as if she were getting rained on. Deborah found Wendy's attempts at leading a discussion about freedom and order banal, pat, self-congratulatory.

Deborah knew this carping was a symptom of her mood. She remembered Dick Rubinstein, a rabbinic school professor of homiletics, telling her a story during office hours. It came from a book by Claude Lévi-Strauss about South America. Dick had been a hippie in the sixties, had traveled widely in the East, and had almost become a Buddhist. He wore sandals and socks even in winter and Deborah, who came from California seeking a more hard-core East Coast sensibility, had mild contempt for Dick and for his class. After one class, in which Deborah had mercilessly critiqued a student's sermon, Dick had asked her to visit him during office hours. Without a word he had taken down this book by Claude Lévi-Strauss from the shelf and read the epigraph aloud. It was a story about a medicine man in a certain tribe who one day lost his faith in the magic he was performing. This was a terrible trauma and the effect it had on him was profound. What saved him—though in a way it was also his undoing—was that he became a critic of other medicine men, exposing their tricks because he knew them so well. But he did not stop practicing medical magic. On the contrary, he hurled himself into his practice even more. He became, in his own confession to the anthropologist, the best faker of all.

After reading this story aloud to her, Dick had pushed his glasses up on his head and said, "It's a good warning for every rabbi, don't you think? Denouncing the practices of others is often a measure of our own religious insecurity. We'd like to denounce ourselves but that's not convenient so we train our criticisms on our fellow practitioners. Meanwhile, we're convinced we're simply the smoothest fakers around.

"You're too young," Dick continued. "Too passionate. Too gifted at this to give in so early, before you've even begun."

It was, Deborah often felt, the best lesson she had ever received. And though she had never wholly lost her critical impulse—she couldn't help it—she had kept it in check and found that good things came to her when she did. But watching Wendy she felt all her critical instincts rise to the surface. She looked like a blind person with her soft, slightly averted, flinching face. How pretentiously she swayed! There was something mannish in her manner. After kiddush, Wendy sat down before drinking, leaning exaggeratedly to the left, as the Haggadah prescribed.

It's all ersatz, Deborah thought. *Cobbled together. An act.*

Even as she had these thoughts Deborah felt ashamed of them. Wendy noticed her staring and flashed her a warm smile.

The group was chanting *"Ha-lachma"*: *"This is the bread of affliction which our forefathers ate in the land of Egypt."* On her right, Lev was staring hard into his Haggadah as he joined in. He wasn't so much singing as mouthing the words in his noiseless, shy-man, lip-synching fashion. He seemed suddenly foolish. She looked away.

THAT NIGHT, after Lev had fallen asleep, Deborah got up and sat by the kitchen window smoking cigarette after cigarette. The moon was visible, high and round and faintly pink.

Deborah loved the full moon. It signaled the start of many Jewish holidays and Deborah had always been moved that she could look up the same as the ancients had—even in New York, over the tops of skyscrapers—and that a reckoning could still be made. Judaism often seemed at odds with the natural world, and she was grateful for this lunar alignment with Jewish time. She sometimes thought of the moon as being pregnant for the holidays, ready to give birth to a new season.

But when Deborah looked out the window and saw the pale full moon, signaling the arrival of Passover, she did not feel her customary elation. The moon seemed incomplete, a limbless bust of marble.

She looked at her life suddenly, so filled with ritual objects and calendric rhythms, the Passover candlesticks, boxes of matzah, her grandmother's dishes, two sets of boiled silverware, and she felt like someone who had been expecting a baby and in preparation had bought a bassinet and a swing and baby clothes and a baby carrier and a bouncy seat and many books on child rearing. But then the baby hadn't come. She was surrounded by objects that reminded her of the baby and yet she was alone.

There was an emptiness at her core that Deborah had not experienced for a long time. She felt it almost like a physical weight, a tumor inside her, and she wondered fleetingly if perhaps she was sick; perhaps she was dying.

"God, source of life," she began in a mental whisper, just as she did when she prayed by the bedsides of those who were sick. "*Elohim, Makor ha Chaim* . . ." But she got no further. Something choked her prayer and she began instead simply to weep.

After several minutes she mastered herself and even, her face still wet, smiled at her own childishness. She got up from her chair, washed her face at the kitchen sink, and blotted it dry with a paper towel. Then she sat back down and lit another cigarette.

The Yarzheit candle for her father was burning in its little shot glass. She'd never found a satisfactory prayer to accompany the lighting of that candle but repeated a verse she had uncovered somewhere and often shared with mourning congregants: "*Ha neshama ner L'adonai*"—the soul is a candle to God.

It was a comforting phrase, but it had seemed unusually abstract this time. It was the hands she missed, and the face. The cheeks she had pretended to shave and the lap she sat in. The vague chemical odor of his dyed hair, a mixture of Clorox and licorice, that seemed peculiarly virile though it turned out to be Superior Preference by L'Oreal. She hadn't realized until after he was gone that he had dyed his hair at all, though he always emerged from the shower with a sleeveless undershirt tied around his head like a pirate. Rachel had enlightened her after the funeral—what are we going to do with all Dad's hair dye? The comment had seemed so obscene that Deborah had flown into a rage of absurd denial until her sister had led her into the bathroom where there were three boxes each bearing the same photograph of a brunette model smiling seductively. Rachel pointed and said simply, "Mom's blond."

Deborah, who had become observant after her father's death, understood the possibility that there was a connection between her personal loss and her embrace of Judaism. She knew that her mother, the psychologist, believed Deborah's religious life was merely mourning gone wrong. And her sister, the pathologist, if she bothered with a theory at all, no doubt thought that Deborah believed in a giant benevolent deity with a sleeveless undershirt tied over his head.

But Deborah had long ago come to distinguish between the loss that had propelled her toward her religious inquiry and religion itself. Her journey had moved beyond the thing that motivated it. It wasn't a simple answer to her loss that had mattered or lasted. It was the discovery of community and of ritual, the reclamation of a culture that two generations before her had been sustaining for generations of her family. It was the kindness of Rabbi Mahl, a Reform rabbi, who had encouraged her to say Kaddish all on her own, every day, if she could not find a morning minyan. It was the suggestion by Rabbi Borowitz, an Orthodox rabbi, that she keep kosher as a way to replicate in her home an aspect of God's conception of the universe—behind the great unity were myriad distinctions that filled the world with holiness. These men understood the needs of her soul.

And it was the discovery that her soul had needs at all that had liberated her. She had felt such hunger before her father died but there was no vocabulary in her home for it. Her father's death merely sent her searching. Her mother, who'd had the children share their dreams each morning at breakfast, found Deborah's discovery incomprehensible and wrote it off first as healthy rebellion against her and then as unhealthy rebellion against reason itself.

Deborah believed she had worked through all of this. She'd had her struggles, religious and psychological and political. She'd had bouts of intense observance and bouts of laxness, times when she felt like abandoning her profession and times when it seemed like the only way to be a Jew, but always there had been a simple sense of something powerful and benevolent that was outside her and yet that lived in her, too, and spoke to her directly. Not in the language of common speech but in the language of feeling, of nameless love and invisible companionship. It was what Lev had referred to when he described her as a plant that made her own energy, processing the sun directly. And now she felt that a clear, bright element had drained out of her understanding of the world. It was not that Mrs. Fink had told her something she had not considered. It was that she *felt* in a new way what people like her mother must feel all the time when they contemplate the world beyond the intellectually knowable: nothing.

Deborah had never been particularly afraid of blankness. If that was the price you paid for unity with God, it seemed small. But what if there were no unity either? What if, as Lev had suggested, we were all blind physical processes, randomly conceived? What if her whole adult life had been based on a lie? Deborah was afraid that if she tried to touch the bottom of this doubt she would drown. She thought of Neal, with his hunger for secret meanings. That look in his eyes, that mad need.

She took a long drag on her cigarette and felt the smoke muffling an inner cry. She had an impulse to wake up Lev but something held her back. Her therapist had suggested that it might be Lev's arrival and not God's departure that was unsettling her. Deborah had dismissed this; her therapist was not good when it came to religion and Deborah often marveled that she had chosen a shrink so like her mother, though that of course was part of the point, wasn't it? In any case, she knew that she would not wake him.

Was it shame, she wondered? Lev seemed so to admire her religious life, despite his joking about it. She had felt deep down that they were kindred spirits sharing the same hidden sparks of conviction. Lev had sought her out and she believed she was helping him find things buried deep inside him. She watched him recite *modeh ani* in the morning, not to please her but because something stirred in his soul. She did not wish to disappoint him. She was much too proud, she thought with sudden self-loathing, to expose herself that way.

At the same time, she feared he might confirm her doubts. She did not trust him, really. If she weren't the teacher, dominating him somehow, would he care? Or would all his own doubts and fears rise to the surface, intensifying hers? Deborah did not wish to be confirmed in her fears.

She did not quite ignore his endless evolutionary talk of men and monkeys; she had listened to him with careless attention. She was touched that he gave these questions so much thought, but the details of his reasoning slipped past her because she did not have faith in that sort of reasoning. But now she feared his logic and the things he knew.

Of course the opposite might also be true. Was it so hard to accept that he might console her? That he had his own way of looking at things that could help restore her to herself? But although Deborah did not want her fears confirmed, she also did not want anyone to try to talk her out of her fears. She knew she would see through any attempts at persuasion. You felt what you felt. She really was like that medicine man in the Lévi-Strauss story, she knew those tricks. Hadn't she used them all herself, didn't she use them to console Mrs. Fink?

The thought of Mrs. Fink's frightened, shrunken face brought a wave of gloom over her. She imagined that it was she herself lying in that bed, old and helpless and without belief. Her whole body numbed by a sick, dull sensation. She felt a sudden need for air. She tried a deep yoga breath but somehow the air failed to enter her lungs fully. The cigarettes certainly were not helping.

Deborah stood up and, with a cigarette between her lips, opened the kitchen window wider. The air was soft and cool; she could almost smell flowers and a saltier, marshy smell wafting from the East River. Stirred by an old impulse, she sat right up on the windowsill, leaning back against the frame, her long legs drawn up, the ashtray now in her lap.

She looked down fifteen flights into the courtyard below and felt immune to the plunge, almost as if she were drunk. She'd never had a fear of heights. She'd sat like this at home as a girl until a neighbor would see her from the street and call her parents.

Deborah wondered if she could be seen. The lights in the kitchen were off, though there was light in the courtyard, light from the moon and, behind her, the flickering of the Yahrzeit candle. Perhaps a neighbor would call the police. But no, that was absurd. Her father was not going to appear and order her down with a half-admiring smile.

She was wedged in safely but she felt a dead weight in her chest almost literally pulling her down, making her feel precarious. A great knot of sadness came loose inside her and she began to weep and this time she made no effort to master herself.

What would it matter if she rolled over into darkness?

The tears streamed down her face and she did not bother to blot them. She sat and wept.

DEBORAH'S ABSENCE woke Lev shortly after midnight. He felt a surge of panic and jumped out of bed.

He found Deborah lying on the living room carpet, her legs drawn up. She often did yoga breathing lying on the floor. The eerie glow of the Yahrzeit candle leaked from the kitchen doorway but scarcely dented the darkness.

"Deborah," said Lev. "Have you been smoking?"

He sounded like a parent. Though he did want her to stop, he was more surprised that Deborah, who never lit up on the Sabbath or on Jewish holidays, would smoke on Passover.

Deborah didn't answer him. The moon was higher and smaller than it had been but from the floor Deborah could see it easily, resting against a water tower.

She felt a tremendous urge to talk to Lev. To tell him what had been happening to her, even though she didn't quite know what *had* been happening. She tried to formulate the words, though the more she groped for what she wanted to say the deeper an abyss she felt opening up inside her.

Lev sat down beside her. He touched her cheek with the flat of his hand. He followed her gaze into the murky Manhattan sky.

"The moon is full," he said.

"I've been watching it," Deborah said. "It's shrinking."

"Every year," Lev said, "the moon moves a few inches away from the earth. Someday, it may break out of orbit altogether."

Lev felt the unhelpfulness of his observation; when he was nervous he spouted useless information.

Deborah made no reply. She felt all her words slipping away.

Lev was beginning to see her more clearly though she still seemed like a ghostly form on the floor. They both glowed faintly—Lev's pale, luminous skin; Deborah's darker body, her thick hair loose around her shoulders.

"Deborah," he said, "why won't you talk to me? I can tell something's been bothering you terribly."

He put his hands on her shoulders. It was hard to read her expression, which seemed masked in the dimness, fixed like a statue's. Except that her eyes shone. Was she crying?

He was peering at her through the darkness and Deborah felt a sudden resentment. She who enjoyed so to be admired up on the bimah did not, she realized, want to be studied in her own home this way. This was too close.

Perhaps her therapist was right. Lev's emptied suitcase stood in the corner of the living room, enlarged by shadows. It seemed enormous, as if he were planning never to leave.

"Don't be so insistent," she said with unexpected vehemence. "I can't just unpack my feelings like that."

He took his hands away and she saw in the dimness how penitent he looked. His face was full of concern, full of love. And what did she feel? Under the irritation, a strange, encompassing blankness.

"Is it your father?"

She leaned forward as if she were going to whisper a secret but instead she kissed him, sealing up his lips. She tasted of sleep and cigarette smoke.

"Deborah," he said, in an imploring voice.

She did not answer him. Instead, she pulled her shirt off over her head. Her breasts were the color of the moon. The sharp star hung between them.

"Shouldn't we close the blinds?" he whispered.

Deborah said nothing, turning her face away. The movement of her body, her shifting breasts, suddenly filled him with desire. Instinctively he reached out for her.

She was pulling him down, onto the floor.

He knew he was failing her utterly. But he could not help it and followed her down.

DEBORAH WAS IN THE HOSPITAL looking for Mrs. Fink. It was the third day of Passover and she felt an almost mystical urge to sit beside the old woman. Deborah had been back only once since hearing about her near-death experience; on that occasion, Mrs. Fink had been taken down for testing and Deborah, who'd had appointments to keep, could not wait. This time, Deborah found that Mrs. Fink was no longer in the ICU. She wasn't on the floors. She wasn't anywhere in the hospital. She was in a private rehab facility in White Plains. The old woman had all but lived in the hospital until she had gotten really sick, when she had vanished like a dream.

Deborah received the news of Mrs. Fink's departure from the charge nurse and felt a crush of disappointment. She had dreaded seeing Shirley again but she realized now how much she needed to. She half determined to get her car and drive to White Plains, though she immediately dismissed this idea as impractical. But it seemed to her that there was something oracular about Mrs. Fink and that her disappearance from the hospital was itself full of meaning.

Leaving the ICU, Deborah was already in an unsettled state when she was stopped by a young internist named Kenny Widman. Kenny sometimes flirted with her—"I'm not a very good Jew," he liked to say, "maybe you'll help me get better." He had an earring and a blond goatee and a lean athletic body, even in scrubs and clogs. But this time the swagger was gone and he had a pale stricken look as he begged her to follow him. She hurried after him down the hall, and heard strange, irregular, otherworldly cries growing louder and louder.

Kenny led her to a room where a boy, no more than eight, lay dead on a hospital bed. He had black hair and olive skin that had not yet taken on the waxy luster that Deborah, who had seen several corpses, associated with dried Elmer's glue. The boy might easily have been asleep except for the scene around him. A man, short and burly, in a faded paisley shirt and black jeans, was sobbing with his head on the boy's chest while a distressed nurse had her hand on the man's shoulder and was half comforting him and half trying to pull him away. Two orderlies with a gurney were waiting to transport the boy. They looked ashamed and afraid and frustrated and slightly bored.

Most horrible for Deborah, though, was the woman standing at the boy's feet. She had wild dark hair, which she was pulling at, pulling *out*, with one hand. With her other hand she gripped a crucifix hanging from her neck by a silver chain that she stretched out taut. She was shouting in Spanish at the tiny body of Jesus, imploring the naked, metal figurine to help her son. Occasionally she would stop her pleading, press the crucifix to her heart, and simply shriek. This was the sound Deborah had heard in the hall.

There was a time when Deborah would have rushed in, undeterred by the chaos and the grief, not caring at all that they were Catholic or that they were hysterical or that there was a corpse on the bed. She would have stood beside the woman and let her scream. She would have taken the man's hand. She would have spoken to the orderlies so that they did not stand in such strange isolation. She would have soaked up some of the rage and grief like a sponge until the priest came. She would have gathered them all into a circle around the dead boy. But she did not even enter the room. Like Kenny, who had vanished without a word, she simply fled.

Deborah got into the first elevator she could find and took it down, her heart pounding. She was filled with shame and a nameless fear. In the lobby she stood for a moment under the high cathedral ceiling, regaining her balance and watching the merging elements of the hospital world: the Indian family escorting its silver-haired matriarch, in orange sari and sandals, to the front desk; the pregnant woman with her small suitcase—where was the husband?; a woman bent double, creeping with a walker; a man with a bloody bandage over his eye;

doctors in powder blue scrubs; Filipino nurses in white; a child in an electric, high-backed wheelchair, steering through the crowd.

Suddenly she saw, to her surprise, the dapper, bearded figure of Reuben hurrying toward a bank of elevators. She noticed his kippah before she noticed him, a black disk flying by. Despite the somber garb, Orthodox men were the white rabbits of the religion, always rushing past—late! late! late!—except on Shabbas when they sauntered with time-killing ease.

Yes, it was definitely Reuben. He had once played for the Yeshiva University basketball team. Deborah had found this hard to believe— she was taller than he was—but watching him navigate the lobby with darting grace she could imagine Reuben on a basketball court. He was in many ways the last person she wished to see at that moment and she turned toward the exit, but something impelled her to change direction and run after him.

He was waiting by the elevator when she caught up to him, wearing his navy pinstriped suit jacket draped over his shoulders with the macho effeminacy of a bullfighter. He did not notice her until she stood beside him and said in a low voice, almost a whisper, "Reuben."

He turned and, blushing slightly above his beard, smiled.

"Deborah!"

And then—the same infuriating gesture she remembered—he glanced quickly around the lobby before leaning forward and kissing her cheek in greeting.

"How are you?" he asked.

"Oh, all right," she said, vaguely. She wondered suddenly if he might not be sick. A horrible premonition flashed through her. Cancer!

"And you?"

"Thank God," he said, bobbing his head.

"You're not here for yourself?"

"I'm seeing a cousin. Triple bypass."

Deborah was moved that Reuben, who was very busy, would visit a sick relative in the middle of the day. But then it was part of his culture. Visiting the sick was simply what you did, like praying three times a day or setting aside a portion of your income for the poor. This had always given him, almost in spite of himself, a matter-of-fact godliness that she admired.

The elevator opened and closed but Reuben did not get on.

"I don't want to keep you from your visit," said Deborah, reluctant, somehow, to let him go.

"Shmiel's not going anywhere," said Reuben, with a wry smile. "And you're really doing all right? Still making the rounds, I see."

Reuben reached out a hand and gently lifted Deborah's ID card, which hung around her neck. Staring at the picture and not at her he said, with that mixture of insolence and diffidence, "You look good. I'm glad you're well."

"Actually," said Deborah. "I'm not doing so well."

Reuben immediately dropped the card and looked at Deborah more closely. She seemed, he realized, on the verge of tears. Again his eyes danced to the right and left—he was, after all, visiting a relative, and other family members might be about. But he said, in a kind voice, "Do you want to sit down somewhere?"

"OK," said Deborah.

There was a little snack area in the lobby and she was grateful that Reuben did not object to sitting at one of the small tables out in the open. She bought an apple and Reuben bought an orange—he insisted on paying—and they sat facing each other. Reuben adjusted his large black cloth kippah, held in place by several invisible hairpins, and murmured the blessing for fruits before popping a section of orange between his bearded lips. Deborah wondered if it was from him that she had derived the habit of praying before every morsel or if she had started before that. Somehow, she could not remember. But she felt, as she had on hearing that he was visiting the sick, a sense of his authenticity, of his participation in a culture with deep roots in faith.

"There was a dead boy upstairs," she said.

Instinctively, Reuben's lips formed the traditional words, *Baruch dayan ha'emet*—blessed be the true judge—recited on hearing of a death.

"A Jewish boy?" he asked.

"No," she said. "A Catholic boy."

Reuben nodded.

"I ran away from the whole scene. I didn't know what to do. I felt afraid. I felt . . ." her voice trailed away.

"It's frightening to be near the dead," said Reuben. "And a different faith makes it harder. Jews, you could have recited *tehilim*."

"Reuben," she said. "No. It's not about saying psalms. That's not . . ."

He looked at her with his deep black eyes. There was something familiar in her reproach, as if they were still together, and something new and alarming as well.

"I can't pray anymore. I don't feel there's anything to pray to. I . . ." Deborah lowered her voice to a whisper. "I don't think there's a God I can pray to. I don't feel . . ." She fell silent.

Reuben shifted uncomfortably. His dark beard gave his lips a pink and fleshy look. He swallowed what was in his mouth.

"In Judaism, you don't feel to pray," he said. "You pray to feel. Or not to feel. You pray to pray."

He was saying it half ironically, mocking the person he had been in their relationship and yet still was. His own world was often a tyranny for him and he had, for all his derisive jokes, admired hers. And yet he'd anticipated just this moment for her. It made him angry somehow that she was in spiritual crisis, almost as if some warning of his own had gone unheeded.

"You always put too much faith in feeling," he said. "Too much faith in faith."

It wasn't what she wanted to hear. He could tell from her face, which was looking at him with so much need—unusual for Deborah, who had always seemed so self-sufficient, almost defiant. He was being unhelpful. He was lecturing her.

Deborah winced and looked away. And still he made it worse. His eyes fell on her hands. She had so many rings it was hard at a glance to tell.

"Still single?" he asked.

"Yes," she said, instinctively withdrawing her hand.

"I wonder," he said, "if your lifestyle"—a word Reuben regretted as soon as it passed his lips—"if you wouldn't be happier with a husband and a family. These are stabilizing forces. You love children so much."

Everything was coming out wrong. He scowled, which only made him appear all the more judgmental. Deborah seemed to shrink away from him. Her full lips grew thin with anger.

"I only mean, a beautiful woman like you should have no trouble . . ."

Deborah stood up. What a mistake it had been to run after Reuben.

He reached out and grabbed her arm with surprising force.

"Wait!" he said loudly, almost a shout.

Deborah stared coldly into his imploring face.

"I'm sorry," he said in a lower tone.

She looked down at his hand on her bare arm.

"You shouldn't be touching me," she said in a voice rich with sarcasm. "I might have my period."

He let go. White marks remained on her olive skin.

"Please sit down," he said softly. "I'm sorry. Please."

A tiny spark of orange pulp clung to his mustache.

Deborah sat down.

"You know," he said. "I went into therapy after we broke up. I still go. It turns out you were right, I really am a narcissist."

In spite of herself, Deborah laughed.

"I'm so sorry you're suffering," Reuben said, very gently. "You don't deserve to. I never met anybody with such a soul as yours. You made me a better person."

She looked at him with a face suddenly rounded with gratitude, a full moon of emotion.

"*Al tasteer panecha mimeni*," Reuben quoted, adding, in English, though Deborah knew the verse well, "Please God, don't turn your face from me."

"Would we ask if it didn't happen so much?" Reuben said. "You're lucky to have felt what you usually feel. Some people never do, like a person who can't ever love. But people who have loved once can always love again. You have to be patient."

Deborah smiled wanly; her face was heavy with sadness.

"I wish I had what you have," she murmured.

"I don't have anything," said Reuben. "I always envied you."

They were speaking so softly, the conversation had grown so intimate, that they were leaning their heads toward each other close enough almost to kiss. She noticed that his beard was turning gray at the edges. He must be forty, she calculated, still single, while many of his friends had four or five children. No wonder he preached the value of marriage. In his community, it could not be easy.

"I've been falling for a long time," said Reuben. "In fact, no, that's not true. I was never up on the trapeze, like you were. I was always down in the net."

He *has* been in therapy, thought Deborah. He had never spoken this way to her. It was almost disappointing—she half wanted the cocksure Orthodox boaster. Wanted him for his sake as much as her own.

"But how do you have the strength to pray three times a day and put on tefillin and keep kosher and live the way you do? Surely you believe? . . ."

Reuben shook his head sadly.

"But then how can you do it?"

"Jews aren't expected to feel God's presence," said Reuben. "That's why there's the Torah."

How often had she herself said this, though she realized now that she rejected it utterly.

"You always felt God was for the goyim."

Reuben didn't smile.

"I've done these things since childhood," he said. "And I need the net," he added. "Without the net I'd really fall. Maybe the net *is* God. As close as we're supposed to come . . ."

"Oh Reuben," said Deborah, pity welling up for him, and for herself. At the same time, she felt a deepening sense of loneliness. An illusion gone.

"It's hard for me to talk here," said Reuben.

Deborah nodded. She felt flattered that he would share these things with her at all. The Orthodox were so locked into their own world.

"Would you like to come back to my flat?" he asked, almost in a whisper. Almost as if he weren't saying it at all.

He had always said *flat* instead of apartment, a weird affectation, she thought, though she suspected it came from studying in Jerusalem where the Britishisms of Mandate Palestine crept even into the lives of Orthodox yeshiva students.

She shot him a questioning look that he studiously avoided. He was staring down at his hands. How could he have played basketball with those little hands?

"It's upside down for *paysach*," he added, apologetically.

She'd always liked the way he pronounced the Hebrew name for Passover, with its heavy Ashkenazic flavor. It was like tasting a recipe cooked right. The word never seemed convincing on her lips.

"Deborah?" he asked. He was looking at her now with burning intensity. "I have really missed you."

And to her amazement, almost in a dream, Deborah got up to follow Reuben through the busy lobby as he went outside to hail a cab.

Book

Four

LEV LEFT WORK EARLY and stopped at his apartment to pick up a few last-minute things. Bill wasn't there, though he had returned from Africa. Lev watered his plants, which he was sure Bill would kill, and gathered up a few forgotten items. He stuffed underwear and socks into his knapsack and tucked his squash racquet under his arm.

Moving in with Deborah had worked out much better than he had hoped. How different this was from his feelings when he moved in with Jenny. Then he had felt swept along by forces outside of himself. Now he felt driven by an inner impulse. He knew Deborah was in some kind of crisis, but in spite of this awareness, he felt an uncharacteristic surge of optimism.

Outside, he heard the flapping of wings and noticed pigeons flying back and forth from one side of his street to the other. New birds kept rising off grimy ledges and joining the panicked flock. Lev looked up farther and there, high above his head, was the dark silhouette of a redtailed hawk, hanging in the blue air like a living shadow. The hawk drifted over a water tower and out of sight. The pigeons settled back onto their perches, but Lev felt a lingering elation.

Lev had found the seder a moving experience. Deborah's friends were a strange group, and, at the beginning, Lev had viewed them with condescension. He would enter a room where they were congregated in shlubby intimacy and think, "Yikes, Kikes!" Many, like Wendy, were rabbis and Lev had felt that these observant and semiobservant Jews weren't quite American, but in fact he had come to realize that they were more American than he was. They never doubted their place in the culture. They chose to be Jewish and to be observant and, like Deborah, did it with a kind of joy. It was part of the freedom the country gave them. Lev felt a great hereditary weight, inescapable despite his boundless ignorance. Secretly, in some shadow fashion he could never have articulated, he viewed himself as a soldier in a great and ancient religious war. He had, however, given up Krav Maga for a class in Hebrew prayer.

Lev did not go straight to Deborah's apartment but stopped in a coffee shop. He ordered a cup of vegetable soup and only after he had eaten an entire packet of saltines did he realize that they were prohibited on Passover and that the soup itself contained forbidden noodles that fell under the broad category of chometz.

Lev had determined to eat only kosher food for the duration of the holiday, but already the yoke of obligation and guilt crimped his earlier expansiveness. He pushed aside the soup, feeling almost physically contaminated. Had he been seen? He resented this new cringing self-consciousness. How strange that a holiday associated with freedom could make him feel trapped. How stupid to feel guilty about a bowl of soup.

A moment before he had felt that all his life he had been asleep and that suddenly, with Deborah, he was awake. But now he wondered if perhaps the reverse were true—if he hadn't been lulled into a relationship that cut him off from larger life. Deborah seemed to him a sort of mythical figure waiting for him on the far side of an abyss. Leaping off would bring him liberation tinged with the entangling shadows of death.

What would life with Deborah really mean? Would it mean marrying the members of her congregation, and her grandmother's dishes, and the rabbis of the Talmud, and a great deal more besides? Suddenly Lev had a hard time separating out the woman he loved and the world that trailed after her like the great endless train of a gown.

Lev sat considering all this when he noticed that at the counter of the coffee shop a young priest was just getting up from his own meal. Lev had overlooked this man earlier. He had spent most of the meal staring at an obese woman in a green floral tentlike dress who appeared to be eating two servings of rice pudding simultaneously. Lev owed *Eureka* a story on obesity in America, just the sort of article he hated to write but that the magazine wanted from him more and more. He had written twice about the subject for the magazine already, which made him the resident expert. As always, the real questions at the heart of the story lay beyond the purview of the magazine and, seemingly, the scientists themselves. What loneliness might drive this woman at the table to bury herself in blubber, to weight herself down to the earth? What problem inherent in being human made the body a burden? And where, amid the layers of mortality, was the soul?

The priest was slender. His black, collared shirt had short sleeves and his arms were surprisingly muscular. He looked like a Vermont carpenter; there was something neo-hippie about his beard and bearing. He stood next to the stool he had sat on and, with a tight movement of his right hand, made the sign of the cross over his empty plate. Then he placed a few dollars on the counter and left.

To his surprise, Lev felt a kinship with the man. It was not the sign of the cross, which made Lev shudder inside, but the acknowledgement of an invisible presence connected to the meal that Lev found so stirring. A sense that even in this coffee shop prayer was appropriate and that something higher than himself was present, like the hawk hanging over his head that he had only noticed when he saw the pigeons. He realized that this was the same coffee shop he had sat in the night he had rushed back to Deborah's and taken her in his arms. He might easily have gone home that night, and he remembered that evening and his decision with a flood of gratitude and an impatience to be with Deborah.

Lev had not made any sort of blessing over his food and was unsure whether it was a mistake to give thanks for food he should not in fact have eaten. But he stood beside his chair, as the priest had, and uttered the little postmeal prayer Deborah had taught him, *Blessed are you God who feeds everyone*. As he did, he felt, almost physically, Deborah's presence and beyond her presence the presence of something more.

LEV FOUND A NOTE from Deborah on the dining room table.

> *Dear Lev,*
>
> *I hate writing this but somehow calling you at work seemed worse. You are a wonderful man. I love you, but I need to get away for a little while and have gone to Rachel's. There are certain things I need to work out alone. I know you're aware of how distracted I've been. I'm not proud of what I've become. I have to clear my head and figure some things out. Please don't feel any less at home because I'm not here. I just need to get away. Even if you had your own place this month, I'd still want to get out of town. There's lots of food in the fridge—you know where everything is.*
>
>

Love,
Deborah
>

Lev felt sick when he read the note. It recalled the confused sensation of reading his father's suicide note except that somehow Lev read his own death in the letter. It was signed "Love"—there was hope in that—but it was a letter, not a person. Not the body he had imagined coming home to and holding. His squash racquet was still tucked under his arm, which, when he became aware of it, compounded his feeling of foolishness.

This was how Jenny must have felt when he told her that he could not go through with the wedding. He had also said, "I love you." He had also blamed himself. Well, he had come full circle and perhaps deserved no less. But he still could not believe it. Why? What had happened?

His first impulse was that he should track her down. He had never met her sister, Rachel, but he knew she was a doctor in Westport, Connecticut. She could not be hard to find. But even as he dialed information he realized that she did not wish to be followed and hung up the phone. He should give her a little room. Deborah, he reminded himself, wasn't calling anything off. There wasn't anything *to* call off. She was just going away for a few days. But that was what so surprised Lev. He was the one who was supposed to run away. And yet here he was, in her apartment. Deborah's sister was completely unobservant—hostile, even, from what Lev had gathered, which made Deborah's decision to go there seem stranger and more desperate. She had spent hours scrubbing her apartment, changing over the dishes, and stocking it with kosher-for-Passover foods.

Lev felt humiliated and confused; he wanted to get angry but in fact he realized with shame that there were tears in his eyes.

Lev ate a dreary supper. There were precooked meals from Mealmart stacked up in the refrigerator like astronaut food in foil containers—potato kugel and stuffed peppers and quartered chickens. But Lev ate a hard-boiled egg and a tin of sardines, in keeping with his mood. He felt a certain custodial urge toward the old-lady dishes. "You know where everything is" had a special meaning coming from Deborah—the milk, the meat, the parve, the Passover-ready. He might have disappointed her but would preserve everything, and Deborah would return and find him keeping Passover alone.

But two days later, when Deborah still had not come back and still had not called, Lev found himself filled with a growing anger. Perhaps she was not at her sister's—perhaps she had gone to her former boyfriend's. Rationally, he dismissed this possibility, and yet his feeling of abandonment and betrayal grew stronger as the day progressed.

By evening, Lev was in such a state that for dinner, rather than heat up the dreadful kosher-for-Passover kugel and schnitzel, he went downstairs to Pick a Chick and bought an unkosher rotisserie chicken. He and Deborah had passed the store many times. The mouthwatering smell of roasting flesh was pumped onto the street by a fan above the door. "I want one of those!" Deborah would sometimes say, pausing in front of the plate glass window, where a giant neon chicken blinked on and off.

Deborah often gave a vegetarian impression, since in nonkosher restaurants she ate only vegetables or fish, but she loved meat and Lev had on several occasions accompanied her to Kosher Delight near Herald Square, a vast, kosher version of McDonalds. There, young orthos dated discreetly while the numerous children of large observant families scampered and *fressed* and a bearded, skullcapped *mashgiach* gloomily patrolled the premises, ensuring that everything was in accordance with Jewish law. Lev watched with amusement as Deborah unwrapped her greasy Garden of Eden burger with childish delight.

Lev felt an angry thrill as he stood in Pick a Chick and ordered a whole chicken. It came with a free pound of potato salad and—at this Lev's heart beat faster—two buttermilk biscuits. He paid—half the price of Mealmart—and took his tinfoil-lined bag back to Deborah's, gripping the top of the bag tightly as if it might cry out like a stolen goose in a fairy tale: "Help! Help! I'm *tref*!" But the chicken said nothing.

Back in Deborah's apartment, Lev set the table with sadistic care, neat even in his anger. He chose one of the ceramic plates with the little horse and cart, and laid out a milk knife and fork, boiled with such care by Deborah, for good measure. He pried open the lid of the potato salad and stuck a soup spoon into it. He ripped open the tinfoil-lined bag and pierced the juicy back of the chicken with a serving fork. But when he lifted the barbecued bird, with one hand under it to catch the drippings, and carried it over to introduce it onto her grandmother's dishes, he found he could not.

He stood, holding the chicken like a head on a pike, poised above the table. He felt a twinge of disgust at his own weakness. He realized how easily he might plop the bird onto the plate. The sky would not fall, nothing would change. Deborah's dishes were only what they were because Deborah believed that is what they were, as had her grandmother before her. And a wider, invisible world that thought the same.

In a sense, the homey dish was part of a set table that went back in time and outward in space. His own grandparents had a seat at that table and so did many others, the living and the dead together. He stood absurdly holding the chicken in the air, unable to create the chaos he had fantasized about. He simply did not wish to undo Deborah's world, even if she herself had abandoned the kitchen.

As a compromise, Lev carried his bird into the dining room and ate it on top of that day's *New York Times*, with the torn-open bag spread under the chicken to keep the grease from soaking through. He ate without silverware or plate, a kind of medieval feast, tearing off a leg and then a thigh. He was preserving Deborah's dishes but eating like a savage, pinching out bits of potato salad with his fingers, feeling a grotesque hunger. He didn't bother with a napkin. After this, he told himself, he was going to call Jessica, a former grad student in zoology who sat next to him at work and whose mysterious tattoo he glimpsed whenever she bent forward in her chair. *She's dessert!* he thought wildly.

But already he was worrying what to do with the contaminated spoon and fork he had put into the potato salad, carefully extracting them and laying them on the newspaper. Scraps of bad news flashed at him—AIDS in China, civil war in Ethiopia, Milošević on trial (did it matter what he ate in such a world?). And yet, grease dripping from his chin, he felt implicated in the barbarity. He ate the buttermilk biscuits last, cramming them into his mouth and chewing, though there was nothing to drink and he nearly choked.

There was a good deal of chicken left over, but when he was done he wrapped it in the *Times* and threw it in the garbage, which, after washing himself carefully in the bathroom (so as not to contaminate Deborah's carefully boiled kitchen sink), he threw down the chute in the hall, feeling on his face the cold, cindery draft that rose when he opened the trap door before shoving the bag in and hearing it fall with a whoosh.

As he was walking back to the apartment, feeling purged despite his indulgence, Lev realized the phone was ringing. Deborah! He felt sure it would be her, as if he had conjured her.

"Hello!" he said breathlessly.

"Rabbi Green?" A woman's voice asked.

"No," said Lev, his voice falling. "She isn't here."

"Can you tell me when she'll be back?"

"I'm afraid she's away for a couple of days."

"She's away?"

The woman sounded tremendously disappointed.

"I could take a message," Lev offered.

"Does she have a cell phone or some kind of pager?"

"No," said Lev, put off by this pushiness. "As I said, I can take a message."

"My mother died," the woman blurted out.

"Oh," said Lev. "I'm very sorry."

"I don't have a rabbi. We don't belong to a temple. But my friend Nancy went to a wedding Rabbi Green performed and said she was just wonderful. Nancy thought she'd be good for . . . funerals, too. I think she's the kind of rabbi that Mother would have liked."

"I'm sorry she's not here."

The woman said nothing but he felt her presence on the phone, a sort of audible silence. An almost palpable need. He wished the woman would get off the phone. Her stressed and stricken voice made him uncomfortable and her silence was killing him. But he asked, in a kind voice, "When did your mother die?"

Lev remembered how practical Deborah could be in the face of tragedy, and he thought he might need to pass this information along. His question seemed to have an instantaneous, therapeutic effect.

"Yesterday. She died in the morning. I know we should have had her buried today, that's what my husband says. But my daughter lives in California and . . ." The woman launched into a long explanation involving the details of her mother's stay in the Intensive Care Unit and how her system had suddenly failed, there were blood thinners for a stroke but heart medication that interacted badly with the blood thinners and then of course the dialysis—since it was ultimately her kidneys that went.

As she was pouring out all this information, Lev wandered with the portable receiver to the bookshelf in Deborah's bedroom, where he found a tattered copy of *Gates of Mitzvah: A Guide to the Jewish Life Cycle*. He thumbed through it and found the rituals for mourning. Perhaps there was something useful he could tell her.

"Well," said Lev, "it's true that Jews do emphasize immediate burial, but forty-eight hours is sometimes all we can expect in this day and age when people are so scattered."

"Yes," said the woman, sounding relieved. "That's what I felt. There's been so much to do."

"You have to take care of yourself," Lev said. "And others have to take care of you. This time is referred to as"—he checked again the page in *Gates of Mitzvah* he had been scanning—"*aninut*—the time after death but before burial. A time almost of suspension. You have no obligations."

"Ha," laughed the woman. "My husband isn't well and my kids aren't even back yet. Lisa's flying in tonight. Philip is still in Chicago. It happened very suddenly, even though she'd been in the hospital a long time. I'm the one who told them to get back to their lives. It looked like she'd turned a corner."

And then, with a kind of hopeful awakening, she said, "You must be a rabbi yourself."

"Well," said Lev, evasively, "I don't really function as one."

Shocking himself further, he heard his own voice say, as if someone else were conducting the conversation, "When would you hope to have the funeral?"

He realized he did not even know this woman's name.

"I reserved a place at Levine's for tomorrow at ten a.m. Would that be convenient?"

"Convenient?" Lev thought with a horrified thrill. Good God, what was he doing? Take a message and get off the phone!

"I also spoke to someone at the Plaza. They've got an afternoon slot—although my mother's already *at* Levine's."

"The Plaza Hotel?" asked Lev.

"The Plaza Funeral Home," said the woman. "On Amsterdam."

"Ah," said Lev. "Of course. You'd be surprised where some people have their funerals."

"Really?" The woman asked.

"Your family's coming in tonight?" Lev asked, to change the subject.

"Yes. Please," said the woman, with a kind of desperation. "I can't tell you how terrible the last few days have been. And I have so much to do, so many arrangements. They want to know how many limousines I need and I have to figure out food and people keep calling and I have to call people—" her voice broke.

"What time did you say?" Lev asked. "At Levine's?"

"Ten. Thank you! Thank you so much!"

"Ten o'clock would be fine," said Lev, as if a demon were speaking through him. But it wasn't a demon. He was imitating Deborah's manner, compassionate but businesslike. Someone has to be in charge, she often said. You're just the point they organize their grief around.

And indeed he told himself that the second he got off the phone he would call Deborah—here was a reason to summon her home.

"Ten's fine," he said, "but we should meet beforehand." This was a conversation he had overheard many times.

He scribbled down the woman's name—Estelle Kalman—and her mother's name—Myrna. He scribbled down *9:30* and *Levine's* and the exact address on West 100th. In a moment he would find Deborah's sister's number, call her up, and explain the situation.

He scanned the book before him again, as well as Deborah's rabbi's manual, which he had also taken off the shelf. He was looking for the appropriate thing to say to a mourner on parting. Was there such a phrase? He wanted one last rabbinic flourish. He caught sight of himself in the bedroom mirror flipping frantically through the books. He felt like Mickey Mouse in *Fantasia*, putting on the sorcerer's hat. Any minute, he would take it off.

"I'm very sorry for your loss, Estelle," Lev ventured, preparing to hang up. He realized that this was what the police officers on *NYPD Blue* always said and so he added, in Hebrew, a phrase he had just lit on and thought he had heard Deborah use when informed of a death: "*Baruch Dayan Ha emet.*"

Somehow it didn't seem quite right.

"Thank you," the woman said awkwardly.

Clearly she knew no Hebrew at all.

He should have left well enough alone. His head was spinning a little. But really, the woman sounded much better. With awakening curiosity, she asked, "What is it you do if you don't usually work as a rabbi?"

"I'm an educator," Lev said, repeating what a number of Deborah's nonpracticing colleagues often said. He hoped the term was sufficiently meaningless to suggest many things and deter further inquiry. "It's my wife who's the full-time rabbi."

Whoever said that lying leads to lying certainly knew what he was talking about. He had to get off the phone.

"I didn't catch your name," the woman said, with an apologetic laugh. "Is it Green, too?"

"It's Friedman."

He was afraid that if he invented a name he would never remember it.

"Well thank you Rabbi Friedman. You're a lifesaver."

"Please," said Lev, feeling now quite dizzy, so that he sat down on Deborah's bed. "Call me Lev."

DEBORAH DID NOT GET ALONG WELL with her sister but they were bound by blood and shared history and there was nobody else she even considered going to stay with. She could hear the surprise in Rachel's voice when Deborah reached her at her office.

"Isn't it Passover?"

"Yes," said Deborah. "Can I come stay for a little while?"

"Of course—are you in trouble? You must be."

Rachel sounded at once like an older sister, as if Deborah had smashed the car or got caught smoking pot in school. Deborah heard the concern and felt both touched and also fearful that she would disappoint Rachel's expectations of calamity. Rachel was, after all, a doctor, and always suspected medical crises. The sudden death of their father had stamped her, too.

But Deborah was feeling as though her emotional state really was a physical one, that something was breaking. She was running away from her synagogue and her congregation, she was running away from her own scrubbed apartment during the holiday she cared most about. She was running away from a man she loved. She was asking to stay in an unkosher house with a sister who judged her harshly and often seemed contemptuous of the very choices that Deborah was now doubting.

Deborah said, in an almost supplicatory voice, "I can't really explain now. Is that all right?"

"Fine," said Rachel. "Anyway, I'm with a patient. Just call Dawn and let her know you're coming."

That was Rachel. Would it have killed her to let Dawn know she was coming herself? But as a matter of fact, Deborah found it easier to talk to Rachel's partner than to Rachel. Dawn had an easy, open manner, and Deborah often suspected it was Dawn who chose the birthday gifts and wrote the holiday cards.

Dawn wasn't home when Deborah called but she was cooking dinner when Deborah arrived in the late afternoon. Dawn was a big-boned woman, mannish but maternal, with hair cropped at the sides but high on top with a skinny braid in the back. Deborah was fond of her but an inner voice always whispered *dyke* when she saw her. Dawn was wearing an apron and she gave Deborah a big welcoming hug.

"Rachel told me you were coming," she said.

So why did I have to call? thought Deborah, but she suppressed this feeling. Better not to start out resentful.

"Thanks for letting me crash here," she said, sounding in her own ears like a teenager.

"What else is family for?" said Dawn. "Besides, we don't see enough of you."

Dawn's own family was a disaster. Her parents had died when she was very young. She had lived with an abusive uncle and then in two foster homes, but she had a placid, deeply consoling presence. No wonder Rachel loved being with her.

A timer sounded and Dawn hurried into the kitchen to flip the chicken she was roasting. Deborah was always amazed that her sister, with almost no domestic inclinations at all, had found someone so happy to make elaborate dinners and who was responsible as well for the garden of wildflowers and herbs that took the place of a front lawn. Dawn had worked full-time as a physical therapist at the hospital where Rachel was on staff, which is how they met, but she only worked three days a week now while she got a master's in education.

Deborah set her overnight bag down at the foot of the stairs and joined Dawn in the kitchen. It was a small but beautiful house, with a back porch on an inlet of the Long Island Sound. A big picture window looked out from the kitchen and Deborah saw a white bird standing in the water, its long neck very thin, frozen for a moment before plunging its head into the water and coming out with a tiny silver fish gripped in its strong yellow beak.

Dawn was stirring butternut squash soup. She was left-handed and Deborah watched her large hand move the wooden spoon with great delicacy. There was a tattooed ring on Dawn's ring finger; Rachel had a matching one. On Rachel, the narrow inked band looked wrong, Deborah thought, but on Dawn, the intricate faded arabesques of purple and red and black looked mysteriously beautiful.

"Do you want a drink?" Dawn asked. "A snack?"

"Oh I'm fine," said Deborah. "Everything smells terrific."

But even as she said this she wondered how much she would be able to eat. Her kashrut always offended her sister, though for Deborah, just being in her sister's home on Passover was a massive compromise—a fact that would only offend her sister the more.

As if reading her thoughts, Dawn said, "I bought a kosher chicken. They sell them now at Wild Oats—free-range kosher organic. It's cooking in a disposable pan. And we have plenty of matzah."

There was something so offhandedly tender about this statement that Deborah, in spite of herself, burst into tears.

Dawn dropped her spoon and wrapped her big arms around Deborah.

"Oh honey," she said.

AS IT TURNED OUT, Rachel called from the hospital to say she was swamped, and that Dawn and Deborah should eat without her. Deborah couldn't help feeling hurt. She hadn't come to see her sister so much as to get away, and yet she realized she wanted Rachel to come and be with her.

"Don't take it personally," Dawn said with weary understanding. "She's married to her patients."

Deborah recognized, as she inevitably did when she visited her sister, that though they appeared so different they had many temperamental similarities. One of them was a devotion to strangers in need. Rachel's job required the sort of detached intimacy Deborah also excelled at.

Deborah and Dawn ate without Rachel, killing a bottle of Baron de Herzog Chardonnay, also bought specially for Deborah, and when they had finished eating they sat smoking on the deck, in the fading spring light. The white bird had returned and stood in the darkening blue water. Deborah noticed a single, gauzy feather trailing from the back of the bird's flat head, like a bridal veil.

It was chilly and Deborah had put on her sister's fleece, though the sleeves were too short and she knew Rachel, a fanatical nonsmoker, would resent the smoke clinging to it.

"Did something bad happen?" Dawn finally asked. "Or is it just things in general? I know you may not want to talk—or at least you might want Rachel here."

"It's easier talking to you," said Deborah. "Rachel's never really forgiven me for the wedding."

The two sisters had never much gotten along, but things had gotten worse around the time of Dawn and Rachel's commitment ceremony. Deborah had performed two same-sex marriages but she would not perform interfaith marriages, and Dawn was not a Jew. It had taken a lot for Rachel to ask her sister and she had interpreted Deborah's refusal as discomfort with her sexual orientation. Deborah kept bringing it back to religion and Rachel would say, "What kind of religion excludes people who love each other?" and Deborah would say, "It doesn't—I just can't do the wedding," and around and around it went.

Deborah still heard some of Rachel's accusations in her head.

"You like big *normal* families; you think that's the divine order of things. Mom, dad, kids. But you know what—love makes a family. Not some accident of birth."

Why couldn't her sister defend her choices without attacking Deborah's? She found Rachel's words a hurtful refutation not only of her religious commitment but of their sisterly relationship, a mere "accident of birth." But she suspected deep down there was a tiny grain of truth in her sister's accusation and she was disgusted with herself for her own conventionality. She did want there to be a natural order to the world, and she wanted to believe that her own family reflected it.

She sometimes thought Rachel had eliminated men to get revenge on their father for dying, an irrational notion, she knew. And yet she felt that her sister's anger came from fearing that she herself was out of tune with nature. Dawn seemed far more comfortable with her identity, and Deborah, sitting beside her, felt embarrassed by the memories of those fights, which Dawn had witnessed.

"Oh, the wedding's ancient history," said Dawn. "We're an old married couple by now."

She did not say, as Deborah would have hoped, "She understands your position. You did what you had to do."

Deborah reached for another cigarette from Dawn's pack of Parliaments.

"Your sister loves you," said Dawn. "It's just hard for her sometimes. Here she's a doctor and you've managed to pitch your tent on even higher ground. Your mom's so proud of you."

"My mother thinks I'm a witch doctor," said Deborah.

"That's not true," said Dawn. "We were out there last Christmas and she talked about you with such admiration. The work you do in the hospital."

The hospital, thought Deborah, not the synagogue. But she felt a thrill that her mother had spoken approvingly of her, followed immediately by bitterness that her mother's approval mattered so much. And by shame, because she felt that now that she had the approval she didn't merit it because she was feeling so lost inside her own calling. And by resentment, because she didn't want to be thinking of herself in terms of what others thought of her.

"My tent isn't pitched at all," Deborah said. "It's blown right off the mountain."

The wine had warmed and relaxed her. She told Dawn about Mrs. Fink and about the dead boy she had run away from. She told her about Reuben.

"Did you fuck him?" asked Dawn.

Though she blushed at the question, Deborah was grateful for

Dawn's blunt manner, which allowed for no pseudopietistic assumptions that rabbis stood outside the realm of human nature.

"No," Deborah said. "I jumped out of the cab."

She had, in fact, bolted in the middle of traffic and come very close to getting hit by another cab. She had actually been nicked by a bicycle messenger who had turned around in his seat and called her a cunt.

Dawn waved her hand dismissively.

"I thought Judaism's all about *behavior*. There's no 'sinning in your heart.' I had enough of that bullshit with the Baptists. It'll kill you."

Deborah wanted to believe that it was the image of Lev that had sent her from the cab but she knew that it was only when Reuben had said, in his offhand way, that he was engaged to be married, and that his fiancée had the key to his apartment and that perhaps they should go to a hotel, that she had awakened with a start from a sort of dream.

"I did betray Lev," said Deborah. "Not just by getting in that cab with Reuben. I can't really explain. I think Lev saw something in me that isn't there anymore."

"What did he see?" Dawn asked.

"God."

"Oh, is that all?"

Deborah smiled ruefully.

"Did he tell you that?" Dawn asked.

"Not in so many words" said Deborah. "But I feel it. It's like I was the burning bush and I just flamed out."

"He wanted the burning bush! Just like a man."

The two women suddenly burst into laughter, Deborah laughing so hard the tears came, a kind of hysterical continuation of her earlier outburst. The wine had gone to her head.

She recovered herself and wiped her eyes with the sleeve of her sister's fleece.

"Not to sound too pop psychological," said Dawn, "but isn't it possible you've disappointed yourself and you're pinning it on Lev?"

This was precisely what Deborah always thought about her sister.

She blamed others for her own discomfort with herself. But it was true that she hadn't really given Lev a chance to talk to her. She had simply run away.

"It's possible," Deborah said after a while. "I'm not proud of it, if that's so. I just feel so disappointed in everything, myself included." She was looking down at the smooth, silver wood of the table. "I feel . . ." her voice trailed off.

"Depressed?" Dawn asked, gently, touching her arm.

Deborah shrugged. It wasn't the word she wanted.

"I keep thinking about this friend of Lev's," Deborah said.

"Uh-oh," said Dawn.

"No, not like that. He had a psychotic break and he goes in and out of hospitals. He's obsessed with this one story from the Talmud about the four who enter *Pardes*."

"Tell it to me," Dawn said.

She was looking at Deborah with open, serious eyes. She was much more interested in Judaism than Rachel was and read a lot of books.

"It's a very simple story," said Deborah. "Four men enter what's called *Pardes*—it might be Paradise, or heaven, or God's presence, or the Garden of Eden. It's murky. Anyway, they're all famous rabbis. It's a kind of spiritual test for them. One of them goes mad. One of them dies. One of them loses his faith and becomes a convert. Only Rabbi Akiva enters in peace and leaves in peace.

"I keep thinking about that story," said Deborah. "Because . . . I guess I always thought of myself as being Rabbi Akiva. I thought I was chosen somehow, immune to something. Singled out for something. And now I feel like I'm . . . not. I'm one of the others . . ."

It would have been impossible to tell this story to Rachel. As it was, Deborah felt the shame of admitting to Dawn her own craving for specialness. As if she really believed that God had chosen *her*! The very thing her sister had resented her for and accused her of. She knew that Dawn would pass the conversation along but it was different telling her; she had a calm, nonjudgmental manner. The heavy jaw and dark eyes gave her face a kind of stability as she listened.

Deborah looked out at the water. The white bird was gone, though flocks of sparrows blew in and out of the tall bearded reeds that grew along the tide pool. The wind was on the cobalt water and the visible current made Deborah feel as though she were in a fast boat. She felt her own soul racing away from her.

"Rachel will think I've just come to my senses. About myself. About the world. About the fact that there's nothing out there."

"Oh there's something out there," said Dawn. "We don't always feel it but it's there. We don't always see it but it's there."

Dawn was one quarter Native American, as she had told Deborah in the past, and there was something about the black hair and skinny braid, the smoke drifting from her cigarette, that made her look, in the failing light, like an Indian chief. But this, Deborah knew, was her own fantasy. People had it about her all the time—the need for a shaman. The hunger to be told the truth by someone who saw it and could pass it on. But still, she liked hearing Dawn say, "There's a spirit in things."

"I just can't speak that way anymore," Deborah said. "I had nothing to say to that mother howling in grief with a dead child on the bed."

"No," said Dawn, "grief is something else."

Deborah nodded. That was true. And yet she'd wanted something to say—to herself if not to the woman.

"You know, your sister once told me a story that was very helpful to me when I was going through a hard time," said Dawn. "You'd be surprised, she has a spiritual side, you just don't see it that often. But she told me a story about a man who was a minister who lost his faith. He just couldn't believe in the God of Scripture anymore. And he slowly starts to die inside, and to die literally because he just doesn't feel God's presence. Meanwhile the minister's son has a terrible dream. His son dreams that God craps right on top of the church and that a big turd crashes through the roof and lands in the sanctuary. The strange thing is that the son, instead of deciding he must be crazy, takes enormous comfort from this dream and develops a whole new kind of faith that makes room for chaos and strangeness. Meanwhile, the father dies . . ."

Dawn's voice trailed off.

"It sounded better when Rachel told it," she said, laughing at herself. "It's hard to tell a story about God taking a shit. It's not from the Talmud, needless to say."

"You told it very well," said Deborah smiling. "It's actually a story Jung tells in *Memories, Dreams, Reflections.*"

"Rachel stole it from Jung?"

"No," said Deborah, "she stole it from me. I told her that story years ago. It was very important to me once, even though I don't really like Jung—and my mom really hates him. Which is probably why I read as much Jung as I could find in college."

"Well," said Dawn, "I'm telling you what you know."

"Hardly," said Deborah.

The story seemed to her almost embarrassingly juvenile. Once she had identified utterly with the boy and his dream but now she felt a painful sympathy with the minister father, losing his faith and his world.

But Deborah felt deeply stirred—not by the story, but by the fact that her sister had cared enough about that story to pass it on to Dawn. And because she recognized, with a pang, an aspect of her adolescent self in it. The hunger, a kind of violent craving, for direct contact with religious experience, however extreme. The belief that most religious authorities are trapped inside a dead logic and that the roof falling in is a liberation. The possibility that defilement can make you holy. She had savored these eruptions in the Bible—God wrestling with Jacob or striking poor Uzzah dead when he put out his hand to steady the shaking ark. Lately it was the psalms, and even the humble list of generations, that moved her most. Rachel weeping for her children.

Deborah sat in silence, listening to her younger self telling a story to her older self. She flicked the ash of her cigarette over the railing of the porch and turned her face to the breeze blowing from the water.

THE TRIP TO ATLANTA had exhausted Henry, who slept, it seemed, through half of it. Back in his apartment, he lay on the sofa, listening to the Brahms sonata for violin and piano in G major while Oleg manipulated his limbs. This wasn't part of his job but Oleg wanted to be a physical therapist and practiced massage on Henry's body. Henry didn't mind. His body didn't seem to belong to him anymore; he was always turning it over to others like a man handing someone the keys to his car, though Henry had never learned to drive, something his sons had often held against him. It was Helen who had taught the boys, in a parking lot in Brooklyn. And now Jacob had three cars in his ridiculous house in the Atlanta suburbs.

Henry had begun walking with greater difficulty; mini strokes in the past year had eroded his gait, and he marveled at the ease with which Oleg lifted him out of his chair to lay him out on the couch like dough on a baking sheet. Oleg was a good man; he turned his back when Henry was on the toilet. He reminded Henry of the attendant in "The Death of Ivan Ilyich," the strapping peasant who hauls Ivan around at the end. Henry had always wanted to write a story like that, a man waking to inner consciousness. Who didn't wish to be Tolstoy? But he was living that story now, which meant, of course, he was beyond writing it, though perhaps not. Perhaps he would rally.

He tried to orient himself. On this couch. In his apartment. In New York City. It was, he reminded himself, the year 2000. This was something he found difficult to hold onto, though Lev and Deborah had spent New Year's Eve with them, a Friday night. A Shabbat. He had gone to bed early without making the toast he'd wished to make. He belonged, he knew, to the century that had ended. He would not see much of the new one, though he hoped for his children's sake it would be better than the last.

One of the many essays he had always hoped to write—surely the notes were somewhere in his desk—was the way in which the twentieth century wasn't really the American century, which everyone claimed, but the Jewish century. The great mass of immigrants flooding out of Europe and Russia, remaking the United States. The work of Freud and Kafka and Einstein. Psychoanalysis, relativity, the creation of modern consciousness. Jews were victims of the century's worst crime and participants in its noblest struggles. Establishers of Israel, the most miraculous nation, though on his own visits he had been repelled by the nationalism, the macho swagger. It shamed him to feel that way since of course Jews weren't nationalistic enough most of the time and he considered himself a Zionist. These paradoxes had once consumed him, though he no longer experienced them with any urgency at all. His mind kept jumping the track.

It was Passover. He knew that was why they had been in Atlanta, though Jacob had barely conducted the seder and Henry had not been up to it. It was his daughter-in-law, Penny, who insisted they return to the table after dessert for the second half of the Haggadah and the songs.

Henry fell into a long dark passage of Brahms during which he lost his train of thought and found himself thinking of Kate Maybank. Penny always reminded him of Kate. Of all the Maybanks, Kate was the kindest. He'd had a toothache once and she had taken him to the dentist in London. On the way there'd been an air raid and she had led him to a shelter in the basement of a church, filled with crying babies and old men and the smell of dank earth and wet wool. She'd held his hand and afterward kissed him and called him a brave lad. To this day the faint tingling of pain in a molar gave him an oddly pleasant expectation of something exciting about to happen. Later that night, he had crept out of bed and peeped through the crack of Kate's door, watching her say her prayers in nothing but her drawers, an angel in underwear. He had pined for Christian Kate while his poor parents . . .

Henry turned away inside from the terrible contradictions. The century was over. Good riddance, it had been a disaster. Shabbat still came and went. Oleg laid down one leg carefully and lifted the other. Henry felt the Russian's strong hands along his thigh. Every moment someone was dying, suffering. You lived inside that knowledge, alongside it, in spite of it. He had been a boy, what could he do? And now? What was he now?

But Oleg had stopped what he was doing and was speaking to somebody. He heard a familiar voice inside the music and there was Lev, kneeling down beside him. Real? Real.

Lev kissed him.

Henry seldom ventured speech but he attempted a smile. He would like to have embraced his son. He thought about both boys a great deal—as they were as children, as he had been with them, to them. He sometimes felt that the childhood he returned to most wasn't his own but his children's. In these visitations he was somehow his own children, suffering blows from an angry, irrational man.

Oleg was explaining to Lev that his mother was walking the dog. Lev held his father's hand and looked at him as if he were saying goodbye before a long trip.

Lev wasn't sure why he had come, though he'd had some unspecified hope that his father could help him.

He had failed to get in touch with Deborah—Rachel Green's number had been withheld at the request of the customer. He did not know where Deborah's sister practiced medicine and though he knew she lived with a woman named Dawn, he could not remember Dawn's last name. Deborah did not discuss many details of her sister's life. Lev had left a message on Deborah's answering machine at work. If only she would call in.

Meanwhile, his hope of rescue had evaporated now that he knelt beside his father. What could possibly say? *"I'm on the verge of performing a stranger's funeral. Help me, please."*

Lev often discovered, stuck into the books on his father's shelf, drafts of notes his father had written for him years before (his poor father could not write even a few lines without multiple versions). *Please excuse my son from gym class, he has a cold. Please excuse my son from his mathematics test today, he has been unwell. Please excuse my son from performing this funeral—* He's not a rabbi! They could tape it to the coffin.

He had, it sometimes seemed to Lev, received from his father perpetual permission not to attend. Excuse me from death. Excuse me from life. But of course that is not what his father wanted. He had meant only to shield his son from pain.

Words were failing Henry. He was afraid even to say his son's name for fear it would come out wrong, a curse, an obscenity, or merely gibberish.

But he managed to say, "Is it raining?"

"No," said Lev. "It's not."

His father appeared to be struggling for more words and Lev, who had once fought a stutter, felt a visceral sympathy in his own throat. His father had once given him tips on how to eliminate his stutter— exaggerate it in the privacy of your room. That, apparently, was how Henry had eliminated his accent. Henry had done such a good job that he claimed to have forgotten German as well as his accent. The method was less successful for Lev, who required years of speech therapy.

"Dad," Lev said, eager to save his father from his visible struggle. "I want you to know how much I love you. And . . . I read your letter. I'm doing the best I can. I'm so glad you're alive."

He wasn't sure his father heard him. He looked at Lev with a kind of fear. Henry's eyes were watering, a symptom of the strokes. For him, it was always raining. He wept the way some people coughed or sneezed. Lev kissed him again, stood up, wrote a note for his mother saying only that he had stopped by to welcome them home, and left.

THE RABBI'S MANUAL and *Gates of Mitzvah* lay open on the bed when Lev returned home from visiting his father. It had been no dream. There was the scrap of paper on which he had written: "Levine's—9:30," the woman's name—Estelle Kalman—and the name of her deceased mother, Myrna Epstein. He had also, he realized, written "Rabbi Friedman" on the page. Was he mad?

There were no messages on his machine. He would call Estelle back right now and inform her that he had not realized it when they spoke but he had checked his calendar and he had another engagement. A wedding. A bris. An animal sacrifice—why not, now that the lies were tumbling out? He realized to his horror that he had neglected to take down her number.

Lev considered calling Zwieback, but he knew from Deborah that the rabbi performed funerals only for members of his own congregation, and besides, how could he explain the situation to him? Lev left another message for Deborah at Temple Emunah. Surely she would be checking in—they were in the interim days of the holiday when she would certainly use the phone.

This time, he left Estelle and Myrna's names on Deborah's machine. He left the name of the funeral home. He prefaced it all by saying, "I've done something unbelievably stupid." He called back and left another message asking if she would call one of her friends even if she couldn't come back. He called again and said, "I love you." He did not mention that in the eyes of Estelle Kalman they were now married.

LEV CALMED HIMSELF with the thought that while death may not be avoidable, funerals were, especially if they were not your own. And despite his present emotional state, Lev realized with a kind of surprised relief that he was not the one being buried. The worst that would happen when he did not show up was that a relative, some competent lawyer with a Jewish education—there was always one—would step forward and read a few psalms. Or the funeral director would pinch-hit. Or perhaps they had a hot line for such emergencies. They would find someone. Deborah herself often said you did not need a rabbi for most of the things that rabbis in modern society were called on to do.

Meanwhile the phone began to ring. Deborah! There is a God!

But no, it was Estelle Kalman once more.

"Rabbi, I'm glad I got you. It's not too late?"

"No, I'm glad you called back," said Lev, preparing his escape.

"Why?" asked Mrs. Kalman, instantly suspicious. "Is there a problem? You're all I've got!"

Lev astonished himself by saying, "I need to know your mother's Hebrew name."

"Oh," said the woman, with relief.

There was a pause as Estelle gave the question some thought and Lev reflected on his own weakness.

"When she was growing up everyone called her Feige," Estelle said slowly. "Except her mother who called her Fanya. My mother had an older sister who died of scarlet fever when she was just a few months old and who had been called Fanya. Nobody wanted my mother to be called after a dead girl and everyone called her Feige, except for her own mother who had never really recovered from the girl's death and who always called my mother Fanya. But when she started going to school they called her Miriam. That's the birth certificate name. But then my mother started calling herself Myrna. But use Miriam," she said at last. "That's Hebrew, isn't it?"

This tour of her mother's names seemed to have stirred up strong feelings and she gave a deep sigh.

Lev was still marveling at his failure to take advantage of this moment to cancel. But he would get her phone number and do it later in the evening, if not in the course of the conversation. By then, he might have word from Deborah, and it would be better to be able to say, "Good news, Rabbi Green is on her way."

"Miriam is a beautiful name," said Lev, jotting it down.

Coward! Fool!

But then he remembered that it was Estelle who had called him.

"But you called?" . . .

"Yes," said Estelle. "I'm very embarrassed. I forgot to ask your fee."

"Oh," said Lev, feeling very embarrassed himself. "It's nothing, really."

"Nothing?"

The thought of money made his own culpability greater. But saying nothing surely made him look like a fake. What did Deborah do? For members of the congregation she took nothing. For friends she took nothing. Otherwise, she left it up to the family.

"Nothing fixed," said Lev. "Please, it's up to you. And while I have you," said Lev, to steer the conversation away from money, "give me your phone number."

Estelle gave it.

"I didn't ask you if you planned to speak?"

"At the funeral? Oh I don't know," said Estelle. "My daughter wants to. And my son. And Alex—my son's son." She said this with grandmotherly pride. "He's eight, and he's written a letter he'd like to read. So has his sister, Zoe, who's ten."

Already? Thought Lev. *That was fast work. What are they, obit writers?* But he said only, "That's beautiful. She must have touched a lot of lives."

"She was an impossible woman and she made my life miserable," Estelle blurted out.

"Oh," said Lev.

There seemed to be some repository of ready-made rabbinical responses lurking in Lev because he added, without hesitation, "This is an enormous loss. But that doesn't mean it isn't a complicated loss."

"I wasn't prepared," said Estelle. "And the worst of it is that she called me from the hospital the night she died. She wanted me to come over. I'd already been there but she wanted me back. She wanted me to spend the night with her. I said I'd try to come but I didn't. I went to sleep. I knew I'd come in the morning and I knew she'd be mad and I felt mad knowing that. She was a very demanding woman. She didn't talk to me for weeks after I told her I was marrying Herb. Can you imagine? But she was afraid and I should have gone over there. They called me at three o'clock in the morning. They found her dead. I just didn't want to spend the night in the hospital, in that chair . . ."

Estelle groaned. He believed she was crying.

"She died alone," she said. "Nobody should die alone. And she must have known beforehand. She asked for me."

Lev had once reported a story on the death-and-dying movement. He had interviewed Stephen Levine who had told him that "nobody dies alone." There are, according to Levine, always beloved and loving people who have already died who are there to welcome the new spirit. The tone of his article had been mocking when he wrote it, but now this idea seemed weirdly plausible. Certainly it had a positive effect on Estelle when he shared it.

"Levine," she said. "Is he a rabbi?"

Does everyone have to be a rabbi? Lev thought. *Especially for this woman who doesn't even belong to a synagogue?*

"No," said Lev, who did wonder if he wasn't compounding the evil of his imposture by quoting a New Age guru in the name of Judaism. But who knew if Judaism didn't have similar beliefs that had become lost? And surely Levine himself was Jewish.

"Judaism has lots of beliefs about the soul that people don't discuss," said Lev.

"I hope that's true," Estelle said.

Something else had occurred to Lev that he had heard Deborah say before, which he knew did derive from Judaism though it had surprised him to learn it.

"You know," said Lev, "the rabbis believed that the soul still hovers around the body after death. It takes time to separate from the world. And so in some sense the window isn't closed. Especially while your mother is still aboveground. You can speak to her and tell her you're sorry that you didn't go to the hospital. There's still time."

Mrs. Kalman gave a sigh that was almost a muffled cry. Lev himself felt the awful strangeness of what he was saying. Deborah had said these words before but Lev no longer felt he was quoting anyone, they came from some mysterious well of truth. The window isn't closed! What an idea.

"Just speak to her?" said Estelle.

"That's right," said Lev.

There was silence on the line and he wondered if Estelle wasn't addressing her mother right there and then. He felt a shiver run down his spine.

The realization, known but seldom felt, that everyone dies, had staggered him. He was thinking of the people he loved and the impossibility of imagining that the window should close on them and on him and on all the known world. He ached for Deborah.

Everyone dies! In the face of that strangeness, his own impersonation seemed less bizarre. But even as he thought that he said, into the silence on the phone, "Estelle, I'm afraid there may be a problem about tomorrow . . ."

"What?" Estelle sounded panicked.

"I didn't mention this before," said Lev, "but I've got a bit of stomach virus. It's been brewing . . ."

This hardly seemed like a lie. He felt a genuine urge to run to the bathroom.

"Well, go to bed right now," said Estelle Kalman. "Because I need you for tomorrow."

"Yes," said Lev, like a dutiful child.

"And just have toast and tea," she said.

"Matzah," said Lev.

"Of course," said Estelle. "Matzah. Although between you and me, couldn't it be the matzah?"

"No," said Lev, trying to be firm. "This feels different. But let me get some rest now. And I'll try to track down Deborah."

"Who?" Mrs. Kalman asked.

"Rabbi Green," said Lev. He did not add, "My wife."

"Ah," she said.

Lev could not suppress a perverse feeling of pride that she had accepted him utterly as a rabbi, even though Deborah always said it is the office people see, and that they create you as they need you. Still, he felt he had already given Estelle something and that she sounded calmer, less tormented. He drew strength from that. Before getting off the phone, he took down the names of family members who would be at the funeral.

"I'll see you tomorrow if you don't hear from me before then," said Lev. "Get some rest meanwhile."

"You too," said Estelle.

He still had no intention of doing the funeral. Indeed this knowledge made him calmer as he got off the phone. Surely Deborah would get his message.

But, he found himself thinking, how hard could it be? Deborah always said there was nothing to it. She was just the facilitator, an emcee of sorts. The grandchildren alone would fill ten minutes.

Really, Lev said to himself, a rabbi isn't even required.

THE FIRST NIGHT Deborah was in Westport, Rachel had not come home at nine but at ten-thirty, by which time Deborah was already in the little upstairs room where she slept whenever she visited. Dawn had set out towels at the foot of the bed and there were a few tulips from the garden in a little earthenware vase on the night table next to the lamp.

The room faced the front of the house and overlooked a tiny sliver of the Saugatuck River, which Deborah glimpsed by the light of the round, bone white holiday moon.

The room she was in was used as a guest room but doubled as an office shared by Rachel and Dawn. There was a desk and a computer, and the shelves were filled with Rachel's old medical school books and organic chemistry texts from her college days, with an assortment of women's studies books, some eclectic poetry, and a few popular spiritual works like *The Tibetan Book of Living and Dying* and *Women Who Run with the Wolves* that vaguely depressed Deborah.

Deborah had also noticed, nailed to the door frame, the mezuzah she had given them as an engagement present. It was made by Ethiopian Jews and wrapped in woven, brightly colored fabric.

"I thought you'd like the colors," Deborah had said and Rachel, bitter over the quarrels that had already broken out about the ceremony, said, "You know how we just *love* purple."

But they had nailed it to the door—not the front door, as Deborah had intended, but still, it was a room they both used. Deborah could not help noticing it was nailed to the left-hand side of the doorway— the incorrect side. Perhaps the next day she would offer to put it up correctly.

She opened the top drawer of the desk, thinking—or so she told herself—that there might be a hammer there. She noticed instead, amid the bills and receipts, a manila folder labeled: "California Cryobank Donor Catalog." Despite her better judgment, she lifted it out of the drawer and opened it on the desk.

Inside were pages of donor information in rows under various headings: Ethnic Origin; Occupation; Height; Weight; Hair Texture; Hair Color; Eye Color; Skin Tone. There were categories like "Baby Photo" and checkmarks indicating whether or not previous donations had resulted in pregnancy.

Several of the entries were circled. An Iranian mathematician with olive skin, five nine; a Bulgarian musician, six feet tall, with brown eyes; a Greek physicist with curly hair, six foot two. Deborah scanned the list obsessively as if she were looking for someone in particular— her father? Lev? It was interesting that the company was in California, as if her sister wanted to go home to spawn, though she suspected Dawn would carry the child.

Deborah had long lamented the fact that her sister would have no children. Finding the packet made her feel pleased and strangely sad. It was Deborah who suddenly seemed outside the natural order of things, childless and alone.

Deborah heard steps on the staircase and quickly stowed the file. She slipped into bed just as her sister opened the door.

Rachel was smaller than Deborah, with a delicately boned face and narrow hips. Her hair was the same wavy texture as Deborah's but was cut short in a way that was both chic and severe—it made Deborah think of cancer patients whose hair had begun growing back. Rachel also tweezed her eyebrows, which helped account for the etched gamine delicacy of her face. Deborah always felt shaggy beside her.

"Hey, Debbie," Rachel said, approaching the bed. It was not an abbreviation Deborah liked and her sister often gave it a vaguely ironic tone. But Rachel's voice was gentle and subdued. She bent over and kissed Deborah on the forehead.

"I saw your light."

She sat down next to Deborah.

"You doing OK?" she asked.

"I'm doing OK," said Deborah. "How about you?"

"I had to tell a thirty-two-year-old woman she has breast cancer today," Rachel said. "It's spread to the spine and the lungs."

"Well," said Deborah. "That puts things in perspective."

"I didn't mean—" Rachel began, awkwardly.

"No it really does," said Deborah, not sure if she meant it.

"I'm sorry things are rough for you," said Rachel.

Deborah shrugged.

"Dawn fill you in?"

"A little. Who wants to be a dead male rabbi anyway?" said Rachel.

Deborah gave a little, sad laugh.

"She told you the story about the garden?"

"Yeah," said Rachel.

"I guess it comes as no surprise," Deborah said, "that I turn out not to be so special."

Rachel was not one to say, "Oh but you are special. And I love you," which is what Deborah realized she wanted to hear.

They were both silent for a few moments and then Rachel said, "Remember how Mom used to make us tell her our dreams in the morning?"

"Of course," said Deborah.

"Well, you know what she always told us, when we were explaining them. That you're never just the person in the dream pushing someone down the stairs. You're also the person getting pushed down the stairs. And the person at the bottom of the stairs watching. You're everyone in your dream."

"Yes," said Deborah, smiling in spite of herself because there had been several family sessions about the famous "stair dream" in which it had seemed quite clear to Deborah, and even to Rachel, that it was Deborah getting pushed down the stairs in this oft-repeated nightmare of her sister's.

"Mom wasn't just saying that to diffuse my dream. I really did want to push myself down the stairs, if you know what I mean. I wanted to push you, too, of course. But also myself. And it was Mom watching. And me watching. And you watching . . ."

Deborah nodded. It seemed like a kind of apology, or matching confession.

"Don't you think," Rachel said, "you should think of yourself as being all those characters in that story? Do you have to be the one guy who leaves in peace? Can't you be all of them—not to mention none of them?"

It was good advice, she supposed. Nothing was fixed. Lev, who was always going on about mutable species, was certainly right about that. Though it didn't really address the hunger and disappointment she felt.

"You'd make a good rabbi," Deborah said.

"No need to insult me," said Rachel, shuddering a little too much to be funny. "Hard enough being a doctor," she added quickly.

As she spoke, Rachel's eye was caught by the drawer of her desk, which Deborah had left slightly open. She glanced down at Deborah whose face immediately betrayed her.

"I'm sorry," said Deborah. "I was looking for a hammer."

"A little late-night carpentry?"

Surprisingly, Rachel did not seem angry. She only arched her tweezed eyebrows and stared at Deborah, who was lying back on the pillow, her hair fanned out around her.

"Your mezuzah's wrong," Deborah said.

This came out in a corrective voice Deborah had not intended.

"If you'd like I can put it up right tomorrow."

"Maybe," said Rachel.

"I'm sorry, Rache," Deborah said quickly. "I didn't mean to snoop."

Again she sounded in her own ears like a pleading kid. She wanted her sister's gentle manner to return.

"You saw what's in there?"

Deborah nodded.

"I think it's great," she said.

"Yeah?"

Rachel's face had a probing, skeptical look.

"Yes. I'd love a niece. Or a nephew."

"You don't care it won't be Jewish?"

"It will be Jewish," said Deborah. "It will have a Jewish mother."

Rachel smiled, and it suddenly seemed to Deborah that it was in fact her sister who was already carrying the child. Her lean face looked fuller, there was a little extra flesh plumping the skin around her throat and giving Rachel's expression a softer look.

Deborah wanted to ask but held her tongue.

"I think you'll be a wonderful mother," she said.

"Really?" Rachel sounded doubtful. Frightened almost.

"Yes," said Deborah.

They sat in silence.

"Thanks for letting me come here," said Deborah finally. "It really means a lot to me."

"Of course," said Rachel, looking at Deborah with her gray eyes.

A great awkward weight of unspoken things hung on them both.

"Do you remember," Rachel asked suddenly, "how Mom used to come into our room at night and trace our faces?"

"I loved that more than anything in the world."

"Close your eyes," said Rachel.

Deborah shut her eyes. For a moment there was nothing. Her eyelids flickered in anticipation. Then she felt her sister's breath—their mother had always begun by blowing gently. And then the light touch of Rachel's fingers as they slowly traced the oval of her face.

Deborah smelled the hospital soap still on her sister's hand as her fingers passed around the orbits of her eyes. Rachel let one of her fingers trail gently down Deborah's nose and around her lips. Rachel had a cool, light touch, so light it almost tickled. Deborah heard the jingling of her sister's bracelet, with its little MedicAlert tag—she was allergic to penicillin. Her fingers passed around Deborah's chin, up along the jawline, and rested murmuring on her ears, as if they were whispering a secret. Rachel gave each lobe a little tug, just as their mother had done.

Deborah felt her face floating in space. She was a child back in the lower bunk at home. Her mind gathered up scattered images. Her congregants, like a field of poppies. Dark water. The white bird; its filigreed feather brushed her cheek.

Rachel ended by resting the ball of her finger in the little niche just above Deborah's lips, where the Talmud says an angel touches us just before we are born so that we forget all we have studied in the womb. Deborah felt her mind emptying of all she had known.

"We'll talk more tomorrow," whispered Rachel.

"Good night," Deborah murmured, pretending to be on the verge of sleep. She kept her eyes closed. Rachel leaned over and switched off the reading lamp. Deborah heard her walk out of the room and close the door behind her.

But Deborah stayed awake late into the night.

She heard her sister in the bathroom. The murmur of intimate conversation. The irregular knock of a bed board. Intermittent cries? Better not to untangle the sounds.

Deborah got out of bed and looked out at the sleeping street. She opened the window. The air was cool. She smelled the heady odor of the blossoming trees and saw, in the far distance, the little flash of darkened river, lit by the holiday moon.

LEV HAD READ SOMEWHERE that the rabbis of the Talmud considered sleep "one sixtieth part of death," but when he opened his eyes at 7 a.m. he felt his waking life, too, was mingled with oblivion.

Of course, he had hardly slept. Deborah had not called and yet he kept imagining that she was coming through the door and getting into bed beside him. At 4 a.m. he had dozed and dreamed a horrible dream involving his own burial. He was naked and it was snowing and the coffin was too small. He woke in a panic and considered calling Rabbi Zwieback, despite his reservations, but he didn't want Deborah to lose her job and felt somehow his irresponsibility would implicate her. Toward dawn Lev drifted off so that when his alarm rang at seven he felt torn out of sleep as if it were the middle of the night.

There were still two and a half hours before he had to be at the funeral home and Deborah might yet call. Nevertheless, he made himself coffee and matzah with butter, propping beside him the rabbi's manual so that he could review the order of the service.

Everything he did he told himself was provisional. "Just in case," he had printed the names of all the children and grandchildren on a sheet of paper torn from one of his reporter's notebooks. He had memorized them at 3 a.m. There were two great-grandchildren—Alex, eight, and Zoe, ten. There was Estelle of course. Estelle's two children, Lisa and Philip. Philip's wife, Joanne. And Estelle's brother, Milton, who lived in Long Island but who was on bad terms with everybody. It was unclear if Milton's ex-wife would come but Lev had written "Nicole" in parentheses next to Milton's name. He pored over these names as if he were cramming for a final exam and had made two copies, one for his breast pocket and one that he simply kept like a bookmark in the rabbi's manual. He had inserted it at the Twenty-third Psalm, which he thought he would open with, "just in case" he actually went through with it.

He read the psalm aloud in Hebrew and English, for practice, and was just reciting "Yea though I walk through the valley of the shadow of death" when the phone rang.

"I hope you're feeling better. You don't sound very good," said the by now familiar voice of Estelle Kalman.

"Actually, I'm a little weak," said Lev.

"We'll take you as you are!" said Estelle.

She was filled with a sense of the business of the day. A friend of Myrna's, someone who knew her from the day program at the senior center where she had spent three afternoons a week, wanted to speak, too. Would that be all right?

"Of course," said Lev, and added the name Edna to his list.

Estelle wanted to talk. She kept saying, "I can't believe this is really happening." And her brother, Milton, had been making trouble, suggesting at the last moment that Myrna be cremated.

"He left the plans to me," said Estelle, "and now he makes this cockamamy suggestion."

"Jews don't really cremate," said Lev, though he had read in *Gates of Mitzvah* that the Reform movement did permit "above-ground" burial. "After the Holocaust, especially . . ."

"Don't worry," said Estelle. "I told him over my dead body. My mother's going in the ground!"

Lev smiled in spite of himself.

"You're doing the right thing," he said. "You're doing something for her that she can't do for herself. That's what makes a funeral such a large mitzvah."

"I know," said Estelle. "Thank you, Rabbi."

As soon as he got off the phone, Lev ran to the bathroom and threw up his breakfast.

Maybe he really did have a stomach virus. Or perhaps his divine punishment was already beginning. But afterward, Lev felt calmer. Better to keep an empty stomach, he thought, though he did not want it completely empty. He had already popped a Xanax at 4 a.m. and had set out next to his orange juice a couple more, along with a beta blocker that acted as an antianxiety medication and that he had been given by his friend Tony who played the French horn and who took the pills whenever he auditioned because otherwise his fingers got so sweaty they slipped off the keys.

Lev showered and dressed. Somehow it was already 8:30. He was beginning to panic and to rush. His blue suit was still at his apartment and the thought of explaining to Bill why he needed it persuaded him to make do with the blazer and dark gray pants he had brought to Deborah's. He wished he had a robe to wear and went so far as to remove the black rabbinical gown, a spare, that Deborah kept hanging in her closet. It was much too small and his arms stuck out pitifully. He looked like a giant in drag.

Lev took two kippot from the top drawer of Deborah's night table, where she kept a collection in different colors, almost, he could not help thinking, like condoms. Lev selected a small leather black one and a dark green one for backup. He put the black one on his head and fastened it with bobby pins. He wished he could wear a false beard, a hood, a mask. But it was unmistakably his own face, though very white, that he saw in the mirror. His hair looked redder above the pallor of his skin and Lev wished his kippah were larger.

And then he was outside in the cool spring morning, waving the rabbi's manual at a passing cab.

In the cab, the Xanax, a double dose, kicked in and gave Lev a detached, otherworldly feeling. He watched the joggers and the dog walkers and the green light filtering through the trees and felt like a visiting angel, marveling at the embodied world.

As the cab made its way across town, Lev found himself thinking of the kibbutz in the Jordan valley where he had worked briefly in college before relocating to a Jerusalem yeshiva. He had harvested sod, stacking squares of grass chopped from the ground by a machine hooked up to a tractor. Earth clung to the squares of grass, which were heavy and warm, like pelts cut from a live animal. Work began at 4 a.m. He had a visceral

memory of standing in darkness under the date palms in front of the dining hall waiting for the tractor to pick him up while overhead fruit bats
crashed from tree to tree, gorging themselves. In those heady first weeks
he'd begun an affair with a French volunteer and one late night they had
wound up in the fields. There was no place else to go; they each had
roommates. Her English was terrible and neither of them spoke Hebrew
well; everything was gesture and touch. They had lain down in a furrow
of the field, it was like a dream. And then, when they were undressed, the
sprinklers had come on, great silver jets of water, like a romantic movie
except that the water was reprocessed sewage and the woman began to
scream, running with her clothes pressed against her breasts, her naked
ass clad in damp earth, while Lev jumped into his jeans and ran after her
until he heard the laughter of men and saw two *shomrim*, kibbutz guards,
leaning against a fence with their rifles slung over their shoulders, making lewd gestures. The episode in the fields had humiliated him but he
kept longing for it while he studied in the yeshiva, just as he had contin-
ually felt on the kibbutz that something was missing from his life . . .

The cab stopped in front of the funeral home. When Lev saw
the cluster of mourners gathered outside he felt a jolt of adrenaline
and almost told the cab driver to keep going but, impelled by some
mysterious force, he got out and stood on the sidewalk. There was a
high-topped ambulette from the Sinai Center letting out its load of
elderly mourners who had come to pay their last respects. Though she
had lived on her own, Estelle's mother had spent three days a week in
the center's day program and volunteered in its library. It was the
home where his father had rehabilitated from his stroke and Lev half
expected to see his father lifting reproving eyes at him that said, "This
is not what I meant at all!"

Lev made his way past the canes and walkers and entered the
darkened lobby. He approached the gloomy man standing guard at
the door and said, in a voice barely above a whisper, "I'm performing
the funeral of Myrna . . ." good God, what was her last name?

"Epstein," said the man, looking at Lev skeptically. "Second floor.
The family's already upstairs."

There were a few mourners milling around in a sort of anteroom where an open guestbook rested on a high table, but Lev made his way toward the little room where the immediate family was. He reminded himself of Deborah's philosophy—the mourners will treat you with the authority they require.

And indeed, no sooner had he entered than a woman came toward him.

"Rabbi Friedman!"

It wasn't a question; Estelle Kalman knew it was him.

"Your hand is freezing!" she said. "You really do look unwell. Thank you for making it."

She introduced him to everyone as "The Rabbi," and every time the title was used Lev felt a little stab of nausea and uncertainty. But he rallied and shook hands all around, nodding and murmuring. They were impressed that he knew so many of their names. One woman was sobbing—Gloria, a sister of the deceased, whom Estelle had somehow forgotten to mention. Lev embraced her.

"May the Lord comfort thee," he murmured.

Good God had he really said *thee*? He was talking like a Quaker in a movie, though perhaps so softly she hadn't heard. He was relieved to see the flesh-colored hearing aid affixed behind her ear like chewing gum.

Estelle had seated herself on a couch. She was more than middle aged but not at all old and surprisingly stylish in a long black skirt with little zip-up boots and a dark blouse. She had red hair, like Lev, though hers had a teased and puffy look. She was flanked by her husband, a gray-faced man with a bad toupee, and her daughter, a young, darker version of her mother with long brown hair, too much lipstick, and a worried face. Everyone looked at Lev expectantly.

Lev produced a slender reporter's notebook and set about interviewing the family, gathering up stories he could use in his eulogy. It wasn't so different, he told himself, from writing an article; people shared with instant trust. When he had transcribed a good collection of anecdotes in his precise shorthand, he slipped away, found a water fountain, and took another Xanax. Then another for good measure. He tipped his head back like a bird to help the pills go down. He panicked briefly that he had taken too many and would simply fall asleep drooling among the mourners, but shook off his fear and returned to face the family. The funeral director, a small man with manicured nails and a large red-stoned ring that gave his hand a papal weight, touched Lev on the shoulder and said, "We'll be starting in about fifteen minutes."

"I'm going to do *k'riah* now," said Lev, swallowing hard.

The funeral director, who had already asked those not in the immediate family to please take seats next door, shooed the stragglers out of the little room. Lev pulled up a chair, opened his manual to the section marked "*k'riah*—Rending the Garment," and said, "I'd like us all to come together for a moment."

Zoe and Alex were called over and sat on chairs, looking at Lev curiously. He felt their eyes on him but he also felt a strange self-confidence.

"Herb, come here!" Estelle called, addressing her husband, who was now sitting off by himself reading the *New York Post*.

Lev could see why Myrna would oppose marriage to such a man and his sympathy for the dead woman increased. Herb grudgingly got up and sat beside his daughter. Alex scrambled onto his lap.

"For hearts that are torn," Lev declaimed, reading from his manual, "we perform this act of *k'riah*."

A hush fell over the little group at this first rabbinic utterance. Lev then added, by way of explanation, "As a sign of mourning it is customary to perform a token tearing of the garment. Only the children of the deceased, and the siblings, perform this custom. Milton, should we begin with you?"

Though he had been described as a black sheep, Milton had actually been very gracious to Lev. He was an overweight man—perhaps he had the gene; Alex was also a fatty—and seemed more uncomfortable than grieving, as if something were physically afflicting him. When he had interviewed him earlier, Lev had been touched that Milton would say only, "She was an angel. She brought us up after my father died and never complained. She ran the clothing store all those years. People loved her. She was tough but people loved her. I loved her."

Lev leaned over and with trembling fingers grabbed Milton's lapel. Locating the seam, he tried to make a small rip. The material did not budge. Zoe and Alex giggled. Lev tried again without success. He had a pocket knife on his keychain and at last he fished it out, opening the tiny blade.

"It's just a few stitches," Lev said. "I'll do it on the seam."

But as he was aiming his knife at Milton's swelling front, he felt a tap on his shoulder and, turning around, saw the funeral director with a badly suppressed smile on his lips. In his little hand he held several black ribbons and a scissors.

"It's also possible," said Lev, "simply to affix one of these."

Everyone laughed, even the sister who had not stopped weeping. Somehow he had missed the ribbons. And though Lev now remembered the black ribbons Deborah organized at the funeral he'd watched her perform, the actual tearing ceremony had taken place behind closed doors.

Milton all but grabbed a ribbon out of Lev's hand and, opening the safety pin at the back, stuck it himself onto his own lapel.

"There's something you say," Lev said, collecting himself.

He made a point of reading the little one-line prayer in Hebrew as a way of reclaiming authority. He then read it in English and Milton repeated the phrase in a sullen voice.

"We praise You, Adonai our God, who has implanted within us everlasting life."

Lev had thought he might use the little family huddle to try a sort of free-style prayer of the sort Deborah excelled at but his embarassment was now too great for this. When the black ribbons were all attached and cut, Lev merely reviewed with them the order in which people would speak. He made a few emendations to his notebook page and then the funeral director, who had by now returned to the little room, nodded to Lev.

It was a relief to let the funeral director take over for a while. He fussed people into position with his anxious, fawning, bossy manner. They lined up in front of the double doors leading to the room where the mourners had already gathered and where the coffin waited. Lev was at the front of the line. At a sign from the director he began to walk, the family behind him, into the large room.

Deborah had a way of walking that was humble yet somehow commanding. He tried to capture her posture. The crowd stood up at the funeral director's command, a sign of respect for the family. Lev thought for a brief moment, looking out, that he was going to be sick. He was a little weak in the knees, though whether this was from the medication he had taken or nerves or both he could not tell. But he breathed deeply and kept going.

The black fact of the coffin brought him up short. The coffin looked like polished ebony. He should have urged Estelle toward a plain pine box; he knew the funeral homes shamed you into extravagance. But the thought that there was a corpse inside trumped all other reflections. There it was, the great show stopper! And yet he was connected to that box, like a bullfighter to a bull.

The funeral director, who behaved like a maître d' seating a large party, was trying to get Lev's attention. Everyone had sat down by now—the family first and then the crowd—and Lev realized that he had forgotten to take his place at the podium. Instinctively, he had simply taken a seat. Hurriedly, he rose and ascended the steps to the lectern like a man ascending a gallows. Oh to run away! But he was fixed by forces beyond his control, and by all those eyes, now looking at him intently.

He opened his manual and rested it on the tilted surface. He looked out over the mourners while trying not to see any one of them, though this was impossible. The white heads of the old people were visible toward the back. In front of him was the immediate family and just below him, a little to the right, the coffin.

"Forgive me," he breathed in the direction of the coffin. "I know you deserve better than me."

Speaking to this woman, though she was dead, had an oddly reassuring effect on him. He turned a few pages and cleared his throat.

Don't be afraid of the silence, he told himself, one of Deborah's tricks. But for a moment he became hypnotized by it, listening to the rustling, the coughing, the loud whisper of an elderly man toward the back saying, "I can't hear!" and the hissing return of his neighbor, "He's not talking!"

Could he really do it? He felt dizzy and he wondered if he had overdosed on Xanax after all. A beam of darkness emanating from the back row entered his vision and diminished his sight. There was a dark spot growing in his brain, threatening to engulf him in shadows. He was sweating and had forgotten to bring a handkerchief. Indelicately, he mopped his brow with the sleeve of his blazer. He felt the cold steel button on his forehead. Silence from the coffin had spread to engulf the entire room.

Lev blinked and cleared his throat again. Then he heard his own voice say, " 'Adonai, what are we, that You have regard for us? What are we, that You are mindful of us? We are like a breath; our days are like a passing shadow; we come and go like grass, which in the morning shoots up, renewed, and in the evening fades and withers. You cause us to turn to dust, saying: Return, O mortal creatures! Would that we were wise, that we understood wither we are going! For when we die we carry nothing away; our glory does not accompany us . . .' "

Well, he had their attention. He felt the power of what he was saying and his own littleness. Though the passage, an amalgam of several psalms, ended with a word of consolation—"Adonai, You redeem the souls of your servants and none who trust in You shall be desolate"— the bleak power of the opening formulation hung in the air, and the coffin reinforced it like an exclamation point. His dizziness had scattered and he was no longer sweating, though his forehead was still damp. He had managed not to stutter at all. A cool breeze seemed to blow on him.

Truly, he was nothing before the universe, before God. This insight emboldened him. Still looking down, he launched into the Twenty-third Psalm.

"The Lord is my shepherd I shall not want . . ."

The funeral director appeared beside him and adjusted the microphone so that suddenly "he leadeth me beside the still waters" leapt out of the speakers. Had no one yet heard him? Disheartened but no longer in danger of fainting, Lev read on.

When he had finished reciting that psalm he noticed that Estelle and her daughter were both crying and this, perversely, gave him confidence. He read the same psalm in Hebrew—he had always been a good reader, despite poor comprehension—and once this hurdle was passed he felt a rising sense of authority, an unexpected feeling of power.

He turned a few pages, enduring the silence in which one or two people blew their noses. Filling in the name of the deceased, he read, "Death has taken our beloved Myrna. Our friends grieve in their darkened world. In their silence, there is lamentation. In their tears, there is loneliness. Lost in their sorrow, may they find the presence of loving friends. Hear them, O God. Be with them . . ."

When he was finished with that section he consulted his slip of paper and said, "There are some people here who want to say a few words. Myrna's beloved great-granddaughter, Zoe, will now read a letter she has written."

Lev stepped down so that Zoe could come up, and for a moment he thought he might keep going, out the door and down the steps and into a cab. What could they do to him? But to leave that body up there was worse than leaving a bride at the altar. There was no running away.

After Zoe's letter, in which she recalled going to Rumplemayer's for ice cream sundaes, Lev introduced Alex, who stood up and, after a brief catalog of memorable toys his grandmother had given him, said, "I'm sorry you're not here now and that you won't be coming to see us for my birthday!"

After Alex, Lisa spoke—her grandmother had taken her shopping at Bloomingdale's and Saks when she was a teenager for things her own mother would never buy her.

A Polish housekeeper who had also been a kind of home-care provider rose to speak but wept so profusely that no words came out of her mouth and Lev was forced to usher her off the stage. Estelle did not get up to speak and neither did Milton, but two of Myrna's friends from the Sinai Center spoke and it was most moving of all to see the elderly, so close to death themselves, eulogize their friend.

"Too soon!" Edna, who looked about one hundred, said. "You've been taken too soon." On her way back to her chair, she touched the coffin in farewell and murmured something Lev did not catch.

When all the speakers were done it was Lev's turn to say a few words. His plan was to keep it very short. This was the part Lev had dreaded the most. He tried to imagine that Deborah was with him, whispering in his ear, speaking through him.

"Friends," he began—more Quaker language, and yet it sounded right—"we are here to mourn a death and also to celebrate a life." (Was that true? Celebrate seemed wrong.) "To some it might seem an ordinary life, but it was, as we can tell looking out at all of you, a life that touched many other lives and that leaves a great hole in our midst."

He had scribbled some facts about Estelle that he repeated now. Her birth on the Lower East Side. The loss of her sister, before she was born, to scarlet fever. The death of her father, who, having pulled himself up to prosperity from immigrant poverty, dropped dead of a heart attack one day after opening a new clothing factory. The death by cancer of her mother, whom Myrna nursed in her final illness, and of her own husband, and how she had raised the family alone in a tiny apartment in the Bronx where she had a clothing store that somehow grew into two stores under her tireless management. The love she lavished on her grandchildren and on her friends, and the volunteer work she found time for, the knitting she organized, despite arthritis, for people with AIDS. A good woman. And though, said Lev, she did not belong to a synagogue and was not someone who cared much for organized religion, she really was what Judaism calls "a woman of valor."

He then read from "A Woman of Valor," which the manual reprinted as a possible reading. He saw several people nodding their heads and he thought, *Let the tradition speak for you. Invent as little as possible.*

And yet he felt compelled to say a few words more. Holding up

Deborah's rabbi's manual he said, "I look into this book and I am reminded by it of all the terrible things that can happen. There is a section for an infant not yet thirty days old. A section for a young parent who dies. A section for someone who dies in great pain. In a way, Myrna had experience with all these terrible things. And yet she survived and endured them."

He paused, still holding up the book, no longer sure what he wanted to say. He looked out over the faces, which seemed so familiar to him. It was like looking down from a tightrope and yet he did not fall. He forced his mind back to his task. Deborah was no longer present; he felt utterly alone. It was too hard to think through her, and what he thought was how he wished he had known his own grandparents, any of them. And he realized, almost for the first time, that he was eulogizing an actual individual, a life that didn't exist anymore. He had been to the library at the Sinai Center to get newspapers for his father when he was rehabilitating there, and Lev suddenly remembered a white-haired woman signing out books, her walker parked beside the desk. Was that Myrna? He found, to his astonishment, that there were tears in his eyes.

But he needed to conclude. He lowered the manual and his eyes rested on Milton, sitting gloomily next to Alex at the end of the aisle.

"Myrna's son, Milton, said to me before the funeral that his mother was an angel," said Lev. "What's so moving about that for me is that he wasn't saying she is one now. We don't know what happens to her now." This, he realized, was maybe going too far and he saw a cloud pass over some of the faces. He added quickly, "Though our tradition speaks of a world to come. But to be an angel while we're here— isn't that the point?"

And then, by way of closure, he said simply, "She will be missed by many."

Then he took his seat. He was utterly spent. Estelle's daughter, Lisa, reached out a long arm and handed him a tissue; his cheek was damp. She was smiling at him in a kind, almost pitying way, he thought. He remembered Deborah saying defiantly, *So what if I cry? I'm human. I'd hate to be one of those rabbis who act like they are just dead wood. I'm not an anchorman doing the news. I'm receiving the news myself. I'm affected by it. Otherwise, the whole thing's bullshit.* Lev was not sure why he had wept—the medication, the stress, the fear were enough to make him break down and sob like a baby. And yet he felt something else had affected him, too.

The funeral director was now standing at the podium, announcing the location of the cemetery. Nothing was said about shivah, which Estelle wasn't really having, though everyone was invited back to her apartment after the burial for bagels and lox.

Lev, relieved and exhausted, was surprised to see the funeral director motioning him back to the podium. Had he left something out?

When Lev got there, the man whispered, "*El Maleh Rachamim.*"

Somehow, Lev had neglected this prayer in his preparations, though of course he realized now it was the central prayer, the final farewell, and in some ways the one fixed element of a funeral. He also realized, glancing into the manual, that there was a space for Myrna's Hebrew name but also a space for her parents' names and he did not know those. It seemed a mistake to go ask Estelle now. Furthermore, he could not remember the tune and had not practiced the Hebrew.

How could he think it was possible to escape without humiliation and without detection?

For a moment as he stood again at the podium he considered confessing.

"Ladies and gentlemen, I stand before you a sinner." But who would that benefit? Not the people crying in the front row. Not the busload of visitors from the Sinai Center. They wanted a rabbi and so for them he would be a rabbi.

He cleared his throat and began to chant in a tuneless but heartfelt moan, in English, "Compassionate God, eternal Spirit of the universe, grant perfect rest in Your sheltering presence to Myrna Epstein, called in Hebrew Miriam, who has entered eternity . . ."

He got through the prayer in English, having added what he hoped was a Hebrew flavor with his chanting. Beyond this he had committed only one unfortunate error—in his anxiety he read "let him/her find refuge in Your eternal presence" without selecting a gender. He did it again at the end: "May he/she rest in peace and let us say: Amen."

Perhaps they would think it was a new sort of egalitarianism. In any event, he was done. He was simply too spent to tackle the Hebrew and so, after the assembled had echoed back "Amen," he nodded to the funeral director, who looked as eager as Lev to bring things to a close and who waved in the professional pallbearers, dark-suited men with a mafioso air who wheeled the coffin down the aisle, followed by the family and by Lev himself. Lev walked in a kind of trance, though several people pressed his hand and said, "That was lovely." Only one or two, he thought, looked at him askance, though Lev was primarily thinking, *I did it! It's done!* and feeling a relief bordering on euphoria.

This feeling followed him to the lobby where he was embraced by a weeping Estelle who said, "You are a prince for doing this so sick." He embraced Milton and praised Zoe and Alex to their parents. He then detached himself from the family and wandered outside where a large crowd was already gathering. The senior citizens had all beaten him down the stairs.

A tiny woman in a large, superfluous fur coat came up to him and said, "Young man, I couldn't hear a word you said."

"Thank you," said Lev, before he realized he wasn't receiving a compliment.

"You seem like a nice fella, though," the woman continued. "Are you single? I have a granddaughter about your age."

Lev was about to say yes, merely from a truthful impulse, when someone in the crowd said, "He's married, Ma. And he's not Cindy's type at all. Besides, you shouldn't bother him now. Can't you see he's sick?"

The old people all backed away from him. But the persistent woman with the granddaughter said, no longer addressing Lev, "Where's his ring?"

"They don't always wear rings today," said a stooped man with a cap.

"They wear them in their *pupiks!*" said a woman with a cane, before boarding the ambulette that had now backed up into position, beeping loudly.

Lev felt a light touch on his hand. He turned and almost screamed. It was the white-haired woman Lev had recalled from the Sinai Center library. The ghost of Myrna Epstein come back to torment him!

"That was lovely," the ghost said.

"Who are you?" Lev brought out.

"Rita Goldfarb. I worked in the library with Myrna."

Ah.

"She would have liked the service. She didn't like rabbis but you don't seem like one."

"Thank you," Lev stammered.

"But you shouldn't call people angels. People aren't angels," Rita waved her hand dismissively. "It's enough they should be human beings."

The old woman had a European accent that Lev immediately felt chastened by.

Lev had moved himself greatly with his own words but he realized now that they had nothing to do with reality, only with the wish for what reality might be.

Myrna wasn't an angel. Estelle had told him his mother was an impossible woman. He felt a double sense of sadness; he had gotten her life wrong even as he was fucking up her death. He felt like a murderer. Can you kill the dead?

He would like to have spoken to the old woman a little longer but she had already vanished, as if she truly were a ghost. It seemed to Lev a good time to make his own exit. He began moving away from the increasingly congested entranceway but he was grabbed with surprising force by the funeral director.

"Where are you going?" the man asked. "You're in car two."

Lev looked and saw two great black limousines lined up behind the bus from the Sinai Center.

The burial! Lev had completely forgotten.

In front of the bus, a little way up the block, was a hearse into which the funeral home goons were sliding, with surprising difficulty, Myrna Epstein's coffin. He still had to go to the cemetery and shovel this woman under. At the sight of the tilted coffin with its terrible load his remaining strength drained out of him. He watched the men wrestling the coffin into position.

Lev was unclear about the Jewish belief in Hell but he had a good idea that if such a place existed he would be going there and the woman in the coffin would be the first to testify against him.

"I have to tell you something," he said to the director, who was no longer holding on to him.

The director nodded.

The man's face, Lev realized, was not unkind. It had simply worn its mask of artificial consolation too long.

"I've never buried anyone before," Lev said.

"You don't have to. There are men there who will do it for you."

Lev was not sure if this was sarcasm or consideration. But he knew that there was no relief. Having finished with the coffin, one of the funeral home men was now holding open the door of Lev's limousine, beckoning him inside.

Lev stood rooted to the pavement while Gloria, the sister who had wept so, ducked into the limo, along with two cousins whose names Lev had forgotten. The director led Lev into the street and for a moment Lev fantasized that he would whisper, "Get into a cab and get out of here!" but he was only taking Lev to the passenger side. At least he would not have to talk to anyone. Dutifully, Lev folded himself inside and put on his seat belt. The door slammed with a muffled limousine thunk and Lev found himself seated in the overheated car, watching as the driver got into a fight with the driver of the ambulette, who was occupying the space behind the hearse. One old person after another inched slowly into the idling vehicle.

Lev shut his eyes and when he opened them he was out on the Whitestone Bridge. Mercifully, the driver did not speak to Lev but merely stared impassively ahead. Snatches of conversation drifted forward from the back seat—"I think she found him on the Internet." "No, he's the friend of a friend." "I'm worried about her."

On the Cross Island Parkway, a police siren blared and Lev thought fleetingly that they had come for him; the funeral home director had ratted him out, or someone who knew that granting "his/her soul eternal rest" was not a rabbinic formulation. Was impersonating a rabbi a crime? But the police car shot past and Lev drifted off to sleep again, no longer caring what happened to him. He had so nursed the impression that he was sick that he half believed he was, and indeed he was shivering slightly, despite the heat in the car. Stuporous, he watched the roadside ugliness flit past, drifting in and out of consciousness until at last, in Elmont, the car turned into the Beth David cemetery where Lev realized his mother's parents had been buried many years before. He could not escape the feeling that the dead, at least the Jewish dead, all knew each other.

The limousines lined up in front of the cemetery office, where there were bathroom stops and a slow wait for several lost cars. Lev realized that he had left the rabbi's manual at the funeral home. He was now wide awake, feeling trapped not simply because he was in a car but because he could no longer imagine getting away.

He turned to the limo driver, who Lev kept imagining was going to dump him in the East River when all this was over, and said,

"I've lost my rabbi's manual. I'm not going to be able to finish the job."

The driver, without saying a word, leaned toward Lev and flipped open the glove compartment. He extracted a little booklet with the funeral home name printed on it. Inside was the graveside Kaddish and the Twenty-third Psalm.

"Thanks," said Lev.

The cars began moving again, snaking their way down the tiny lanes of the city of the dead where vast monuments with single names—"Kramer," "Ziff"—rose above the lower field of graves where an occasional bunch of flowers withered against a tombstone and where, here and there, a funeral was in progress.

Lev opened his window to revive himself. The air was cool but it was unmistakably spring. The cemetery went on for miles and yet looked peripheral, not the ultimate destination of all flesh but some marginal spot under the great carpet of Queens where the dead were swept. He fixed on a distant crabapple tree, all white amid the desolation. Close by, a lone magnolia tree put out pink, waxy, corpse-fed flowers.

Lev could not remember where his grandparents were buried. He glanced down at the little booklet he had received and studied the graveside Kaddish, subtly different from the Kaddish said in synagogue, as if to trip up mourners when they most needed a familiar prayer.

None of this would have happened if his father hadn't asked him, in his non-suicide note, to say Kaddish for him when he died. From there he had sought out Deborah and now here he was, preparing to say Kaddish for a total stranger, pretending to be something he wasn't.

Well he would see it through, despite his exhaustion and shame. What else could he do?

Lev slid the booklet into his breast pocket.

It was a long walk to the grave. Another funeral, now finishing, had blocked off the little street closest to the Epstein family plot.

My dear friends, Lev rehearsed in his mind. *My dear friends.* The rest would come to him when he stood there.

Suddenly, someone screamed.

Gloria, the weeping sister, had tripped on a footstone and flopped into a shrub. There was something obscene about the sprawled old woman, her skirt hitched up, embracing the bush. Lev and several others raced over and helped her to her feet. Her cheek was scratched but she waved everyone away angrily—all but Lev, whose arm she grabbed as she hobbled forward.

She would be joining her sister soon and seemed to be marching grimly toward her own fate. There was a moist red line on one cheek, like a dueling scar. He had been told she resembled her sister and Lev apologized to her silently. Gloria was sniffling and her tears and aged face brought home to Lev again the full weight of his terrible deception. He could barely take in the field of graves stretching all around him. Each headstone reproached him with his sin. But at last he forced himself to look toward the gravediggers and toward the freshly dug grave itself. As he did his heart gave a sudden lurch.

There, next to a mound of red earth, stood Deborah.

SHE LOOKED VERY TALL, as if she were standing on the mound of dirt, not next to it. She had on a long gray skirt, a white collared shirt that flared at the wrists, and a red velvet shawl Lev had never seen before that was draped over her shoulders like a tallis. Her hair was pulled back and her broad face was watchful and composed.

Lev had to resist the impulse to break into a run. He extracted his arm from the grip of the wobbly Gloria and handed her off to Milton, who was just behind them.

"Will you excuse me for a moment?"

Then he walked as quickly as he could toward the spot where Deborah stood, cutting through a low shrub and trampling on several graves before arriving at the Epstein family stone.

The gravediggers, in heavy shoes and smudged navy jumpsuits, were unceremoniously lowering the coffin on long canvas straps. It pitched against the steep dirt walls like a boat against its moorings.

Deborah's face remained serious but her eyes were smiling as Lev came up to her.

"I only got your message this morning," she said. "I came right away."

"Thank you!" was all Lev could say.

He had an impulse to throw himself down at her feet, right there in the dirt.

"Did you do it?" she asked.

"Yes," said Lev.

"I knew you would," said Deborah, with pride.

The coffin settled with a hollow thud. The men yanked the straps hissing out of the pit.

"You've got to take over," said Lev.

Estelle and several others were by now approaching. Lev began speaking in a speedy whisper, like a spy transferring information.

"They think I have a stomach virus. I told them last night I'd try to get you, so it won't seem so strange that you're here. I botched *El Maleh Rachamim* so you should do that one again. Myrna's Hebrew name is Miriam. I never found out the names of her parents."

Deborah nodded, taking it all in.

"Anything else?" she asked.

"They think we're married."

Deborah raised her eyebrows at this, but Lev had turned to Estelle, who was by now standing before him on the arm of her son Philip. She was eyeing Deborah with perplexity.

"Estelle," he said. "I'm afraid I really am unwell. Miraculously, Rabbi Green is here. So please, excuse me."

He had the night before committed to memory the Hebrew phrase meaning, "May God comfort you along with all the mourners of Zion and Jerusalem," but it had flown completely out of his head. The arrival of Deborah had broken his brief enchantment. All competence went out of him and he only put out his clammy hand and said, "I'm so sorry."

"You're a trouper," Estelle said distractedly.

She had caught sight of the great mound of earth, badly concealed by a green tarp, and the spades stuck into the exposed dirt. She was not yet near enough to look down into the grave itself, but the long shadow of final things had fallen across her and she scarcely noticed as Lev drifted away.

Deborah stepped forward and, with firm, tender confidence, introduced herself and offered condolences.

Lev spotted Deborah's little red Honda parked on the narrow lane perpendicular to the one his limousine had stopped on. As he headed toward it, a mockingbird landed on a gravestone a few feet away from him and cocked its tail so that its body formed a wide V. Lev was close enough to see the bird's red eye and to read, "Loving Son, Devoted Husband." He slowed, hoping the bird would sing, but with a flash of white wing patches it flew off into a large solitary chestnut tree. The gravediggers were leaning against the trunk having a smoke.

When Lev reached the car, he turned back and saw Deborah gathering the mourners toward her with outstretched arms. Then he opened the passenger-side door, ducked inside, reclined the seat back as far as it would go, and shut his eyes. He sank into a deep dreamless sleep and woke only when the car door slammed.

He opened his eyes with a start.

Deborah was settling herself behind the wheel. There was dirt clinging to the hem of her dark skirt and she had that look of serious exhilaration she got after a full burial.

"Was it a dream?" he asked.

"Nope," Deborah said.

She smiled at him, but then she noticed that her shawl had a streak of dirt on it.

"Shit! My sister lent this to me. I'll have to have it dry-cleaned."

She began brushing at it with her hand.

Lev brought his seat upright. Whatever elation he had felt at his audacity had ebbed away. In Deborah's presence, he felt like an impostor.

"What have I done?"

"A funeral," Deborah said, her eyes merry. "And from what I understand you did a very good job."

She withdrew an envelope from her little pocket book and tossed it into Lev's lap. Meanwhile she started the car and drove slowly down the little lane.

"What's this?"

"Look inside," said Deborah.

"Oh God," he said.

Deborah could not contain herself anymore and burst into laughter.

Lev counted five crisp one-hundred-dollar bills.

"We have to return it," he said.

"Hey some of that's mine," said Deborah. "Don't forget my dry-cleaning bill."

"You can keep your cut."

"We can give it to charity if you want," said Deborah. "You can't return it to Estelle."

"We'll give it to charity."

"Except let's go out to dinner with some of it."

Lev shut his eyes. "Isn't it a sin?" He could not yet see the humor in the thing.

"You didn't break any *halakhic* rules," said Deborah. "On the contrary. You helped somebody in need."

"But they thought I was a rabbi!"

"Would that all the people were prophets!" said Deborah.

"What does that mean?"

"That's what Moses says when these two guys start prophesying in the camp. The spirit of God has come down on them, but Joshua gets very upset and tells Moses to kill them. It's like they're operating without a license. But Moses says, 'Would that all the people were prophets.' We're supposed to be a nation of priests, you know. Not a nation of congregants. Or a nation of clerical administrators."

A funeral procession was now going by. While they were stopped to let the slow heavy hearse and fat black limos slide by, someone rapped on Lev's window. It was a young, plump woman with bright blue eyes. Lev recognized her from Levine's. He had found her face a pleasant one to look out on. She stooped as Lev rolled down his window. He tried not to stare at the tops of her breasts, bunched before him in a scoop-necked sweater.

"Excuse me, Rabbi," she said.

"Yes?" said Deborah.

"No," said the young woman. "Rabbi Friedman."

Lev gave a wan smile that was really a grimace.

"I was wondering if you perform weddings?"

"Oh," said Lev, pride and mortification mingling. "I'm sorry. My schedule just doesn't permit. This was an exception."

"That's too bad," said the woman. "That was a very beautiful service."

"Thank you," said Lev, who had laid his head back on the seat.

"What's the name of your congregation?"

Lev pretended not to hear. He simply closed his eyes.

"I'm afraid the rabbi isn't feeling too well," said Deborah, from her side of the car.

"I hope you feel better," the young woman said to Lev, before turning to go.

Deborah doubled over with laughter when the woman had walked away.

"Oh God I'm going to pee in my pants," she said. "We have to get out of here."

But they paused at the exit gate and Deborah, who had recovered herself, took out a bottle of water, opened her door and ritually washed her hands, first the right, then the left, three times. When she was finished she passed the bottle to Lev. Silently he took it, opened his door, and washed his hands, too. When he was done he handed the water back to her.

Before Deborah turned off into traffic she reached into her bag and handed Lev a hard-boiled egg and a piece of matzah.

"Didn't I tell you to bring food to a funeral? You look like you've seen a ghost."

And then, imitating the sensei from *Kung Fu*, she said, "Grasshopper, you have much to learn."

It was only when they pulled onto the highway that Lev said, "Deborah, why did you run away?"

Deborah wasn't laughing anymore. A sadness had settled over her that made her earlier hilarity seem like passing mania. She had decided, for the time being, to withhold her encounter with Reuben. She knew that she did not want to be with him and, she told herself, nothing had happened. Besides, the larger answer was just as painful.

She was silent for so long, staring ahead so intently that Lev began to wonder if she had heard him.

"I'm sorry," she said suddenly. "I was sinking. I had to get away."

"From me?" asked Lev.

"From myself. And you."

"You wouldn't talk to me!" said Lev.

"I know," said Deborah. "I felt like I was becoming invisible around you. More of a 'rabbi' and less of a person. And at the same time, I felt inside like less of a rabbi than ever. And I thought if I lost the things that made me a rabbi . . . if I lost God . . . I'd be nothing to you. But it wasn't really about you. I was afraid of becoming nothing to myself . . ."

"Did you?" he asked.

"Did I what?"

"Did you lose God?"

"Would it matter?" she asked. "To you?"

Deborah was squinting at the road. It had begun drizzling—too little to bother with the wipers but it made visibility through the speckled windshield poor. He looked at her profile, her thick eyebrows, drawn together in concentration; her shoulders slightly hunched. The wide open face and pursed, pouting lips. A car cut her off and she swore with helpless irritation. If she hadn't been driving, he would have put his arms around her. He had a great urge to gather her up and shelter her, as if, despite the windshield, she were getting rained on.

"It's you that I want," Lev said softly. "It's you I love."

Deborah stared straight ahead but her eyes filled with tears.

BACK IN THE APARTMENT, Deborah unpacked the little bag she had taken to her sister's. She had brought along her grandfather's tallis but had not used it. Nevertheless, as she put it in her drawer next to the little velvet pouch containing his tefillin she felt hopeful. Perhaps tomorrow, she thought.

Lev watched her unpack.

"You're back?" he said.

"If you'll have me."

"It's your apartment," said Lev, wanting to say more but smarting again at the memory of her sudden disappearance. He knew her flight had to do with more than her fears about God or his own need for her to have faith. Rabbis were spiritually promiscuous—they belonged to everybody and nobody. His presence demanded something different and he wondered if she could commit herself to ordinary life with a man like him.

"Deborah," said Lev, sitting on the bed. "There's something I have to tell you."

Deborah froze.

"While you were gone, I . . ."

"Who?" said Deborah, cutting him off. She had not told him about Reuben but he had gotten revenge anyway! Men always did. She suspected Jenny, the ex-fiancée. They'd run into her once together, a pretty, petite girl with an angry underbite. Deborah could tell she still had feelings for Lev, despite the blow he had dealt her.

"I brought a chicken up to your apartment."

"A chicken?"

"From downstairs," said Lev.

"You mean from Pick a Chick?"

"Yes," said Lev.

He waited for her to laugh but to Lev's surprise she looked upset.

"You bastard!" she burst out. "My grandmother's dishes can't be *kashered*—they're ceramic!"

"Nothing happened!" Lev shouted. "I couldn't go through with it."

But Deborah raced to the kitchen and flung open the cabinets as if she expected to find evil doings inside. She was staring at her grandmother's blue ceramic dishes when he joined her.

"I didn't eat on them," said Lev. "I ate on newspaper. I *treifed* up a fork and a spoon—they're wrapped in tinfoil."

Deborah closed the cabinet. She was laughing at herself.

"Bubba's dishes are safe," said Lev.

"Somehow I need them more than ever," said Deborah. "Even though at my sister's, you should have seen me. I ate baked potatoes cooked in their microwave."

"You heathen," said Lev.

Back in the bedroom, Deborah stepped out of her skirt. She slid off her pantyhose, businesslike, in pre-shower mode. But Lev drew close, unsnapped her bra and placed his hands over her breasts from behind.

"I need to shower," said Deborah. "I didn't have time this morning."

"My day began with death," Lev said.

He felt her nipples waking under his palms, but Deborah, sniffing her armpits, declared, "I really do stink! All that digging and no de-odorant. I'll just be a minute."

Lev ignored her. He kissed the prickly hollow under her arm, in-haling the warm earth odor, faintly rank. His hands strummed past her ribs and over her soft belly. Kneeling, he slid her underpants down past the bearded arrow of pubic hair, resting his cheek for a moment against her cool ass. A double portion.

"You certainly seem to have regained your strength," Deborah said, laughing as Lev all but pushed her onto the bed. She lay back, set-tling herself against the pillows as he hastily removed his clothes.

He did not hurry to hide himself under the blankets. His lean freckled body made Deborah think of a leopard or cheetah reared up on hind legs.

"Oh Rabbi Friedman," she called. "Aren't you forgetting some-thing?"

She tapped her head and Lev, naked, reached up and removed the kippah, still clinging by its bobby pin to his hair.

THE FOLLOWING SHABBAT, Deborah returned to Temple Emunah. Lev sat in the back row during services. Deborah saw him and felt warmed by his presence. Afterward he met her in her study where she peeled off the heavy black robe.

"It feels like I was away for a long time," said Deborah.

"And does it feel OK?" Lev asked.

"For now," said Deborah.

Her robe lay on the floor where she had dropped it. It always looked to Lev as though the Wicked Witch of the West had just melted. He hung it up for her.

"You're not going to run away again?" he asked.

"Not from you," said Deborah.

She had told him about Reuben. He had taken it badly, as she knew he would, but she wanted to smash the idol she feared he might make of her, for her own sake as well as his. He had stormed and called her names but it was a short-lived outburst. After all, nothing had really happened.

Outside, they walked in silence, holding hands.

"You always look so confident up there," said Lev. "However you may feel."

"When I'm up there I do feel confident."

"At the funeral," Lev said, "everything I did was an impersonation. I was imitating you. I was reading from the manual. But somehow they took it as real. And that made it real for me. Do you know what I mean?"

"I know exactly what you mean," said Deborah. "Rabbis are all impersonators."

"But does that make them false?"

"No," Deborah conceded. "That's how tradition works, I suppose. As long as you don't lose sight of the thing that inspired tradition in the first place."

"All through the funeral, it was as if you were beside me," said Lev. "Whatever good I did, I did reflecting back your light."

Deborah shook her head.

"That was you," she said. "I'm not sure I have any light."

"You must. Because I'm just a moon. And you know, two moons can't reflect each other's light."

"Maybe they can," said Deborah. "Maybe that's the whole secret."

Book
Five

LEV AND DEBORAH DECIDED on a six-month engagement, not long, but somehow they both felt in a hurry. They were getting married right before the high holy days. A crazy time for Deborah, but she liked the idea of starting married life just before the Jewish New Year. They had agreed to defer their honeymoon until after Yom Kippur.

Though her mother lived in Palo Alto, Deborah wanted the wedding to be in New York, where she had lived since becoming a rabbinic student. Deborah's father had been raised in Brooklyn and a lot of his family was still scattered throughout the metropolitan area. Her sister was in Connecticut. All of Lev's family, with the exception of his brother, lived in the Northeast. Even Deborah's mother had grown up in Scranton, Pennsylvania, and lived in Philadelphia before fleeing to California.

But her mother wasn't happy with the decision.

"I'll still pay," Laura Green told her daughter, "but I won't pretend I don't wish you were doing it in the Bay Area. Even Rachel had her thing out here."

Deborah didn't want her mother to pay. Her father had had a large life insurance policy, which, after funeral expenses, Laura had cut in half and invested for her two daughters for them to draw on as they needed. Deborah had dipped into her fund for rabbinic school and to buy her apartment when she came east and had always seen it as her father's participation in her religious journey. Besides the money her father left, she earned a good salary and had been saving money. Lev, who still felt guilty about squandering someone else's money the last time he helped plan a wedding, was willing to shoulder half the burden. But Laura Green wouldn't hear of it.

"Debbie, my money's for you and Rachel. You'll have it all when I die—you know that. And there's the fund from Daddy. There's nothing to fight against. I just wanted to see you married here, where you grew up."

"I had a very good childhood, Mom," said Deborah. "But my life is here."

One of the more frustrating things her mother did was continue to describe as rebellion the life that Deborah had chosen, as if its primary motivation was to negate the world she came from.

More than her mother's disappointment or the precedent of her sister's West Coast commitment ceremony, it was the thought of her father, who had so loved the Pacific Ocean that they had cast his ashes into it, that made Deborah waver. But she did not wish to move the wedding for the sake of the dead. She felt her father's spirit would attend wherever it was—if in no other place, it was in her. And the living—with the exception of her mother and stepfather and a handful of her mother's friends and colleagues—would be spared the schlep.

Deborah settled on the Brooklyn Botanic Garden. The place was usually booked a year in advance but Deborah had learned of a cancellation through a colleague who had been scheduled to perform a fall wedding there; the bridegroom had been diagnosed with testicular cancer and the couple had gotten married earlier than planned.

"Don't tell me that!" said Lev, blocking his ears.

"You should be glad I have inside information."

"Your inside information is always about men losing their balls or children dying," said Lev.

"He's not losing them—he's getting chemo. They can probably still have kids. They froze a lot of sperm beforehand just to be safe."

Lev relented. As far as he was concerned, anyplace that wasn't Tappan Hill—intended site of his aborted wedding to Jenny—was fine with him.

"And if you want to use the temple that's OK with me, too."

"You know I don't," said Deborah. "The food is terrible there and the dance floor stinks."

Deborah was, in her own words, behaving like some JAP from

Long Island, even though she had always vowed that her own wedding would be different from all the weddings she performed and that she would be different from all the brides she had worked with. Discovering that it would not, that she was not, humbled her but also uplifted her. Here she was, one of the girls after all.

She called Lev all the time at work now. The klezmer band that played swing, or the swing band that played klezmer? Did he have an opinion about day lilies? Chicken and fish or steak and fish? Perhaps they should eliminate fish altogether and have some truly vegetarian option. Was lasagna too tacky for a wedding? And then there was the unresolved issue of what the string trio should play as they marched down the aisle. She had always loved "*Erev Shel Shoshanim*," but then "*Dodi Li*," taken from the Song of Songs, had deeper meaning: My beloved is mine and I am his. She didn't care if it *was* a wedding cliché.

It was amusing for Lev to watch Deborah throw out one prejudice after another as she planned her own wedding, though she drew the line at uniform bridesmaids' outfits. Lev had been through his own earlier wedding drama and had vowed he would be different, too. *Then* he had hurled himself gamely into all the details—in part to hide his mounting fears of the marriage. He had learned the difference between a "sweep train" and a "chapel-length train." He had scouted locations like a movie producer. He had auditioned one bad nine-piece band after another—no klezmer for Jenny.

This time, though he joined her whenever she asked him, he was happy to allow Deborah to report from the field. Lev disliked the planning but he discovered that he was eager to *be* married, and this realization filled him with happiness. He had already learned the little Hebrew phrase he would have to recite when slipping the gold band on Deborah's finger—*Behold, with this ring I consecrate you to myself according to the laws of Moses and Israel.* He found himself reciting it aloud at odd moments.

The ceremony itself was going to be simple and traditional. No passages of the Ramayana, no poems by Lorca or Neruda, no homemade vows, no tantric chanting from well-meaning friends. Deborah's friend Wendy was going to perform the ceremony. Lev had grown fond of her and Deborah wanted her, despite the size of her ass.

It had been Lev's idea to fashion a wedding canopy by tying his father's tallis to the tallis that Deborah had inherited from her grandfather. She had always counted on using her grandfather's tallis, the prayer shawl she wore when she prayed, or tried to pray, in the morning. But she loved the idea of adding to it the one that Henry owned. It was the only thing Henry had that had belonged to his murdered father.

For Lev, the tallis was a token of survival and triumph. His father had been put on a train the way Superman was put on a spaceship when he was a little boy before his home planet was destroyed. The tallis had its own story of escape and survival and that it had somehow been reunited with his father seemed part of a hopeful miracle.

Lev had believed that his father would be deeply moved by his request but to Lev's astonishment, Henry had refused.

What he had actually said, with uncharacteristic clarity of speech, was, "I don't know where it is."

"Can I help you look for it?" Lev asked.

But his father only shook his head.

Lev feared that his father had not understood the request. Or that it brought up too much pain. He did not press the matter. Perhaps, he thought, it was the wrong thing to get married under after all. Deborah told him he was crazy. She was determined to get it and decided to bring it up with Helen Friedman. They were scheduled to visit the Botanic Garden together.

Lately, Deborah saw a great deal of Helen. To Lev's amusement, his mother often joined Deborah on her wedding-related forays. Though Helen no longer shot weddings herself but dispatched photographers, she had a deep familiarity with every aspect of matrimonial mechanics and had felt hurt to find herself shut out entirely of Jenny and Lev's plans. Jenny's mother lived in Short Hills, New Jersey, and had skipped across the Hudson at a moment's notice. Deborah's mother was not coming east until the day before the wedding.

Helen and Deborah, two jaded professionals, hurled themselves like high-school girls into the planning. Both had witnessed outrages of taste and favored clean elegance. There would be no train at all on Deborah's gown.

The two women often made a morning of it—a trip to the florist's or to the shoe boutique or the dressmaker's, and then lunch at some downtown spot before they rode uptown together so Helen could get back to her studio or check on Henry, and Deborah could put in an appearance at Temple Emunah.

Helen had a very different view of Deborah from the one she had formed the first time they had met, when Deborah had offered to pray with Helen in Henry's hospital room. Deborah seemed older, not as self-confident and yet more substantial. There was something chastened about Deborah, less assured but more mature.

What Helen admired most was not the spiritual but the professional achievement of Deborah's life. Once or twice Helen and Henry had joined Lev at a Friday night service and Helen had enjoyed the sheer competence and command of Deborah's movements up on the bimah, even if the service itself left her cold.

Deborah and Helen wandered the grounds of the Botanic Garden together. Helen was providing the photographer and looked the whole place over with an eye toward light and shadow. Deborah, who had been there before with Lev, wanted a map in her mind of where everything would take place, not just the ceremony and the reception, but the ketubah signing and the ritual isolation of the couple following the ceremony.

"Really?" said Helen. "We didn't have symbolic sex in my day."

"Weddings used to be consummated right after the ceremony," explained Deborah. "This is a reminder of that."

It was a beautiful June day. The cherry blossoms had fallen but the pink and white lily pads were blooming in the reflecting pools in front of the Steinhardt Pavilion and the whole place had a heady, honeysuckle odor. Helen, in one of her flowing, belted summer dresses and sandals, with her white braid and heavy jewelry, looked like a Roman empress. She surprised Deborah by knowing the names of all the flowers, particularly the beds of wildflowers. She pointed out yarrow and cinquefoil. Like Lev, the names and the knowledge seemed to delight her and she kept bending down to touch a leaf.

When they had finished scouting they visited the Bonsai Museum and then strolled across the meadow toward some flowering linden trees.

"I shot my first wedding here," said Helen as they walked along.

"Really?" said Deborah. "Then this is the perfect place. Why didn't you say so sooner?"

"Because I hated it."

She saw the stricken look in Deborah's eyes.

"It's not the place," she added quickly. "It's beautiful, of course. It's the memory. I'd been a photographer for years but not of people's weddings. I dreamed it up after Henry's heart attack. I didn't want to do it. It was purely for the money and I'd never worked for money before. Just teaching, which you do for love. The bride was a bitch, the bride's father was a monster. I kept telling everyone to smile; meanwhile I was cursing under my breath the whole time.

"But it worked out," she added. "Eventually I didn't have to go myself. I had all these talented students who needed cash. There is no shortage of hungry photographers and, as I'm sure you, too, have discovered, no shortage of weddings. And it turned out I had a good head for business, unlike my husband, poor man."

"How is Henry doing?" Deborah asked gently.

Helen shrugged.

"All right, I suppose. Stronger in some ways. Weaker in others. He lives more and more in his own world, less in mine. He's—harder to read, now." Her voice trailed off.

Deborah told Helen what had happened when Lev asked for the tallis.

Instead of answering, Helen said, "Have I ever told you how I started out, taking pictures of DP camps in Europe?"

Deborah had in fact heard the story.

"That must have been quite a time," she said.

"It was terrible," Helen said, "the poverty, the suffering. The sheer horror of what had happened. But it was all so exhilarating. You could still hail a cab with a pack of cigarettes—they were a kind of currency. I was incredibly young and really quite callous. Everything fed me."

Deborah nodded.

"I was photographing Bergen Belsen in 1950. I was nineteen, if you can believe it. The place had been turned into a DP camp right after the war and became a whole little society. By the time I got there, the British were in the process of closing it down, but there were still schools. They had their own government. People got married. It's quite inspiring what the human spirit can do.

"But," said Helen, "I talked to a lot of survivors. People opened up to me. We think of survivors as being old because they're old now, but then they were almost all young. A lot were my age. The old people had died. I heard unspeakable stories. Just unspeakable. The girls in particular. What they did to survive . . ."

Helen seemed full of something that needed to come out. There was an urgency to the way she was talking to Deborah.

"I was just a tourist in that world," she said. "I came home, I finished school. I lived here in ease. A few bad dreams—not many.

"But Henry," she said, "is really the reverse. He has been here a long time, but he is still only a tourist here. You have to realize that about him. I haven't always and it's cost me. Suffering is picturesque, you know. His scars were somehow beautiful to me. They put me in contact with something and I felt like a healer. But for some things there's no healing at all."

"I'm sure that's true," said Deborah. "But I would like to think, for his son . . ."

"For his son Henry would do anything. But this is just a piece of cloth, you know."

"It's a symbol of something," said Deborah.

"Yes," said Helen. "It's a symbol of God's total abandonment of the Jewish people."

"Or of the opposite," murmured Deborah.

"We all have our interpretations," said Helen crisply. "You know what happened to my husband's parents and to his sister. And the number of relatives he lost—cousins the age of my granddaughter. Babies. Innocent babies!"

She drew deeply on her cigarette. She had quit smoking after Henry's first heart attack but occasionally stole a cigarette from Deborah's pack, though Deborah herself, who smoked more and more, had vowed to quit after the High Holy Days.

Deborah wanted Helen to go back to talking about the difficulty of shooting against the willow trees and where the light would be at 11 a.m. in late September. But Deborah felt fated to receive the religious confessions of everyone around her the way therapists receive sexual secrets. She remembered something a Jewish philosophy professor, European born, had said to her during office hours after she had poured out her heart to him: "You do not lose one out of every three people and go back to life as it was. We have only begun to reckon the effects of our losses on the Jewish soul. People think it's over but it's only beginning."

Deborah had no desire to speak but she found herself saying, "God wasn't responsible for the Second World War or the Holocaust. It was all a man-made horror."

"Well," said Helen, "either God doesn't care to intervene, no matter how much suffering there is, in which case he might as well be the devil. Or he doesn't have the power, in which case he's just some chicken-shit deity I can't be bothered about. Or he's not there. Whichever, it doesn't make much difference."

She spoke like the angry young woman she must have been.

"Perhaps," said Deborah. "But it's people . . ."

"You can't lose your faith in people," said Helen, with surprising vehemence. "That's suicide."

Deborah certainly had no logic with which to counter Helen's comments. Another person angry at God. This, as far as Deborah was concerned, already put her in a category of belief, even if it was angry belief. If anything, it made her feel closer to Helen, though Helen clearly saw it as a difference between them she needed to get off her chest. Deborah sometimes joked that being a rabbi was like working for a boss that everyone hated, like collecting rent in a bad neighborhood. She was glad Helen did not ask her to unpack her own mysterious relationship to faith or to Judaism, which for Deborah lived more and more at a wordless level of simple doing.

They sat down on a bench and looked out over a slope of grass toward the Palm House, a great glass and iron structure, gleaming like an enormous birdcage. Deborah said nothing. Helen broke the silence by saying, "I'm sorry I lectured you like that."

"Please don't apologize for speaking your mind," said Deborah.

"I really don't know what came over me," said Helen.

"I have that effect on people sometimes."

Helen waved her hand dismissively.

"He keeps it in the bottom drawer of his desk. You should just ask him for it. He'll give it to you. You speak to something in him. Some lost part of himself."

"Thank you," Deborah murmured.

"I realize," Helen continued, "that I've never thanked you for all your kindness to Henry. Your visits mean an enormous amount to him, I can tell. I think he accepts you as part of the past that ended before I came along."

This was said without bitterness, though Deborah knew it was something that must cause her pain. She wanted to say something but Helen stood up and began walking back toward the main buildings, pausing for a moment to take in the great sweep of the garden, the low buildings of Brooklyn barely visible beyond. Deborah came and stood beside her. A Japanese woman in a wedding gown had appeared with a little entourage to have her picture taken.

"You don't have to tell Lev how bitter I sounded about taking pictures here," Helen said. "I think this is an absolutely stunning place to get married."

"I once cried in the bathroom after performing a wedding at Wave Hill," said Deborah.

Helen put her arm around Deborah.

"Poor us," she said.

The two women started to laugh. And because they understood each other, and because they were imagining the wedding that was going to take place, and because they both felt inside their own bodies the mysterious passage of time, and because the Palm House looked like a building in a fairy tale and the grass was a sort of childhood green, they also began to cry.

They walked across the fragrant lawn and laughed and wept.

HENRY FRIEDMAN was sitting at his rolltop desk, where he spent a
great deal of time, lost in thought. Thought was lost in him, he had
liked to joke when he was well, but now he was not well and did not
joke. Strangely, his command of speech had improved even as his inner
clarity declined. He could speak his mind, but it didn't always feel like
his mind anymore. Since the last big stroke, three tiny strokes—possibly more—had continued to carry away clarity the way persistent ants
carry away a loaf of bread one crumb at a time. The crust was all there,
he thought, dragging a comb through his rust-gray hair in the mirror,
but the inner loaf was growing airy. He knew that things were breaking
down, or knew it sometimes when he tried to leap from one island of
thought or recollection to another, or when—much worse—he tried to
jump into the present. Much of the time he felt surrounded by water.

His desk was an island. He did not work at it but he liked to sit
there.

Occasionally he had tried to return to *Joy Comes in the Morning*, but
had found it almost impossible to reenter the manuscript and was unsure if that was because it was unreadable or because he himself had
lost the ability. He had stopped trying but he looked at the manuscript
without removing the rubber band and it worked as a kind of memory
stone. It stirred up in him deep corresponding memories. Whether he
had put them in his book or not he was not sure. He had a feeling that
the things he remembered occupied the invisible spaces between the
facts he had tried to set down.

The silence of his own father, praying alongside him, he thought of
more than anything his father had ever said directly to him. Including
good-bye? He could not remember. His mother he remembered, the
embrace at the train station, the rough weave of her coat on his face.

And the chocolate bar given him by Inge Rosenfarb, who lived in their apartment building and who, he realized later, could only have been a prostitute.

The train was always leaving—not for horror in the east but rescue in the west, its own guilty torment. He wore around his neck, like the other children, a black square placard with a white number painted on it. He could not remember his number. He had been placed in the car of a neighbor's child, an older boy named Heinrich whom he could not stand and who had, almost as soon as the train was out of the station, relieved him of the chocolate bar so that at the Dutch border he was regretting the loss of his chocolate—though of course he had an inkling even then that he would never see his parents or sister again.

He sifted the contents of his desk. Things were always turning up—old yearbook photographs of his sons, a wedding photograph. His? The incomplete manuscript of the book about trains. Years ago he and Helen had gone to a resort in the Adirondacks—they had wanted to swim but the lake was "turning over." The bottom rose to the top, fistfuls of seaweed floated free, trailing their muddy anchors. His desk was like that. His thoughts.

He scribbled notes occasionally, though his handwriting was illegible, even to himself. *If I forget thee O Jerusalem.* Thank God it was his left hand that had lost much of its grip, its—what was the word? *Cunning!* His right hand worked fine, though it seemed to have had a kind of sympathetic collapse of ability when it came to writing.

But he did not forget Jerusalem; he thought of it all the time. The divided city of 1952 when he had visited and determined to move there and change his life. Just home to pack. He had already spoken to someone about teaching English at a middle school in Rehavia.

"You're never coming back," said Gabor, who was calling himself Dov, one of his few surviving cousins, a shrewd old Hungarian who had come to Palestine in the thirties and painted signs, despite a degree in fine art and an apartment full of unwanted landscapes of the Judean hills. "You're already a soft American."

But Henry had been sure he would come back—if not for

Jerusalem then for Greta, from Berlin, who had changed her name to Penina. A freezing flat on Keren Hayasod, under the thick wool blanket that smelled of damp sorrow. Penina had been from a well-to-do family. An icy Jerusalem rain outside. Naked bodies, white as wild mushrooms under the dark cover. After the war the girls did everything.

Henry's heart ached. Why had he never gone back?

Sick of war. Sick of deprivation. Sick of Jews and Jewish fate. He cringed at his own weakness.

Perhaps it wasn't too late. For here she was, with her dark Jewish eyes.

Deborah placed a hand gently on Henry's arm to wake him from his reverie. Beatrice, the housekeeper, had sent her into Henry's study. Helen was at her studio.

Henry strained to fix his attention on the young woman before him. His son was going to marry her. Deborah.

She still visited him on a semiregular basis, though lately she had been busy with wedding plans. She often came on Saturday afternoons. While Lev visited with his mother or walked Mephisto or occasionally sat with them, Deborah chanted the Torah portion to Henry from her *tikkun*. She did not recite the whole reading, just a few columns, while Henry shut his eyes and listened, letting the words and singsong melody bathe him. When she was done she always sang "*Eyts Chaim He*"—it is a tree of life to those who hold fast to it—and as always when she sang these words, the tears came. Singing them to Henry, Deborah felt again the inner umbilical attachment to something large and mysterious that often eluded her at other times.

But more and more, he asked for Israeli folk songs, the early ones he knew from his youth and those that he learned in Israel, dancing in the evenings. How he had loved to hold hands and dance in a ring. With Greta. With other girls and young men whose faces came to him more vividly than the faces around him. Though he suspected they were superimposed, transported faces, and sometimes he was aware of imagining his mother and sister and childhood friends, and Helen, who hadn't been there, of course, and his sons and even Deborah herself, all dancing with him. It was the Hebrew and the youthful beauty of Deborah's voice and the open-eyed way she looked at him, even though Henry often shut his own eyes and felt the ageless part of himself respond to the music and to her voice.

When Henry saw Deborah he grew flustered and confused and wondered suddenly if it was Shabbat—he had gotten particularly bad at the days of the week. But Deborah assured him he was not wrong about the day—it was Tuesday.

"Henry," she said, when she had settled herself next to him and felt sure he had recognized her. "I've come to ask you for something."

Henry shook his head no.

"I told Lev," he said in his slow, careful manner.

Despite his many lapses, he could be extremely sharp and intuitive.

"I don't believe you," said Deborah, gently. It was a gambit—she knew Henry had a hard time finding anything. But she was sure he did know where it was.

Henry smiled in his vague, ambiguous way.

He had been thinking a great deal about the tallis since his son had asked him for it. A few months after Henry's departure on a youth transport to England, his father had been taken to Buchenwald concentration camp. He had brought his tallis and tefillin with him. When he died—in what manner Henry had never learned, but he had read the testimonies and discovered how inmates were tortured in life and that, in death, many were flayed, their tanned skins used to bind books—his ashes were improbably returned to Henry's mother along with his tallis. It was late 1939. Nobody knew what became of the tefillin. All this Henry's sister, Estie, had written him—he was in England at the time. The tallis had been given to a friend who had a visa to go to England. But somehow the tallis had been left behind. Estie had then given it to a neighbor who was headed to the United States but getting out via China. Estie was supposed to go, too, but stayed behind because Henry's mother had fallen ill at the last minute. His mother and sister had both been deported to Izbica in 1942 and from there to Belzec, where they were gassed.

But the tallis had spent the war in the Shanghai ghetto and then traveled to Palestine where, through a series of chance encounters, it was returned to Henry on the trip he made in 1952 when he went to the Jewish Agency searching for evidence that his sister had perhaps survived the war and gone to Palestine as she had always spoken of doing and found instead the neighbor who had not gone to the United States after all but was living in Herzlia and who still had the tallis with her.

For Henry the story was a bitter one and for years he hated the tallis and could not open the pouch. And when he did, and unfolded the white and black fringed cloth, striped almost like a prisoner's outfit, he half expected to find blood on it.

It was during this period that he had turned his back on Judaism. He lost himself in his bookstore, in Helen. In America. Once, he had come close to throwing the tallis down the garbage chute in his apartment but had felt such terrible remorse that he had worn it as penance on Yom Kippur—it was the first time he had gone to shul in many years. Gradually, he began to wear it once a year, when he went to services for Kol Nidre. By then, he was a father with two small sons. The tallis would not let him go.

"Why didn't you give it to Lev?" Deborah asked, rousing Henry.

"I need it," he said quietly.

"But we're getting married before Yom Kippur and can give it back to you."

Henry was silent for a long time.

"I need it," he said again, as if this was a new response.

"But why?" Asked Deborah, growing annoyed for the first time.

"There are explanations," said Henry, though he did not offer any.

"We want to get married under it," said Deborah. "We want to tie it to my grandfather's tallis."

"How many do you need?"

Deborah wasn't sure if this was a detached sentence or part of the conversation, but she said, "We want two. My family and your family."

"Stars and Stripes Forever," murmured Henry.

The exasperation Lev sometimes expressed about his father Deborah felt now. It was as if she was being taunted.

"My grandfather worked in his store every day but Shabbat," said Deborah hotly. "And I think he worked on Shabbat, too, because he needed the money. He didn't want to be a jeweler. He wanted to be a teacher."

"I need it," said Henry again.

"Lev needs it!"

But Henry was shaking his head, no.

She wondered suddenly, with remorse for her outburst, if he wasn't lost inside a dream. It was often impossible to tell when he was following things and when he was lost. He retained all the outward habits of clarity. But she could not let it go.

"What do you need it for?" she asked.

In a near-whisper, Henry said, "A shroud."

A shiver ran through Deborah. For a moment, she was stunned into silence. She felt great concern and an unexpected wave of irritation. They were getting married and he was thinking of shrouds! Selfish man, she thought, though at once she felt embarrassed by her thought. Was he thinking of killing himself again? The question flashed through her with sudden panic.

"Henry, I hope you're not planning to harm yourself?"

Her words startled him. They had never spoken about his suicide attempt. He himself was often unsure he had really done it. The question shamed him. He reached out his right hand and took hold of her left hand with surprising force, shutting his eyes as he did so.

DEBORAH CALLED LEV from the first pay phone she could find.

When Lev answered the phone, he wasn't surprised to hear Deborah's cheerful voice.

"Guess what I'm holding?" she asked.

"Tell me," said Lev.

"Superman's cape."

Lev laughed but he felt a pang.

"He gave it to you?"

"I'll tell you the story tonight," she said. "I've got to get to the temple before they forget I work there."

They kissed into the phone.

HELEN FOUND HENRY lying on the couch in the living room.

Beatrice had gone home, but someone had covered him with the woolen afghan that usually hung over the back of the sofa. Unless he had lain down and covered himself after Deborah left.

He looked younger as he slept. His face was handsome and composed though his hair, which he combed himself, looked insecure on his head, as if you could blow and scatter it like dandelion seeds in September. Helen cut his hair for him and realized he was overdue. His beard was getting wild.

She had gotten used to his sleeping in the middle of the day. She wished he was on his bed because she felt a sudden urge to lie down beside him and sleep herself. She still flared up in irritation from time to time, but seeing him now, peacefully asleep, she felt a great surge of protective love for him. The dark intractable mystery at the heart of him, which had made him alluring and elusive and exasperating for forty years, seemed less pronounced. She would like to have run her hands over his head, to smooth his hair, but was afraid of waking him.

The doorbell rang and Henry did not stir. The downstairs security men were very lax, Helen thought. Delivery men were always ringing the bell without being announced first, and often they had the wrong apartment.

When she saw Neal Marcus standing in the doorway she gave an involuntary gasp that made him start back.

"Oh my goodness, Neal," she said. "I wasn't expecting to see you."

It had been a long time since she had seen him, though Neal and Lev had been such close friends for so many years that his face was etched into her consciousness. But it was as an open-faced boy at birthdays that she remembered him best and it was a shock to see him encased in a man's body, his face ravaged, unshaven. She felt a maternal urge to embrace him and a simultaneous desire to slam the door and bolt it.

Neal's curly hair was matted and greasy and his glasses, owlish round frames of the sort most people had given up for understated ovals, were crooked on his nose. There were two deep scratches on one cheek and one on his nose, as if he had slept in brambles. Helen, with her keen eye, took all this in at once, and took in too the strange shuddery way Neal stood in his overcoat, a handsome navy raincoat that was splotched with dirt. Why was he even wearing a coat in July? His right hand was thrust deep into his coat pocket from which it looked as though some wooden object were protruding, half concealed by his hand and arm. But she forced her eyes back to his face, which had a wild look. He was rocking from one foot to the other which reminded her, incongruously, of her grandfather *shoklng* as he prayed.

"Neal, how are you? I'm afraid Lev's not here."

She was glad her son wasn't there.

"I need to see Mr. Friedman," he said, with husky urgency.

"Why?" Helen asked, closing the door a little and stepping laterally to block the opening with her frame. If Neal leaned farther into the apartment, he would have seen Henry sleeping on the couch, and Helen wanted to prevent this from happening. Neal's eyes were already straining to see past her, beyond her. Mephisto had gotten out of his basket and was now peering through Helen's legs at Neal's feet. The dog did not bark.

Every fiber of Helen's body warned that there was danger, though she tried to counteract this, not wishing to let her instinctive aversion to Neal affect the way she treated him. She did not want to punish him for his illness; the poor boy had suffered terribly and clearly was in the middle of some new calamity.

"Mr. Friedman's in danger," Neal said.

He wasn't looking at Helen as he spoke; his face was tilted down at her feet and at the dog. His eyes had an unfocused fixity as if they were seeing another reality.

Was that a hammer sticking out of Neal's pocket? Helen felt some fierce protective element in herself stiffening.

"What kind of danger is my husband in?" she asked, more to keep him talking than because she wanted to hear what Neal would say.

"He's in mortal danger," was all Neal said. "There are—"

He cut himself off and raised his eyes as if seeing her for the first time.

"Neal, you're bleeding. What happened to your face?"

Neal drew his left hand up to his nose. A shadow passed over his face and he shuddered it away. Helen produced a small packet of tissues she kept in her dress pocket and handed it to Neal. He took the tissues without a word of thanks and slid them into his coat pocket.

"Where are you living these days?" she asked, trying to figure out whom to call, beyond 911.

Neal bristled. He was rocking back and forth on the balls of his toes as if he might pounce on her at any moment and had begun a muttered, imperceptible conversation.

She told herself that if Henry had not been at home she would have let Neal in and allowed him to wash up and calm down at her kitchen table while she called around and figured out what was to be done. But his interest in Henry—Helen had gleaned little glimmerings of Neal's delusions from Lev; Nazi plots and double agents, and an intense fascination with Henry's story of survival—made her feel it was impossible, particularly in her husband's weakened state.

"Stay right here!" Helen said in a forceful voice, as if she were giving a command to a dog.

Neal shrank back and Helen quickly shut the door.

"Stay there," she called out to Neal, "I'll be right back. I think something's burning!"

It was an absurd thing to say, but she needed to say something. She raced to the phone in the kitchen. She had never been particularly close to Carol Marcus, though she felt sorry for her. She had suffered through her son's illness without the help of her husband, who had divorced her—divorced them both, it seemed to Helen—but Carol had maintained an almost defiant cheer in the face of her troubles that Helen found a little batty. Still, who could blame her? They had been friendly when the boys were young and occasionally had lunch after they had gone off to college.

Carol's number was still in her book. What would she say: "Your son's outside my door acting strange. Please come get him"? Meanwhile her own son was getting married.

To Helen's surprise, a man picked up.

"Oh," said Helen, flustered. "I was trying to reach Carol Marcus." Did Carol have a boyfriend? Good for her.

"Who is this?" the voice demanded.

Was everyone crazy?

"It's a friend," said Helen, giving her name. "I need to talk to Carol. Who are you?"

"This is Detective Riggio," the man said. "I'm with the Twentieth Precinct. I'm afraid Mrs. Marcus has been taken to the hospital. She's been the victim of an attack."

"Her son is outside my door," Helen said, suddenly whispering.

"Don't let him in!" the detective said. "We'll be right there."

Helen gave her address to Detective Riggio, though in her present state she half wondered if he really was a police officer. She then crept to the door and peeped out the peephole.

There was no sign of Neal.

"Helen," said a voice behind her, so faint and faraway she nearly screamed.

But it was only Henry, sitting up after his deep sleep.

WHEN THE PHONE RANG, Lev was sure it was Deborah calling him back and was surprised to hear his mother's voice. Usually so calm, his mother sounded panicked and he thought at once something had happened to his father.

"Thank God I got you," she said, breathless.

"What happened? Is Dad all right?"

"Don't go home!" his mother blurted out. "Or if you do, lock the door."

"Mom," said Lev, genuinely perplexed but feeling a kind of intuitive horror. "What are you talking about?"

"Neal Marcus beat his mother unconscious with a hammer. He was just here looking for Dad but I shut the door and he left."

"Did he try to hurt you?"

"No. But he had a hammer in his pocket. Or maybe he didn't. I thought I saw something. He looked terrible. Very agitated."

"Why wasn't he at the home in Brooklyn?"

"I don't know. Something must have happened."

"What makes you think he'll try to find me?"

"Lev, I just feel like he might. Why did he try to find us? He always came here when he was having trouble at home and you've told me he has a thing about Dad, and how there are still Nazis in the world and nobody is safe. And I just feel like he'll try to find you. Promise me you'll be careful. Does he know where you work?"

"He's never been here," said Lev. "I'm sure he could find it if he wanted to. But I doubt he will."

Lev was trying to stay calm though his mother's panic was infectious. She was not prone to worry and hearing the distress in her voice unnerved him. Instinctively Lev opened the drawer of his desk to see that the large scissors was there, which it was.

"Just keep your eyes open."

She gave him Detective Riggio's telephone number.

He scribbled it down on a yellow Post-it.

"Mom," he said. "I have to go."

He was thinking of Deborah. They were no longer living to-gether—Bill had returned to Africa and Lev was officially back in his own apartment, though he often stayed at Deborah's. But as the wedding drew near she seemed to want them to separate more, as if to heighten the sense that the wedding was a union. The last few nights he had stayed in his own apartment.

She had called him from a pay phone—the last person in New York without a cell phone, he thought bitterly—but she had said she was going to the temple. Neal might indeed seek her out at Temple Emunah. Lev dialed her office and got her answering machine. He left her a message, trying to sketch out what had happened without hysteria.

Then he left a message on her home machine for good measure. A sick foreboding took hold of him. She had given Neal her home ad-dress and Lev had known it was a mistake. He wondered if he should go straight to her apartment. But she was on the West Side and he wanted to be with her; somehow that seemed like the only safety. He opened his drawer and threw the scissors into his knapsack as he got up to go. At the last minute he thought better of it and tossed it back into the drawer, swung the knapsack over his shoulder, and rushed outside.

THE TEMPLE was quiet and cool. Things were dead in summer. The security guard knew him and nodded. Lev had forgotten there was someone stationed at the door. That calmed him. He trotted up the stairs to Deborah's office. Sonya, a stylish young émigré from the for-mer Soviet Union with frosted hair, smiled at him warmly.

"Is Deborah in?" Lev asked.

Sonya shook her head. He noticed that the glass of Rabbi Zwieback's door was also darkened.

"I think she's running some errands," Sonya said with a wink. "I saw those shoes she bought last week—gorgeous gorgeous gorgeous! And I told Rabbi Green she can dye them afterwards. They'll be perfect for evening wear." She seemed to see Lev for the first time. "Are you all right?"

Lev was thinking it was strange that Deborah hadn't arrived yet. It had taken Lev half an hour to get uptown and Deborah was a ten-minute walk away. He hesitated and then said, "Someone who might be dangerous might be looking for her."

Sonya gave a little gasp. She leaned forward, intrigued, serious, a little thrilled. She had, Lev knew from Deborah, been forced to get a restraining order against a former boyfriend who once had given her a black eye.

"Who is it?"

"Someone with . . . problems. An old friend of mine. I just think he might try to find her. Please. If you see her tell her Neal is in a dangerous state. And tell her to play her messages; sometimes she doesn't."

"Tell me about it," said Sonya. "She's terrible. But I'll tell her. Is there anything I can do?"

But Lev was already bounding down the steps.

DEBORAH HAD TOLD LEV that she was going to Temple Emunah but decided suddenly to stop by Roosevelt Hospital. None of her doubts had been answered or laid to rest, but she felt more at peace with herself and drawn in a new way to the bedsides of sick people. Her patients saw something in her even when she did not see it in herself. They looked at her with a belief that she drew strength from, even if their belief was only a reflection of what they thought they saw in her. Imagining it there somehow placed it there.

Sometimes Deborah felt that if God was revealed anywhere it was in the space between her and the patients she visited, where it ceased to be possible to tell the origin of a feeling or a belief. What had once lived inside her she now found outside herself, though subtly it was drawn back into her where it grew and gained strength. Perhaps, she thought, this is what is meant by community.

She walked south on Broadway, which was crowded with people, baby strollers, men selling used books on card tables, their tape decks blaring opera. It was a hot July day; the sunshine seemed heavy, coating everything with butterscotch brightness. Deborah felt soothed by the heat, though it clearly oppressed the old Jewish ladies pushing wire shopping carts that doubled as walkers. She looked with good will on the pregnant women drifting past in their billowing summer dresses. A voice whispered in her ear: *You're getting married*—and she felt overcome with joy.

An old man with a hunchback and a tragic Jewish face was playing the violin in front of Fairway, some sort of Gypsy air. He did not play well but he played with great feeling. She stopped and watched him for a moment. He winked at her and she dropped a dollar into his violin case, open at his feet like a tiny coffin.

Suddenly she did not want to go to the hospital but home. She was afraid of losing Henry's tallis and did not want to bring it to the hospital. She wanted it safe in her apartment, where she could unfurl it next to her grandfather's prayer shawl and see how they looked side by side.

She felt a kind of triumph with the tallis in her hands. She had not tried to talk Henry out of a shroud. She felt that everybody was so focused on preventing him from ending his life they stopped talking to him as if he might ever die—and clearly he wanted to think about it. Whether he killed himself or died of natural causes, he would still one day be dead and Deborah thought it was cruel to deprive him of a conversation.

"You should definitely have a shroud," Deborah had said, after she had sung with him a little, "though I hope you don't need it for many many years. But there's no reason it has to be your father's tallis."

Deborah suspected that for a part of Henry, only those things from his childhood were authentic. It was an understandable impulse but it eliminated too many things—including his own children.

"It is possible," Deborah had said, "to buy a new tallis, you know."

Henry had smiled vaguely.

"Why not get a new tallis and wear that to shul?" Deborah suggested. "Or give it to Lev when he gives back your father's? When you die, the new tallis can become your shroud and Lev can keep your father's. Maybe someday there'll be a grandchild married under it who can say, This was my father's. It was given to him by *his* father who got it from his own father, though he had to go to Israel in order to recover it."

It was remarkable to realize how quickly new generations sprang up.

"You'll still have a shroud," said Deborah. "But let your father's tallis stay in this world to remind people about the world that's gone."

Helen had told Deborah that Henry kept the tallis in the bottom drawer of the rolltop desk.

"Shall we see if it's in one of these drawers?" Deborah asked.

Henry had not responded but he had done nothing to keep Deborah from wrestling open the bottom drawer of his desk and there, amid papers and notes and envelopes and old playbills from Carnegie Hall and a yellowed *New York Times* with a headline proclaiming the first moon landing, was the worn velvet pouch. Deborah had reached in and taken it.

She felt vaguely troubled by the feeling that Henry had not wholly followed what she was saying and that she had stolen the tallis rather than received it freely. Henry seemed surprised when she started to leave with the tallis bag. But he was very tired and she stayed to settle him on the sofa. She removed his shoes and lifted up his legs for him. She covered him with the blanket and sang to him as he shut his eyes, as if she were putting a child to bed.

Outside, she had dismissed her doubts. Jacob stole his blessing from Isaac and that made it no less a blessing. She phoned Lev from the first pay phone she found. The tallis that was going to be a shroud had been turned into a wedding canopy. Could anything be more beautiful?

The sky was darkening and charged suddenly with summer electricity. Grit blew through the quickening wind. Impatient to be home, Deborah stuck out her arm and hailed a cab—the driver saw her and signaled, but the light changed before the taxi could pull up to her. She had to cross Seventy-fourth Street and by the time she did, a man in a business suit had opened the door of the taxi.

"Mine!" Deborah shouted, as the first drops fell. The man sheepishly stepped aside.

Deborah laughed at herself as she settled into the back seat. She had always felt more like the spider than Miss Muffet. She'd stolen a tallis and frightened a businessman, but she felt peaceful. She was humming the *Sheva Brakhot*, the seven blessings from the marriage ceremony. She did wish Wendy had a better voice, but she made up for it with good intentions. Mostly Deborah was glad that Lev liked Wendy—he took her part now when Deborah mentioned her deficiencies.

"You should do the wedding yourself, with mirrors," Lev teased, "like those doctors who take out their own appendix."

Deborah laughed but she always said, "I'd rather be a bride."

The cab driver, a man with a long Greek name on his license, was listening to her sing.

"You happy," he said, as they sped across Central Park. "You are in love, yes?"

Deborah smiled from the back seat.

It was hot in her apartment—the rain had stopped and the sun was out again—but she did not put on the air conditioner. Instead, she changed into a T-shirt and a pair of shorts and opened the windows a little wider. In the bedroom she retrieved the blue velvet pouch with her grandfather's tallis and brought it out into the living room. But she wanted to look at Henry's tallis first.

Deborah drew the tallis out of its maroon bag and spread it out on her couch.

It was yellowed like old ivory, and there were several small holes in the fabric. The material felt almost damp. One of the tassels was half gone as if it had been chewed off. The tallis wasn't kosher and if Lev was ever going to use it to pray in they would need to get it repaired. But it did not need to be kosher to be part of a chuppah.

Deborah felt moved thinking that this garment had once covered Lev's grandfather in prayer, though she felt at the same time how paltry, how inadequate it was—a mere scrap of cloth. She saw the tallis with double vision: the outer layer of onion skin; the inner essence of everything.

She knew Lev was pleased to have it, but again she felt a small tremor of disappointment. What Lev had said about Henry seemed accurate. He never actively gave you anything, but then you discovered something from him in your pocket as if it had been there all along. Lev's desire to have the tallis was itself the gift.

It was, Deborah realized, Lev's model for God—almost the reason he seemed to expect so little direct communication from above. She wanted someone to say: "Here, Deborah—this is for you."

She hoped the tallis would not tear during the ceremony, but the material, despite the holes, had a spongy resiliency. She had confidence in its durability.

Deborah was just about to spread her grandfather's prayer shawl beside it when the downstairs phone rang. It was Charlie the doorman.

"There's a man here asking for you," said Charlie. "Won't give his name. He wants to talk to you himself." He added in an undertone, "I know you deal with all kinds, Rabbi, but . . ."

"Can you put him on?" Deborah asked.

There was a crackling as the device was transferred; a panting silence during which Deborah knew that it was Neal.

"Rabbi Green," said a voice at last—husky and denatured but familiar, too. "You gave me this address."

"I certainly did, Neal," said Deborah, reassuringly.

She had been meaning to find out how he was doing and had even begun a letter to him. She had been so taken up with her own life and work and wedding plans that she had not followed up as she wanted to.

"Neal, please come up. Give the phone to Charlie and I'll tell him."

Charlie came on the phone.

"Let him up please, Charlie," Deborah said. "It's all right. I know him."

"He's on his way," said Charlie. "I'll be right down here . . ."

"It's all right," Deborah cut him off, feeling protective of Neal. "Thank you."

Deborah felt a strange excitement knowing that Neal was coming up. She looked at herself in the mirror and smoothed back her hair, which she had gathered into a coarse ponytail. She had an impulse to put away Henry's tallis—it made the sofa look like an unmade bed. But the doorbell rang before Deborah could do more than fold it in half.

Neal burst into the apartment as soon as she opened the door so that all of a sudden he was standing behind her, as if *he* had answered the door and she was the visitor.

"Shut the door," he said urgently.

Deborah did as Neal said. She felt no fear, only pity and an unex-

pected exhilaration in her soul. She noticed that he was holding, between his thumb and forefinger, the little slip of paper with her address on it that she had given to him. He suddenly handed it to her
with subdued politeness, as if his number had come up at the fish
counter.

"Neal, would you like to sit down? Let me take your coat."

Neal drew back from her. He seemed surprised to find himself in
Deborah's apartment. He stared at her suspiciously and she felt self-
conscious, underdressed. She was wearing the shorts she slept in and
there was a tear up one seam. Her feet were bare, the polish on her
nails blood red. But he did not keep his glance on her.

He was noticing, with great consternation, the number of unused
outlets in Deborah's apartment. At home he had filled the sockets with
childproofing plastic plugs but here the number of places through
which his thoughts could be sucked was overwhelming. He felt his
brain energy diminishing and other voices creeping in.

The berating voice of Henry Kissinger was back. *Fool! Toy! Fuckup!*
There was no time for shuttle diplomacy. God wasn't put off like that.
Go or die!

Neal shuddered. He swept the apartment again with his eyes and
noticed the tallis. It lay on the couch like an old battle flag.

Deborah had a feeling Neal did not know about their wedding
plans and sensed they would upset him. But he did not ask about the
tallis. He only put out his left hand and touched the fabric with a kind
of fearful delicacy, as if he were touching the hem of a forbidden garment.

He poked his finger gently into one of the holes.

"This is all that remains," he said in a pained voice. "We have to get
the rest back."

"The rest of what?" Deborah asked.

Neal didn't answer. But then he said, as if in answer to a question
she had not asked, "I don't know which way to go. I'm being sent one
way but pulled another."

"Are you sure you don't want to take off your coat?"

The filthy garment was buttoned to the throat.

Neal ignored the question. Deborah might help him, unless she wasn't Deborah but only an ingenious impostor, like the woman pretending to be his mother. *She* would have killed him and eaten his brain if he had not acted swiftly. He had not been fooled by her cries or by his own name on her lips or by the pet names *pupik* or *honey boy*—on the contrary, it only inflamed his outrage that these things had been stolen from his true mother and he brought his hammer, the hammer of God, down on her with holy vengeance.

"Neal!" said Deborah, trying to use the kind forceful voice she had heard psychiatric social workers use. "Did you come for a particular reason?"

"I need to consult your books," said Neal, as if emerging from a trance. "You have to help me before it's too late."

"Should I call someone?" Deborah asked, thinking that the people at the group home should be notified.

At that moment her telephone actually began to ring and Neal looked at her as if she had made it ring. She did not answer it. There was something frightening in his eyes; they narrowed with cold suspicion as if they saw concealed malevolence in her. She noticed for the first time two long scratches running down his cheek.

Deborah cast a glance at the intercom by the door. Three big steps and she could have a finger on the button. Neal followed her glance. He regretted that he had dropped his hammer down the garbage chute of Helen Friedman's apartment. *Weakling. Fool. Shithead.* The tide of blood and darkness was rising.

They stood listening to the telephone ring. Neal felt the cables in his brain tightening. God had his number. *Go or die! Go or die!*

"I'm going," he said aloud.

"Where are you going?" said Deborah.

The phone had stopped ringing. Neal looked at her without comprehension.

"What book do you need to consult?" Deborah asked.

She would wait until he quieted down, then call Lev and ask him to call the group home.

Neal had crossed to her bookshelves, where he was rocking back and forth, moving his hands, hugging himself, as if he needed to keep burning energy to stay warm despite the heat in the room. His eyes were scanning the titles.

"Forest of words," he said. "Our first resting place. No going back, unless . . ."

He stopped himself. He was thinking: *Four went in, one came out. But who among you has the heart and the nerve? My Hebrew name is Nahum, a prophet but a minor one. Someday I'll come of age.*

He laughed suddenly in a way that frightened Deborah. She picked up the telephone but Neal put his hands over his ears and emitted a piercing screech.

Deborah put the phone down. She crossed the room and stood beside him, but not too close. Her heart was racing.

"Four went in, one came out," Neal said aloud. Or had he only thought it?

"You want the story about Rabbi Akiva," said Deborah quietly.

Neal gave her a penetrating look.

"Do you know where it is?"

"Yes," said Deborah. "Wait here."

She ran into the bedroom, where she kept her grandfather's Talmud. It was a chance to use the phone—she could close the door, lock it. But she found herself squatting down before the shelf and hunting for the proper volume. Quickly, quickly. It was in *Hagigah*. She felt Neal looming behind her, his shadow bearing down on her. He had followed her in!

She stifled a cry, gripped the heavy volume like a weapon. But when she stood up and whirled she saw that Neal was not behind her, had not followed her. He was in the living room, where he had taken hold of the tallis and had flipped it on over his coat. The top portion was over his head like a hood and hung down over his eyes. He looked like an enormous child dressing up as a ghost on Halloween.

"Take that off!" she wanted to shout, but she did not dare.

Deborah had recaptured her composure. She brought the brown book over to the dining room table. Neal drew close. He had grown very quiet and seemed calmer inside his tallis. Deborah opened the book on the table and flipped through its fragile pages. She thought perhaps studying would calm him further and then she would call. There was a doctor she had gotten friendly with on the psych ward at Roosevelt, Marc Blumenthal, and Deborah decided she would page him if she could not get Lev. There was always Charlie downstairs and of course the police, though for Neal's sake it would be better to avoid that if she could.

Stay calm, thought Deborah, humming softly to herself.

"No singing!" Neal said, from inside the prayer shawl. "That's the worst thing you could possibly do."

"I'm sorry," said Deborah. "Here, I've found it."

"Can you read it?" said Neal, almost apologetically. "I have trouble focusing."

She was amazed at how rational he suddenly sounded. His madness seemed to rise and fall like gusts of wind. Deborah felt that only the tip of his consciousness poked through a private delusional world and occupied the same space that she herself inhabited. And yet there was something persuasive about the way he spoke.

He sat down uneasily beside her at the table, the large book open before them. It was hard for Deborah to concentrate. Neal had calmed down a great deal but she felt his feet tapping and stirring under the table. A disconcerting odor came from him, sweat and something stronger and more penetrating. The phone rang again. She was itching to answer it but she forced her attention on the words and pointed. She began reading aloud, translating as she went and offering elaborations on the translation.

Neal, draped in the tallis, tilted his head back and listened.

" 'Four entered Pardes.' Literally, that means an orchard," Deborah began. "The four are sages. They were also friends."

She was trying, for some reason, to humanize the reading. The blunt staccato rendering of the Gemarah had a piercing force she wanted to buffer, like a telegram bringing news of calamity. She didn't know how much of the commentary to go into so she offered her own gentle asides.

"Two of them," she said, "Ben Azzai and Ben Zoma, were students of Rabbi Akiva. Ben Zoma married Rabbi Akiva's daughter."

"The orchard is heaven," said Neal.

"Well," said Deborah, "we don't know. Some of the commentators suggest it might be."

"How did they enter?" Neal asked.

"The Talmud doesn't say," said Deborah.

"Someone says," Neal answered.

"Yes," said Deborah. "Rashi says they meditated on God's name and that's how they ascended."

She pointed to the place. Neal nodded. Deborah continued: "Akiva said—this is before they entered—'When you come to the place of pure marble stones, do not say, "Water! Water!" for it is said, *'He who speaks untruths shall not stand before My eyes.'*

"That last part," said Deborah, "is a quotation from Psalms." She wasn't quite sure what it was supposed to mean. She knew it had something to do with the creation of the world, whether water came first or land.

Neal said nothing. She could not see his face—it was hooded in the tallis—but she heard him muttering. She caught only stray sounds.

Deborah continued reading and translating:

" 'Ben Azzai gazed and died. Precious in the eyes of God is the death of His pious ones.' That's a quote from Psalms," said Deborah. She continued: " 'Ben Zoma gazed and was harmed.' " She did not say, "that means he went nuts," though she imagined Neal knew this. The verse commented with a quotation from Proverbs: " 'Did you find honey? Eat only much as you need, lest you be overfilled and vomit it up.'"

Too much honey, Deborah thought, *the Talmud's idea of madness.*

"Acher," continued Deborah, "tore up the plantings. That means he became an apostate. And Rabbi Akiva," she concluded, "entered in peace and left in peace."

Neal was still muttering, still hooded, rocking back and forth. Deborah wished she could see his face.

He had lapsed into a murmuring trance. Could she safely leave the room? One of his arms was resting on the bottom half of the book, covering the commentary. He shifted suddenly, in his itchy, twitchy way and Deborah noticed a dark streak, almost fecal, that shot across the page. She felt a sense of terrible violation. Dirt on her book! But then her stomach tightened and told her what her mind was slow to recognize: Blood! There was blood on his sleeve, in his sleeve. The whole dark arm of the coat was soaked in blood, so thoroughly it did not show as a stain but more as a kind of darkened cuff.

Deborah stood up—Neal was still murmuring as if sealed inside some deep private prayer—and went quickly and quietly into the bedroom. She closed the door behind her and pushed the metal button in the center of the knob that locked the door.

She was breathing hard, trying to stay calm. She must call the police.

She picked up the phone but there was no dial tone. Instead, Lev's voice said,

"Hello? Hello?"

"Lev!" Deborah whispered.

"Deborah? I can't really hear you. I'm in a cab. Did you get my messages? You must think I'm crazy. I'm sorry—I panicked when I heard about Neal's mother. I—"

"He's here," said Deborah.

"What?"

"Neal's in the living room."

"Deborah, where are you?"

"I'm in the bedroom," she said. "The door is locked."

But even as she spoke she heard movement in the next room. Loud sounds—had his chair toppled or the book fallen to the floor? She felt a terrible foreboding.

"I've got to go," she said.

"Where are you going?"

"I've got to help him," she said.

"Deborah!" said Lev sharply. "Stay put. He attacked his mother!"

"He needs help."

"For God's sake, I'm almost there. Deborah!" Lev cried in desperation, feeling he had already lost her. "I'm calling the police. Don't move!"

"I love you," said Deborah.

SINCE STOPPING HIS MEDICATION Neal had, intermittently, sensed his true self blooming, bursting free. But there were competing voices, too many suggestions and whispers to be clear. Voices that swatted him down even as others lifted him up and led him on. Sitting at the table, robed in his tallis, he felt God booming in his blood cells. The words of the book spoke in an angelic voice. He waited for the book to speak again but in the meanwhile he felt an unfolding realization—first a whisper, then a roar, a tide of truth overwhelming him.

He was God!

The answer was so simple. Four entered the orchard and one came out. But one was already there. God was there! A fifth presence in the orchard; a fifth way he had never realized before. You didn't enter, because you were already there; you didn't leave because you were everywhere.

Was it true? Was this what Henry Kissinger and the Reproving Voice did not want him to understand? But he did understand.

The way to the orchard was opening up, right here, right now, a garden all around him, blooming in his blood. It was time not space. It was now. It was forever.

He had left the table and was looking out over his kingdom. There was the marble sweep of his palace, a shining city of God. He leaned into the wind. It was necessary to claim his place before the others caught up to him. Doubt was the enemy and *they* sowed seeds of doubt. But this was larger than his own puny fate. Hammer or no he would cut them down like wheat if they tried to stop him. The sickle of his thoughts was sharp as ice.

Great discs of bright light gleamed up at him from the marble depths.

"Do not," a voice reminded him, "say 'Water! Water!' "

Neal shuddered. Someone called his name. The Reproving Voice was catching up to him, but he was God and could say what he liked.

Water! Water!

Deborah did not see the leap. She saw only an overturned chair; the tallis on the carpet in front of the open window. A terrible piercing cry filled the apartment. Deborah did not at first realize that it came from her throat. The only other sound was of metal crunching, as if Neal had broken into hard pieces. It was later determined that his foot had caught on an air-conditioning unit which became dislodged and accompanied him as he plunged headfirst into the courtyard below.

CAROL MARCUS did not regain consciousness in time to attend her son's funeral. The funeral was arranged by the Lubavitchers, with whom Neal had studied in Brooklyn. Consequently the service was held at a small synagogue in Fort Greene. Helen Friedman rode out with Lev and Deborah.

Henry, who had wept so much when he was told that Helen at first suspected he mistakenly believed it was Lev who had died, remained at home with Oleg.

Deborah found herself unable to sleep the night before the funeral. She kept reliving that afternoon in her apartment. What if she had called the police immediately? What if she had not left the room to call Lev? She felt implicated in Neal's death.

"He could have killed you," said Helen in the car. "And if anyone is responsible, it's me. I could have asked him in and then called the police. My windows are closed because of the air-conditioning."

"After what he did to his mother I'm not sure he would have wanted to live," said Lev. Nobody answered him.

Lev had arrived in Deborah's apartment a moment after the police. She was already telling her story to a cop with trembling composure. Lev had been so fixated on rescuing Deborah that Neal's death did not fully register on him even though—despite police instructions—he peered out Deborah's window and saw the sprawled body of his friend, facedown, a dark, amoeba puddle surrounding his head.

Lev continued to feel that Deborah was in danger and had to keep reminding himself all that day and the next that the danger was past. He continued to imagine himself racing in and hurling Neal off of her. The violence of these fantasies disturbed him.

He stuck close to Deborah as they entered the little room where the service was to be held. The room was barely half full. Lev recognized Neal's father, whom he had not seen in many years—a handsome, thickset man, with the same dark curly hair as his son, though sprinkled with gray. He stood alone with a stony expression on his face. Lev did not approach him.

Lev had telephoned the one or two people he was in touch with who had known Neal in college, but it was last-minute notice and he was, as far as he could tell, the only friend of Neal's there from the time before his illness. There were several familiar faces from the group home, however. Not merely Mildred, the social worker, but Joe, the attendant, and several of the residents, who looked somber, almost stricken.

Lev had never seen a true plain pine coffin before—it looked as if it had been banged together out of old planks. The paleness of the coffin made it seem naked, and filled Lev with pity. It did not seem big enough to hold the body of his friend. Was his friend really inside? That seemed impossible, one of those mad delusions that Neal himself was always articulating in his moments of clarified insanity.

Nothing felt quite real to Lev, who sat in his seat as if at the theater. A blanket seemed to lie over his emotions. He was watching, not living, the scene before him. He tried to summon grief but felt only numbness at his core.

Lev was sitting between his mother and Deborah. Deborah was deep in her own world, already dabbing at tears and staring fixedly at the coffin. His mother kept looking at him with quizzical concern. Did she expect him to break down? She held his hand during the service, and Lev allowed himself to believe that it was for her own sake.

The service was conducted by a slight, nervous man with a pointed salt-and-pepper beard who kept the dark fedora on his head as he spoke. He was the man who had studied with Neal, the man who had first read with Neal the passage about the four who entered Pardes. He did not speak of that reading. He chanted several psalms in Hebrew. Then he spoke briefly about the Torah reading that was coming up that week. It was the story of Moses smashing the tablets and having to go back up the mountain to get a second pair.

The man cited a passage from the Talmud, from Brachot. He told the mourners that according to the Talmud, a man who has lost his mind is like the broken tablets that Moses shattered, which were gathered up and carried in the Ark of the Covenant along with the new pair. The broken tablets are also precious, the man said, though we do not know what role they were meant to play.

He did not ask if anyone wanted to speak but Mildred, the social worker from the home, stood up in her place and said, "I just want to say that Neal Marcus was a very brave young man. He never stopped fighting, never stopped trying. I found him an inspiring person to work with. He had a wonderful, intelligent, gentle spirit. He was simply overwhelmed by a terrible illness that doesn't discriminate against race or religion or sex. It strikes everybody and sometimes despite all our efforts there's nothing we can do. He made the most of his life until his disease got the better of him. He would never hurt a fly when he was well. May God bless him. And may God bless and heal his mother, Carol."

Lev had been considering what he might say but the man running the service did not ask if anyone else wanted to speak and more words did not seem necessary or even possible. The man recited another psalm and then chanted *El Maleh Rachamim*—he had a very beautiful voice, high and tremulous. Neal's father, Lev noticed, was weeping.

Lev resolved to speak to Steve Marcus after the ceremony but he was not among the handful of mourners who traveled to the cemetery, which was in New Jersey. This included a few people from the Lubavitcher community; Joe, but not Mildred, who had to get back to the home; an uncle and several cousins whom Neal had played with as a boy.

"He couldn't bear it," the uncle said. "How can a man bury his own son?"

Deborah and Helen took their turn shoveling dirt on the frail coffin.

Deborah, to Lev's surprise, did not shovel more than the symbolic three shovelfuls, despite her usual penchant for full burials. She retreated to the periphery with Helen, who was wearing a large straw hat. It was a cloudless day. The sun was blazing hot.

"He died a long time ago," someone behind Lev muttered.

Lev wondered if this was true. Perhaps this was why he felt as he did. He was aware of a great inner heaviness, a sympathetic part of himself allied with the body in the box. But also a detached feeling of freedom as he took up one of the shovels.

Why did he not feel grief? He tossed a shovelful of dirt onto the coffin and tried to summon sorrow. He pictured Neal's broken body, folded inside, but felt only blank revulsion. *Dad is inside,* he told himself, and threw down a load of dirt. *Mom is in there. Jacob. Little Margaret. Deborah.*

He was appalled to discover himself engaged in this sick exercise, as if he were an actor in need of tears. He succeeded only in making himself feel dizzy. *Am I crazy, too?* he thought, not for the first time. It had always been the question Neal induced in him. Did he too have hidden savagery in his heart? He stuck his shovel into the diminishing mound of dirt and imagined Neal crushing the skull of his mother in a paroxysm of rage.

Lev shook his head to dispel the vision. He was not Neal. Yes, his mind did strange things, it poured out of its little container and roamed where it wanted, but it always came home again. He was sane, and he felt lonely in his sanity.

Jenny had accused him of a morbid attachment to his sick friend and felt it hurt his ability to form new friendships. This was unfair. But did he hold back some part of himself? Perhaps. Nobody shared all his feelings. With Deborah, though, he felt known and unafraid. He wished Deborah would come and stand beside him.

The black kippah he wore was a magnet for the sun and his hair felt on the verge of combustion. He burned easily and the back of his neck was exposed. But he kept digging, flinging dirt onto the pale coffin. If he could not mourn, then he could shovel. He had removed his blazer and given it to Deborah before taking up the shovel. His white shirt was clinging to his back. He had left his bottle of water in the car and desperately wanted a drink.

He found himself shoveling beside a young pale Hasid with a blond, goatlike beard. As the man labored, the fringes of his undergarment came untucked and the sweat poured down his face, but he did not pause.

Lev kept pace with him and had a strange momentary hallucination that it was in fact Neal standing beside him, shoveling dirt. If that was so, then who was in the coffin?

He felt he was burying himself and then realized, with a strange hallucinatory clarity, that he was. He was in the coffin. There was a great heaviness in his chest, as if dirt were being heaped on him. The pity of it overwhelmed him. His childhood friend, his childhood. It wasn't the grown man but the boy that Lev had played with every spare moment growing up. It wasn't crazy Neal but well Neal behind the wall of madness Lev longed for. Lev and his brother, Jacob, were close in age but different in so many ways; Lev and Neal had shared an interest in everything.

Lev felt a great shattering loneliness and a rage that frightened him. He wanted to strike something. But as he drove his shovel into the dirt, the rage melted into a deep ache of loss. A memory of Neal came to him. They must have been about eight or nine years old, biking through Central Park collecting "samples." They had formed an explorer's club and routinely went on expeditions, bringing back everything they could find—bugs and stones and leaves, sifting through them on the dining room table of his parents' apartment. They had parked their bikes and were wandering along the bridle path west of the reservoir when Neal pointed to a rounded square object about the size of a piece of coal.

"Look at that rock," said Neal, with great excitement. "Break it open, there's a fossil inside."

Even at that age Lev knew that there were virtually no fossils in New York City—the rock was too hard. And certainly none that would be lying out on the path. But Neal had such a persuasive manner and Lev, who had an older brother, was so used to following fraternal directives that he did as he was told. He picked up the dark object and realized at once from the weightlessness and fibrous texture that it was horse shit.

Neal burst into immediate laughter and Lev threw the calcified turd at him and hit him in the head. It exploded on contact. Neal, though it could not have hurt much, began to cry, jumped on his bicycle, and rode away with Lev in hot pursuit, not to pound him further but to apologize and beg him to come back.

Lev's head began to throb. He was exhausted and leaned against the shovel as if he had grown very old all of a sudden. The coffin was only half covered. Pebbles still danced across it.

"Lev," said a voice just behind him. "I think you ought to let someone else shovel for a while."

It was Deborah. Her arm was around his waist. Joe from the group home took the shovel from Lev's hand.

Deborah led Lev to a bench in the shade where his mother was already sitting.

"Sit down, honey," his mother said. "Look at you."

Lev sat between his mother and Deborah. Helen produced a bottle of water from the bag of woven straw she carried over her shoulder and Lev gulped down the little that was left in it.

"I'm sorry I don't have more water," his mother said. "Do you want a hard candy?"

Lev was unable to answer. He covered his face, ashamed of the tears whose absence had caused him shame a moment before.

"It's all right," murmured Deborah, her hand on his drenched back as the great sobs came. "It's all right. It's all right."

Two days later, despite predictions of recovery, Carol Marcus died of a blood clot and was laid beside her son. It was a private ceremony organized by her sister. Lev did not learn of it until after the funeral.

DEBORAH HAD A THEORY that when Jewish men entered their sixties they started to turn into Jewish women. This was evident in Miron Salamon, the president of Temple Emunah, who had been honored earlier that year for his sixty-fifth birthday with a "dinner-dance" held at the temple. A stern man who had been the head of a small independent bank, he had developed a layer of soft tissue under his chin and pouchy folds under his pale green eyes that gave him a grandmotherly look and promised gentleness that he did not possess.

When Deborah was summoned to a meeting with Salamon she felt instinctively that it was to talk about Neal. The funeral had taken place a week before and she had never mentioned the incident. She had been taken up with the wedding and something else—guilt?—held her back. But she knew that word had spread. Certainly Sonya, her secretary, was aware of the story. Neal's death had not made *The New York Times*, though it was in the police blotter of the *New York Post*—"Schizophrenic Man Leaps from Rabbi's Window." It was hardly a scandal and yet she realized the synagogue was, through her, involved. She ought to have informed them.

The meeting was in the board room of Temple Emunah. The room was lined with photographs of former senior rabbis and past presidents of the synagogue, a gallery of smooth, male, black-and-white faces so drained of personality as to remain totally indistinguishable to Deborah.

Deborah was surprised to find that Rabbi Zwieback was sitting at the large polished table, with its pot of coffee and stale rugelach left over from the board meeting that morning. Henrietta Pilch was also there, the vice president of the synagogue and a famously successful fund-raiser who was herself the daughter of a fabulously wealthy real estate developer.

There were a few initial pleasantries exchanged. Henrietta asked Deborah how her wedding plans were progressing. Deborah said that everything was going well except that last week there had been the painful interruption of a funeral—a young man who had jumped from her window. Perhaps they had heard?

"Yes," said Salamon, "that was just terrible."

"It's an awful disease," said Zwieback. "Several in our own congregation have children who have been afflicted that way."

"The young man's family weren't members here, were they?" asked Salamon.

Deborah said they were not.

"And you performed the funeral?" asked Salamon.

"No," said Deborah.

"Your boyfriend performed it?"

The question surprised Deborah and filled her with new alarm.

She glanced at Zwieback, hoping for a sign of some sort, but his face gave away nothing and seemed to be practicing for its place alongside the facial eunuchs on the wall.

"The funeral was performed by someone from the Lubavitcher community," said Deborah.

"But your boyfriend has performed funerals in the past, hasn't he?"

"He performed one," said Deborah, feeling her stomach tighten.

Salamon nodded.

"He's not a rabbi, though?"

"No," said Deborah.

"I'm told he did a very good job," he said, smiling affably. "Perhaps we should hire him."

This was just too strange for Deborah and she had an impulse to say, "Get to the point, would you please?" when Salamon said, "It's funny how things come about. My wife knew Estelle Kalman years ago at Queens College. Quite by chance they bumped into each other in Bloomingdale's and got to talking about this and that. Estelle told

Mimi that her mother had died and that the funeral had been performed by two rabbis, a husband and wife. The husband conducted the service, the wife did the burial. Imagine her surprise when half the team turned out to be you."

Deborah felt herself coloring strongly. What had seemed innocent and dreamlike now sounded sordid.

"What you do on your own time is your business," said Henrietta Pilch, "but you're a representative of this synagogue and there are rules and norms. You're a model for the community. There are teenage girls—and boys—who look up to you."

"I've always tried to be a role model," said Deborah, aware of an edge of anger in her voice as she said it.

"Have you been living with your boyfriend?" Salamon asked.

So that was the point. They didn't care how many funerals Lev performed, they didn't want them living together. Zwieback's predecessor had turned out to be a sex addict who had screwed everything but the stained-glass windows—the synagogue had faced an awkward period of scandal. This was fallout from that.

"He has his own apartment," said Deborah. "But at the time Estelle Kalman called he was staying in my apartment. That's why he answered the phone. She had called for me."

"You know that's not allowed."

"I'm marrying Lev in two months," said Deborah.

"Estelle Kalman thinks you're already married. Fortunately Mimi had the wit to keep her mouth shut."

"I'm sorry," Deborah said. "That was unfortunate."

"What were you thinking?" asked Salamon.

The marriage was Lev's lie, not hers, but she was not going to pin this on him. She had invited him to move in. Professionally, it had been a foolish thing to do, though she did not feel morally culpable. They were getting married. He really was the one.

"It was a foolish thing to do," said Deborah.

She looked at Henrietta Pilch.

"Very foolish," said Henrietta.

Deborah had hoped for some sort of feminine solidarity from her but her face was fixed in prim severity. She dressed, like a lot of petite rich ladies, in Chanel suits that made her look like an old-fashioned flight attendant. She was only missing the little hat.

"Am I being fired?" Deborah asked.

"Not fired," said Henrietta. "But we do think it would be best not to renew your contract. We need to protect ourselves. We'll extend your present contract through October."

"I was told in June my contract would be renewed," Deborah said.

It was only her own disorganization that had prevented her from actually hammering out the details and signing the thing.

"That was before we learned what we have learned," said Salamon.

"In that case," said Deborah, holding her head up defiantly, though her cheeks were burning, "it's probably best if I just leave now."

Nobody thought such haste was necessary. Who would run the overflow service for the high holy days?

Deborah said she would think it over.

She went to her office and sat down at her desk, her head whirling. Deborah, who had cried so often in the fulfillment of her job, did not cry now. She felt a strange mixture of anger, defiance, and sadness. But also release. After the incident with Neal she felt half deserving of some sort of punishment.

Deborah was startled by a knock on her door. It was Rabbi Zwieback, who stuck his head in shyly. She stood up and invited him in but he remained standing awkwardly in the doorway.

"Deborah," he said, in a low voice. "I'm very sorry."

Deborah nodded.

"My own contract," he began, "is up now, too. They've promised me two more years but nothing has been signed. There are some de-tails . . ."

His voice trailed off. He realized this was not a good excuse for his failure to say a word in her defense. Personally, he hated Salamon, whom he considered a boor and a bully. Deborah knew this.

"I want you to know," he said, "that the job doesn't make the rabbi. It's a gift that dwells within."

He touched his heart with his hand.

"You will always be a rabbi."

Deborah felt the tears welling up though she was determined not to cry.

"Truly," said Zwieback, looking at her with great kindness, "you have the divine spark."

"We all do," said Deborah. "Otherwise, what would the point be?"

He nodded, though it was more a bowing of the head.

" '*Hazor'im bedim'a berinah yiktzoru,*' " he said, quoting in Hebrew a verse from Psalms and smiling his weak, wise, weary smile: "Those who sow in tears will reap in joy."

He opened his arms but she did not run into them, as part of her would have liked to do. He turned the gesture into a modified shrug, took a step toward her, and kissed her in a grandfatherly way on the forehead. At which point she did begin to cry—though it was not until he had closed the door behind him that the tears began to fully flow.

ON THE MORNING OF THE WEDDING, Deborah walked alone to the shabby townhouse in the West Seventies that housed the mikvah.

It was 7 a.m. and the slanting sunlight set the empty sidewalk on fire and gave even dented garbage cans an otherworldly glow. Deborah had been online for a week checking the forecast, but the rain that had seemed inevitable had spent itself the night before. Central Park, when she crossed it, had been littered with leaves and branches. That morning, the little weather haiku at the top of *The New York Times* predicted: "Seasonably cool and gusty, some sun."

It was time to stop thinking about the weather. She had woken up at 5:30 a.m. and prayed, though without her tallis, which had already been bound to Henry's and artfully attached to chuppah poles, wooden dowels eight feet high that Lev had bought at a lumber store.

Deborah had wanted Lev to go to the mikvah, too, but he had declined.

"Not yet," he had said, a line he liked to quote ever since Deborah had told him that this was the response of Franz Rosenzweig, the great Jewish philosopher, when asked if he put on tefillin. Privately, Lev had doubts about the hygiene of the place—how often did they change that water, anyway?—though he added, when he saw her disappointment, "I'm taking the plunge in other ways."

This was certainly true. It was not simply a reference to their wedding, but to Lev's decision to leave his job and go with Deborah to Israel for six months.

Deborah had decided not to stay on at Temple Emunah until after the high holy days. Let someone else handle the overflow. Instead she had discovered in herself a great desire to get away from New York.

She and Lev had already decided to spend their honeymoon in Israel—why not extend their stay? Lev blamed himself and his funeral folly for Deborah's dismissal and would have followed her even if he had not felt, as he did, an urge to go, too.

The year 2000 seemed a hopeful time of new beginning. The world was changing. Deborah had called a friend who administered grants for people who wished to become Jewish educators and she had been given a six-month stipend with a chance for renewal.

They were going to live in Jerusalem—they had already found the apartment of a professor on sabbatical. Technically, Lev was taking a leave and not quitting, though he did not expect to go back to *Eureka*. There was a book he was thinking of writing about the Carmel Caves, where there was evidence of the encounter between Neanderthals and homo sapiens, which had taken place one hundred thousand years ago in what was now Israel. Meanwhile, he was planning to study Hebrew, string for a few papers, and take classes at the same coed yeshiva where Deborah had spent a year after college. That it was called "Pardes" Lev found both appealing and disconcerting.

"Let's hope," said Lev ruefully, "it turns out better than Neal's quest."

Deborah thought about Neal a great deal. His yearning for flight and union, for pure knowledge, stirred and disturbed her. Why should mental illness mock our deepest desire? She felt great pity for him and his mother. She did not believe that she had caused his death, but she still felt a chastening sadness whenever she thought of him. It was part of the stripping away of rabbinical illusions.

The mikvah lady buzzed her in and Deborah trekked up the dark stairway. She smelled the food smells and the pool smells, drinking in the cindery air of the old walk-up.

Mrs. Lubkin seemed perplexed to see Deborah alone. She was used to her escorting others.

"Where is the *kallah*?" she asked, using the Hebrew word for bride.

"I'm the kallah," said Deborah, with sudden shyness.

Mrs. Lubkin paused for a moment, then stepped out of the shadows of her doorway and folded Deborah in her arms.

DOWN IN THE ECHOING, damp chamber, Deborah stood naked at the edge of the pool. She had gotten her legs waxed in honor of the wedding. She liked seeing her smooth thighs and calves, a fuller form of nakedness.

Deborah had worked up a sweat on the walk over and was glad to shower in the changing room. She would not shower again that day—you were supposed to keep the purifying water of the mikvah on you as you entered marriage. She decided she would cab it back home.

Deborah had wanted to come alone, though her mother had arrived the day before and was staying in a hotel in midtown. Now, however, as she looked at the little pool, she felt a great ache of solitude. She tried to dispel the feeling. After all, she thought, she was not alone. She was on the brink of marriage. Her friends and family were in town to celebrate with her, and Lev was getting ready in his own way in his apartment. Lenora, the convert with whom she had become increasingly friendly, was going to do her hair and makeup after the mikvah. Terri, another friend whose wedding she had performed in the last year, was helping her dress.

But still she was alone. Before God one was always alone. She had no job and felt like a warrior without a shield. She felt free and terrified, as if she were starting her religious life all over again—as if she, too, were a convert. Though she believed what Rabbi Zwieback had said: The spark of her calling lived within.

Deborah descended the steps and stood up to her knees and then up to her thighs in the warm water. She descended the final step; the water came up to her chest.

She had meant to bring her little book of Psalms into the room and recite some before immersing herself. She felt a need to pray and found herself singing a Shlomo Carlebach arrangement of two verses from Psalm 126:

Return our exiles, God, as you return streams to the Negev.
Those who sow in tears, reap in joy.

Was it because she was going to Israel? Did she think of streams in the Negev because she was dipping herself in water? She always marveled at what words rose to the lips at certain times. Perhaps it was only because, in accordance with tradition, she was fasting before the wedding and already hungry and the lines were part of the psalm sung as the introduction to the grace after meals. It had always been one of her favorite psalms, a "Song of Ascents."

Deborah stopped thinking about the words and the reason for them and merely sang, repeating the verse several times. Her own echoing voice came back to her in the tiled space. She paused, as if hoping for another voice. She looked into the pool and at the chains of light and shadow that formed and broke in the gently stirring water. She looked into the clear water, past her breasts and belly, toward her thighs and the beard of pubic hair.

"Please God," she prayed in her heart, "stay near me."

Then she shut her eyes and plunged.

THAT MORNING, Lev woke up at 6 a.m. He recited *modeh ani* and felt the "lionlike resolve to serve his creator" that the prayer book spoke of, along with an overwhelming sense of gratitude, not merely that he was alive and well—unlike poor Neal—but that he was going to spend his life with Deborah. After calling off Jenny's wedding he had suffered many months of self-doubt in which he envisioned a life alone, a life without love. And now it hit him, with great delayed gratification, that he had earned a new life for himself that he could not have imagined. He felt heroic. He did not dwell on the shivering panic and shame that had made him ill in the months after his busted engagement, the long conviction that he was a coward, fleeing life and commitment. He was a gambler who had won big. *Thank you, God, who gives me back my soul.*

Lev dressed quickly—not in his formal clothes but in jeans and a sweatshirt. He had planned a quick hour of birding in Central Park. It was early fall migration—the birds that he watched fly north in the spring were now flying south, but there were more of them because they had their children with them, juvenile birds in cryptic plumage that made them hard to tell apart. He was stopping by his parents' apartment to pick up his mother.

For the longest time, Lev had promised to take his mother birding. When he had mentioned casually that he was planning to clear his head the morning of the wedding by going to Central Park for an hour she had insisted on coming along. He had been looking forward to the solitude but he did not want to say no. He and Deborah would be leaving for Israel a few days after the ceremony and he knew his mother wanted to spend time with him.

There was not much time, though Deborah had more to do than he did—mikvah, hair, makeup. She had to put on her dress, which, though simple, still needed an extra pair of hands to do up the hook-and-eye fastenings in the back. Lev had laid out his dark blue suit and starched shirt, his shined shoes and festive tie. He did not need much more.

There were puddles on the sidewalk but the sun was shining; the air had been scrubbed by rain and wind. Lev, nervous and excited, felt slightly outside of time, the way he felt when he was traveling to the airport and looked out at familiar sidewalks at an unfamiliar time of day and saw the people scurrying to work and felt removed from the daily bustle, like someone back from the dead.

And here in fact was Riverside Chapel, quiet at this hour but no doubt preparing for business in the hidden rooms within. Lev detected, alongside his eager happiness, a lurking sensation of nameless dread.

"What's the difference between a wedding and a funeral?" asked the old Jewish joke.

Answer: "The musicians."

Was it from his father that he had heard that joke? Lev thought it was, which surprised him, not only because his father was such a devoted husband but because the line between life and death did not seem like something his father would joke about. And yet, had it not been for his father's suicide attempt, Lev often thought, he would not have met Deborah.

Lev was not fasting, and he stopped for a bagel at a coffee shop on Broadway. He saw no reason to feel weak and wobbly under the chuppah, or to link the day with Yom Kippur, which was coming up. Bad enough to have to drive funeral thoughts from his mind. Fasting had never felt like purification to him. It gave him a headache and clouded his thoughts. He lacked the metabolism for orthodoxy, though he made *motzi* over his bagel before biting into it. He had adopted from Deborah the desire to make all aspects of the day feel sacred—this day above all. Though even now he knew that if he found himself suddenly on the other side of the wedding, like a man coming out of a coma, he would be happy. Deborah's whole life seemed devoted to being alive inside the moment, which is why ritual mattered so much to her. Lev appreciated this and had vowed to attempt it more fully himself, though his habit of looking at himself from without and thinking his way past events died hard.

"I'm getting married," he said to the plump, dark-haired owner of the coffee shop, unable to contain the news. The owner, a Greek with a bushy mustache who was manning the cash register, smiled and hesitated before taking Lev's money, but then he did take it.

"Congratulations!" he said, impaling the check on a spike.

Walking to his parents' apartment, Lev felt as if he were not merely thinking the day but inhabiting it. His body felt in possession of secret powers. Were women staring at him? He thought they might be. He certainly was noticing the women on the street with more sidewalk promiscuity than usual. That narrow skirt, plumped like a basketball net filled by a falling ball. *Swish.* What's inside those jeans; that sweater? What did it mean to choose a single person amid all this profusion?

Now that he thought about it, hadn't he dreamed about Jenny? He tried to recall the particulars of the dream without success, though he summoned with ease her taut, well-waxed body and green eyes. Strange she should visit him now.

Perhaps he should have fasted. He powered along, feeling roosterish, ready to crow. He tried again to summon his dream of Jenny. But he knew that it was because of Deborah that he felt so alive. He thought with pleasure of Deborah's body, which still surprised him with its fullness. The erotic modesty with which Deborah lay on her side and looked back over her shoulder. He wished he had spent the night with her.

And yet he quickened his step to draw even with a woman in tight jeans and a bomber jacket. He glanced stealthily sideways, only to see a withered, warty face, much older than he expected.

What's the difference between a wedding and a funeral?

It seemed possible that his father had told him this joke around the time he had broken things off with Jenny to cheer him up. Or perhaps his father only intended something that Lev himself was aware of feeling. That every choice means the death of infinity; the birth of the particular. Inside which, one hoped, a new infinity would be born.

LEV'S FATHER was still asleep and so was his brother. Jacob and his family had been staying with his parents for the past week. Jacob was thinking of moving back to New York and had interviewed with a high-flying securities firm with offices at the top of the World Trade Center. Everyone was hopeful about his chances and excited about the possibility of his return, especially since Lev and Deborah would be going away and it was good for Henry to have one of his sons close at all times.

Lev's sister-in-law, Penny, was awake with their new baby, Zoe, and Margaret was up and running around after Mephisto and already wrinkling the pink velvet dress she was supposed to wear at the wedding, which she had insisted on putting on first thing even though her mother had begged her not to.

"So, groom," said Penny, kissing him. "Doing all right?"

"Fine!" said Lev, grabbing Margaret and turning her upside down while Penny, in an other-people-are-sleeping voice, cried, "The dress, Lev, the dress!"

When Lev had set the giggling Margaret down, Penny handed Lev his tiny niece and said, "Do you mind? I've got to run to the bathroom. Your mom will be out in a minute."

Lev did not mind at all. Zoe was two months old and already able to smile and gaze with fixed attention at objects and people, without much caring who held her. She was wrapped like a burrito in a yellow cotton blanket, one tiny chubby foot sticking out that Lev encircled tenderly in his hand. Despite the unformed baby-blur of the cheeks, the infant bore an uncanny resemblance to Jacob. Lev had read somewhere that this was adaptive—an early resemblance prevented murderous fathers from killing babies they suspected of belonging to others—but it stirred in him a feeling of mysterious kinship. She had

Jacob's hairline, though the soft fringe of her hair showed signs of turning red. She gripped Lev's finger with surprising force.

He and Deborah had already talked about having a family. Lev was aware of the elation and sadness of wanting children. Time would not stop with him. He was in it now, part of the generations. And this, too, was a reason that a wedding was like a funeral, however different they might be. The death of illusions of immortality. Had this been his father's message?

Lev surrendered Zoe reluctantly to Penny when she reappeared. A moment later his mother emerged.

She looked outfitted for a safari, with two cameras, a great tele-photo lens, and a shoulder bag for assorted gear.

"Ready?" said Helen, kissing her son.

Helen told herself that had he been well, Henry would have wished to do something with Lev—go to synagogue or at least take a walk. Whether he would actually have done anything was another matter. But she felt a parental urge to be with her son before his wed-ding—for her husband's sake, and for her own. She had not been alone with him since Neal's funeral, and she wanted to make sure that he was doing all right in its aftermath. She herself had been terribly shaken, though it had hit her only a few days later, after the news of Carol's death, when the poor boy had posthumously become a murderer.

Why should this calamity have befallen Carol Marcus and not her? That thought terrified her and made her more afraid of Lev's upcoming trip to Israel than she ordinarily would have been. Children could die, they could lose their minds. Blind chance seemed to rule—some-thing she had always believed intellectually but felt now viscerally in a way that troubled her dreams. She felt a great urge to be with her son.

Helen also had another motivation for going to Central Park with Lev. She had discovered a desire to begin taking pictures again and wanted to try her hand at nature photography. The thought had oc-curred to her at the Botanic Garden, where she had felt the simple pleasure of looking at all those flowers that, in her youth, she had taken the trouble to learn the names of. But she was less drawn to the idea of shooting flowers than birds, which, because they were high up and evanescent, presented some of the challenge she had always savored as a photographer.

Lev hurried them along. They'd have about an hour to wander before they had to go home to shower and dress.

Lev and Helen entered the park at Seventy-eighth Street, crossed the transverse, and then cut into the Ramble, passing over the wooden bridge that bisected a boggy lobe of the lake where Lev looked without success for phoebes. They walked under a stone bridge, moving in silence along the snaking path where Lev pointed out a hermit thrush and a kinglet that Helen was too slow to get her camera on.

Lev was not in a talkative mood; he wanted to free his mind and he moved as if he were by himself, binoculars at the ready, eyes fixed upward. He kept losing himself in mundane absorption and then waking with a jolt, that was by now half terror and half joy, into an awareness of the actual day. Today. It's happening today. *Behold, with this ring I consecrate you to me . . .*

He sensed his mother watching him and gradually realized that she had stopped trying to photograph birds. She was photographing *him*.

Helen watched her son straining after a tiny movement high above. She knew, with maternal intuition, that when he moved his lips after seeing a particular bird, he was muttering a prayer thanking God, though she did not ask him about it. He was, like his father, private about his religious life. But it wasn't the prayer she wanted to know, just how he looked squinting into the binoculars or bending over to pick up an acorn that he slipped into his pocket, as he had done since he was a boy.

She photographed Lev. She photographed other birders. She photographed dog walkers. She photographed the police officer in his little blue and white electric cart, drinking coffee from a thermos. She photographed the parks department people in their green jumpsuits and dark green pickup, with their shovels sticking up in the back and a great load of branches and vines tangled in the bed of the truck.

Leave the sky to others, she thought. She couldn't help looking level. People! People! There was no getting away from them. She wasn't done with the earth. When she reloaded it wasn't with the Fujichrome 100, the color slide film she had started out with, but with black-and-white Tri-X 400, which she had always used for portraits of people.

Lev lowered his binoculars and watched his mother work. She was training her camera at a homeless man, asleep in the wooden pagoda across from the pin oak where Lev had imagined he saw a rusty blackbird. He heard the muted mechanical swish of the shutter, repeating in rapid fire.

Helen smiled sheepishly as she turned and noticed him.

He came and stood beside her.

"The birds are too far away," she said. "I'd rather shoot fish in a barrel."

"Is that what I am?"

"No," she said. "You're already in flight."

Lev said nothing. He looked at the sleeping homeless man, who, he noticed, had a cigarette burning between his blackened fingers.

"You think Jacob will get the job?" he asked.

"Jacob always gets the job," said Helen. "It will be great having him back—though of course it would be wonderful to have you both here."

She had run off to Europe at nineteen against her father's wishes and had always prided herself on encouraging her children to follow their dreams. And she had always wanted Lev to cut loose a little. But Israel scared her. Two days before, a terrorist had blown himself up at a bus stop in Jerusalem, and beyond the physical danger a nameless dread nagged at her. To counteract it she said, "Your father would be very pleased, I think, about your going to Israel."

The grammar was confusing.

"He does know," said Lev.

"I know," she said. "He does know. He forgets, and then he knows again. And the other day he spoke to me in Hebrew, I think, so that I had the feeling that in his mind maybe he was going, too."

Lev looked pained. He was still gauging his father's mental state, which was impossible for him to get a fix on.

"Poor Dad," said Lev.

"Yes," said Helen. "It's what he feared—but he's at home in it, too. It's still him, I try to tell myself that. But I know he's fighting a great battle."

In spite of himself, Lev smiled.

"That's one of Dad's," he said.

"Yes," said Helen. "It's Philo, I think. But as far as I'm concerned, it's your father."

" 'Be kind to those you meet,' " Lev quoted, " 'for everyone is fighting a great battle.' "

They had begun walking slowly back along the wooded path, littered with twigs and fallen leaves from the rain the night before.

"I never knew a man to quote other people and make everything seem like his own words," said Helen. "I used to think, why can't he use his own words? What's he hiding behind? But now it gives me hope—I find his voice everywhere, even though he speaks so little. I'd like to think that could be true for all of us. That my pictures of other people are pictures of me, too."

Lev nodded. He had debated asking her about the other quotation of his father's that had been haunting him that morning—but decided against it.

"You may turn out to be the most religious member of the family," he said.

They walked in silence; birding and photography were over. As they were leaving the Ramble, Helen said, "Are you all right with today?"

So far, everyone had avoided a head-on reference to his canceled wedding.

"Yes," said Lev. "More than all right. I feel very lucky."

"You are," said his mother.

"Thanks," Lev said, laughing.

"Of course, she's lucky, too," said Helen. "But she is a special woman. Those bastards didn't deserve her."

"I agree," said Lev, but since he continued to feel responsible, he didn't like to dwell on her firing and had fudged the part about the funeral in telling the story to his mother.

"Is Deborah still shaken up about Neal?" Helen asked.

"Yes," said Lev. "She doesn't blame herself, quite, but it was a trauma. It will be good for her to get away for a while."

"And then come back," said Helen, in spite of herself.

He did not answer.

"I know you were shaken, too," Helen said, probing gently.

"Mom," said Lev. "It was a funeral. I was burying my friend." Lev had wept again on the car ride home and, overcome by heat, had vomited by the side of the road.

"I know," she said, soothingly. "Of course. You were friends for such a long time."

"Yes we were."

"But different people," said Helen. "Always very different. Even though I know you sometimes link your fate to the fates of those around you. When you were little, if you saw a lame man you started dragging your foot."

"What makes you say that?"

Helen could see she risked insulting her son but could not help pursuing her thought. Lev had been so rattled after Neal's initial breakdown that she had feared Lev might induce some sort of collapse in himself. She wondered what effect Neal's death had produced.

"After Neal got sick the first time, you seemed to expect to get sick, too. I think that's normal. I feel it with your father. I have to remind myself it's him, not me. But even if we all express each other and are all connected, we all have individual destinies. Otherwise the sadness of one generation would crush the next."

Helen embraced her son suddenly, all her camera equipment pressing into him. She held him tight, as if she did not believe all she had said about individual destinies and even now some power could come and snatch him away.

"I'm tougher than you think, Mom," said Lev. "I'm going to be just fine."

"I know," she said. "I know."

IT WAS ALREADY ELEVEN O'CLOCK and the photographer had taken all the pictures it was possible to take without the bride. Lev was beginning to panic. He kept looking at the milling crowd and then, in distraction, up at the sky, as if she might come sailing over the Steinhardt Pavilion. But then Deborah suddenly appeared beside him, breathless and beautiful in the sleeveless white beaded antique dress and little matching wrap that she had picked out with Helen. It was a dress for spring or summer, not fall, but Deborah was defiant—it was part of her theory that fall should be regarded as a kind of spring. There were goose bumps on her bare arms.

She wore no veil but had a small crown of white flowers woven into her hair, which had been swirled up on her head in a loose elaborate bun that exposed her long neck and strong, graceful shoulders. It had taken longer than expected, she explained, for Lenora to do her hair—not that she was happy with the results. Her hair, she felt, looked like a high holiday challah.

"I think you look wonderful," said Lev.

Deborah smiled gratefully and kissed him, very gently, so as not to diminish her lipstick, and because in some vague way they were pretending not to see each other.

Sally, the wedding coordinator—an obliging woman provided by the Botanic Garden who made sure the rabbi had a microphone and that the glass for smashing was wrapped up on the table along with the other ceremonial accoutrements—did not give them any more time together but hustled them over to where the photographer was waiting.

Afterward, Wendy, with Sally's help, corralled the immediate family and necessary friends onto the terrace alongside the lily pool for the ketubah signing. By this time the guests were already seated.

Lev was touched to see his father escorted to the spot by Deborah's mother while his own mother consulted the photographer. Laura Green had short auburn hair and the same fine elfin features as Deborah's sister, but her large brown eyes were Deborah's. Lev had met her only the night before, at the rehearsal dinner. He had liked her, though she had a slightly detached manner, ironic where Deborah was earnest. He and Deborah had promised a long visit when they were back from Israel. Laura's second husband, Stan, was a hearty, easygoing widower with a handlebar mustache and a sea captain manner. Deborah got along well with him, but had determined that though he would march down the aisle, he would not walk beside her.

"Everyone, please," called Wendy. "We need to come together."

Margaret was running around, her pink velvet dress long ago swapped for a violet corduroy jumper. She was holding the little basket of confetti she was going to scatter before Lev and Deborah walked down the aisle and leaving a trail wherever she went. Deborah had suggested the use of paper instead of petals, gently observing to Penny that rose petals were intended to represent the blood of Jesus.

It was windy, and Wendy drew everyone into a tight circle around the bride and groom and the two witnesses who were to sign the ketubah, which had been designed by a friend of Deborah's who made Judaica. There was a great tree at the top of the document whose roots encircled the text and whose branches were filled with birds and flowers and hung with pomegranates.

There was silence as the witnesses signed. Deborah, after waiting a moment, couldn't help herself and started humming a *niggun* softly under her breath that was immediately taken up by Wendy and then by others in the small crowd. Deborah's mother did not sing but she watched everything carefully and rubbed her daughter's back to keep her warm.

After the signing Wendy invited the parents of the bride and groom to bless their children.

Lev noted Deborah's pained expression as her mother asked aloud, "Is this a requirement?"

Laura had a memory of her own father blessing her as a child on Jewish holidays. She had not liked it, or rather, she had not liked him. He was an impossible man, though her own daughter worshipped him and treasured his religious artifacts like holy relics. That was his tallis tied to the poles alongside Henry Friedman's. But Deborah had never experienced his rages or his cruelty to his wife, who slaved and cooked for him and on whom he vented all the frustration of his thwarted life. Laura had needed to go to California to get away.

But she did not resist when Wendy said simply, "It's only a beautiful custom, a way of sending your daughter to the wedding canopy with your love and good wishes."

First Rachel and Dawn read aloud the single sentence: "Our sister, may you be the mother of thousands of myriads." Then Wendy directed Laura to lay her hands on her daughter's head, and as she did so, careful not to disturb the flowers, Laura felt a great surprise of emotion. She read the English words out of the little booklet Wendy held up to her, not bothering with the transliteration: "May God make you like Sarah, Rebecca, Rachel, and Leah. May God bless you and watch over you. May God's face shine upon you and be gracious to you. May God's face turn to you and give you peace." Her voice caught as she read the last line. She did not want to take her hands away from her daughter's head and there were tears in her eyes as she kissed Deborah and whispered, "I love you."

Rachel and Dawn, crying, embraced her as well. Lev's forecast for the wedding had been: scattered tears for much of the day punctuated by emotional downpours.

"Did you hear that?" asked Rachel, elbowing Deborah like a big sister. "May you be like Rachel."

Deborah had stood for her blessing but Lev sat before his father and mother—otherwise he was too tall for Henry to reach his hands to the top of his head. Henry put only his good hand on Lev's head; his mother placed both her hands over Henry's. Lev had wanted his father to say something to him earlier in the day—to offer a blessing of his own, but his father had been silent whenever he had gone and stood beside him. But Lev was moved to feel his father's hand on his head, pressing down on the brown suede kippah, trimmed in gold, that he had bought especially for the wedding. Henry murmured the blessing in Hebrew in a voice scarcely above a whisper and then his mother read in English: "May you be like Ephraim and Menaseh," followed by the same priestly benediction Deborah had received. Lev glanced at his father. He wanted something more, but his father's eyes were closed.

Jacob gave him a bear hug and said, "Remember, my boy, just keep breathing. It's all about the breathing."

Wendy rolled up the ketubah. The wedding coordinator, while still maintaining her cheerful air, was pointing out that they were running a full forty-five minutes behind schedule. She shepherded them all toward the spot from which they would march down the aisle. They drifted toward the meadow, where the white folding chairs were set up and filled with guests, swiveling in their seats to watch the wedding party descend the hill.

Lev wanted to walk beside Deborah but Bill appeared at his elbow. Bill was being transferred to London from Africa and had timed his return to coincide with the wedding. He'd gotten his newspaper to put him up in a hotel for a few days so that Lev could sleep apart from Deborah before the wedding, as Deborah wished.

"Still plenty of time to call this whole thing off," he said, with a grin. "Plenty of time."

Bill had been slated to be Lev's best man at his wedding to Jenny. He was getting a second chance and was holding one of the chuppah poles.

Deborah found herself walking next to Rachel. Dawn was up ahead, and though they had all been together the night before at the rehearsal dinner, it was only at the ketubah signing that Deborah thought she had recognized a slight bulge in Dawn's belly.

"Am I right that Dawn looks a little different?" she asked in a low voice.

Rachel smiled awkwardly.

"*B'sha'a tova!*" said Deborah. And then added quickly, because Rachel always shrank from Hebrew, "May it happen in a good hour. May it all go well."

She slipped her arm around Rachel's waist and Rachel put her own hand, delicately, on the beaded back of Deborah's dress.

"Mom doesn't know yet. I wanted to wait till after the wedding."

Deborah was touched by this consideration.

"Somehow," Deborah said, unable to restrain herself, "I thought it would be you."

Rachel shrugged and Deborah, aware of how easily her words could be misinterpreted, said quickly, "You know how much I love Dawn. It doesn't matter, it's just what I thought . . ."

Rachel said nothing. Deborah was sure she had offended her—why was she always blurting things out? They walked along in silence but then Rachel whispered in her sister's ear, "It's my egg."

SALLY, CONSULTING HER CLIPBOARD, was lining everyone up in the order they were going to march. The chuppah bearers were out in front, already holding their poles aloft like standard bearers in a medieval pageant. The two talleisim had been lightly stitched together by Penny, who had passed the threads through the embroidered collars of each prayer shawl.

After Neal's suicide, Deborah had discovered a single rust-red smudge on Henry's tallis. The garment was too fragile to dry-clean. Deborah had dabbed at the spot with diluted Clorox until it faded into a kind of tea stain on an old tablecloth. She dared not do more, afraid that the fabric would begin to dissolve. She didn't mention it to Lev and regretted it now. Not that she was superstitious. The whole point of a chuppah, as she reminded herself, was that it was open to the elements, like the tents of wandering ancestors. The world beat down on you and it was only the witnesses around you, and God, and most especially the person by your side, who helped you endure the storm. But she shuddered inwardly as she thought of Neal and Carol Marcus.

"Ready?" Her mother asked gently. She was standing beside Deborah. They were last in the procession.

Deborah slipped her hand through her mother's arm and felt the emotion well up in her, though she did not wish to ruin her makeup. She had already wept once, during the blessing.

Lev was in front of her. His mother was on his right, his father on his left. She was amazed at how much taller Lev was than both his parents. He turned and glanced back at her. He looked very handsome with his sharp features and pale, freckled face against the dark blue of his suit. He smiled and lifted his mobile eyebrows.

The trio began playing "*Dodi Li*."

Wendy walked first down the ruckled rice-paper runway, clutching her little rabbi's manual and smiling at both sides of the aisle in her awkward, averted way.

Then came the chuppah bearers.

Next came Stan, who had been paired with Dawn. They walked arm in arm, Dawn's midnight blue, tentlike dress flapping behind her. Then little Margaret was loosed with her basket of confetti, which, instead of being scattered as planned, was dumped in a single heap halfway down the aisle. Penny, who followed holding baby Zoe, tried to distribute the confetti with her foot as she passed the pile.

Then came Lev, escorted by his parents. His father's limp seemed more pronounced. The rice paper made it hard to walk. Lev was prepared for his father to fall and braced his body as he walked, which stiffened his own gait. But they all made it to the spot where the seats ended. Lev kissed them both and continued alone down the aisle. Henry and Helen sat down.

And then the bride came. Lev turned to watch her walk. Deborah's mother was on her left and he knew that in her mind her father was on her right. Her face was beaming with that yearning soul-brightness in her eyes, that brimming look that had once frightened him and that now made him want to rush toward her. Her eyes were fixed on his and he felt an overwhelming sense of joy.

The music spoke in his ears. *I am my beloved's and my beloved is mine.* He remembered what Deborah had said: *So what if it's a wedding cliché?* It spoke for him anyway. Just as his father's blessing was no less a blessing because it came from a book. But he stopped thinking as he watched Deborah walk toward him.

Deborah stopped a few feet away from him and kissed her mother. Lev took a step toward her and then drew her toward the chuppah with him. Together they turned their back on the assembled guests and faced Wendy.

The two talleisim billowed above them like a kind of sky, splotched, imperfect. Instinctively, Deborah's eyes sought out the stain on Henry's tallis. But she was too happy to dwell on it. Beyond them stretched the green expanse of the meadow, sloping upward. The leaves of the chestnut trees were turning yellow, though there was a great deal of green left, and a green light hung in the air. Leaves were whirling to the ground.

Deborah had imagined this moment—this very moment—and here it was. The sense of wanting something and actually getting it made her feel almost weightless. Lev was beside her. Wendy was in front of her, where she herself had stood so often. And at the four corners of the chuppah stood friends and family, holding their poles like Masai warriors, smiling at her and Lev with love.

The musicians had failed to taper off at the end of the processional and were now playing *"Erev Shel Shoshanim,"* which Deborah had also crammed into the program, from beginning to end. She felt a flash of irritation—the violinist had struck her from the beginning as a nitwit—and then amusement at herself. Let Sally go and shut them up—or not. She did not mind stretching the moment a little longer. She looked at Lev.

His brow was clouded, though he smiled when he saw her looking. He had been thinking of his father. His father should have given him the tallis himself. It shamed Lev to feel anger at this moment, at his incapacitated father sitting so helplessly in his chair, but he could not help it. What has he ever given me? Lev asked himself, and then realized, with grateful astonishment, that the answer was Deborah. He had given him Deborah.

Henry was seated in the front row, in the aisle seat that Helen had helped him into. He had always wanted the aisle, even before he was sick, as if it might be necessary—in a movie theater, in synagogue—to get up and run.

The music had taken hold of him. *Erev shel shoshanim. Evening of roses. Let's go out to the grove. Myrrh, spices and incense are a carpet to walk on.* He knew the song. Where did he know it from? *At dawn a dove is cooing. Your lips are like a rose. I'll pick it for myself.*

Was he marrying her?

Helen had pointed out his tallis. It was painful to see it stretched out in the open air, flapping and straining against the meager stitching that bound it to its fellow. He had an impulse to cut it down and bring it back to his seat, gathered in his arms.

The things that mattered most had always made him ashamed. The tallis brought him shame. His own survival. His love for his wife—desperate, almost childlike, even after all these years. *Your hair is filled with dew. Your lips to the morning are like a rose.*

He ought to have destroyed the tallis but he liked wrapping himself in it and praying. It went against reason and experience but he could not help it. That he continued to pray even now was a source of shame. One more in a long list—perhaps the greatest of all. That after Darwin and Freud and Nietzsche and Marx and even, God help him, after Hitler. After the murder of his mother and father and Estie and so many more—as many as stars in the sky, too many to count—still, he continued in some vague and wordless way to pray. He couldn't help it. He could not break free of his dependencies any more than he could break free of life itself, as on that day in the bathtub—he suddenly remembered it—when a desire for life had welled up in him and he had leaped out of the water, jumping out and running—where? Where was he running?

But the question dissolved into a patch of deep and spreading green right at his feet that seemed to speak to him in its own language and that occupied him completely until Helen rubbed his shoulder and he looked up and saw his son standing beside Deborah and felt the silence. The music had stopped. He realized what was happening and tried to smile.

Wendy tapped the microphone clipped onto the lapel of her lavender pantsuit and looked at the assembled guests before turning to face the couple. At that moment a great wind blew up—you could hear it growling into the microphone—lifting Lev's kippah and separating the two prayer shawls. The tassels at either end, where the prayer shawls had been tied, still held, but the middle of the chuppah tore open, the stitches ripped out by the force of the wind. There was a collective gasp as each tallis billowed out like a sail.

Dawn, who was sitting in the front row, jumped up, ducked inside the chuppah and, reaching up, grabbed hold of the two separate pieces of cloth before they could pull apart completely. The wind died and she brought them gently together as if she were drawing a pair of curtains. She remained standing there, trying to hide herself behind Wendy but her large draped body and upraised arms stood out like a statue holding up a building.

She nodded at Wendy as if to say, "It's fine, I've got them. Don't worry."

Wendy, satisfied with this arrangement, turned back to face the couple standing before her. Another gust came up. The chuppah flapped and fought. Deborah shivered and moved closer to Lev, who took her hand.

The rabbi began to sing.

ACKNOWLEDGMENTS

I WOULD LIKE TO THANK my wonderful editor, Jonathan Galassi, for his suggestions, insights, and enthusiasm. His assistant, Annie Wedekind, was not only a terrific reader but helpful in every step of the process that turns a manuscript into a book. I am deeply appreciative of the care that went into making this book, from the outer cover to the inner design. Sarah Chalfant, agent, friend, and reader, was, as always, always there. My friend Cindy Spiegel lent an expert eye to the manuscript and a sympathetic ear to its anxious author, for which I am very grateful. My Nextbook colleagues have been a splendidly supportive community. My mother, Norma Rosen, continues to inspire me with her creativity and devotion to writing. My family—in New York and Albany and Brookline and Ann Arbor—have kept me on course with their love and support. Finally, and most of all, my wife, Mychal Springer, has done more for me, and for this book, than words can ever express.